The Beast

ALEXANDER STARRITT has worked
or written for a wide variety of
publications, including the *Daily Mail*,
the *Mail on Sunday*, the *Guardian*, the
Huffington Post and *Newsweek*. He
grew up in the north-east of Scotland
and also translates from the German.

The Beast

by **ALEXANDER STARRITT**

APOLLO

An imprint of Head of Zeus

First published in the UK in 2017 by Apollo,
an imprint of Head of Zeus, Ltd.

9 7 5 3 1 2 4 6 8

A catalogue record for this book is available from
the British Library.

ISBN (HB): 9781784979942
ISBN (XTPB): 9781786694003
ISBN (E): 9781784979935

Typeset by Adrian McLaughlin

Printed and bound in Great Britain by
CPI Group (UK) Ltd, Croydon CRO 4YY

Head of Zeus Ltd
First Floor East
5–8 Hardwick Street
London ECIR 4RG

WWW.HEADOFZEUS.COM

The Beast

Real blood, real intestines, slither down
the likeness of a tree.
—BRIAN PATTEN

TUESDAY

FIRST CHAPTER

YOU know that feeling where everything suddenly seems *more real* than it did before? It struck Jeremy Underwood, a paunchy, slightly downtrodden sub-editor in his mid-forties, when he arrived back at the office from a week's holiday and – while pausing outside to have a cigarette and adjust to the idea of re-entering the uproar within – noticed two figures hanging around the entrance, both of them draped in the lazy folds of rich black burqas.

He worked at a newspaper that in liberal London was a synonym for brazen bigotry, hypocrisy and enraged hatred of those on whose fears it fed; and that in the rest of England was bought and read every day by two million decent people. No name was emblazoned on the wall above its revolving doors. The entrance was functional, like the short gangplank and side door by which you board a huge transatlantic liner. But a pale clock face marked with Roman numerals was bracketed above it in an octagonal iron case, and the crown it wore was the paper's name, hammered out in the heavy gothic type that adorned its masthead: *The Daily Beast*.

One of the burqa-draped figures pointed up at the building while they spoke in what Jeremy presumed was Arabic. The other one bulged slightly at the right-hand side, as if carrying something under her cloak. Conscious of a slight acceleration in the labours of his tired, smoke-clogged heart, Jeremy remembered a story he'd worked on just before going away: a group of terrorists – how many? Four. Four terror suspects on bail – had escaped the oversight of the law by joining the crowd at their mosque, cutting off their electronic tags and leaving dressed in burqas.

The *Beast*'s leader column had been incensed by a police spokesman's offhand remark that, even if the squad cars had arrived in time, they were hardly going to strip-search the lot of them. The column had excoriated 'a country so enfeebled that its "authorities" are unwilling even to defend it'. The heads of the mosque and various Muslim community groups had been incensed in turn, and 'vowed' that they would not stand for this harassment.

And now these two shapeless figures were here, on the *Beast*'s own doorstep, carrying something under their cloaks.

From deep within him emerged a memory of having been struck by this sort of shock once before. It had been when he was a cub reporter in Margate, long ago. He'd been in the cinema on a date, hypnotized by the huge lights and colours, when, with startling speed and size, a gargantuan black shape loomed across it. The illusion was ruptured and, with a flash of vertigo, he was pulled backwards into his surroundings of movie theatre, Margate, the rustle of hands in popcorn.

He'd flinched in his seat, and his date – one of the assistants on the paper – laughed at him, thinking he was clowning. It was just someone sticking a hand in front of the projector. But he'd been confident then, and young, and hadn't minded her laughing. He'd actually clowned a little more, amusing them both; and, despite a lingering unease, he'd soon slipped back into the movie.

Now, as he stood outside the *Beast*'s offices, the two black-clad figures gave him that same vertiginous shock. Around them all was normal: the workaday lunchtime backdrop was going on with its business. But they were here. He kept smoking, trying not to give away that he'd noticed them, and realized that his fingertips were trembling. He'd drunk half a litre of coffee in the car. Were they trembling more than usual?

He listened in, but couldn't understand what they were saying. They continued to talk. And as he watched them, the shock receded. He told himself he was being paranoid, his perceptions warped by too many years of news. They were doubtless just two perfectly ordinary Muslim women dressed in burqas. Bombs and terrorists might appear in some places, but what he saw before him was the entrance to the paper's offices after a week off, spent with his wife in Dublin. He'd felt almost free over there, without his daughters or any obligation to work; and, even though Louise had made him carry their passports everywhere in a scratchy security belt, he'd been lifted by a certain lightness that was still with him.

Implicit beyond the entrance was his mind's habitual setting: the shift pattern and the late finish; the print deadline and the pension plan; the front bench and the back bench; the commute and the catchment area. Jeremy decided to think no more about terrorists, and pressed the stub of his cigarette into the soil of the raised flowerbed beside him. Then looked at the rotating doors. On every panel was stamped 'Cardholders Only'. His card was in his pocket.

But he'd still not fully shaken off the feeling of disorientation, and to settle he addressed himself by his secret nickname, which he'd not told even his wife or his closest colleague and friend, Max. He spoke to himself in a needling but encouraging tone, the way he imagined a public-school games master might address a hopelessly un-athletic child. 'Come on, Drudge. Come on, Drudgy. One foot after the other. Card out, through the door, up the escalator. You can manage that, can't you?'

And up he went.

SECOND CHAPTER

THE escalator carried him at a stately pace up to the vast, sun-flooded atrium, six storeys high, and deposited him full in the marble glare of Lord Copper. His glory was magnified by two tall black-backed waterfalls that slid silently past him on either side, and by the gold letters inlaid above him in elegant Roman type: Copper House. In front of him, facing each other, stood an honour guard of six more busts on slim pedestals, lesser viscounts and founders, their heads set two feet lower than the great man's. And down this avenue Lord Copper stared in undimmed fervour at all those who entered.

Jeremy gave him a nod of recognition. Despite everything, the tired old charger in his chest did still paw the ground as he came once more into this last confident stronghold of the Press. How could it not, when it felt the sheer self-belief of a paper that built in marble, that commissioned busts, that constructed waterfalls and imported carp to patrol their lower pools in seamless tessellations of red and gold?

And not just the self-belief, but the bullishness. The two newspapers in the building that were not part of the *Daily*

Beast Administrative Trust – the *Impartial*, which reported mainly on conflicts in the Middle East, and the *London Trumpet*, which reported mainly on parties in Mayfair – were permitted no visible sign of their presence. That applied most blatantly in the new 'Editors' Hallway', a Doric arcade in smooth Italian marble that led – because there was nowhere else for it to go – from the canteen to the service lifts. Inside it hung the black-and-white portraits of every man who'd achieved the highest rank on his paper: Editor of the *Daily Beast*, the *Beast on Sunday* or *BeastOnline*.

When the arcade was opened, the current Editor's portrait photo had attracted sightseers from every floor of the building. By some complex system of grimaces and contortions, he'd succeeded in twisting his features into the perfect semblance of a light-hearted, affable grin. Only a man with his keen sense of posterity would have put himself through it.

Underneath Jeremy's deep reluctance to return to work, under the slow despair engendered by years of every day doing things that he didn't want to do, he had, in some peculiar way, missed being here, as someone moving away from a railway line misses the clanking of the trains. But even the atrium and the arcade were only outworks of what was upstairs, the *Beast*'s most sacred citadel.

He took the glass lift up the side of the atrium, rising above his Lordship; above the pools where the carp's stubby snouts breached the surface to engulf spiders that had fallen from the ceiling; above the raked-gravel Zen gardens where the reporters made their phone calls, and the terraced cafe-bar where they did their scheming, and finally arrived at the outer edges of the organ from which the *Beast*'s bellow issued forth: the newsroom.

He pulled open the glass door and heard the relentless

sound of a thousand fingers rattling across their keyboards. These belonged to the rows of exhausted twenty-five-year-olds who wrote *BeastOnline*. They were kept in a battery of ten desks with the most senior furthest from the door through which Jeremy had entered. On one side they had a bank of windows on to the atrium; on the other was a wall of filing cabinets and a narrow passageway. As Jeremy walked along it he watched the fever with which they gobbled whatever scraps of information they could, trying to keep up the unrelenting pace that the *Beast*'s website required: 'Whinging mass murderer hunger strikes for PlayStation' – 'Is overpopulated Britain on the brink of CANNIBALISM?' – 'You're fired! ISIS executes downed pilot with flamethrower.'

None gave him so much as a glance. They were leaning into their screens, racing, racing, always racing to be first in the world. 'Peanut butter contains cancer-causing fungus' – 'Shocking pictures: Law students forced to fund degrees by stripping online' – 'Yew were always on my mind: the tree that looks like ELVIS.'

He was lucky, he thought, that he'd been born early enough for the print edition to see him through to retirement. Some friend of his wife's had asked whether he could arrange work experience for her teenage son, who wanted to be a journalist. He'd prevaricated, sort of agreed to look into it, and done nothing, out of equal parts apathy and protectiveness. But really he should show the boy and his mother the state of those who wrote for *BeastOnline*: young skin made pasty by lack of sunlight, dulled gazes, lank hair, stress-related acne and forearms that cramped with repetitive strain injury as they lifted the Maltesers, crisps, chocolate biscuits and tea that kept the onliners alive and awake while they ruined their eyes, their health and their profession. Office legend had it that if you stood outside the *BeastOnline* toilets at any time of day or night you would hear the sound of weeping.

It made Jeremy want to tell them that they were still childless and re-trainable and not yet inescapably committed to this life. For him, his two daughters were like hostages – beloved, all-important hostages – held against his continued compliance. Particularly the elder one, Elsa – who was already a teenager but whom he could somehow still picture most vividly at about four or five, when her hair had been a brighter, purer hue of blonde and every feature of hers that was strangely his but not his own had enslaved him with love. She especially was a beautiful little blonde hostage, whose power to condemn him to work he accepted absolutely. With the younger one, Jenny, it was somehow less complicated and less intense; she was simply another hostage, of course also adored, backing up the first.

But even if he warned this teenage candidate to stay away before he ended up trapped in it and having paranoid thoughts about women in burqas, what good would it really do? Every kid thought he'd be the Editor one day. He himself hadn't believed in the shackles until he was wearing them.

He walked on, past the onliners and their overseers, who were huddled around a screen and peering at a photo of the environment minister posing on a beach in skimpy Speedos. One was saying, 'Is that a wink? Is he winking? Oh, he's going to regret that.'

Beyond them, the noise grew louder and more diffuse as the space opened up. The whole of *BeastOnline* occupied just one outlying arm of the newsroom.

Before him, hundreds of people typed or talked on the phone or asked each other questions in a low maze of desks spreading out under a pressboard ceiling. It was broken up by square pillars festooned with rotas, complaints and marked-up pages, and at the distant edge was a glowing strip of frosted windows on to Kensington High Street, whose natural light hardly encroached on the room's artificial brightness. Everywhere were loose sheaves of printed paper, empty cups and sandwich wrappers, and all of it and everyone was slightly scruffy, slightly neglected; the computers old, the bins full, the desks not decorated with anything personal.

Demarcating the territories within the newsroom were flimsy partitions on which the departments pinned A3 prints of their best work. Features had a picture of an apparently decapitated Princess Beatrice pulling her own head out of a top hat. Health had one that looked like a malevolent crab. In front of this the Health editor, a carelessly dressed woman in her fifties, was saying into a phone, 'Then find out what kind of fucking growth it fucking well is. And if you can't find out, get one yourself and ask a fucking doctor.'

To Jeremy's left, on the wall towards which the newsroom pointed, was a grid of bright, fuzzy squares. These were the English and American news channels, projected there soundlessly alongside an unending scroll of *BeastOnline*. In one square, a serious blonde in a trouser suit was belabouring a group of surly proletarians. In another, a reporter was talking earnestly into a microphone while behind him dense black smoke chugged from a burnt-out petrol station. The slug at the top left of the screen read 'TERROR', and Jeremy's mind jumped to the two people in burqas he'd seen outside; he wondered whether they were still there. In the next square, someone in Parliament was shaking a roll of paper at the indifferent opposition, the green benches almost empty. Beside that was the spool of *BeastOnline*: 'How romcoms can turn you LIBERAL' – 'Shhh! 60% of women can't keep secrets'

– 'Rejected migrants given luxury mosque, and YOU'RE paying for it.'

Set just off from the flat but ceaseless movement on these screens was his own department, around which all others were arranged: Production, the very belly of the *Beast*. From this cluster of grey desks were reporters sent out to sleep in hedges and pick through bins; from here were photographers told to get closer to the fighting; from here were envelopes of cash dispatched to prostitutes, to PAs, to political advisers. And to here copy was returned, to have its grammar disentangled, its ignorance corrected and its significance identified; it was here that raw, mud-caked nuggets of information were cut and polished to have revealed in them the shine and sparkle of the news. And fixed to one of this department's pillars was the symbol of the newspaper's – of all English newspapers' – true home, prised loose and taken the night they went into exile: a metal road sign reading 'EC4 Fleet Street'.

In the line of desks closest to the TV wall, and facing away from it into the newsroom, the bosses were already seated and typing. That meant the Editor was in personal charge today; otherwise they would still be standing around drinking coffee. In front of that back bench were the subs' desks, taken out of their traditional rows by management consultants and arranged into what Jeremy had reluctantly become modern enough to call 'pods'. Some of the men who'd traditionally been middle-bench subs and were now 'pod leaders', men his age, were already at their desks. Of the younger generation, only one, Lauren, was wandering around. She must have come in early.

Max stood up when he saw him, took the pencil he was chewing from his mouth and raised his hand in a loose salute.

Jeremy broke into a wide grin and on impulse gave him the finger.

Max made his swaggering walk towards him. By right of being generally acknowledged as the best sub, he was allowed to come as close to not wearing a tie as a news sub ever could: a black one that was almost invisible against his black shirt. The shirt was tucked loosely into black trousers, from which it escaped behind him. His black hair was gelled, and it glistened as if newly glued along the deep comb-furrows from forehead to nape. He hunched a little from years at the keyboard, one shoulder slightly higher than the other.

He put out his hand and said, 'Alright, Jez?'

Jeremy shook it. 'Alright?'

Max didn't usually stoop to the banterous riffing that was the newsroom's idiom and pastime, but was so pleased to see Jeremy that, not knowing how to express it, he reached for the nearest mode. 'Your face is a bit blotchy. You didn't shave all week, did you, till this morning? Were you trying to hide your ugly mug from the Irish?'

'Thanks for that.' Jez was very pleased to see him too.

'Go on then, get your holiday anecdotes out of the way. How are you?'

'Oh, you know, glad to be back.'

Max chuckled. 'You lie so well, my friend.'

Before they could pick up all their threads, the chief sub bustled up, bald, voluble and menacingly avuncular. 'Hold on,' he said. 'Did I just hear you say you were glad to be back?'

Jeremy slipped into the newsroom tone: 'Back in England, not back *here*. I've not gone mad.'

The chief sub pretended to wipe his expansive brow. 'Phew. I thought you must have caught some sort of brain disease out there. Where were you again?'

'Dublin. It was—'

The chief sub pantomimed horror and grasped for Max's arm to steady himself. 'He *has* gone mad. You went on holiday to *Ireland*? What's wrong with you? Don't you get enough violence and alcoholism in this office?'

Max watched, amused.

The chief sub carried on. 'Did you like it?'

Jeremy shrugged. 'Well, it wasn't—'

'Of course not! No one likes Ireland. Not even the Irish. Why do you think they're always swarming off to other people's countries? Australia, America, New Zealand. Imagine *wanting* to move to Australia – what a noxious fart your life must be.'

'Or Canada,' prompted Max.

'Canada, right. Canada's lovely. No one for thousands of miles. It's like being dead. Wonderful. Of course, the food's shit, but they don't know any better. Go there next time. You won't come back spouting gibberish about being glad to be *here*.'

'Look at him,' said Max, egging on the chief. 'He's gone on holiday and not even managed to get a tan.'

The chief sombrely shook his blocky head, as at someone beyond the reach of reason. Jeremy was smiling openly at all this attention and went to speak. But the chief was already back to thinking about edition, and spoke over him: 'I've put you under the supervision of Max today, just in case you do anything mental now you've had a sniff of freedom.'

'What do you mean, under his supervision?'

'You're not on the middle bench, Little Miss Shamrock. Just one of Max's grunts. Front bench. Front rank. Cannon fodder. Just like the Irish.'

'What do you mean?' Jeremy flushed as if he'd drunk too much hot tea at once, and his shirt collar seemed to tighten around his neck. 'I'm not one of the grunts. I've been on the middle bench for... since I came here.' He heard how plaintive it sounded. 'That's fourteen years.'

'Not today, Gerry Adams. Britain says no.'

'But who's on the middle bench instead of me?'

'Lauren.'

'Lauren? But she's about eight years old.'

Max tried to explain. 'She started doing it while you were in Dublin.'

And the chief blared over him, 'Do you really think the job's so hard it can't be done by an eight-year-old girl? We'd train monkeys to do it if they weren't all immigrants. Don't go on holiday next time. Or if you do, go to Canada and stay there. Marry a Canuck, eat pancakes, get a job on the *Toronto Courier*. You'll love it.'

Jeremy was about to complain, but the chief clapped him on the arm and said, 'Good to have you back, you mad bastard. Now where's that eight-year-old with my flatplan?' And he bustled off.

THIRD CHAPTER

'WHAT the hell?' said Jeremy to Max, too surprised and embarrassed even to really swear, and opened his arms out wide as if to draw some referee's attention to what had happened. The pleasure of return was jostled from its glass and in it was left a grainy sediment of nastiness, monotony, the killing feeling that he was running on a wheel that moved no faster or slower whether or not he was on it. And, as if that weren't bad enough, he'd been demoted to a smaller wheel.

He could see Max, his round shoulders hunched up to his ears, considering before he spoke. Jeremy knew him well enough to predict that he would try to preserve the lordly feeling of professional mastery – the sense that nothing could disturb their command of what was in front of them, nor their steady ascent in rank and remuneration – though Jeremy always wanted to point out that that applied more to Max than to him. And, indeed, Max said: 'So, after all your griping, you've realized you *do* want to be a pod leader.'

'I don't want to be pushed out of it by a kindergartener. Come on, Max, I've been here for fourteen years. And in one week away they just... It's just...' He felt as if he were about to lie down and capitulate.

'I think you'll find it's thirteen years. If it was fourteen, you'd be almost as senior as me.'

'What the fuck, Max?' His voice was still plaintive, with no fight in it. 'You take one miserable week off in a dump like Dublin and they turn on you before you've even had time to come back and sit down. One day, when I keel over and die right here in the newsroom, they'll just complain that my body's too big to stuff into the bin.'

'If that was true, they wouldn't bother making all those pension contributions.'

'Max...' Jeremy sat down heavily in a chair. His shoulders slumped forward and he looked at his hands. 'Fourteen, OK, thirteen years I've been here. And I was editor of the *Sentinel* before I came. Twenty-five years I've been a journalist. Then you take one week off – *one week* – and you're back with kids who've just left uni.' He shook his head again.

Max, a little worried about him now, lowered his voice. 'It's not like your pay's getting cut though. Less work, same money. That's not a bad deal, is it?'

Jeremy raised a hand and wearily pushed that consolation away. 'That just means in a year's time they'll notice I'm getting paid too much and give me the boot.'

'Listen,' said Max. 'This'll only be temporary. I'll talk to the chief. I can just tell him the truth – that it's a waste not having you in charge of one of the pods. Lauren'll probably only be on till he writes the next rota, then she'll just fill in when someone's away.'

At that, a sound of rage escaped from Jeremy, but it was the sound of rage escaping. He shook his head again in surrender. 'Fuck me,' he said.

And Max, who, although not fond of banter did like a well-turned one-liner, said, 'No thanks, Jez. Not pretty enough,' and patted him on the cheek.

At that, Jeremy half-laughed and then sighed. He could see that his surface self wanted to be angry, but what would it bring him? More than a decade of something indistinguishable from loyalty had brought him only demotion.

While Jeremy logged in to his computer, Max tried to further buoy up his mood. But Jeremy was only half-listening. His thoughts had been cut loose of the present and drifted away and out on to the enormous past. Across his mind's eye flickered an image of his youthful hands gripping handlebars as he cycled through a night sky thick with gently drifting snow. He'd been a cub reporter on his way to cover he couldn't remember what; probably some council meeting in one of Margate's satellite towns. His hands had been stiff and pleasantly sore, his breath had come hot from inside his layers of coat and he himself had been ardent in his eagerness to bring back the news. He remembered the glamour he'd associated with it then.

His thoughts kept being interrupted by subs touching their hand to his shoulder or hailing him from across the desk as they passed: 'Alright, Jezzer; decided to come back, did you?' or 'Escape attempt unsuccessful, was it, Jez?' And there were still a few old-school enough to call him, and everyone else who was on the inside, 'darling'. The camaraderie made it bearable, as it always did.

He hadn't needed camaraderie at the *Sentinel*. When he became editor there, the feeling had been of strength exerted; to stop the absurd construction of a bypass around Margate and Ramsgate, the main contract for which – this had been the decisive scoop – was tendered for by the mayor's brother-in-law. Or to shame some corporate owners into sprucing up the dirty nursing home in Shottendane, partly with the recurring headline 'Grottendane'. Or to keep alive (by means of a weekly column) the idea of the Isle of Thanet, which a millennium ago had stood 500 yards out to sea with Margate and Ramsgate on its shoulders but was now joined to the mainland by silt and the A28.

That had been regional journalism at its best, making an unbroken line from a Dark Age proto-journalist called the Venerable Bede to the newsroom of the *Margate Sentinel*. They'd deliberated for weeks about what to name the column. Planet Thanet. Isle See You on Thanet. In the end, when the deadline was upon them, he'd played a captain's stroke: Thanets for All the Memories. Even Max would have been pleased with that one.

But what was such strength as he had left being exerted for here? Criminal Immigrant stories, Mucky Teachers, Bungling Bureaucrats, anecdotes of the Feckless Underclass. It was for money, that's what he was working for, and the promise of regular money to come – a promise he'd realized was all-important in the days after his first child was actually born.

He'd then seen his situation with a new starkness: that all the good reporters left the *Sentinel* for the nationals, that his staff had been shaved and squeezed and pared from sixty down to eight. That if someone was going to try to ride out the storm it couldn't now be him. That it was time to get out.

There were plenty of others here who'd made the same retreat from the dying regionals to central London: Ian had been editor of the *Wigan Herald*, Mike of the *Yorkshire Mirror*, Rich of the *Penzance Gazette*. Now they all worked for the *Beast*, an army of generals all simply—

Max interrupted his thoughts. 'What's wrong with you?

Are you still moping about having to do one rota without any real work?'

Jeremy shrugged exaggeratedly. 'You know. Just lacing up my boots.' And indeed, that was what he was doing: just physically making the movements that did the work, filling his mind with it to push out whatever he might be thinking or feeling for himself. Typing in his password, ReadAllAbout!t, opening PagePlanner and InCopy, checking which pages had already been drawn.

Around him, the *Beast* was yawning, stretching out, waking up. At his back, he could hear the Sport subs throwing biscuits at each other. To his right, Turkish Liz and her assistants were answering the phones with their traditional 'Bonjoo-er, Pictures'. Ahead of him, the bright wall of projected TV continuously shifted. In every direction out from the focal point at which he sat were hundreds of other hacks, chatting, typing, butchering the outside world into its various cuts: News, Features, Travel, Personal Finance, Health, Politics, Diary, Property & Gardening...

'Fine,' said Max, though Jeremy could see that he was still treating him carefully. 'Once you're settled in, can you pick up a Tragic Schoolgirl?'

So here he was, back at the bottom of the heap, being told which stories to pick up. 'Got it.'

Max watched him, wondering whether he should make the natural joke about not meaning that Jez should pick up real live schoolgirls. Maybe he could be needled out of his despondency. But if Jez just got back into the work, he thought, it would all settle itself. 'Totally straight-up-and-down story. Nothing unusual about it.'

Something popped into Jeremy's mind. He said, 'Actually, I just saw something quite strange outside.'

'Was it the English summer?'

'No, it—'

'Was it someone paying money for a copy of the *Impartial*?'

'No, it—'

'Was it—?'

The chief sub reappeared at Jeremy's shoulder, grinning horribly. 'What was it, Jez? Go on, tell us, Jez, tell us, Jez, tell us, Jez. What was the strange thing you saw?'

Jeremy recoiled from him. 'Nothing that interesting. Just these two people in burqas.'

And with that, the terrible machinery of the *Beast* was set in motion.

FOURTH CHAPTER

THE two figures in burqas were still outside the building. They'd wandered a little way down the short street, consulted an iPhone, and returned to stand under the old-fashioned clock. One of them, Aisha, said to her cousin Leila, who was visiting from Abu Dhabi: 'I'm sure there's meant to be a Whole Foods here. Google Maps said it was in this building.'

Leila nodded, unable to help in any way. Aisha said this place did a shaved pomegranate salad that Leila just had to try. But Leila didn't understand why anyone would *want* to shave a pomegranate; couldn't you just cut it open and eat it like a normal person? But she didn't say that, because they didn't know each other all that well, despite being cousins, and she felt that her parents had slightly forced Aisha to hang out with her. It wasn't that her cousin had done anything to make her feel unwelcome – far from it; she'd taken a few days off work to show her around – but Aisha was already in her twenties and seemed to have so many friends and other things she could be doing. She probably didn't care about this pomegranate salad either, but had had to find something for

Leila to try while in London; and, now that it had become a thing, they were going to carry on looking for it.

Leila resisted the urge to get petulant. But in fairness she hadn't even wanted to come to London. She'd wanted to spend the college holidays at home reading *Game of Thrones* and imagining she'd come into the world as Daenerys Stormborn instead of as a doctor's daughter from Al Bateen. But her mother had laid on the guilt, reminding her again and again how excited her father was about the trip he was giving her – how he'd never have dreamed of being able to go to London at her age, and all of that.

At least volume four of *Thrones* had travelled with her and, this morning, while one part of Leila's mind was willing her cousin to take her time getting ready, Daenerys, Queen of the Andals and the First Men, Khaleesi of the Great Grass Sea, the Mother of Dragons, had set about subjugating the insolent slave-owners of Meereen. Now the book was lying fat and unread – the Khaleesi paused, the swarm of arrows arrested in flight, the catapult straining at its tether, the city-state of Meereen waiting, just waiting – in the bag on her hip. She felt a bit stupid wearing it under her burqa, but with all the pickpockets there might be in a foreign city, she'd decided it was better to be careful.

FIFTH CHAPTER

UP IN the newsroom Jeremy was saying, 'They were standing outside, pointing up at the offices.' And as soon as it was out of his mouth, he knew it was just a figment, the mind making purely personal associations.

The chief asked, 'What offices?'

'Us, our offices. The *Beast*. It's ridiculous; the funny thing was that it reminded me for a second of that story—'

Max quoted, 'Deadly terror gang escape dressed as women.'

The chief nodded. 'Good story, that. Murderous Muzzers in women's clothes. One to frighten the kiddies.'

'We had a follow-up as well, while you were away.'

The chief said, 'How long was your ordeal among the bogtrotters, Jez? It's been so long I'd started to forget your face.'

'I left last Monday, a week yesterday.'

'Don't go for so long next time; you'll come back and find yourself working in the canteen. But Maxi-pad here's right. While you were off, we had Baroness Ahmad saying she was going to have an inquiry into why poor old Plod didn't take them all to Heathrow to be searched by women border guards.'

Max interjected. 'And there was something else in there, too.'

'There were lots of things in there, little Max. That's why it's called a story and not just a headline. Which one are you thinking of?'

Max's face did not betray whether being spoken to like that annoyed him. 'We quoted someone in the Met saying there was no reason the terror gang couldn't use the burqas to disguise themselves for a bombing.'

'Did that definitely come from the Met and not just Newsdesk's overheated imagination?'

'Yes, it did,' said Max, albeit that, ever meticulous, he provided the caveat: 'It was a Blundering Plod story, though, so we might have just been asking them to imagine the worst possible repercussions they could.'

But the word 'bombing' reverberated unsettlingly, and the chief spoke to himself out loud, no longer being facetious: 'Still, someone in the Met. Jez, did you hear these two say anything?'

Jeremy felt that this was all being taken far too seriously. 'You know, I'm really sure it was nothing to do with that gang. The point is it was just a strange moment.' He tried to think of a way to bring up his demotion again.

'Maybe not, but humour me, young Jezza. I haven't just been on holiday and had my brain softened up. Did you hear them say anything?'

'Well,' Jeremy said reluctantly, 'the one who was pointing was talking the whole time, but it was in Arabic.'

'And was it a man's voice?'

Jeremy raised his hands helplessly. 'To me it sounded like a woman.'

'That doesn't necessarily mean a thing nowadays, though, does it,' the chief said pensively.

Jeremy added, 'Well, it could have been a girl.'

'What do you mean?'

'Not a woman – a girl, a teenager.'

'An adolescent?'

'An old adolescent.'

The chief looked at Max, who didn't need to hear the question, and confirmed: 'One of them was eighteen or nineteen.'

'And voices are all over the place at that age, aren't they?' The chief turned back to Jeremy. 'Did you get a look at their build? Did they look like men or women?'

Jeremy raised his hands again. 'You can't tell, can you? Isn't that the whole point of a burqa?'

'Yes,' the chief said grimly, 'it is.' He considered. 'Was there anything else? Did you see them do anything else? Did they go anywhere? Did they have anything with them?'

'Well, if you really want to know, one of them had a bulge under their right arm like they were carrying something.'

The chief again looked at Max, who ran his palm from his brow back over his hair's stiff black furrows. 'And have you mentioned this potentially hugely significant fact to the Newsdesk?'

Jeremy was pained. 'I really don't think it's anything. In fact, Frank, I wanted to talk to you about the next rota.'

'Just a minute. Have you thought about what would happen if the biggest scoop of the year was on Newsdesk's doorstep and someone in this newsroom knew about it, but didn't say anything?'

Jeremy wished he hadn't mentioned it. But the chief was right about that. He said, 'Fine,' and heaved himself to his feet.

'Have you thought that they might come over here and rip you limb from limb and I probably wouldn't even try to save you, because you'd deserve it?'

'I'm already on my way, aren't I? But I'm going to say I think it's nothing.'

'You say whatever you like, sugar puff. Just make sure you give them the story as well. Talk to Colin, he's one of the saner ones. He'll give it a good going over.'

Jeremy nodded, sighing to himself at the thought of the needless questioning he'd let himself in for, and carried his paunch over to the Newsdesk.

The chief's ever-shifting attention landed on the square pillar where the rota sheets were tacked up, and he bustled over to it. Below the rotas were postcards or letters from subs who'd retired: 'I've mainly been sitting in my lovely quiet garden with a beer and thinking of you poor saps stuck in that newsroom'; 'You can imagine how many friends I'm making here in Spain by spotting inconsistencies in the menu layouts'; 'I've turned around the parish newsletter. Circulation has tripled since we broke a story about the deacon over-claiming his expenses.'

Next to them were pinned thin scraps of newspaper, bearing headlines gone egregiously wrong:

GIRLS' SCHOOLS STILL OFFERING 'SOMETHING SPECIAL' — HEAD

HOSPITAL WAS SO DIRTY I DISCHARGED MYSELF

OUTLAW BUYING PORN — FORMER MINISTER

The chief knew that the Editor disapproved of all this, though not enough to interfere in the culture of the barracks, and he himself was attached to these memorials to subs and blunders past. He knew that Jez wanted to talk about Lauren taking his place. Lauren might not be up to it but, if she was, he would have two trained middle-bench subs where before he'd only had one. And it was no bad thing to keep the rabble hungry. He took a hard-nibbed pencil from his pocket and moved a few more people around the rota in clear capital letters.

He came back over to Max, who tried to read in his expression any clue about the rumour he'd heard in the Lord Wellington: that the chief was leaving. The rumour said he was going to work for the *Brute*, but that couldn't be true. The *Brute*'s circulation was collapsing. Their whole paper was now just dressed-up wire stories and 'my secret shame' by footballers' ex-girlfriends. And neither the footballers nor the shameful secrets were even any good. The revelation that the former squeeze of a Swansea goalkeeper had slept with the manager? It was a long way from 'I pissed on Pelé'. The affectionate old insult that the *Brute* was nasty, *Brutish* and shit didn't even apply any more; now it really was just shit.

No, you would have to be an idiot to join the *Brute*. And Frank, even though his headlines were all fist and no velvet, had never lacked subtlety when it came to his own interests. But if Frank did go somewhere, the next in the hierarchy was... Max. He studied the chief's face. The bastard was, as always, boisterously full of himself. There was no sign to read. Max detested him.

The chief raised his flabby chin in the direction of Jeremy. He was sitting beside Colin at Newsdesk, leaning forward to prop his cheek on his palm and watch what Colin was writing down. The chief correctly distrusted Max as a pretender to his seat, but chatted anyway: 'Probably nothing to it. Just Jez hallucinating with joy at being back.'

'No, probably not. But if there is—'

'The thing to find out would be what they were doing here.'

'Terror attack on *Beast* HQ.'

'Now *that* would be a splash worth coming to work for.'

'The biggest story for years. Could only be better if they did blow part of the place up.'

The chief was amused. 'And even Newsdesk couldn't fuck up the body count if the victims were on the floor right in front of them. Plus with any luck you'd get a bit of shrapnel right in the brain stem and wouldn't have to worry about it.'

Max didn't know whether the chief meant Max or himself. He carefully said, 'Yes,' and diverted the chief back to safer ground: 'But it would probably be Health and Travel that get blown up, since they're closest to the door. It wouldn't be a great loss to British journalism.'

'Hold on – HOLD ON there just a minute, Little Miss Hoity-Toity. The softer sections are keeping us all in jobs. How many full-size British Airways ads do you see in the news pages? Right next to a cheery little story about tourists getting machine-gunned in Sharm el-Sheikh?'

'I thought all our jobs were safe for now.'

The question of whether the chief was leaving hung in the air between them.

He said, 'We won't need jobs when we've all been blown up. And tell Jez not to shoot his mouth off until those loafers on Newsdesk have found out if there's anything there. Because if there is...'

He and Max looked at each other.

'I'll tell Jez to keep schtum.'

The chief nodded and returned to his seat. Grasping the edge of the desk with his thick fingers, he swung himself back into position. If the terror gang really was planning to attack the *Beast*... The idea of getting the paper out while bombs were going off on the doorstep flattered his sense of himself as a tough old hack. If you'd lived in the newsroom as long as he had, he thought, it would take more than a few bangs to throw you off. But he would need to stop anyone getting in, send the non-essential staff home, then also – plans and contingencies branched in his mind and only after several minutes' thought did an instinctual shudder pass across him. He dismissed it.

Max was thinking it was typical of Jez to get snagged up in this sort of mess. By the time Newsdesk had found that there was nothing to the story, it would be late in the evening, which meant things would be hectic on deadline. Maybe very hectic. The team was light because of the summer holidays. Everyone already in – the middle bench – was solid, hardened, load-bearing. Those coming in at half three, however, were casuals, old-timers and new grunts, who might disintegrate in the intensity of first edition.

Max had two of these grunts allocated to his pod: Rosie, who was probably a nice girl but far too timid to get her teeth into the copy, and the boy who'd been sacked by the *Stentorian*, Will, who had all the piss and vinegar he'd ever need but was still just a greenhorn and couldn't be trusted. They'd be in soon enough, but Max would have to get moving.

The Tragic Schoolgirl he'd already assigned to Jeremy. He also had a Dirty Doctor, a Criminal Immigrant and a couple of Scientific Studies that the children could handle. For now, he would take care of the other page lead, a combined Benefits Cheat and Corrupt Establishment story. It was in poor shape; not quite a case of total reconstructive surgery, but it would need substantial work. It was astonishing to him how few reporters could write something as simple as a news story. The intro had come through as:

> A NORTH London council continued to
> pay Jobseeker's Allowance to a woman
> who took a job in their own offices, it
> has emerged.
>
> Not only that, but she was promoted to
> the role of personal assistant to the depart-
> mental head.
>
> Ms Rebecca Yates, 34, had come to
> work for Islington council as...

The *Beast* did not start a story as boringly as, 'A North London council continued...' Max noted that it had been filed by Ben Jessop, who'd come from a round of redundancies at the *Respectable* and was obviously still writing the kind of foot-dragging prose that had made redundancies necessary.

Max checked online that the 'departmental head' was who he thought he was, and tapped the return key three or four times to make himself space at the top of the article. He paused before starting, like a carpenter checking his tools were in their places. He wrote:

> BUNGLING bureaucrats at a scandal-hit
> council paid dole money to a benefits cheat
> who was working in their own offices.
>
> Islington Council even made shameless
> Rebecca Yates, 34, the boss's PA while she
> carried on claiming unemployment benefit.
>
> She was promoted under Michael
> Fenimore, the notorious mandarin who
> last year refused to resign from the Left-
> leaning council after the death in care of
> tragic Baby K.

That was more like it. He made the first paragraph 9.5-point type with no indent. Second par 8.5 indented. Third par onward 7.75.

The pictures had been assigned to the page while he was working: one from Facebook of Yates on holiday, looking drunk, one of Fenimore looking shifty in a car park and a small one of Baby K looking like a baby. Max recognized the picture of Fenimore from the year before. If the story kept running, they'd need to send someone to Islington for a fresh one. He deleted the three bits of dummy copy that read 'KICKER: caption here capti', and his fingers filled them in without his needing to think. 'CHEAT: Rebecca Yates'. 'SCANDAL: Michael Fenimore'. 'MURDERED: Baby Kevin Harvey'.

The first part done, he looked up. At Newsdesk, Jez was now explaining himself to two other reporters, who were standing in front of him and writing shorthand into their notebooks. That meant Newsdesk was acting on the bomb story. He bit his pencil thoughtfully, tasting wood and metal on his tongue. What would a bombing in the newsroom even mean? While his thoughts struggled to dissect something so far from the page and the *Beast*'s internal politics, the first thing that popped into articulacy was a name: the Burqa Bombers, like the Shoe Bomber or the Pants Bomber.

That would do as a tag as long as no one got killed. Then the tag would have to be something understated and momentous, like the 22/6 bombings. There were only so many times, however, that you could use the numbers before it was no longer understated or momentous, but merely a convention, which meant: no bite. It could probably stretch to one more, but 22/6 was nothing like as catchy as 7/7 or 9/11. Perhaps they'd have to call it the Kensington Bombing or – yes – they would call it the *Beast* Bombing and with that, just as a flourish, force every other paper to name the *Beast* in their front-page headlines.

Light of heart, he looked again at the Benefits Cheat. After the first few percussive pars had blasted a path through the reader's indifference, the story filled in the details. The Cheat had registered several months beforehand with a temping agency, which had then called and asked her to start at the council the following morning. She claimed she hadn't had time to inform the Benefits Office. Max contracted it to read that she'd had to start 'at short notice'. That was a fair representation. And it turned out that she'd been 'temporarily promoted' – a quote from an anonymous colleague – while someone was ill. Well, 'temporary' had still happened. He would let the readers make up their own minds.

As he was tidying it up, Jez came back over from Newsdesk in a state of misery. Behind him Max could see the two reporters he'd spoken to loping out the door. He asked, 'So?'

Jeremy dropped unhappily into his chair, 'They've got it into their heads that there's something to it.'

Max absorbed that information. There was no reason to assume that Jez's assessment was more accurate than the Newsdesk's. The story was live. But he did not seriously think that he, a future chief sub, could be touched right here in the heart of the *Daily Beast*'s newsroom. The important thing was to get the edition out smoothly. He said, 'In the time you've been chatting, I've already finished shaming this Benefits Cheat.'

Jeremy leant all the way back in his tilting chair, and said, 'I hate reporters. They're going to find there's nothing there and then whose ear are they going to come and chew off?'

'Yours, it looks like,' said Max, who wanted Jeremy to get on with the Tragic Schoolgirl already. 'But even so, just in case someone is planning to set off a bomb in here, we wouldn't want to spoil the biggest scoop either of us has ever seen just because someone couldn't keep his mouth shut. Don't forget the *Impartial* and the *Trumpet* are right underneath us.'

Jeremy understood, and nodded. He wouldn't say a word.

SIXTH CHAPTER

A HOLLOW, sick feeling had been settling in Jeremy's gut since he'd talked to the Newsdesk. It wasn't so much anything they'd said as their sudden focus, their sharpened intent. In his experience, every reporter in his most secret heart was as lazy as he could get away with. They'd always prefer to copy and paste some regional news article, rewriting the intro and introducing some errors, rather than do any actual reporting themselves. Except, that was, when they caught the scent of something big. And they'd caught a scent from him.

Jeremy had an unhappy presentiment, like reading the paper over breakfast and seeing an error printed and un-recallable, the responsibility his, and having to wait for the chief to ring. At least, he reassured himself, with Newsdesk in this mood it wouldn't take them long to run the trail cold. Then they could come and have a go at him all they liked; by tomorrow it would be over.

He could tell that Max wanted him to get on with the Tragic Schoolgirl and the story of how she'd been killed. But there was no point hurrying to get things out of the way; the big scoop would not be coming. Nevertheless, to oblige his friend, and thinking that it might take his mind off the Newsdesk, Jeremy opened the copy and tried to concentrate. He sighed and read 'terrible accident'... 'schoolmates' grief'... 'little brother's anguish'... 'young life cut tragically short'. She'd died falling off a horse when a car passed too quickly. The horse was helpful; it meant the readers would know at once that she was the right sort of person. Other than that, she was just another Tragic Schoolgirl, fifteen years old, the latest of innumerable sisters who'd fallen off balconies or taken bad ecstasy pills or – as fondly remembered by the newsroom – gone on an Outward Bound expedition to Greenland and been mauled by a bona fide polar bear.

They'd managed to get a picture of this one in her school uniform. Some type of nautical-themed jacket with white piping down the seams and on the pockets. A skirt and a pie-shaped hat. She looked ridiculous; it must be a good school. On impulse, and taking an interest for the first time, he decided to check where the school was: the girl lived somewhere called Middle Rosen, Lincolnshire. The story had her name – Elaine Phillips – but not her school's. Switching to Google Maps, he searched for 'private girls' schools' in the area.

Of course Lincolnshire was far too far away for his own girls, but maybe it was this one: Stamford High School. The uniforms looked different in the site's pictures of eager, high-achieving pupils, and it seemed to be mixed, but he clicked through anyway to find the discreetly concealed section on fees: £4,675 per term for day pupils. Unambiguously beyond the reach of what he could pay; especially so if his career had already reached the phase where he was moving down the hierarchy rather than up. It was £8,250 for boarders.

A dull pain expanded in his chest. The school his girls

went to was, naturally, in a catchment area slightly more expensive than he could afford. That was why he and Louise had chosen to live there – because it meant that the girls Elsa and Jenny sat next to in class weren't Sharons and Traceys but rather Augustas and Octavias or, he admitted to himself, at least Ceciles and Floras. And when they left school, those other girls' dads would be able to connect them with the cushy careers that it was a pleasure for the established middle classes to arrange for one another. No drudgery, no trudging, for them. The thought of his girls feeling every day how he sometimes felt... It was unbearable.

And a private school would be better, a boarding school: the uniforms, the slang, the obscure games and the careers that those girls' fathers would have in their gift. But he would never be able to pay for it, not even if he didn't eat and went back to working extra shifts at the *Beast on Sunday*. He'd done that for nine years after Jenny was born. An extra double shift, 11–11, every Saturday for nine years. When he thought about it now, it staggered him. The sheer number of birthday parties and play dates and painting afternoons he'd only heard about, not seen. Almost all of them, really. One year, he and Louise had tried postponing Jenny's birthday so her father could be there; but she'd hated it so much they'd done it to Elsa only out of fairness and then stopped. He looked at the photos instead.

At the time, he'd been proud of all that working. And on the rare occasions that he'd been around to hear the other fathers' commiserations, they'd usually contained an undertone of respect, as for one carrying a heavier load. At the *Beast*, too, there were gestures of recognition accorded to the new dads who took every extra shift going. Claps on the shoulder when you came in again, unasked-for cups of tea when you were deadened with fatigue, the chief even saying, 'Not such a malingerer after all' when you put your name down for every Saturday till the end of the year. That was what made it tolerable. Meanwhile Louise worked too, but not in the evenings, and went round to her friends' houses, to the cinema, had a life. He didn't have any friends left really, except for Max. His existence narrowed to a single imperative: the kids. It was almost impersonal, less a love than a duty, but there was love everywhere within it.

The one thing that actually hurt was when it seemed that, despite all this, he'd somehow still ended up a bad dad – one of those who'd blunder home, ignorant of their children's days, only to interrupt the family life he'd paid for. The kind who were always the fall guys in children's movies, like Mr Banks in *Mary Poppins*, who worked in a bank and was always at the office when Poppins and the kids were larking around London. He'd banned Elsa and Jenny from watching it. The film was especially galling because the Bankses lived in a stucco-fronted West London townhouse and he was sure they could have figured something out without needing to send the kids to the local comp.

But working for the girls, especially when they were younger, had lent purpose to all he did. Sometimes he would look at them with amazement and think: everything you've ever eaten, everything you've ever worn, every bed you've ever slept in, I've given you. Whenever he'd asked himself why he was doing it, driving to the office, shattered before he even started, the answer had been at hand. But now they somehow seemed to need him less. Not less money, of course, and they were still children, young children; but that insistent *they-will-not-survive-without-you* was dissipating. He could now picture the day when they would with blithe and necessary ingratitude simply grow up and out and away. And he didn't know what he'd be left with.

Terribly little of that pride seemed to remain since he'd slackened back to working merely full time. Now he wondered whether, in reducing the strain, he'd undone himself, like an overstretched rubber band gone loose and floppy. No wonder he'd been demoted. And he'd be getting a bollocking from Newsdesk when they discovered there was nothing to this bomb business. He really had spent longer here than was good for him; seeing bombs under every burqa must mean he was getting as institutionalized as the chief.

He tried again to concentrate on the story. The picture was good. Pretty, hair up in her hat, intelligent-looking, maybe a bit of a goody-two-shoes but not too smug to be likeable. And the resolution was high. Much better than in the old days, before Facebook, when all these mug shots had been lifted from school photos. Then it had just been one small head among many, with a light circle around it.

Max said, 'Looking at that page, that's quite a solid wodge of text. Do you have a line in there that could be a pull-quote?'

'Eerrrm. Yes. The mum says, "I look at her clothes and it hurts more than I ever thought possible." I can crunch that down.'

'Yep, that'll do it.'

'That's the nice thing about the posh ones, isn't it? They're a bit more articulate.'

Max nodded. They'd missed each other and wanted to chat. 'Yeah, it means you don't have to spoil the copy with clichés – "she was an angel".'

Jeremy laughed, to his own surprise. '"She was the light of our lives."'

'Hardly worth getting quotes at all.'

'You could give them a list of phrases to avoid.'

'While you're on the doorstep? You are a hard-nosed old hack, aren't you, Underwood? Anyway, they'd just start giving you synonyms. "Oh, she was a cherub; she was the lamp of our existence." Do you fancy a tea?'

'That'd be great.'

Max stood up and touched his hand to the pocket where he kept his staff card. 'Assam, semi-skimmed? Or did you pick up some new habits in Ireland? Builder's, whole milk, six sugars?'

'Normal's fine, thanks.' Jeremy leant back in his chair and brought his hands together on his paunch, the demotion and the Newsdesk temporarily unimportant. 'I know it sounds stupid, but everything is *so* Irish over there, though. I thought – you remember – that it would all be pretty much the same, except you'd pay in Euros.'

'But what, they all wear leprechaun hats and say "begorra" at the end of sentences?'

'Nah, just, I know it sounds obvious, but they've got the accent and the chattiness and, I don't know... It's just so different that you really feel *away* from all the usual. You know, you go into a pub and people buy you a drink and talk to you as if you're all actually human beings.'

'You took a whole week off and went to Ireland just to get blabbered at by the local drunks?' Max shook his head, sincerely amused. He always went to the Algarve.

'Yeah, it was great.'

'You should call the Irish office; see if you can get a transfer.'

'Funnily enough, Louise mentioned that as well. But that's what you do, isn't it, whenever you go on holiday? You think, let's just fuck it all off and come live here. But it's not really the place, is it, it's just being away.'

Max had never had that feeling. He made a non-committal expression and asked, a little stiltedly, 'Did, er, Louise have a good time?' Families were taboo in the newsroom rambunctiousness. He remembered a detail: 'She'd been there once before, hadn't she?'

Jeremy nodded. 'Years ago. But she really did like it. She loves all that kind of stuff, the mist, the folk songs, she finds it, you know, romantic. And she liked that it was just the two of us.'

'Good,' said Max. 'Great. Well,' he said, leaning forward to tuck the back of his black shirt under his belt, 'I'll get the teas.' And he swaggered away past the rows of *BeastOnline*, too disdainful of them to hurry.

Jeremy tried to get on with the Tragic Schoolgirl. But he couldn't get on with her. Elaine Phillips, 15. Her horse reared and she fell off; that was the whole story. Yet there were all these individualizing details to be fiddled with: when it had happened, what her headteacher had said, how many *l*s and *p*s in Phillips. The kind of thing that mattered only if it was wrong, but that made readers ask themselves: 'If they can't even get that right...'

Even before he'd gone away, he'd been finding it harder to actually make himself do the work. It was fine at nine o'clock, with edition forty-five minutes away and the alarms screaming. Then some of the old speed and facility returned. It was the only time he felt fully awake. But at three? The gears wouldn't engage.

Max came back with the teas in two cardboard cups. Jeremy unhooked the plastic lid and dropped it into the bin beside him. Steam and heat rose from the milky brown liquid. He realized he'd still not done any work. The gears kept slipping back into neutral and in his mind there was the heavy churn of foreboding. Newsdesk were going to pitch his non-story to the Editor at conference.

He should leave it to Lauren to deal with and see how much she liked being on the middle bench then. He glanced up at her. All he could see was the back of her head, the thick, mottled blonde hair sitting on it like a wig. She seemed focused on the screen in front of her, concentrating on the work as you do when you've just been promoted.

His own work was sitting undiminished in front of him. Alright, he said to himself. Come on, Drudgy, let's do some subbing. Come on, Drudge of Drudge Hall. Come on, at least you're not young. Then you'd have another thirty years of this.

He began to put some things in order. They certainly couldn't call her 'peppy' in the third par. And he was a bit unsure about the phrase 'The schoolgirl died when a car...' It seemed too stark. He put in a 'sadly': 'The schoolgirl sadly died when...'

The intro, as usual, would have to be rewritten. Reporters didn't understand that the *Beast* did not sensationalize. Its base note was deep earnestness, the tone of the newsreader. It was just that the world it reported on was, unfortunately, often sensational.

He worked, his mind sometimes flicking through its other channels, and around him the other subs did the same. Each man's thoughts landed on his story and lifted again, like a nation of bees. Meanwhile, their bodies sat in their chairs. Their pupils flickered. Their fingers twitched. Sometimes they unconsciously rubbed the ache in their forearms.

Fragment by fragment, tile by tile, Jeremy got it done, until only the headline remained. He clicked his cursor into the text box and pressed Ctrl+A to select all the dummy copy. It used to say:

|HEADLINE IN HERE|
|PLEASE HEADLINE |
|IN HERE PLEASE |

But since the minister for culture, media and sport had proposed independent regulation of the Press the dummy copy at the top of every story read:

|CAROL CRAWLEY IN|
|HERE PLEASE GET |
|CAROL CRAWLEY IN|

He deleted it and wrote:

|FAMILY'S ANGUISH|
|AS SCHOOLGIRL KILLED
|IN TRAGIC FALL |

Didn't fit at all. And really he needed to get horses in there somewhere.

|FAMILY AGONY AS |
|HORSE-LOVING GIRL
|KILLED IN TRAGIC FALL

Horse-loving. The newsroom was so saturated with ribaldry it was hard to tell whether the readers would hear the same innuendo.

|FAMILY ANGUISH |
|AS KEEN RIDER, 15|
|DIES IN TRAGIC FALL

He could squeeze in that comma and that extra *l*; but, on reflection, 'fall' wasn't enough. He had to get in that there had been some kind of coming together with a car. Otherwise it would sound as if she'd just lost her grip. And he wondered for a moment about 'keen rider'. It was fine. No one else would be thinking of 'horse-loving'.

> |FAMILY AGONY AS |
> |KEEN RIDER KILLED|
> |IN |

Killed in what? 'Car crash' was too dull, and inaccurate. Car smash? Still inaccurate. Road tragedy? Road horror? Or maybe, yes:

> |FAMILY AGONY AS |
> |KEEN RIDER DIES IN|
> |ROADSIDE HORROR|

He could squeeze the leading so those extra letters fit, and that would do the job. It was a shame they didn't have a picture of some carnage on the road – the shape of the dead horse under a police blanket, one leg sticking out, that sort of thing. But apparently the horse was fine.

He checked whether *BeastOnline* had the story. They did, and had headlined it *DEAD pretty – girl at £25,000-a-year school killed in horse tragedy*. Someone was going to get a strip torn off him for that. He turned his screen to show Max, and said, 'Look at this.'

Max's expression hardened into scorn. 'Amateurs,' he said. 'There was one like that while you were away. About a mix-up in a cemetery that meant this family spent years bringing flowers to the wrong body. They'd lifted it from the paper, so it had all the right lines – heartbreaking mistake, grieving all over again, that sort of thing. Even the headline was OK. But they got a photo of the headstone that we didn't and captioned it GRAVELY MISTAKEN.'

Jeremy laughed.

Max said, 'Can you imagine someone doing that on the paper? They'd get sacked. I mean, I would sack them.'

As they were both imagining Max with the power to sack, the two young grunts assigned to their pod, Will and Rosie, hurried into the newsroom. They'd happened to meet on the way in and Will was trying to talk to her while she rushed nervously between the desks, not wanting to be rude but certainly not wanting to be late. She respectfully said, 'Hello Max, hello Jeremy.'

Jeremy said, 'Wotcher,' and Max, with open scepticism, nodded and said, 'Afternoon.' Jez thought Max was too tough with the newcomers, but in the end, he couldn't blame him for it; they hadn't yet earned their seats.

The stocky bald form of the chief bustled over and said, 'Afternoon, Will; afternoon, Rosie. So nice of you to join us.'

Rosie flushed. 'We're not late, are we?'

The chief sub clasped his fat hands together. He didn't know how to cope with someone who put up so little front. 'Um,' he said. His voice strained and creaked as he tried to make it gentle, 'No, no, not at all, just get settled in and I'm sure Max'll find something for you to look at.'

The children sat down and the chief, shaking his head quickly as if to clear it, came around the table to talk to Jez. 'Alright, fuckwit,' he said. 'Let's have a look at this schoolgirl of yours.'

He stood beside Jeremy and they both cast their eyes about the page. Jeremy had zoomed out enough to fit the whole story on his screen. The copy became a blurred approximation, apart from the first paragraph, which could still be made out along with the other important elements: headline, quote, photograph of the dead girl in her school uniform.

'Not bad, is she?' said the chief. 'You definitely would, wouldn't you, Jezza, you dirty dog.'

Jeremy said: 'She's backlit, though, in this shot. Probably makes her look prettier than she is. But yeah, not bad-looking at all.'

'She won't be as pretty now. Just a pint-sized corpse lying down there in all that lovely peace and quiet, thinking, "Thank God I'm dead and don't have middle-aged pervs like that Jezza Underwood leering at me any more." Lucky bitch. But listen, look in standby. Turkish Liz has put another Tragic Schoolgirl in there. Apparently we've got a glut of swishy-haired corpses today. There's a whole stack of ugly ones she hasn't even put through. This one got choked by her abseil rope.'

Jeremy flicked back to PagePlanner, feeling, as ever, bombarded by the chief. In standby there was a picture of another pretty young schoolgirl, this one wearing a navy jumpsuit and a red helmet, making a trout-pout with two other girls, their faces pressed against each other for the camera.

The chief put his fleshy hands on the desk and leant forward on to them, assessing the picture. 'Taken literally ten minutes before it happened. Got tangled in the rope somehow. She's prettier than the horse girl, isn't she? And we can definitely get a better headline out of it.'

Max, who'd been listening in, quick-fired: 'Strangled up in blue.'

The three of them, and Will, laughed. Rosie looked harder at her screen.

The chief said, 'OK, drop the horse girl; put this one in instead.'

Jeremy didn't want to have to do all the work again. 'But the other one's really middle class. She's got a horse. Maybe we could get a picture of it.'

The chief, who precisely understood his reluctance, gave him a look of pantomimic disbelief, and said, 'This one's fucking abseiling. Is that what they do on the sink estates where you live?'

Jeremy, despite knowing it was ridiculous, was slightly annoyed by the suggestion. 'There are no sink estates where I live.'

'And have your kids gone abseiling?'

'Yeah. One of them.'

'Exactly. The sink-estate kids aren't abseiling; they're shanking their pals and raping each other's sisters. So boot out the horse girl. It's not even that tragic, is it, that she can't stay on a horse? Not so much tragic as just shit at horse riding.'

Jeremy groaned inwardly at the thought of having to do the last half-hour's work again. He said, 'I don't have to make a new file, do I? I can just copy and paste the new text into this document.'

'Fine. I'll get the Art desk to switch the pictures.'

He bustled away. Jeremy, sighing, hit Ctrl+A to select all the copy, then pressed Delete.

SEVENTH CHAPTER

AT TEN past four, the strained voice of the Editor's PA spoke with audible politeness on the address system. As every day, she'd already come on at four to say 'News conference please.' But the middle and back benches and the heads of Newsdesk and Pictures had failed to show any sign of having heard. So the Editor made her, as every day, come on again to say, 'News conference *now* please, everyone.'

Still no one moved, until the chief finished the story he was on, hit the return key and, in one movement, spun sideways and up out of his chair. His pod leaders rose as one, Max still typing while he stood up. With thumb and forefinger, he flicked Ctrl+S, then checked it had saved. He glanced at Jez, with whom he usually walked to conference. Jeremy shook his head unhappily: he didn't even want to go; this bomb bullshit was going to go all the way to the Editor and he wanted as little part of it as possible. As Max left, Jeremy saw him fall in next to Lauren. Everything was going to shit at once.

The back bench supposed they'd better go too and got

to their feet. Seeing all this commotion, Geraldine, the head of Newsdesk, said to her deputy, 'Off we pop then,' and the whole crowd shambled, talking, past the Fleet Street sign and down the corridor to the Editor's office.

The newsroom relaxed. Several people stopped pretending to work. One of the casuals, pale with hangover, put on his coat and went out to buy a McDonald's. The remaining subs stood up or stretched their arms above their heads. Rosie crouched forward to lift a phone from the handbag beneath her desk. It looked big in her hands. Will swivelled his monitor to show her the Dirty Doctor story Max had assigned him.

'Look at this,' he said. 'This guy persuaded eight hundred women that they needed to be examined naked, and took pictures with a camera he'd hidden in the light fitting.'

'Oh my God,' said Rosie. 'That's awful. What a horrible man.'

Will had thought it was quite funny. 'But how can people be so stupid? You go to the doctor with a sore throat and he tells you to take off your pants...'

Rosie shuddered. 'Ugh. But you trust them, though, don't you, doctors? That's what's horrible.'

'I wouldn't trust one who looked like this. Look at the picture. You can *see* that he's a pervert.'

Rosie had to admit that he did look a bit shifty.

'And the amazing thing is,' said Will, 'he's a complete cretin as well. The way he got caught was he started putting them online. How dumb can you be?'

Jeremy thought it was endearing that they were still interested in what the stories revealed about the world outside the newsroom. Maybe, he thought with unexpected cheerfulness, it wasn't so bad being a grunt again after all, lolling around chatting while the bosses did the worrying. He rolled his chair to the side so he could see past his screen, and said, 'It's a thing that doctors do, take pictures. That story's been popping up every few months for as long as I've been here. There are forums where they swap them.'

It wasn't Jeremy whom Will wanted to speak to. 'Yes, that's what it says.'

'There was one a few years ago who had it going so well that he got the patients, once they'd gone home, to send him more naked pictures for check-ups.'

Will laughed and Rosie shuddered again. 'I just think it makes you never want to go to the doctor again. I can't believe people in positions of trust behave like that.' Saying something earnest made her defensive, and she made as if to carry on working.

'But you wouldn't undress just because someone told you to, would you?' said Will, flirtatiously.

She paused to let that dissipate. 'Surely the point is that these are sick people. They're desperate. That's why it's so sick to exploit them.'

'Yes,' said Will, 'it's terrible. Especially when people are at their most vulnerable.'

'Exactly.'

The conversation seemed to have come to a close, so Will went back to editing his story. He'd wanted to make her laugh and somehow it had turned sour. Frustrated, he checked the style guide for whether 'underway' was one word or two. Two: 'under way'. He wanted to tell her about something he'd heard, though he couldn't work out how to introduce it: that the news conference was nicknamed the Vagina Monologue, because only the Editor spoke and he called everyone a cunt.

But she probably wouldn't even like that. She could be so difficult. And it wasn't as if that were justified by her being especially attractive. Her hair was short and boyish, but bulged on top like a mushroom. Her limbs were narrow, her ribcage bony. She jerked her head about like a small animal and picked at the bean salads she sensibly brought from home. He wouldn't be surprised if she'd had an eating disorder at some point.

There were certainly prettier girls around. It wasn't like at the *Stentorian*, from where Will had been sacked a week after finishing the traineeship and where it had been all clever, vicious boys. The *Beast* had decided to replace its journeyman casuals with ambitious girls who'd been to Cambridge. Will had been told he was lucky to have a job here at all; the *Beast* needed girls to whisper prompts for when it spoke to women readers. But Rosie should by no means consider herself the only lobster in the tank.

He tried again, differently. 'Oh, God, look at this. He took pictures of this poor woman and of her daughter, separately, then Photoshopped them together. Isn't that awful?'

'It's gross,' said Rosie. 'I don't want to think about it.'

Jeremy spoke up again. 'Just to save you getting told by Max later, that'll have to come out.'

'Why? It's such a good detail.'

'It's too much for a family newspaper.'

Will had thought that ludicrous term must be ironic. 'But the *Beast* is constantly printing stories about perverts.'

'The readers want to know about perverts, they just don't want to know too much.'

'So they want to be teased.'

'Got it in one.' Jeremy made the sign of the cross as if blessing Will. 'And I say you are a journalist, my son. I can see you're destined for a glorious career.'

Will blushed. He felt a thrill of excitement. Was that true?

Was there something about him that people could see from the outside? Would people who met him now one day be saying that, even when he was young, you knew he would go on to great things? His being sacked from the *Stentorian* would be one of those curious factoids like Einstein failing his university entrance exam.

But when he read through the prose he'd reworked, and caught the unmistakeable tone of gloating excitement, the shame of his situation again consumed him. To find himself, after his first from Oxford – he'd never while there imagined he would catch himself thinking like this, but from *Oxford*, for God's sake; where had Jeremy or Max got their degrees? Hull? – and after an essay on Browning's metrics that his tutor had called 'extraordinarily promising' – *extra-ordinarily* – he found himself working in the gutter, for the gutter press. And this was no Wildean 'in the gutter, but looking at the stars'; he was working for the *Beast*, and '*Beast* reader' was a shorthand he himself had previously used for the worst kind of person – vulgar, ignorant and bigoted.

Its pages seemed to him the product of a mind that was morbidly drawn to decay and corruption, and that displayed the filthy-fingered rectitude of one who needs to examine so that he can judge. Paedos, molesters, murderers, thieves and cheats, its mental landscape was a teeming darkness made only more hideous by the pure white light of Tragic Schoolgirls, Tragic Babies, Tragic Soldiers, Tragic Anything.

Every page was tainted. But, he realized with horror, it was in the *Beast*'s own voice that he was condemning it. The idiom of contamination – *he* was contaminated. It was like tar that stuck and sucked as you tried to rise out of it. And he couldn't. But in despair he thought that if he had to live in filth he would plunge himself into it. He would swim in it.

He would revel in it and eventually he would be its king. If they wanted hammering headlines, they would have them. Striking down hard on the keys, he wrote it one sweep:

| 'DR FILTH' TOOK |
| VILE PICS OF |
| SICK CHILDREN |

And there below the headline was the newly dubbed Dr Filth's wispily bearded face, which Will captioned 'SHAMED: Dr Steven Franks' of Eagleton Road Practice, Norwich. Name him, shame him, ruin him, bankrupt him, have his neighbours smear shit on his door, his colleagues strike him off, his wife disown him, his children get beaten up at school. Have the public call for prison. Have the jury convict him, have the judge send him down, down into the blind pit where he belonged.

Slowly, Will's despair broke up and dispersed, like a mob after violence. With it went its attendant fantasies, leaving him still there, in the newsroom. He felt empty, as if after a bout of tears.

Glancing across at Rosie, he saw she was engrossed in what she was doing. After trying in vain to catch her eye, he desultorily remembered that there'd been something he intended to look up in the style guide, but not what it was. He clicked haphazardly through the alphabetical folders with their tens of thousands of entries, like 'Kings Road, Chelsea, NOT King's Road' or 'The Yemen, NOT Yemen' or undeleted assertions that the currency of France was the Franc and that of Italy the Lira.

There was a comprehensive section on correct forms of address for the aristocracy. 'If there are two peers of the same name but different rank, as in Viscount Pill and Lord Pill of

Piltdown, the first should be given his formal style to avoid confusion. Eldest sons of dukes, marquesses and earls use the courtesy title – i.e. Lord Pillock (usually one of their father's lesser titles).'

Wasn't 'pill' very old, very posh slang for someone who was a bit of a bore? He might have read it in Wodehouse. And 'pillock' was from a very different slang – he wondered who'd written this passage. There was something about the style guide that appealed to the academic manqué in Will, particularly the remnants of older versions still extant within it. The first had apparently been written when the paper was founded in the 1890s, and subsequent generations of subs had altered and edited it to match their times. You could still peel apart some of the layers. The word for such a thing broke free and floated up to him from a previous life: a palimpsest.

He imagined much of the style guide had been revised into blandness when it was computerized in the eighties. But, since it was unlikely that anything was ever de-prohibited, he opened the folder of Banned Words, which turned out to be compendious:

'Argie – A white-van man's coarsely jingoistic term for the Argentine. Do not use. Britannia is gracious in victory.'

'Choke back tears – A bizarre mix-up of eyes with throat.'

'Disgraced paedophile – Who used to be what? One of the most respected paedophiles in Britain?'

'Evacuation – Since almost no one is capable of using this word correctly, please avoid unless you are both confident and right. See also: enormity, mutual, pristine.'

'Filly – You are not a landowner and women are not horses (despite your desire to ride them).'

'Frog, for French. Also Krauts (Germans), Nips (Japanese), Micks (Irish), Spics (Hispanics), Taffies (the Welsh), Wops

(Mediterraneans), Yanks (Americans), to say nothing of nig-nogs, gollywogs, Sambos, "our dusky cousins", "the Hottentot MP for Tottenham" and all the rest of it. No mention, however jocular, must ever be made of "Wogs begin at Calais". Jocks (the Scots) is probably all right in light-hearted copy.'

'Impacted – Management speak. If you want to write like this, get a job in PR. The word you're looking for is "affected".'

'Rumours – the *Daily Beast* does not report rumours. On occasion, however, it may report speculation.'

'Socialist – For MPs, say Labour, NOT Socialist NOR Red NOR atheist.'

He looked up from the guide. The Sport subs, men his age to whom he would never speak, marked out by their mutton chops and young beer bellies, were beginning to bash their heavy fingers on their keyboards as the first results came in.

To his left, Turkish Liz and her deputy were chatting while they flicked through pictures on her screen. The deputy said, 'You know the whole band's full of nancies. Even that Freddy Giles.'

'So he prefers cock? Maybe he's not as stupid as he looks.'

'No, but they say he never wears a rubber, because he's shooting blanks.'

Liz was amused. 'You can tell him to stop taking me up the arse then.'

Will suppressed a startled laugh and looked away quickly before they noticed him eavesdropping. Liz was one of the few people in the newsroom whom Will's mind found restful, partly because she was a woman and partly because she was on Pictures, ergo: not competition. Her petrol-black hair was chopped into a bob that swung around her face when she hurried, and her nose curved towards a scarlet-lipsticked mouth that puckered and pouted whenever she was concentrating. Will had already heard that it was the after-mark of a long coke habit, from the days when Liz had been alluring and highly sexed. He'd never spoken to anyone remotely like her. In fact, he thought many of the newsroom veterans were like over-bred dogs, forced by the constant pressure to become extreme versions of themselves.

Even though it was rude, he glanced across at Rosie's screen to see what she was up to. She was diligently examining the opening paragraphs of a Criminal Immigrant story and did not seem especially open to some frivolous chat. But the bosses were in conference and after they came back everything would pick up speed until deadline.

A pretext came to him. 'Sorry, Rosie,' he said, again swivelling his screen towards her, 'do you think this headline is alright?'

Rosie's body started to turn, but her eyes finished the sentence they were reading before they flicked across. She asked, 'Sorry, what was that?'

'Um, I'm not sure about this headline. Do you think it's alright?'

Rosie read it and said, 'Hmm. Calling him "Dr Filth" is very... He's named and pictured, isn't he?'

'He's been convicted, so there's no legal problem.'

Rosie twisted her hands together uncomfortably. 'I don't know; it's hard to say. It's obviously very strong. Is "Dr Filth" just from you, or does someone in the copy call him that?'

'Someone says: "You don't expect a doctor to be so filthy."'

'Hmm.' Rosie considered. Will didn't see what there was to consider – it was the strongest headline he'd read all week. 'I don't think it'll get through.'

Jeremy spoke up from the other side of the desk. 'The *Stentorian* wouldn't have printed that, would they?'

'No,' said Will, 'but the *Stentorian*'s going down the pipes.'

Rosie was interested. 'Do you think so?'

'Oh yes, it's dying from the inside out. All that's keeping it going is subsidies from the TV channels. Really it should have gone bust already.'

'Yeah,' said Jeremy. 'But they haven't turned a profit in 200 years. I suppose the difference nowadays is the losses keep getting bigger.'

Rosie wanted to ask Will whether that was why he'd left, but thought that might be awkward. Instead she said, 'A friend of mine from uni, Leo Draper, works there. Do you know him?'

'Oh, a bit,' said Will. 'He did the journalism master's at City, didn't he? Were you on that too?'

'No, I went straight on to the trainee scheme here. But if I hadn't got a place I would have done a master's and then tried some other way.'

'When I started,' said Jeremy. 'No one did any kind of training to be a journalist. I'm from the first generation where it started to be normal even to have a degree. And the *Brute*'s second-last editor, Myles Crawford, started on the Newsdesk at sixteen; that wouldn't happen now.' Actually, he'd come over from Ireland, Crawford, from the *Evening Telegraph* in Dublin. Jeremy wished he'd never heard of the place.

To Will, being told the oral history of newspapers always felt like an induction. He asked, 'But you didn't do that?'

'No, I got a degree and then started as a cub reporter on the *Margate Sentinel*, and worked my way up to editor before I came to the middle bench here.'

'How come you're not in conference today? Don't all the pod leaders go?'

He noticed that Rosie shifted in her seat and absented

herself from the conversation, appearing to examine what was on her screen.

'Because I'm taking a break from the middle bench today. Lauren's doing it.' And before Will could ask him anything, he said: 'The idea is to let you whippersnappers have a go at the middle-bench jobs, so the paper won't collapse when we retire.'

'Really?' said Will, forgetting all about Rosie. 'And how did Lauren end up being the one doing it?'

'Well, she's been here a few years; she knows what she's doing.'

Will turned this over in his mind. Yes, she did seem securely embedded. He'd heard her call reporters 'a bunch of fucking primadonnas' and she had an immediate certainty about the *Beast*'s voice, as well as the tired eyes and irritability of someone who'd given many hours to ventriloquizing it. He asked: 'Did she apply, or how did it work?'

Jeremy leant all the way back in his chair, as if it were nothing to him. 'I don't know. I suppose she let the chief know she'd like to give it a try and then when I went to Ireland there was an opportunity and he asked her. Pretty straightforward.'

To Will this was very intriguing indeed. He'd already known in principle, of course, that promotion here was not like in, say, the civil service; you didn't wait your turn. And as he examined this shard of information, his colleagues, too, returned to their own preoccupations. Rosie asked herself how anyone could be so tactless when they were obviously very smart. She liked Lauren, as well as that there was a girl on the middle bench, and knew that Lauren was clinging to the pod-leader job by her fingertips; Jeremy being wound up might mean she was demoted again.

For his part, Jeremy was restless with what he told himself was merely nicotine withdrawal. He and Max always smoked after conference, that being the latest possible moment before they were locked in until edition, and he kept glancing up the corridor to the Editor's office, thinking he'd spotted them. He could vividly picture Max coming back, telling him the Editor had spiked the whole bomb thing and asking whether he wanted to go out for a smoke. It was about time; conference was usually ending by now. The casual who'd gone to McDonald's had already hurried back in, licking his fingertips.

Jeremy had to wait a few more minutes before the people who'd been in conference streamed back into the newsroom. On a normal day, they sauntered and laughed and came to a standstill to finish their conversations before they parted. But today they strode in silence back to their seats. Geraldine and her deputy on Newsdesk were moving almost at a jog. Everyone noticed. Those subs still standing up got back to their desks. Those writing emails or shopping online quickly closed their tabs and found their places in the copy. Will's antennae quivered; he saw that Jeremy knew what was going on.

Even Max was not swaggering. When he arrived at the pod, his pencil jigging rapidly between two fingers, there was no mention of a cigarette break. Aware of Will's attention, he simply said, 'Jez, could you go and lend a hand to Newsdesk? They're working on a story that could benefit from your experience.'

EIGHTH CHAPTER

THE faces clustered around Newsdesk were all unfamiliar, except for Colin, to whom he'd spoken earlier, and Geraldine, the head of Newsdesk, to whom he'd been warned never to speak. He certainly did not want to speak to her now. Jeremy wished as hard as he could that he'd never mentioned the burqas to anyone. But no magic happened and his legs kept carrying him closer.

Geraldine was voluminously coiffed, a head shorter than him and dressed as if for a country wedding in a navy-blue jacket over a floral summer dress. She'd crumpled the sleeves up to her elbows and delicate silver bracelets clinked expensively on her wrists as she gestured at her reporters. When she saw Jeremy coming, she exclaimed, 'There you are, old thing! We thought you'd already been blown up. Jeremy, isn't it? Come and sit down, there's a good fellow, we've saved you the place of honour.' With the flat of her palm, she tapped the top of an office chair standing empty at the centre of their cluster, as if for an interrogation.

Jeremy sat, surrounded by standing reporters. That Geraldine had been told his name made him feel that what he'd been dreading was now taking place. The newsroom gossip was that there hadn't been any 'old things' when she'd started out in the pit as a hungry crime reporter on the *Fun*. But with every rung she'd schemed and bullied and toiled her way up to the level of executive, she'd more completely adopted an oddly placeless and timeless posh-person's voice. Her sons were at Eton, so she'd made it work, but it implied a willingness to sacrifice bits of herself to reach what others might have liked to. Although, given that she'd worked the crime beat on the *Fun*, he presumed that more of the sacrifices had been made by other people.

Geraldine gave him a practical smile. 'So, you're the one who spotted the terrorists?'

'Well, kind of.'

A wrinkle of dissatisfaction disturbed her brow. 'What do mean, "kind of"? Did you see them or not?'

Jez had to try very hard to appear relaxed. 'Listen,' he said.

Geraldine's eyebrows jumped; it had been a very long time since anyone told her to listen. She appeared to indulge him.

Jeremy could see that that had been the wrong way to put it, but he pressed on. 'They were just two people wearing burqas. It could have been anyone.'

'Yes, I suppose it could have been Mahatma bloody Gandhi, but it wasn't, was it?'

'Erm.'

Geraldine feigned astonishment. 'Was it?!'

'Well, no, it wasn't—'

'Now *that* would be a splash! Gandhi, back from dead, becomes suicide bomber. Man of peace turns to hate. Second-ever instance of Lazarus phenomenon, scientists baffled, Jesus unavailable for comment. My dear man, that's the story of the century! You're quite sure it wasn't him?'

Jeremy was hating this. He said, 'Yup.'

'Rats!' said Geraldine, facetiously clenching a fist so the bracelets trembled, entertaining herself and her reporters while she stared Jeremy right in the eye. 'But at least we've succeeded in getting one fact established. Gandhi not one of the bombers. Lennard, take that down.' A few of the reporters sniggered.

Jeremy tried to interrupt. 'Yeah, but—'

'Now let's try for a second fact. It was *you* who saw them and *you* who brought in the story, or didn't you?'

'Yeah, sort of, but—'

'Stop.' Geraldine held up one admonitory finger. Her amusement had ended. 'Let's get this settled, shall we? It was you who saw them, yes or no?'

'Yes, but—'

Geraldine again stopped him with a finger. 'Would it be alright with you if we kept in mind that we've a deadline in a few hours? And that if we don't get this finished by then there'll be no newspapers in the shops tomorrow morning. Or didn't anyone tell you that that's how it works?'

Jeremy stared miserably at his hands. One of the reporters looked up at the clock behind the back bench.

'Well, didn't they?'

He shrugged helplessly.

'Good chap. Next question. How did you know it was them?'

'I *didn't* know it—'

Geraldine threw up her hands in rage. Her usual delight in her job was being severely impaired. 'Have you come over here to take the bloody piss? Or are you honestly trying to tell me that the story you've brought in and pitched and sold to the Editor is that you don't know anything at all?'

'No, of course—'

'They were pointing at the *Beast*. You saw them pointing. Is that accurate?'

'One was pointing.'

'One was pointing at the *Beast* and talking in Arabic.'

'Well, one was pointing at the building.'

'What the fuck's the difference?'

'There are two other newspapers in this building, and Whole Foods. Not counting the *Beast on Sunday* and all that.'

Geraldine's momentum was halted. Her forehead tensed into deep furrows and she opened her mouth as if about to say something. The subs were hopeless pedants, but this was a good point; it put the story to the test. If the bombers had been pointing at the *Impartial*... It didn't bear thinking about. Geraldine looked around her reporters for suggestions.

A blond boy with a face like an overweight cherub's spoke up. 'Actually, though, they aren't both on that side of the building. You were on the Usk Street side, weren't you?'

'Yeah.'

It was to Geraldine that the blond reporter continued. 'The *Impartial* doesn't go all the way round. Neither does Whole Foods. On that ground floor, you've got the escalators and then, above them, the canteen. The *Impartial*'s only on the High Street side. Its offices don't go all the way round the building. It's only us and the *Trumpet*'s floor that go all the way round.'

'And who on earth would bother to blow up the *Strumpet*?' asked Geraldine. 'Good journalism, that man.' A thrill went through the reporters; the test had come up positive. 'So,' she said, 'they were speaking Arabic and what build were they, what was their height?'

Jez didn't see where any protest of his could be lodged. He said, 'I don't know, maybe five-six, five-seven.'

'*Magnifique*. One of the ones on the lam from the mosque is five-six. There we go. And the rest were five-eight or five-nine. You said five-seven?'

'Yeah.'

'Seven, eight...' She turned to her reporters: 'What's the difference?'

Jeremy interjected, 'Well—'

'None. There's no practical difference. And who knows how accurate that original five-eight is anyway?'

The cherubic reporter, riding high on his success, spoke up again. 'And a lot of Asian guys are quite short, aren't they?'

'That's got nothing to do with anything.' Inaccuracy irritated Geraldine, but the intimate fear she lived with – of getting the story wrong, of printing the wrong thing and having to explain it – made her ask, 'There's not some special reason you've got a brilliant eye for height, is there? You didn't use to work in the menswear department at Peter Jones? You're not some kind of enthusiastic hobby carpenter?'

'No.' Jeremy glumly shook his head.

'Good.' Geraldine was reassured. 'And you told Colin that one of them had an adolescent voice, like this Atif Kayani, who's what, nineteen?'

Jeremy nodded, capitulating.

'So,' she looked around her staff, 'the descriptions are a match. The voices are a match. One was carrying a package. They were pointing at our offices. So far, at least, it stands up.' She squeezed Jeremy's shoulder and said, 'Well done, old bean, we'll make a reporter of you yet.'

The reporters popped their knuckles or shifted restlessly. A couple glanced at the doors and one asked, 'So does that mean—'

Geraldine interrupted. 'It means we go out and get a marvellous story. Do you really think the *Daily Beast* is going to be intimidated by a bunch of carbuncular teenagers from West Acton? Don't start quaking in your boots quite yet, Davidson; you won't be murdered at your desk.'

Jeremy's lips parted, but his remonstrances all blocked one another and none came out.

Geraldine seemed to have done with him. She said, 'Righty-ho-ho, chaps, off we go-go,' and began to give her orders.

Jeremy's dread seeped into his arms and legs like flu, dragging him towards the carpet. He wished he could go out for a cigarette and clear his head. It would soon be too late to stop them. And he sensed that, if he didn't stop them, everything would in some unforeseeable way become immeasurably worse. He could hear Geraldine telling the reporters not to let anything slip to the police until after deadline.

Jeremy spoke. 'Sorry,' he said. 'There was something else I should mention.'

Geraldine was obviously not often interrupted. She stared at Jeremy for a hard second, then said, 'What is it? They handed you an embossed business card saying Bombs R Us and you're not sure it's relevant?'

Jeremy thought to himself that it was lucky decades in the newsroom had inured him to that sort of talk; otherwise he might have felt a little humiliated.

'Come on, out with it.'

He said, 'It's just that I think this is all being taken too, um, definitively. The descriptions, the packages, there are—'

'You've got some caveats.'

'Yes!' Jeremy was startled into exclamation by this sudden ease of understanding. Caveats were exactly what he had.

'That's fine. Ben,' Geraldine pointed at the doughy-faced reporter who'd spoken before. 'Take his caveats. Tell me if there's anything important.' She did not look at Jeremy again before carrying on, committing reinforcements to the work already begun by the two reporters she'd sent out even before news conference.

Five long London miles away in a Muslim part of West Acton, the first of these was kicking through the heaped contents of the Kayani family's bin: curls of onion peel; cardboard egg boxes; desiccated tea bags; hard black banana skins; orange plastic bags with loo roll and pink Tampax wrappings peeping from under the knot. The heap gradually spread across the pavement as the reporter prodded his shoe through it. It was lucky that this was a residential street and there was hardly anyone about. In any case, Geraldine had said this story was big enough for him not to worry about producing complaints; Newsdesk would deal with them after the story was in.

The Picture desk had also sent a skinny, tracksuited snapper with thick glasses, who was crouching behind the low wall at the front of the house, his camera cocked. He made an ungainly shuffle sideways as a warm, fermenting pong wafted up off what had been the bottom of the pile. A shiny streak of bin juice spilt itself across the reporter's shoe. He swore and started flicking his foot in midair.

As he did so, the house's suburban door, painted dull green around a panel of frosted glass, was torn open. A young-ish man whom the reporter recognized from his Facebook pictures as Kayani's elder brother rushed out with his fist raised. 'Hey,' he shouted. 'HEY!' And the snapper popped up from behind the wall, the camera coming to his eye even as he rose. His immediate hyper-acute concentration slowed time to all but a standstill. Bam. Bam. Bam. The camera recoiled infinitesimally as it stamped those instants into the pictorial record.

The elder Kayani dropped his fist in shock and stared at the ferrety man in the thick glasses and black tracksuit, while the reporter covered the space between them. Bringing up his Dictaphone, he said, 'I'm Martin Harris from the *Daily Beast*. What does your brother Atif think of our newspaper?'

'You're a bunch of—'

Half a mile south, outside the West Acton Friday Mosque and Community Centre, the other reporter, Aamir Malik, one of the *Beast*'s most specialized employees, checked his reflection in the glass door. He smoothed his already-smooth lapels and tightened his pale-green striped tie until the Windsor knot sat snug under the crisp downward curves of his collar. He'd been born in Newham to Pakistani parents with whom he only rarely spoke English, especially now they were growing less independent. One of his maternal uncles had been a political correspondent on the *Mirror of Karachi* and under his influence Malik had become a newsman. The *Beast* had no one better at getting information out of Muslims.

He went inside, introduced himself and asked to speak to the head imam. Ten minutes later, he was sitting in the imam's spartan office and blowing on tea that was still too hot to drink. There was no colour in the room other than some framed gold-on-black calligraphy and a shelf of lever-arch folders in red, yellow and blue. Malik was saying, 'People must have been very angry about the suggestion that the police should search all the ladies.'

'Furious,' said the imam, shaking his head unhappily. 'And I must tell you, a lot of that fury was directed at your very newspaper.' The imam's face gleamed nut-brown beneath a white skullcap, and a white neck-beard marked the line of his jaw. He still had a Punjabi accent and Malik allowed ever more of his parents' gestures and inflections to come through.

'Because of the editorial.'

'Yes, because of that article.'

'I'm sure things must have become very heated.'

'Oh, very heated indeed. People were even talking about going to your offices and burning them down. You must understand – you should already – that you can't say these things. People were very, very incensed. How would your colleagues at the *Daily Beast* respond if someone threatened to –' he did not want to say it and instead circled his hand vaguely in the air – 'to do that to *their* wives?'

'Oh, they'd be very angry. And the families of those four boys must have been especially angry.'

The imam's manner changed slightly. He must have been in on their escape. But Malik didn't care about that today; it could be a follow-up story tomorrow. So he skirted around the boys themselves, kept the imam talking about how angry the congregation had been, and took notes.

Back at Copper House, Maurice Lennard, an ageing and pudgily sexless reporter with fishy lips and floppy white hair, leant against the barrel of the revolving door on to Usk Street. It was going to be a long evening for him, smoking ciga-rettes, trying to work the BBC News website on his phone and guarding against the off-chance that the terrorists came back today. He'd not been on a stakeout for years, but had been chosen because he would not, by panicking, draw the attention of either the building security or the swarms of story-hungry reporters inside Copper House. Despite the danger, it made him feel like an old hand for once, rather than just old.

As Geraldine's other reporters, given their missions, pushed slowly through the doors and then burst out on to the street and away, they saluted him with a raised hand or a grim nod. With the first couple, he was unsure how to respond and sort of waved. But soon he realized that the grim nod was best, and then he felt that he was doughtily sending them out one by one like fighter pilots to do battle above the skies of Britain. Good luck, Davidson. Off you go, Jacobs. If an attack did happen, it wouldn't be members of the public who were killed; it would be journalists, his own colleagues.

He ran his gaze along the hundred yards of street. There were a few expensive cars parked, a stub-nosed Bentley and a wide, flat racer that he thought was a Maserati, not the sort of thing West Acton terrorists would have the funding for. A few girls in short dresses and young men in suits were already queuing for the rooftop bar on the building opposite. He guessed that when the terrorists came it would be from the High Street and not from behind Copper House, where a quiet square with no big access roads lay under a canopy formed by giant plane trees. He could see their upper strata glowing a fresh translucent green as they were caught by the late-afternoon light. At the High Street end, the gap between the buildings flashed red and blue and black as traffic shot past. Pedestrians strolled or hurried past the aperture. The terrorists would be in black cloaks.

He was under strict instructions from Geraldine to call as soon as he saw anything, so that she and the Editor could decide whether to tell the police and the building security. But Maurice had realized even as Geraldine was saying this that there would never be enough time for a phone call. He now decided very easily that he would stop them himself. He'd lived long enough to know that from this point life was mainly a story of decline. He was not fast or strong, but he had a flaring of bravery left in him. He readied himself, and waited.

The reporters rushed past him, not sorry to be putting distance between themselves and the target. They jumped into their cars or ran for the tube while calling their contacts. And in Baroness Ahmad's chambers, in the government's counter-terror unit, in the office of a man at Scotland Yard who could be trusted to act discreetly, the phones started to ring.

Upstairs in the newsroom, Geraldine sent off the last two reporters: 'Alright then, chaps, Godspeed, I wish I was going out there myself, don't get blown up before you land the story.' She then said 'Righty-ho' to herself, clapped her hands together with a clash of jewellery and strode off to the Editor's office before Jeremy could catch her attention.

Ben, with all the manifest reluctance of someone given a tedious task, half-sat, half-leant against the edge of the desk beside him. He crossed one leg over the other and held his notebook flipped open on his thigh. Scratching the inside of his ear, he asked, 'So, what are your caveats then?'

Jeremy wondered what they'd done to corrupt this child, or whether that's just what graduates were like now. He said, 'We can't be sure that the people in burqas were those guys.'

'Those terrorists.'

'Yeah. I only saw them for half a minute, maybe less. *Maybe* they were men, but isn't it more likely that they were just what they looked like, you know, women?'

The child emitted an almost imperceptible sigh. 'So you're saying your caveat is that you don't know anything for sure.'

Jeremy shrugged, opening his palms as if to say: well, there you have it.

'OK, got it. That's great,' he said with transparent insincerity. 'Thanks very much. I'll let Geraldine know when she's got a minute.' With a practised flick of the fingers, the cherub flipped his notebook shut.

NINTH CHAPTER

AS SOON as the chief, periodically glancing over his shoulder at Newsdesk, saw that Jeremy was no longer in use, he bustled over to collar him before Geraldine came back. He and Geraldine loathed each other, each considering the other insubordinate, and didn't speak. He addressed her deputy, 'Alright, Colin.'

Colin stood up. 'Alright, Frank.'

'Have you finished putting the thumbscrews on Jez here? We'd like to mistreat him ourselves if he's free.'

'No problem,' said Colin. 'But we might need to borrow him again later if that's OK?'

'We don't have enough subs today who've reached even Jez's level of near-competence, so we won't be able to spare him for the full water torture. But I'm sure he'll be happy to give you whatever help he has time for, won't you, Princess Jezmin?'

'Delighted,' muttered Jez, getting to his feet.

The chief nodded at Colin and slapped Jeremy on the shoulder. The two subs, one blocky, the other shaped like a pear, walked very slowly and very close together back to their desks. Jez said, 'Thanks, Frank. I really hate reporters.'

'Who doesn't? And if anyone's going to plier out your toenails, it'll be us. We'll need every pair of hands we've got tonight. If this story comes in, and it's as big as it could be, the Editor'll want the edition to go on time.'

Jeremy appealed to him. 'Listen, this story. I really think there are problems with it.'

The chief weighed that up. 'And you've said that to Newsdesk?'

'Yeah, but you know what they're like.'

The chief considered. 'The Editor wants this story. He thinks it could be the biggest splash this paper, that any paper's had in years. *Daily Beast* uncovers terror plot against the newspaper. It's better than the expenses scandal, better than phone-hacking, better than the Rotherham paedo ring. If it stands up, and we don't get blown up in the next five hours, it'll be scoop of the year, splash of the year, every prize going. The Editor thinks it *is* going to stand up and the Editor, despite being madder than an IRA hunger striker, is even more of a journalistic genius than me. So, in terms of getting this story spiked, is there any piece of information you have that Newsdesk and the Editor don't?'

The chief beamed his frightening grin full at Jeremy, who glumly said, 'Not really.'

'Alright, how about let's do some fucking work then?'

He slapped Jeremy's shoulder for a second time, as if to release him from his presence, and, without expecting a response, bustled back to his desk.

Jez watched him take his seat, then turned towards his own. Before he could get there, Lauren, seeing him momentarily unoccupied, jumped from her chair at the head of what was really his pod. She was hunched with apology and squeezing two of her fingertips till they went red and white. The curmudgeon in Jez dug in his heels.

'Hi,' she said. 'How was your holiday?'

Jez put his hands in his pockets and let his paunch expand forward between them. He said, 'Yeah, not bad.'

'OK,' she said. 'Good.' She hesitated, and then plunged in. 'I'm really sorry about being in your seat. They asked me to cover while you were away and then, you know how it is, it's not like they give you a choice. If you want it back, I don't know, we could talk to them and see what they say. It's not like we're always in on the same days anyway, so on Thursday and Friday this week, for example, you're rota'd in and I'm not, and I think the idea anyway was just to train me up a bit to have another person who could step in when they needed someone.'

Note, thought Jeremy with a sub's specificity, that she doesn't quite suggest giving me my seat back on days when we are both in. Which is most days. The others are just, what, a consolation prize? And this 'they' she's been getting ordered about by, there is no 'they'; it's the chief.

But even as he was about to speak his mind he was asking himself what blame could be laid on her, or even on the chief. That was how it worked. Had he himself not, when only a little older than her, displaced the deputy editor of the *Sentinel* in much the same way? Actually, he was lucky he hadn't been sacked. The man he'd replaced on the *Sentinel*, a member of the old guard called Mark Pont, had been. That was what usually happened to anyone whose cost suddenly outweighed his usefulness. Lauren would learn that herself one day. Perhaps she already was learning it. And, thinking like this, Jeremy talked himself out of his job.

To Lauren he said, 'Oh don't worry about it. Better you than me.'

'Really?' He could see her relief.

'Yeah, really. I'd been saying to Frank that I'd had enough of it anyway, so...'

'Oh, I *see*,' she said. 'I didn't realize that.'

'Course I don't mind still doing the days when they're short.'

'I *see*,' she said again. Everything about her relaxed. Her shoulders straightened. Breaking into a smile, she made a noise halfway between 'Huh' and 'Ha'. 'I thought—' She shook her head. 'I was worried you might be pissed off. You know, you slip out for a week and they just close up the gap.' Her voice still held a question.

'I wouldn't put it past them,' he said. 'They'd shackle us to the desks if they could.'

'As long as the leg irons were made in England.'

Jeremy's chest lifted in a single guffaw. 'Yeah, and then write a leader slamming the other papers for using foreign-bought shackles.'

'Especially when hard-working British shackle-making families are struggling to pay their mortgages.'

'And to compete with cowboy Polish shackle-makers who're knocking out dangerously low-quality shackles in illegal workshops, some of which have even snapped, allowing rogue sub-editors to escape into the outside world.'

Lauren smiled again. She said, 'Thanks, Jez,' meaning it.

He nodded her away, pleased to be generous. Telling himself he was an idiot who deserved demotion, he went back to his desk, where Max asked him, 'Had enough chatting, have you? Or are Newsdesk going to invite you back for another chinwag later on?'

Max's concern for the everyday question of how to get the work done by deadline made Jeremy feel as if he'd returned from a foreign ordeal and found his home just as he left it. Everything was going to get worse now that the Editor was involved in this story, but he was sick of worrying and the chief was right: it could be Newsdesk's problem for a while. For now, everything was as usual. That sulky, ambitious kid Will was hammering intently at his keyboard. Rosie was dialling someone on the phone.

Out of middle-bench habit, he scrolled through PagePlanner to see what the pod was working on. Rosie's story fitted into the paper so perfectly it could have been told just in the caption kickers: ROBBED, by a photo of an ancient blind woman with a cloud of wispy white hair; and MIGRANT by a camera-phone mugshot of a *Big Issue* vendor. Apparently, she'd opened her purse to give him the sweetly granny-ish sum of 50p and he'd filched a £20 note from under her nose. Not only that, but she'd been a Wren during the war. Pictures had got a service photo of her, which was captioned HEROINE. In it she was sixty years younger, wearing a thick cloth uniform and a narrow naval cap on her crimped hair, pluckily doing her bit to save Britain from the Nazis.

Rosie was asking the person on the other end of the phone, 'And what about the guide dog?'

Jeremy relaxed a little further. Normal service had been at least temporarily resumed. And this blind woman, Anne Palmer-Hassett, 86, of Taplow, Buckinghamshire, a loyal *Beast* reader, had supplied the perfect quote: 'I'm a Christian and I do forgive him because of that. But what I don't understand is why he's allowed to stay in this country.'

Rosie must just be tying it up. She was having to repeat herself because her voice was too soft. 'I said, but if she didn't have a dog or a stick, there must have been someone with her... Yes, or if she did have a stick or a dog after all... That would be great... I'm on...' She gave the reporter her extension number.

Will had put into revise a Scientific Study about how parrots could predict the future, which he'd headlined 'Polly sees a cracker'. Good headline, that; the kid had talent. He was already on to another about how dogs would reject puppies born of incest, which he'd headlined 'Oedipus Rex'. Jez didn't get it. Wasn't Oedipus that play about a boy who wanted to fuck a horse, the one Daniel Radcliffe got naked in when he wanted to stop being Harry Potter?

Anyway, that headline would have to change. It wasn't for him to mention, he wasn't pod leader. But there was no doubt Max would – and even as he was thinking it, Max said, 'Will, "Oedipus Rex" isn't going to make it.'

'But it's—'

'I know what it is. But you're not writing for your Oxford don any more. You're writing for Mrs Thompson, 56, house-wife and part-time secretary, of High Wycombe, who's reading the *Beast* at the hairdresser's. She doesn't know that Oedipus is a made-up Greek who fucked his mum, and she doesn't want to know. So get it out and write a headline that she's going to like.'

Will looked stung.

'And while we're on the subject, in your parrot story you've said the testing centre was in Camden. But Mrs Thompson doesn't know where Camden is; she only goes up to London once a year to watch *The Mousetrap* and buy her grown-up children's Christmas presents. And Mrs Thompson gets very angry – and rightly so – when the media assume that everyone in England is the kind of dickhead who lives in London. The whole *purpose* of this paper is that it's for actual English people and not for the kind who live in Islington townhouses, give their children foreign names and think it's clever to make jokes about fucking their mums. So go into that story and write "Camden, North London" before you lose us a reader.'

Will's lips bunched as if he were about to spit, but he sucked it down and just double-checked the style guide for whether the N in North London was capped. Max was about to say something more when yelling broke out around one of the outlying desks. Several hundred heads turned to see what was going on. It was Features. A tall, slim old man in an outdatedly formal herringbone suit was weakly holding up his palm, looking dazed.

'Fuck me,' said Max, swearing because he was still angry with Will. 'It's John Dyson.'

Jez looked at the clock behind the back bench. It was five. 'This must be his last day.'

The Features people around Dyson stopped yelling and began to bang their desks with fists or staplers or the flats of their hands. There was an instant of charged quiet like that between the end of a play and the cloudburst of applause, then the long-serving hacks, the back bench, the chief, Max, Jez, and journalists all over the newsroom were on their feet, bending forward to whack the tables with whatever was in reach. Greenhorns like Will and Rosie, who'd never seen a banging-out before, copied them in excited bewilderment. Hundreds of hands thumped the shaking tables, rattling the screens and keyboards and making pens jump and run to the floor. The noise was as arrhythmic and furious as a hailstorm smashing into a car park, and through it people were whooping and shouting.

In Dyson himself, dazedness gave way to joy. He laughed and made an elaborate bow, then clasped his hands together and raised them over his head like an old-time champion. The noise lifted to a new intensity. He picked up a worn leather briefcase and set off across the newsroom towards the glass doors, turning to raise his hand to both sides in acknowledgement. The banging almost coalesced into one beat, went wild again, and then hit a rhythm all at once, a single rapid BANG-BANG-BANG-BANG.

By halfway across the newsroom, Dyson seemed over-whelmed. Trying not to let any tears escape, he began to hurry and then, all at once, he was gone and the glass door was swinging shut behind him.

The newsroom went quiet and it was as if, after this deafening, their thoughts had become briefly audible: How must it feel to get a banging-out like that? ... Imagine working here for that long... I wonder how it'll be when I leave... Julie got made redundant last week and all they gave her was a month's pay... I hope newspapers last long enough to see me out... I've got to get out before it all goes under...

As everyone's ears adjusted, the ringing phones, whining computers and busy voices resumed their usual volume. The scroll of *BeastOnline* projected on to the back wall still spooled; the TV reporters projected next to it still spoke soundlessly in their boxes; the silhouette of someone walking behind the back bench moved across the projections; work continued.

The chief bounded over to them with the eager bulkiness of a baby monster, already saying, 'I haven't seen a banging-out like that since Clive got the heave-ho. I thought Dyson was going to blub. Poor sap. He'll have hanged himself in his underpants by this time next week.'

Carefully edging and laying his words like a row of bricks, Max asked, 'Do you think you'd like a banging-out when it's your time to go?'

If the chief caught the subtext about the rumour he was leaving, he didn't show it. 'I'll never be allowed to leave,' he declared. 'I sold my soul to the *Beast* for magical headline-writing powers and to pay for it I've been damned eternally to the newsroom. They all used to cry, though – do you remember? – when the department was bigger and they had further to walk.'

'Yes,' said Jeremy, strangely moved. 'I remember. With that long room where all the layout subs used to sit, and they used to make a tunnel, everyone banging metal rulers. Even Clive blubbed and he was the meanest bastard I ever worked with.'

'Great journalist, though,' said Max.

'Speaking of which,' said the chief, 'enough fannying about. He's had his two minutes and now he's dead to us. So shove a tampon up your nostalgia holes; it's already five o'clock.'

Rosie shuddered, her eyes briefly closing, but Max and Jez both laughed. This was the longest-running joke in the newsroom: that they were all the kind of crude, callous Neanderthals who would actually stoop so low as to work for the *Beast*. The chief said: 'Can I give you page fourteen, Max? There's a single column about the Treasury being incompetent and a page lead about how the Yanks have stopped bombing other people long enough to execute one of their own teenagers. Supposedly a rapist, but the kid's a legal retard – not unlike some subs I could mention, eh, Jez? – and probably didn't do it. Straightforward enough: family's—'

Max did not like being told how to run his pod by anyone, least of all the man whose job he planned to usurp. He interrupted: 'Family's anguish, miscarriage of justice, inhumane proceedings, etcetera. Just a little nip-tuck job, with—'

The chief interrupted him back. 'Except this story's got a lovely pair of fake tits as well. They've gone and fucked up the execution. Used some kind of own-brand lethal injection to save some dosh and it hasn't worked properly.'

Max *loathed* being behind the story. 'Yes,' he said. 'So what's happened?'

'The kid's still alive. They started executing him half an hour ago and he's still…' The chief stuck out his arms like a zombie, let his tongue loll from his mouth, and started convulsing.

Max asked, 'Does that mean the story still needs to be written?'

The chief put his tongue back in. 'No, it's all there. They've left a space for how many minutes it goes on for. Just follow it on the wires and stick in the number when he stops shaking.'

Max wrote the names of the stories into the empty box marked '14' on his flatplan. 'OK,' he said, 'but if you give me many more pages the pod's going to start to be understaffed.'

'Good thing you're the top sub then, isn't it?'

Max couldn't resist the flattery, and preened.

'Which is why it won't matter that Newsdesk want to borrow Jez again. Apparently they've found their cat o' nine tails.'

Jez sighed with frustration.

'And last thing: that "Dr Filth" headline – who wrote it?'

Max said, 'I've already changed it.'

'I know, but the Editor wants it changed back. He likes it.'

Max tried to think of a response, but the Editor's express wishes overruled any objection. 'OK,' he said.

'So whose was it?'

'Will's.' Max glared at him, and Will tried – not quite successfully – to keep his face straight.

The chief said, 'Keep it up, kid, and you'll get a life sentence like mine. Now, Jez, get over there.'

TENTH CHAPTER

WHEN Jeremy returned to Newsdesk, lugubrious with anticipation, he found that something had driven the reporters into a state of frenetic excitement. They ignored him, which only made him more apprehensive. Geraldine herself was away updating the Editor and Jeremy, summoned to where he was unwanted, tried to fake his way out of how he was feeling by lolling ostentatiously in a vacant chair. He could hear one of the assistant news editors berating a reporter: '... can't be breaking and entering if the window's already broken; just fucking get in there and we'll sort it out later.'

Ben noticed Jeremy and, clamping his chubby hand over the bottom of the phone he was holding, asked, 'Are you hearing this?'

Jeremy tried to protest that of course he wasn't hearing anything, but the reporter shushed him angrily and pointed at the phone. Jeremy bit off the words and instead tapped his fingers on the table. He wished he and Max were outside having a cigarette. He'd missed that on holiday, as well as the familiarity of how their conversations usually went the same way: he moaned about the place while Max criticized people he thought shouldn't be there. Now that the idea of a cigarette had occurred to Jeremy he felt a physical irritation, like hunger in the skin.

A fugitive thrill ran through him: why didn't he just go outside and have a smoke? Who would stop him?

But he knew, of course, that he would stop himself.

Ben was jabbing his finger at a sheaf of paper on the desk beside Jeremy's elbow. Jeremy picked it up for him, the lowermost sheet swinging from its staple. The reporter frowned, put his hand over the phone again and hissed, 'Read it.'

Jeremy read. It was the transcript of a doorstep interview with Kayani's elder brother. The text had been hastily transcribed and was ragged with errors. But there were quotes beside which someone had scrawled big asterisks in red biro:

'Of cuorst my borhter fucjing hates teh beast. Evryone hates it. It shodle bbe fucking burnt down, Yuo think yo're so fhigh and moral, but its al lc omeing to and end ffor you. Weere winning. That;s hwat yuo racsts downt' realize. You'e britain is finsihed, youe ide athat eeryone is a whtie christian is finishdfe. that britains dfead and you haben;t reliazed it yet. Us bwornoskinnd enlgish, w'ere liek baracj obmaa and tigher w oods, were teh best at evhrything, and soont the whoel of england'll by liek London is alredy. Te fuckgng beast is jst the end fo a dyin g cultre, You're dead and you doen't eben knwo it yet. Wwc're comeing, we're already here, we;re everyhwere and you can't stop us.'

The *Beast*'s words formed themselves without Jeremy's having to think – 'terror brother's chilling anti-British rant'. Headline: 'You're dead'. The only thing missing was – he turned the page; another red asterisk, the ink thinning where the nib had accelerated – and, yes, they'd got him to say something about Islam:

'This si agodless country, the churcjh f England, seriosuly, it's a joke, a comeplte joke. Tehy break alll their ownr ueles to fit into your corript culturr. Iand hwen people are lokimg ofor soemthing that that ahs dome fucking intergrity, theyll finalyly aks to be saevd by Islam.'

It could hardly be better for the story. But Jeremy's dread rose up over him. His vision narrowed to the alley of carpet between himself and the double glass doors that led out to the atrium. Dark figures crossed it. The reporters had the story's blood-scent in their nostrils. Hacks were rushing in every direction. No one would notice him slipping out through the noise. Just for a minute, for one cigarette, while he had a think about all of this. And indeed, on long-suppressed impulse, he stood and started to walk.

His shoulder brushed a reporter, who paid no mind, and he'd cleared the first group when Geraldine, returning from the Editor's office, blared 'Ahoy!' from shockingly close beside him. Jeremy's head snapped to the right. Geraldine was staring up at him. 'Where are *you* off to?'

'Um. Fag break.'

'Fag break? *Mon dieu*, you *are* taking the Mickey, aren't you? You don't actually work here, is that it? You're some sort of merry prankster and this is an elaborate ruse. Do I have it right?'

Jeremy thought, I'm a grown man, I'm a full-grown man. I have a house. I have a wife. I've fathered two children. I have a pension. I have savings. I have a heavy glass award for Regional

Newspaper of the Year 1997, Southeast. How can she speak to me like this? This is not how grown men are treated.

But then he thought, Come on, Drudgy. Come on, Count von Drudgenberg. You are not in ze kindergarten now. 'Alright,' he said. 'It just seemed like everyone was busy for the time being.'

'Of course they're bloody busy. So ought you to be.' Geraldine was staring at him as if at an exotic creature that might be a hoax. 'You must be some kind of idiot savant,' she said. 'How you made that spot baffles me utterly.'

'About that—'

'You can forget the caveats now. Hasn't anyone told you? It's been verified. We've got another source.'

'You've got what?'

'Another source. In the Met. We're on the line to him now. We haven't told him about your spot yet but he says he's been hearing things about a bombing, somewhere in central London, involving burqas. He's been hearing about it today.'

'Jesus,' said Jeremy, his mind's foundations swaying. 'Really?'

'Yes, really, you dolt. Pick up that handset and you'll hear it.'

Jeremy picked the handset up off its cradle and put it to his flabbergasted head. Ben's voice was saying, '… you been told about it?'

Another voice – a measured, careful voice – said, 'The information's been circulating in the department. I know that a number of my colleagues are currently looking into the situation and I'll continue to liaise with them about how the investigations are progressing.'

'Can you tell us what information you've got already?'

'At present we're working on confidential indications from our sources that, as I said before, there may be an attack planned within the next few days.'

'By Atif Kayani and his gang?'

'The identity of those involved is still the subject of police investigation.'

'Sure, but if you were to, I don't know, spot some terrorists scoping out a target in burqas, you would be reasonably confident it was Kayani?'

'Hmm. It's very difficult to comment on a hypothetical situation and, in any case, terror networks can be extensive and any individuals sighted, as in your example, might not be the primary members of a particular group. They frequently deploy secondary members for purposes such as reconnaissance. That's been well documented. There's a piece of research we've published in collaboration with King's College London that should be useful to you, about hierarchies within terror groups. You can find it on their website, under "studies".

'But, essentially, if anyone were to be sighted, I would be reluctant to jump to over-hasty identification with particular suspects. After all, it's a very difficult task, as I'm sure you can imagine, to correctly identify what are, ultimately, would-be criminals *before* they've committed a crime.'

'So you're saying that, even if you did spot some people, they might not be the ones actually planning the attack? They might just be hangers-on or something and the attack would actually be coming from someone else?'

'All I can say is that that would be in keeping with observed patterns. I wouldn't make a conjecture about any particular situation without full reference to our sources.'

'And who are your sources?'

The policeman gave a stagy laugh. 'That's not discloseable, of course.'

'But could you give us a way of saying what kind of people they are? Undercover operatives? Informers inside the terror cell?'

The policeman was silent for a moment, then said, 'People in the terror community.'

Jeremy was incapable of believing what he was listening to. This information, like a piece from the wrong jigsaw, would not fit into the structure of his thoughts. It butted, dull but insistent, against his forehead.

Corroborating phrases followed it – 'indications for some time', 'increasingly clear signals', until, eventually, some one of them got into his mind and flipped it upside down.

ANOTHER SOURCE!

Jeremy remembered the distinct feeling he'd had when he saw the two figures in burqas, of a monstrous shadow looming across the cinema screen. He felt it again now. By some astounding accident, he must have stumbled on to something. It must have been intuition, emotional antennae, news-sense, the snap judgement that reached what a considered opinion could not. Another source!

He thought: Fuck. Jesus. Motherfucking holy Jesus, holy fucking mother of God. It's real. It's REAL.

The long years of weariness left him as suddenly as if he'd twisted out from under their grasp. Adrenaline induced the hyper-wakefulness of the newsman who's on to something. He was no longer used to it, and he reeled. There were terrorists planning to bomb *Beast* HQ. The terrorists were coming here. He was inside the room the terrorists planned to blow up. His eyes went to the doors. He half-expected someone to burst in right then. This was the biggest story for... This was the biggest story.

And now one of the Graphics boys – a young guy, more casual than the journalists in a short-sleeved checked shirt – fast-walked over to Geraldine with a sheet of A3 paper flapping in his hand. As soon as Geraldine saw him coming, she pointed at the desk and said, '*Grazie*, old stick, put it down there.' The Graphics man was nervous of her, but put the sheet down on top of all her other printouts, and wiped it flat. It was a map.

Geraldine said, 'Right, where's Stephen?'

The Graphics man looked deeply uncomfortable. 'Sorry, I don't know who that is.'

'The reporter who gave you the information for this map. Where is he?'

'Oh.' The Graphics man twisted around to look back the way he'd come. 'He was just over there.'

Just then Geraldine spotted him and shouted, 'Stephen! Over here please!'

The reporter flinched, as if he'd been caught thinking about something quite else, then hurried towards them. But still there were a few seconds, painful for the Graphics man, in which he alone was responsible to Geraldine. She examined the map, her finger pressing a dell into the abstracted geography.

Jeremy recognized the net of thick and thinner streets and the buildings marked in greyish-blue. The map's centre was Copper House and around it were three concentric rings, spreading across Kensington in angry, then paler tints of red. The first and reddest contained Copper House and their end of the High Street, taking in the square behind them and the blocks around it. The second, slightly diluted, menaced everything down to Earl's Court, up to Notting Hill and east across a corner of the park to Kensington Palace. The third and widest ring, which was almost pink, lay across Hammersmith and Sloane Square to the south and Bayswater and Ladbroke Grove to the north.

Jeremy had recovered from the shock. His mind was as sharp and clear as a frosty morning. He stepped closer and said to Geraldine, 'Where have you got this from? It looks like the whole of West London's going to be blown up.'

'Stephen,' she said. 'What the hell is this?'

'It's the map of the possible damage.'

'I can see that, but this buffoon' – she jerked a thumb at Jeremy, her bracelets jingling – 'can't tell the difference between a terrorist and the Princess Royal, and even he can see it's ludicrous.'

The Graphics man gladly slid to the discussion's edge. 'Well,' said Stephen, 'our guy in the counter-terror advisory said there was a chance it would be a dirty bomb and that there would be fallout.'

'A dirty bomb? Are you serious?'

'He said it was a very real possibility.'

'*How* real a possibility?'

'He said it was definitely possible.'

'How in Heaven's name are four shopkeepers from Acton going to get their hands on a nuclear bomb? Anyone who opens the paper and looks at that is going to think it's nonsense.'

Jeremy asked the reporter, 'What reasons did he have for saying it might be a dirty bomb?'

'He said it was a possibility they'd been worrying about for years.'

Geraldine: 'That's it?'

'Well—'

'It is, isn't it?'

'Yes, but—'

'For fuck's sake, Stephen. This is the biggest scoop you'll ever get near and you're trying to botch it up with this dirty bomb bullshit. Every detail in this story has to be solid enough to build a bloody house on. You' – she was looking at the Graphics man – 'draw this up again with much smaller circles based on the information he' – she pointed at the reporter – 'is going to give you. The first circle wants to be immediate damage, what actually gets blown up, buildings that actually get gutted. Then the next circle is the blast wave – windows bursting, fallen cornicing, car crashes, that sort of thing. Then, last circle, here you go, health risks from inhaling powdered brick, carcinogenic dust, chronic lung disease, all the 9/11 stuff.'

The Graphics man steadied himself and said, 'Might that not be quite a small map?'

'How am I supposed to know? Stephen, you have got us that information, haven't you?'

'Um, yes, I do. It'll definitely be smaller than what we've got at the moment.'

'I know it'll be smaller. That's the whole point. How much smaller?'

The reporter sized up the map, held his thumb and forefinger over a small area, then seemed to change his mind and moved them further apart. 'It'd be about this big,' he said.

'What do you mean, about?'

'He said if it was a conventional bomb – and he really did say a dirty bomb was—'

'Forget the dirty bomb.'

'But he—'

'I don't want to hear one more word about it. You'll make this paper a laughing stock.' She looked at the map again. 'But bloody hell, even this looks like something that's been dropped out of a plane.'

Stephen rearranged his thoughts. 'OK, he said if it was a conventional bomb, he gave me a range for how wide the damage might be. The smaller end of the spectrum would be like this' – he narrowed the gap to one that was close around Copper House and their end of the High Street – 'and the bigger would be like this.' He widened it to again include as far as Notting Hill, Earl's Court and Kensington Palace.

Geraldine twisted one of her bracelets back and forth on her wrist. She asked the Graphics man, 'What do you think?'

'Me?'

'Yes, you.'

'But I don't know anything about bombs.'

'Of course you don't. But how do you think it looks?'

'Oh. We'd have to bring in the frame.'

'It looks better bigger, doesn't it?'

The Graphics man did not want to be asked that question. 'It depends what you want,' he said.

Geraldine clicked her tongue at this feebleness.

Jeremy stared at the map and his hands squeezed each other involuntarily. Geraldine was right; it really did look like something dropped from a plane. The whole building destroyed. He asked the reporter, 'Did your guy say what end of the spectrum was more likely?'

'No, he just said this was the range of what they might be able to build.'

Jeremy ran his eye over the red circles curving across the squared edges of buildings and streets, as if to reassure himself they weren't a mirage. 'We can make it the upper end of the range, since that's as likely as the lower. But let's keep it short of Kensington Palace, because close by will be enough to make the point it's under threat without making the Palace think we didn't tell them Kate and William were in danger. And then, so the map doesn't look too empty, could we do routes of attack, likely escape routes, distance to their houses, the mosque, that sort of thing?'

Geraldine: 'Do we have that information?'

Stephen: 'Yes, we do. Those places are all a few miles west, though.'

Jeremy: 'Then we do a map on a scale wide enough to see all that, and around here, do one of those magnification circles.'

Geraldine asked the Graphics man, 'Would that look good?'

'Yes, absolutely. Um, what colour do you want the route lines and—'

'Red, everything red. And make a panel explaining what the three circles mean. Stephen, give him that copy. And you,' she said to Jeremy, 'now you've woken up, I want you to look at all the copy we get through. You're the only one who's seen the bombers, so read it and tell me whether you notice anything.'

The chief must have been listening in because he bundled himself over to them. He and Geraldine nodded warily at each other. It had been months since they'd exchanged a word. He said, 'Geraldine, I know this story has tits like watermelons, but if we're going to get it off on time, we can't afford to lose one of our most experienced subs from now till deadline. How about Jez here goes back to his desk and carries on subbing and when you get copy through, you ping it over for him to read? If he notices anything, he'll tell you.'

Geraldine, knowing that disagreement would become a test of wills, said: 'Fine,' and turned away.

The chief, for the second time that evening, guided Jez away from the Newsdesk. As they walked, Jeremy's fingertips were quivering with excitement. He told the chief: 'They've got another source. It's for real.'

'Have they done anything to protect the newsroom?'

Jez felt a little thrown that in the shock of the moment he hadn't thought of that. 'No,' he said. 'We've got to secure the building! We've got to—'

The chief said, 'Leave it with me. You go get some pages out of the way as fast as your addled brain can type.' And he bounded off to talk to the Editor.

ELEVENTH CHAPTER

THE pod had fallen a little way behind without him. He could see it in how Max was hunched towards his screen, his chin over the keyboard as he chewed his pencil, and hear it in the tightness with which he spoke, not taking his eyes from what he was typing: 'Jez. Nice you've decided to come back.'

Jeremy leant towards him and dropped his voice so that Will and Rosie couldn't hear. 'Max,' he said.

Max kept typing. 'What?'

'The other story.'

Max blinked as if to detach his thoughts from the copy, then looked up at him.

'It's real. It stands up. There's another source. And Jesus Christ, I almost didn't say anything – I almost didn't believe it myself.'

Max was blinking as if again trying to clear his vision. He ran his palm over his hair's furrows, keeping his cool, and asked himself what a future chief sub would do. 'OK,' he said, 'what show is it getting?'

'They haven't decided yet, but they've got graphics, quotes, comment. A clear spread at least, I'd guess.'

While Jeremy was talking, Max tried to keep his gaze on him, but it flicked involuntarily, as Jeremy's had done, to the entrances. A panic alarm started going off in his brain as it hadn't since he'd first started out as a sub. He saw it now in trainees, in Rosie, the brain jangling so hard all it could think was *Alarm! Alarm!* But he was not a trainee. And as he reasserted control over himself, overcoming this uncharacteristic inner wobble, he scorned the danger. He would be writing headlines even with bombs going off around him.

With conscious calm, he shifted the pencil to the other side of his mouth and said, 'Who's the other source?'

'Someone inside the Met.'

Max had many more questions, but this was not the time. 'OK,' he said. 'There's no copy in yet is there?'

'No, it's only just starting to come together.'

'And we're already behind. Are Newsdesk going to want you again? We're short of bodies as it is.'

'They're going to email me the copy as it comes in and I'm going to read through it.'

'So you're going to spend half your time doing their work for them?'

'I'm just going to skim it, see if I catch anything.'

'Well, that Tragic Schoolgirl's taken another re-draw. Get it out of the way as soon as you can and I'll load you up with some more.'

Jeremy swung himself into his chair as if into a cockpit. He'd been absent from his desk for long enough that his monitor had turned off. He impatiently tapped the space bar until the image of PagePlanner reappeared, fuzzy for an instant before it snapped into focus. He checked on the young ones' progress. Rosie still had her Criminal Immigrant story open; there must be some kind of weakness in it. But more stories had come through and she was also locked into a Scientific Study about how cats could communicate by wiggling their ears. She would need to pick up the pace. Will was editing a celebrity picture story about how the supermodel Kate Kloss's drug-addled boyfriend had been caught with the Radio 1 DJ Edith Bohler, and was thrashing the keys in a continuous clatter. That meant he was rewriting a lot; and he'd already done more stories than Rosie. The boy had no shortage of confidence.

Jeremy again cast his eyes around the room. Reporters were rushing around the Newsdesk with messages and print-outs while Geraldine gave orders and demanded information. Several were standing with telephones wedged between shoulder and ear, trying to block out the noise around them and taking shorthand. Others were already producing copy, leaning towards their screens and snapping at Geraldine's deputy when he hurried them further. The rest of the newsroom, which was anyway moving into the fraught time of the evening, had caught their unease. No one now was chatting or wandering over to other desks to ask a question. They were typing, typing, typing, and their questions were shouted.

Jez opened the Tragic Schoolgirl. The shape had changed again, but thankfully the headline still fit. He saw it with the diagrammatic clarity of an exploded drawing: the news line in par one; how it happened in par two; geography in three; reaction in four. Her father saying, 'I don't even understand. I haven't seen her yet. She was looking forward to the abseiling trip and the school were... How could this have happened?' 'She'd been looking forward to the trip' would do as a pull-quote; and, with a copy and paste, it was done.

The red box at the bottom of the screen told him that he was ten lines over. He snipped, he cut, he ran two paragraphs together. The school's statement was boring and could come down. The reader didn't really need to know what her mother's job was. Four lines over. And there might—

He noticed something happening at the *BeastOnline* desks. The onliners were standing up, pulling on coats, flicking their hair over their collars. They looked afraid and their overseers were haranguing them to move faster. They swept their things into their bags, quickly switched their computers off at the plug and made for the exit.

From among the boys the overseers were selecting a skeleton crew to man a single desk, the one furthest from the door. Others, pale, jittery, some making determined faces, some frankly afraid, were positioned in pairs at every entrance. It looked like a newsroom putsch, except that the boys were facing out.

As they took up their posts, the squat figure of the chief was striding from desk to desk around the newsroom's periphery like a beacon fire passing from hilltop to hilltop. When he passed each desk, the hacks on Travel, on Personal Finance, on Property & Gardening jumped up and fled, leaving only the most senior ones behind to get the paper away.

Will tried to parse what was going on. He'd been right; something big was up. So many people leaving, the onliners at the doors, the reporters like a nest of disturbed wasps, Jeremy uncharacteristically keyed-up, Max driving them on faster than ever – something was happening and he didn't know what it was.

He was like some low-ranking seaman on the night before

D-Day, told just to keep swabbing the decks. Frustration choked itself up in him and he thought: Fine, I'll just keep swabbing the damn decks then. He exercised himself in condemning what he was working on: a story about a 'tragedy at epic ten-hour charity marathon'. It was so *ignorant*. The *Iliad* was an epic; the *Odyssey* was an epic; *Paradise Lost* was a modern epic. Epic was Hector and Lucifer and rosy-fingered dawn and the swift armada of the Greeks. It didn't just mean 'big'. And a tragedy was something else entirely: *Antigone, Lear, Phèdre*.

The *Beast*, despite being so much more powerful than him, was so much worse educated. And that didn't seem to matter to anyone. Nor was it just ignorance; it was a cloth ear for any kind of meaning beyond the literal, excepting of course the pun. Only yesterday, Max had given a Health story about falling sales of moisturizer the headline 'A Farewell to Balms'. Say what you liked about Hemingway – it wasn't just meaningless, since there was no relation between the two things yoked together; it was simply *tasteless* to use a novel about war to sell an article about face cream. And the worst was that, far from hearing how it jarred, the other subs had congratulated Max on his cleverness.

There was always 'something rotten in the state of' somewhere or a 'first casualty of the war on' something. Anything bad in Greece became a Greek Tragedy and any dead painter became an Old Master – categories that occluded the whole complex world behind them.

Well, he could satirize from within, and he and Rosie could laugh together at Max's expense. He clicked the white arrowhead into the headline box, pressed Ctrl+A to highlight the dummy copy and deleted it. He started to write, feeling vicious:

|EPIC TRAGEDY MARATHON|
|UNFOLDS AT CHARITY EVENT|

It was not a good fit. He considered, and his considerations were interrupted by Max: 'We need to get the two dead into the headline. That's the story.'

Will glanced up, hid his glower and brightly said, 'OK, got it.'

He tried:

|TWO DEAD AS TRAGEDY |
|UNFOLDS AT EPIC CHARITY MARATHON|

He retracted his fingers tightly into fists, then drummed them on the air above his keyboard. It was harder when someone was watching.

|TWO DEATHS IN TRAGEDY|
|AT EPIC CHARITY MARATHON|

Losing 'epic' would do it.

|TWO DEATHS IN TRAGEDY|
|AT CHARITY MARATHON |

That second line wasn't a great fit either.

|TWO DEATHS IN TRAGEDY|
|AT CHARITY FUNDRAISER|

But this was far from a subtly sarcastic 'epic tragedy marathon' for him to show Rosie – it was just a commonplace *Beast* headline, and a fairly flat one at that. He felt close to giving up. But at least he'd done it quickly and with Max breathing down his neck. Ugh, 'breathing down his neck'; more of this cliché, these fragments of sense, cracked and bashed together like old stones in a dyke.

Every day he became more accustomed to it. And, if he was honest with himself, Rosie probably wouldn't even appreciate a joke about 'epic tragedy'. Perhaps he should try and get back into academia. He could email Professor Rusthall and ask—

All at once, there was a bellowing and trumpeting from the back corner of the newsroom, a noise like a maddened bull elephant trampling a stand of insubordinate bamboo. As it moved closer, the noise resolved into a voice. It was not a shout, but it resonated. The voice was saying, 'Which motherfucker put this in my newspaper? Which of you fucking halfwits thought this was an appealing layout? Who? You? You're an idiot, man, a blithering fucking cretin. How did you get a job here? What fool hired you? Sit *down*, damn you, I'll draw the page myself. Get me a pencil. Not a *pen*! And stop shaking, man. Good Christ, is this what the Art desk has been reduced to? How the fuck do you intend to cope when you have some real work to do?'

It was a quarterdeck voice, the kind that rang through an Atlantic storm to chase its sailors up the rigging. Or, as it came closer, something like that of an exasperated headmaster on the games field. In this voice was a rising note of querulousness, as if it were surrounded by incompetents, bunglers, amateurs falling woefully short of even the minimum standards of professional journalism, and only the owner of this voice, he alone, truly understood how to spot a story, how to angle that story, how to write it, sub it, draw it, headline it.

The subs tried to make themselves motionless and invisible, like toads under a hedge. Will carefully peeked across at where the noise was coming from, turning his head as little as possible, wanting to be noticed somehow but not to divert the ire on to his own skull. A broad back in a navy-blue jacket, with the height and shoulders of a former rower, was bent over the angled table where pages were drawn, and a navy-sleeved arm was slashing out expert, imperious pencil strokes. 'Panel goes here, pull-quote goes here, big fucking picture, small fucking picture. It's not fucking rocket science. There, make it up like that.'

The figure seemed to have been slightly calmed by drawing the spread. Will glimpsed boxes sketched with architectural clarity. The figure turned and Will saw the strong, still-handsome features, the skin healthily bronzed by trips abroad, the blond hair fading towards grey and receding into a flat laurel wreath, the expression secure, untouchable, the master of its world, both grounded and uplifted by responsibility, possessor of the voice that commanded. It was the Editor.

As he bore down on the back bench, his staff hurried to clear their desks of sandwich boxes and personal phones – anything that might incur the Editor's displeasure – and tried not to let their eyes make contact with anything but their work. The muscles at the base of Will's ears tensed with the effort to listen. But he needn't have bothered. Every word the Editor said could be heard in every department of the newsroom. 'How are we doing?' The clipped consonants. 'Alright. Fine.' The firm full stops. 'Get your people together. You, too, Frank, get everyone together, quickly now.' Already it was taking too long for him. The voice rang out, overtaking the back bench as they scurried towards the outer desks. 'Features! Sport! Politics! Diary! Travel! Health! Showbiz!

Magazine! Gather round. You, too, Newsdesk. The subs can stay where they are.'

The back bench turned in mid-scurry and rushed back. The staff from the outer departments followed, hanging up phones and leaving sentences unfinished. Even Geraldine and the reporters she'd assigned to the bombing stopped their work. Some of the *BeastOnline* door-guards began to drift towards the centre and were pulled back by their overseers. The only person who did not heed the command – and was not expected to – was the deputy head of Newsdesk, who kept answering the incoming calls.

The hundred journalists still in the newsroom crowded into the subs' area, squeezing each other against the edges of desks and making the subs get up from their chairs. The Editor stood in the middle and the crowd left a space around him. He surveyed his people; there was no talking.

Without preamble, he spoke: 'Has everyone gone who isn't working on this edition?' Will tensed even though the question could not be directed at him. The chief spoke up and earned Will's admiration by addressing the Editor with his first name. 'Yes, Charles,' he said. 'They've all gone.'

'Good. Then listen, everyone.' The Editor pointed at the clock on the pillar beside the back bench. 'It is already twenty past seven. There is no time for speeches. Newsdesk are working on what may be the biggest scoop in my twenty-six years as Editor. As we speak, Islamic terrorists are plotting to blow up this newsroom and everyone in it. Your lives *are* in danger. Anyone who wants to leave, go now.'

Though many audibly drew in air or sighed or touched their hair or their faces or twisted their hands across each other, no one left. This seemed to be what the Editor had expected, and he continued: 'You should take that threat as a very great compliment. And be glad, because not only have these murderers named us as the chief enemy of their vile schemes, but we have beaten everyone else to the story. The police have heard from their own sources that something is up, but not even they know about our scoop yet, and they will not know until after first edition. We do not need them to protect us. We will protect ourselves.

'And let me tell you this. When people say that the age of the newspaper has passed, that the glory days of the Press are not today, but belong to hallowed memory, you will be able to point to tomorrow's edition and say: by this are you refuted. In years to come, when I am long dead and you are old and you gather not here but in one another's homes or in St Bride's to remember a dead newsman who stands among you now in mature strength, and you talk about the great papers of the past, you will be able to say: I was there, that day, when they tried to bomb the newsroom. I worked on that edition. In a box under my bed or in a frame on my wall I have my copy, and my work made it.

'So make it right. Because this is the story of a lifetime. It will be pored over by everyone in England tomorrow, and by you for the rest of your lives. Tomorrow we will prove something; we will achieve the highest day's circulation that any newspaper has achieved since before I was Editor. Tomorrow we are going to set a circulation record for this century. And, who knows, tomorrow's record may stand for the rest of it and for all time.

'So for that reason let me be clear: the paper goes on time tonight. Nine forty-five. Every minute after that means thousands fewer copies printed before the vans have to leave the printworks. It means fewer copies in newsagents and on forecourts in Penzance, in Northumberland, in Inverness.

And the printers have been primed for an enormous run. They have cleared the schedules for us. The presses stand ready. We will not be late.'

He looked into the faces gathered around him, and told them, 'Some of you have been doing this as long as I have; remember your expertise. Some of you are far younger; tonight you will earn your seats. Do your work well. Keep your heads. In every man's life, there comes an hour that defines him. Ours has struck. Be worthy of it.'

There was no cheering, but a thrill ran through them. They went to work.

TWELFTH CHAPTER

ADRENALINE like a hundred cups of coffee, like handfuls of coke, like explosions outside the door, pulsed in the veins of the subs. Fingers jittered, lips popped, feet hopped and tapped beneath the desks. Teeth chewed gum to tasteless pulp. The noise rose steadily. Heat gathered, and broke out in sweat across backs and under arms. But adrenaline was what the newsroom was addicted to, what – more than any story – its journalists lived for. They felt as if they would hold back the bombers by words alone, the power of the Press blazing out a charmed circle that none could penetrate.

Eyes gleamed in the light of screens. Tongues darted out of dry mouths. Cheeks flushed. Jeremy was up out of his slouch. This one stunning scoop didn't mean that the rest of the newspaper didn't still have to be produced. He had to cut a dense 600-word story about mortgages into a 200-word space within the next ten minutes, but his too-focused mind was losing its peripheral vision and trying to zoom in on the few words right in front of it. While he tried to zoom out enough to understand the story his thoughts kept jumping back to the bombing. He couldn't believe how easily he might have missed it. But the mortgage story: some kind of tax relief had been promised to lenders and they'd failed to meet the terms. Something to do with lending money to small businesses rather than allocating it to mortgages, the latter being less profitable. There were new regulations that— Max interrupted him to ask about a Medical Breakthrough story Jeremy had spent fifteen precious minutes making lighter on its feet. 'Jez, how much do these tubes cost?'

From long practice, Jeremy split his concentration on to two tracks. His fingers did not cease rattling on the keyboard as he said, 'We don't have that. Just the total cost of the treatment. What do you want it for?'

'The reason we give for the old kind of IVF being so expensive is the equipment cost. We could make a good comparison: old stuff – ten grand; new tubes – 50p.'

'We don't have that, just the total that's in the headline; but Naomi wrote it. I'll give her a call.' Typing only left-handed as he tried to make effortlessly comprehensible a sentence that began, 'Lenders participating in the new scheme, though many on the old scheme have an entitlement to ascribe a percentage…' Jeremy curled the fingers of his right under the hollow black handset and flicked it the half-inch up into his palm. As he wedged it between jaw and shoulder, the chief bounded up and demanded, his voice like an over-tightened string, 'Who are you calling, darling?'

Jeremy: 'Naomi, she wrote this health piece. We're trying to get a breakdown of costs for this new IVF.'

Max: 'But we won't hold the page for it.'

Jeremy was already scrolling down the spreadsheet of reporters' numbers. The chief said, 'Naomi loves getting called. That's why her copy's always so shit. She's sitting at home just *waiting* for you to call her. But don't expect any answers we can actually use.'

Max wished the chief would fuck off and let his pod work. But the chief was already saying, 'These bombers are going to get two clear spreads.'

Jez: '*Two*? How're we going to fill them?'

Max did not let show whether or not he thought that might be difficult.

The chief said: 'Two, Jez, and if you'd rather have some peace, you should have closed your eyes and let us get exploded.'

Naomi picked up and Jez, about to say that that was not the point, said, 'Hi Naomi, it's Jeremy from the subs' desk.'

The chief turned from him and said, 'Max, since you know the story and are sitting next to Jez, you can sub the splash.'

'Am I going to personally sub both spreads or is anyone else in the mood to contribute?'

'Just the news story. We'll portion out the other bits. Do you need help with your pages?'

Max, of course, said no.

'Good, because it's all change. Where's your flatplan?'

The sheet was on the desk under Max's elbow, the pairs of rectangles that denoted his pages already annotated. The chief bent over it. Jeremy was saying, 'But where do these figures come from? Is this just promotion from the people who invented it?' The chief said, 'The prognosticating parrot is moving to thirteen, in bold. The Bulgarian who robbed the blind woman is going on – is that not done yet? Who's got it?'

Rosie piped up before she could be named, rushing out her defence. 'I've called the reporter a few times but she just isn't picking up. I gave the query to Newsdesk and they're trying to find out.'

'Find out what?'

Rosie started to become flustered. 'There's something strange about it. She's blind but it doesn't mention if she had a stick or a dog or anything.'

The chief looked at Max, who said, 'The story's taking a redraw anyway.'

'Fine. Get it through. It's going on seventeen.' Rosie, humiliated, turned back to her screen. The chief carried on: 'The botched execution is going on twenty-two.'

'What, next to the Tragic Schoolgirl?'

'No, she's moving, too, towards the back of the book. Final resting place is...' He scanned the flatplan with the tip of his pencil. 'Page twenty-seven, where, just so it's not all miserable, she'll be next to the couple who bought a Ming vase for thirty quid at a car-boot sale.'

Max said, 'And when can I expect the splash?'

'Any minute.' He barrelled over to Newsdesk to wrest the copy from them.

Max was too professional to rub out the mark the chief had put on *his* flatplan, but said, 'Will, your parrot's moving to thirteen, in bold, the headline'll still fit. Also, the headline for your story about Paul Roux cheating on Kate Kloss with Edith Bohler is going to be:

**NO, PAUL, YOU CAN'T HAVE
YOUR KATE AND EDITH TOO** '

Will opened his mouth to say something about his own idea, recognized he couldn't top that, and closed it again.

'If that doesn't fit let me know and we'll widen the box. Rosie, your Bulgarian's moving to thirty-two; the page's taking shape now. Forget the stick or the dog, just get it in and put it in revise. And Jez, did you hear that? Your Schoolgirl's going on twenty-seven.'

Jeremy said, 'Naomi doesn't have a useable figure for the equipment.'

'What a surprise.' Max had already rewritten the headline assuming that would be the case. Just then the chief shouted across from the Newsdesk: 'Max, sweetheart, the splash is attached to six and seven.'

Max took the pencil from his mouth. This was a moment worthy of him. Subbing a late-breaking splash while revising all his pod's work? No one else in the newsroom would even attempt it. The rising din around him – of the chief asking, with the threatening politeness he affected under strain, 'Is there any reason that page hasn't been sent yet, darling?' and of Geraldine shouting for copy and Turkish Liz cursing down the phone, 'You can go home if you want, but if that terrorist comes out of his house and fist-fucks his girlfriend in the street, and we don't get the shot, it's your head on the block…' – it all dampened down to a distant circumference of information. Max was conscious of becoming calm.

The copy hit the page, and Max began to read at an unstinting pace, nicking away a few words here or reformulating a few words there in rapid flurries at the keyboard. They'd nosed it:

> Terrorists last night were making last-minute preparations to attack central London. The target is the *Daily Beast*.

Max's attention moved across it, and then it read:

> TERRORISTS have been spotted making last-minute preparations for a bomb attack

on central London. The offices of this
newspaper are the target.

Jeremy was using a machete now on the mortgage story.
Quotes from an industry expert – *slash!* Criticism from
the shadow cabinet – *slash!* How this scheme related to the
general economic context – *slash, slash, slash!* He noticed that
the shape of the Tragic Schoolgirl story had changed – he'd
have to write another headline for the new box once he'd
finished this. A message popped up in the bottom right-hand
corner of his screen: an email from Geraldine. As he clicked
on it, Geraldine was already rushing across. It was too close to
edition to simply trust that emails would arrive. She crowed
from close above Will's head, 'Maestro! Have you read
that copy?'

'I'm looking at it now.'

Geraldine rushed back to Newsdesk while Jeremy read,
'Known associates of the West London terror gang used
burqas to disguise themselves to commit terror attack in Syria.
The bombings were carried out on government-controlled
facilities in Damascus and Aleppo in February and March
of this year.' Mother of God, thought Jeremy, this is an even
bigger story than I thought. This isn't just about the Beast.
We can link these guys to extremists in Syria. The connection
is the mosque they've all been to. We can connect the tactics
they're developing over there with what's—

Geraldine shouted to him, 'Have you seen this stuff?
They're bringing terror tactics back to London from Syria!'

Everyone in the newsroom glanced up. The young
BeastOnline grunts guarding the doors shifted anxiously.
Turkish Liz blinked behind her black-rimmed glasses. Remem-
bered photographs were crowding in on her, the unprintable

ones, of damage done to young bodies by a nail bomb in the Manchester Arena, of the stricken London bus in Tavistock Square on 7/7, its back broken by a bomb, and particularly of the dark patches on the walls in the offices of the magazine *Charlie Hebdo* after the jihadis got in. She hoped she would die at once.

Jeremy shouted back to Geraldine, 'We've got them. We've nailed them. We've got the whole thing.' And in those who heard him, spirits were lifted.

He switched back to the mortgage story. He hacked out two more lines and filed it. Immediately he reopened the Tragic Schoolgirl. The headline now read:

> | HORROR ON FIELD DAY AS |
> | SCHOOLGIRL STRANGLED BY |
> | ABSEILING ROPE |

There was no pause for thought or clever tickling of connected words. The pressure shot them into place like rivets:

> | GIRL, 14, KILLED IN FREAK |
> | ACCIDENT AS ABSEIL ROPE |
> | TWISTS AROUND HER NECK |

There was a subdeck, too:

> | Family's heartbreak over tragedy on adventure break

Then:

> | Family torment at adventure tragedy |

He captioned the photo with a word from a quote: '"POPULAR": Schoolgirl Polly Dunbar'. The picture itself he didn't even see. A quick check by eye: the first paragraph was 9.5 point, the second 8.5, the third 7.75. No paragraph ended at the bottom of a column or in the top line of the next. There were two full, un-indented lines above and below the pull-quote – 'She'd been looking forward to the trip'. There were no widows. The copy fitted. He ran a spell check, clicking through all the names it flagged up. A search for double spaces came up blank. It was done. He hit 'revise'.

But Max had somehow managed to read it while subbing the splash, and said, 'Jez, there's a mark from the lawyers. They want us to put the criticism to the ambulance service.'

'But it's a matter of record. They did go to the wrong place.'

'I know, and you're right, and if you want to start a long argument with them about a Tragic Schoolgirl, be my guest.'

'I'll put back in the line about them refusing to comment before they've conducted an inquiry. That'll cover us, won't it?'

'It'll have to.'

'And on your mortgages, when did the scheme come in?'

'Announced two years ago, actually came in at the start of last year – so eighteen months.'

'OK. Will, there's an add on your Dirty Doctor – a quote from his family. Most of it's bullshit. Crunch it right down; we only need a flick. Keep the bit about their shame. Rosie, are you sure you're done with the Bulgarian and the blind woman?'

'Yes,' Rosie was bright pink. 'It's in.'

'OK, then pick up a short about the rare 2p coin worth £1,000; it's on seventeen. Get the two figures in the headline, tell us what's on the coin. Write it straight, no drop intro, nothing fancy. And as fast as you can. Jez, there's a single column about an earthquake in Dorset, on thirty-two.'

Jeremy didn't have to be told what to do. He spotted a problem and told Will, 'Your parrot, it shouldn't be in ragged. Bold is always full-out. It'll get shorter when you change it, you might need to reinstate a line.'

Will had stepped up out of his rookie's quiet and he, Jeremy and Max were in uninterrupted communication. 'Got it. Do you want me to cut in that botched execution story?'

Max said: 'Do it. Also get the figure, that it took forty-two minutes, into the headline. And we need a better pull-quote. I think there is one.'

Will, 'From the prison guard.'

Max said, 'That's it.'

Jeremy said, 'And I saw there's more in strike.'

'I'm on it.'

Like the flying parts of a mechanical loom, each raced his own course, intersecting without touching to run off an ever-extending strip of finished news.

Jeremy said, 'Max, the picture of Kate Kloss is getting bigger.'

Max said: 'Will.'

'I'll trim the copy.'

'Thanks.' And Will glowed.

Jeremy looked above the back bench, where a vertical electronic board had been switched on to display a double column of numbered boxes. They showed the pages in the pairs in which they were printed – one and sixty-eight, two and sixty-seven, three and sixty-six – and were coloured either minatory red – not sent – or summer-sky blue: away. The first forty pages, the News section, were still mainly in red, but Features, Travel, Health and the other pages towards the back of the book had already gone.

Jeremy found the earthquake story and opened it. He could hear the chief, like a distance runner lengthening into his racing stride, begin to raise his voice, 'Jack, darling, would you like to tell me why twenty-four hasn't gone?'

Jack from the Art desk looked up, but it was Jack Brandt, the leader of C pod, a tall man from Darlington, broad and strong-boned with a deep, flat voice, who replied, 'It was ready three hours ago. But the pages have just been redrawn.'

'It has to go right fucking now, darling.'

'It fucking can't.'

'We need it, darling, we need that fucking page.'

'Then stop fucking changing things.'

'That's the job, darling. If you don't like it, go home and I'll send it myself.'

Just then, they both stopped; everyone in the newsroom looked at the doors; there was a commotion; someone was trying to get in.

But it wasn't what they instantaneously feared – it was a white man, in a suit; a hack; the grunts from *BeastOnline* were standing close in front of him, their arms slightly raised in case he tried to break past them. The chief told Jack, 'Get that page ready,' and barrelled for the door. When he reached the would-be intruder, he was too far away for what he said to be heard over the newsroom's racket. But the man soon turned and ran back towards the atrium. The chief nodded at the two young men guarding the door and said something that made them stand up straighter, then bounded back to the subs' desk.

As he arrived, the newsroom's attention was on him. He spoke loud enough for other departments to hear: 'That was a reporter from the *Impartial*, trying his luck. They got wind that we're working on a huge story up here. I said to him,

"Call yourself a newsman? The Queen's been shot."' There was a great shout of relieved laughter.

But even as he was announcing this anecdote, he did not stop moving. It was nine o'clock.

THIRTEENTH CHAPTER

THE newsroom reverberated like the engine room of an ocean liner at full steam. Will had been taken up in the terrible din and was working faster and surer than he ever had before. His fingers could not stop typing long enough to open the style guide and he felt he was claiming his seat as he asked Jeremy and Max the questions he would earlier in the day have checked himself: 'Focussed, one *s* or two?'; 'The Bible, capital *t*?' And Jeremy or Max shot back, 'One *s*', 'No cap', and their togetherness was palpable.

Jeremy was in a state of near-magical alertness and dexterity. Style questions from Will; map questions from Graphics; copy questions from Max; and always him with the answer. He shot each question down the instant it popped up. He was headshot Jez, the deadshot kid.

It was in this moment that Rosie's reporter called her back about the blind woman. The phone rang amid the noise and, as Rosie answered, she felt her body seize. The import of what the reporter said struck her, and she was stricken. But she managed to say 'Thanks' and then: 'Max, the blind woman. She's not blind.'

That was serious enough for Max to disengage his concentration from the splash. He said, 'What do you mean, she's not blind?'

It was all that Rosie could do to speak. 'She's partially sighted. And registered, I mean, she gets disability benefit. She's legally blind, I mean partially.'

'OK, so that's fudge-able. But the money. The whole point of this story is that she didn't see him take the money out of her purse. Did *any* of this actually fucking happen?'

'Apparently he did take the money, the money from her purse. She saw him do it, but she was too shocked to say anything.'

'But we had quotes from her hours ago. We've got her saying she forgives him. How the fuck did this blind old bitch not mention this then?'

Rosie cowered. 'I don't know.'

'*Fuck*,' said Max. Not even having time to look down at his watch, his eyes flicked to the wall clock. Seven minutes past nine. He was close to the abyss. He kept himself together. 'OK,' he said, and unmarked the page as ready to send, while calling across to the pairers' desk: 'Hold twenty-two.' They shouted back, 'Hold twenty-two.'

'So, she was too scared to stop him when he took her money, is that fair?'

'Umm, yes.'

Max looked at the headline:

| BLIND GRANNY ROBBED |
| BY BIG ISSUE-SELLING |
| BULGARIAN WHILE SHE |
| GAVE HIM A DONATION |

'So the headline can stand. She's legally blind, that's true, isn't it?'

'Partially.'

'Partially blind is still blind. Or it's blind enough for now. We'll clarify in the copy. And he *thought* she was blind, is that right?'

'As far as we know.'

'OK, that's more back-up for "blind" in the headline as long as we explain.'

Geraldine shouted, 'Max!' and started striding towards him. Max talked faster. 'So the story is blind woman mugged by *Big Issue* Bulgarian she was giving a donation to. Even though she has some sight, she was too terrified to stop him. Write it like that, and I need it now.'

Geraldine reached their pod. 'I've got some marks,' she said with a measure of deference, since Max was handling the splash. 'Can I make them over your shoulder?' Max nodded and she hurried around behind him. Pushing her hair out of her face, she took an instant to size up the page, whose layout was changing continuously as the Art desk worked on it.

Unfurled across the first spread was the map showing the bombers' routes and the concentric red circles spreading around Copper House. To the right were photographs of the four terrorists. They'd been taken from Facebook and were of varying quality. Kayani, who'd obviously taken the photo himself, his arm stretching to the bottom corner of the shot, had arresting brown eyes and a soft, boyish, sparsely bearded chin. Although Turkish Liz had done her best to find pictures in which they all looked fanatical, this – the only useable one – showed him grinning happily. As she watched, Max captioned it 'MENACING'.

Underneath was a profile panel: where the terrorists lived,

what branch of Nando's one of them worked in, where in West London they'd grown up, the fact that two of them held season tickets at Queen's Park Rangers, that one of Kayani's schoolteachers had said of him, 'He was a nice, shy boy who fell in with the wrong crowd.' For an instant, Max considered using that for the panel headline. But this wasn't the *Conscientious*; this was the *Beast*. He wrote 'Home-grown fanatics'.

To the left of the map was another photo, taken that after-noon. It showed Kayani's elder brother in front of the terraced family house, his face twisted into an ugly snarl and his fist raised. Beneath it was a mocked-up transcript headlined 'You're dead – terror brother's chilling rant'. A selection of the most striking quotes had been written out in a typewriter-style font. 'Your Britain is finished.' Geraldine wordlessly pointed out that it actually said 'Yuor'. 'Jez,' said Max, with audible calm, 'Could you tell Graphics to correct their literal in "your" in the transcript before the Editor sees it?'

Jeremy pushed off from his desk and, before his chair had stopped rolling, was on his feet and moving.

'Righty-oh,' said Geraldine. 'We need to get in quite high up' – Max scrolled to the top of the page – 'maybe in there' – she pressed a fingertip to the screen – 'that these chaps were on bail awaiting trial on terror-related charges, which we haven't actually said anywhere.'

Max said, 'OK. We can do it here, after "The four men". So…' He typed as Geraldine spoke: 'The four men – who had all absconded from bail on charges related to terrorism…'

Max interrupted. 'Can't we say "terrorism charges"?'

'Not really, it's—'

'OK.' Max retyped: 'The four men – who all jumped bail on terror charges… When was it?'

'The second.'

'Two weeks ago.'

'And then we can pick up again.'

'... all belonged to the infamous West Acton Mosque.'

'We've got two "all"s in that sentence.' Max deleted the first. 'And that's not strictly accurate. The West Acton Mosque is a different place. This one's the West Acton Community Centre and Friday Mosque.'

'What's the difference?'

'The other one's moderate and litigious. We've had trouble with them before.'

'So do we have to be careful about how we refer to this place?'

Geraldine was pained. The West Acton Mosque's libel case had gone all the way to court. She'd had to appear. 'You carry on. I'll get the lawyer.' As Geraldine shouted for the Legal desk, Max had an instant in which to hit Ctrl+Tab with his thumb and forefinger, bringing up the pages to revise. As his eye flew down the columns, his fingers, like those of a master potter with his apprentices' work, quickly snicked off twists of clay or thumbed loose joins together. While he did, he said, 'Will, you start proofing out our pages. Rosie, we need that Blind Bulgarian story right now.'

Rosie was caught in an agony of indecision. She'd re-nosed the story as Max instructed, but now it didn't fit properly into the box.

A message popped up in the bottom right-hand corner of her screen. Her friend Caroline, on B pod, had written: 'There's a rumour we're all going to move into some kind of bunker. WTF, we have a BUNKER?!' Rosie nearly cried. If Caroline had time to write messages, all her stories must be through. She must just be proofreading. Rosie sneaked a glance at the electronic board showing which pages had been sent. The whole back of the book was already away. They were as far forward as twenty-two, this page, and even some pages ahead of it had gone. She was panicking. Her mind was sliding off the words as if off wet glass. She could not get her grip. She was not actually *doing* anything.

From the corner of her eye, she saw someone rush up to the chief brandishing an A3 proof. The chief turned and shouted, 'Kill page twenty-one, darling! Kill twenty-one!'

The head pairer, the one who sent the pages to the printers, called back in confirmation, 'Kill twenty-one. Kill twenty-one.' Then picked up the phone that went only to the presses and said, 'Kill page twenty-one, all editions. Twenty-one is coming again.'

Max said, 'Rosie, where's that story?'

She said, 'One minute.'

'Thirty seconds.'

She heard the chief shout: 'Twenty-one is coming again. Twenty-one V-one.'

The pairer called back, 'Twenty-one V-one,' and said into the phone, 'Twenty-one coming again now. Twenty-one V-one.'

Geraldine was returning with the lawyer. Max said, 'Now, Rosie.'

She said, 'One minute.'

'What's the problem?'

'The paragraphs are falling badly across the pull-quote.'

'Put it down; I'll sort it.'

She closed her InCopy window, unlocking the text for Max.

Just as he was about to open it, Geraldine arrived with the lawyer behind her. Jeremy and Max caught each other's eye. Max did not have time to ask him, but just said, 'Move the pull-quote wherever you need. Art desk can fuck themselves if they're going—'

And already the lawyer had reached him and was saying in his South African accent, 'We need to tread very carefully here. They've sued us before. We need to fix it so they have no reason whatsoever to believe someone might even potentially think we're talking about them.' Rosie listened to his accent as if to the radio. She was trying to get on with the next task, proofreading, but she'd had a story taken away from her, and her concentration, like a filament through which too high a current has passed, was blown.

Nor did the lawyer seem on top of things. His gelled white-blond hair was sticking out from one side of his head and the muscle in the corner of his right eye was jumping uncontrollably. He said, 'Can't we be completely unambiguous and refer to this mosque as "the West Acton community centre"?'

Geraldine was disgusted. 'It makes it sound as if they're putting on a bake sale. They're death-dealing fanatics, for Christ's sake.'

The lawyer, out of some unconscious habit long divorced from its original purpose, stretched his mouth into a grin. Max said, 'After first mention, when we'll give it the full community-centre title, we can call it the "terror mosque". If this other lot think that might refer to them, we can say that that can only be because they *themselves* think they're terrorist sympathizers. Making that connection would never have occurred to us.'

The lawyer thought for a second. His eye-muscle hopped as he said, 'Fine, as long we put the full name at first mention. But we've got a heap of other problems. Naming these four men and accusing them of—'

There was a bellowing from the corner; the Editor was back in the newsroom. His great voice rang out: 'Who wrote this headline? Who the fuck put a headline this boring in my newspaper? I don't care if the page has gone. Can't you understand there's no point it going with a headline like that? Get it back and think of something better!'

The chief shouted, 'Kill page sixteen. Kill sixteen, darling.' The pairers replied, 'Kill sixteen,' and said into the phone, 'Kill page sixteen, all editions.'

The voice went off again: 'Damn it, man, write it. What the fuck's the matter with you? Can't you do at least *some* of the work? Delete that; it's gibberish – I don't even want it on my fucking screen. Now type:

THE PRIEST, THE PRINCESS AND
THE DRUG-DEALING BODYBUILDER '

There was a pause, then: 'Of course it fucking fits.' For once, the Editor did not seem soothed by doing the work. 'So what the fuck are you waiting for? Send the cunting page.'

The chief checked the headline for typos and shouted, 'Page sixteen coming again now. Sixteen V-three.' The pairers called, 'Sixteen V-three,' and at Max's pod, the Editor broke on them like a storm.

'Why the fuck has no one seen fit to show me the splash pages? Have you all forgotten that this is still my newspaper? You,' he pointed at Max.

But before he could carry on, the chief was there, saying, 'Max here is subbing the splash copy, so perhaps Jeremy could show you the pages?'

The Editor turned to Geraldine and said, 'Don't stand there gawping, fetch me a chair.' The chief was already back at his desk, a zigzag vein in his temple pulsing as he speed-read the pages being sent.

Geraldine, with mutinous ill-grace, commandeered a chair from the nearest Sport sub, who went on typing at a crouch, and pushed it awkwardly into position beside and slightly behind Jeremy. The lawyer, whose nerves could not withstand addressing the Editor except through an intermediary, looked supplicatingly at Geraldine, who said, 'Charles, the lawyer's got some concerns about naming these terrorists, specifically...'

'Of course he does. We'll get to the nit-pickery later. Now I want to see whether these pages are halfway in order.'

Jeremy, who'd been rearranging the Blind Bulgarian even as Geraldine brought the chair, hit 'OK' and opened PagePlanner. It was exhilarating to be beside the Editor, the source from whom all power radiated. He said, 'This is the first splash spread, the map, the four terrorists, the brother.'

The Editor sat forward in his chair, his forearms resting on his thighs and his large hands dangling between his knees, and assessed the page. He said, 'Why are there no rag-outs on this page? For Christ's sake, you can't expect people to remember every story we covered two weeks ago. Why is there no one here from Pictures?'

At that, Turkish Liz shot from her seat like a hare from its hiding place, her hooked nose sucking in air for acceleration. As she appeared, the Editor said, 'I want two headlines ragged out from previous editions and put on this page, one from the story about their escape from bail and one from the leader column that set them on to us.'

She nodded sharply, her lips bunching.

The Editor pointed at the screen. 'And is there no more sinister picture of this Kayani? He looks like he's at a fucking barbecue.'

Counting them off on her fingers, Liz said, 'We've been through all his Facebook pictures, all his friends' Facebooks, the police, the DVLA, the passport office, his old school. That's the best there is.'

'Fine.' The Editor waved her away. 'Make the kicker "CHILLING SMILE".'

Liz rushed back to her seat, shouting to the Art desk, 'Jack you're getting two rag-outs for the four–five spread. One minute.'

The lawyer twitched forward in attempted self-erasement. If the Editor dismissed his concerns, then it would be on the Editor's head; as long as he hadn't had them explained, it was on his own. He rasped his dry throat. But the Editor told Jeremy, 'Show me the other spread.'

Beside them, Geraldine was rapidly conferring with Max about how to refer to the terrorists' 'probable' or 'predicted' escape routes without either saying anything as weak as 'possible' or over-selling them in a way that would embarrass the paper if someone spotted they'd come from Google Maps.

Jeremy pulled the slider across to show the second spread. The Editor looked for a moment, muttered 'What feckless cunt...' and leapt upright. Geraldine flinched sideways as the Editor's voice boomed: 'Art desk! Get someone over here! Six–seven needs a redraw. And bring me some paper.'

He turned on Geraldine from his splendid height. 'Who the fuck drew these pages?'

Geraldine, still annoyed about being told to bring a chair, blithely said, 'The back bench, I suppose.'

'I AM the back bench.' Then, looking up: 'Where's that artist? Jack!'

Jack arrived at a run with a slim sheaf of A3 drawing sheets and a selection of pencils.

'Good God, man, I'm not planning to draw the whole book. That's your job.' Max, who'd just changed 'Terror brother's chilling rant' to 'sinister rant', so it wouldn't double the editor's caption kicker, checked the clock. The long black pointer was aiming almost vertically down. Eighteen minutes to go and a spread was being redrawn. He spoke below the Editor: 'Rosie, you keep on proofing our pages. If you spot anything, tell me right away. Will, you stop reading the other pages and read everything on the two splash spreads. Read four–five now and six–seven as soon as it's taken shape. There are eight different people subbing these stories. Check everything matches up.'

And above him the Editor was asking the designer: 'Why have you put in this fucking boring picture? Don't you see that it needs to be the bombing these cunts carried out in Syria? It needs wreckage, carnage, aftermath, whatever we've got. Then next to it the unarmed French policeman being executed on the pavement outside *Charlie Hebdo*. Then beside that, like this, the mosque in Acton, smaller, this size. And on the other side, like this, a big picture of some burqas on a street in London. Why the fuck hasn't this been done already?' The pencil slashed across the paper.

'Headline, on top of the picture fade, four decks:

|BURQA BOMBS |
|DEVELOPED IN |
|SYRIA BY WORLD |
|TERROR NETWORK |

'Then, underneath it, Baroness Ahmad goes in here writing about violence in Muslim culture. Then, here on the right, Lord Foltener, with a picture byline and title, "Former home secretary", saying that Britons must stand together and examine how these people came to be in the country. Underneath that, a box this size – Geraldine, is there any reason we're not using the interviews with 7/7 survivors?'

'No, it's good stuff: one of the survivors saying it took her years before she dared get on the tube again – and now this. Also a widow talking about her anguish.'

The Editor's expression grew grimmer. 'You incompetent fucking cunts. That has to go in here. The subs can write the headline to fit. Something like, "Fresh ordeal of 7/7 survivors". That'll fit. Write it in now. And we need an inset picture of the bombed-out bus in Tavistock Square.'

Through a brief intercession of Geraldine's, the South African lawyer succeeded in telling the Editor, 'I'm really uncomfortable with naming these four men, because' – his right eye fluttered – 'if we're wrong and they sue, they've got us over a barrel.'

The Editor sized him up. 'Have you read the story?'

The eye winked uncontrollably. 'Yes, that's why—'

'Then you'll know we're not wrong. There's no way we could have more on them than we do. The Met's practically confirmed it, for Christ's sake.'

'Yes, but we still don't have anything that unequivocally has them planning the bombing. Also, this might even be prejudicial to what they're already on trial for. If we're in court and—'

'How likely do you think it is that four terrorists on the run from the law will want to meet us in court? And are you seriously suggesting we gag ourselves over the most sensational scoop of this century?' He was getting excited. 'Are you out of your *mind*?'

'Alright, that's your decision; I just wanted to flag it—'

'And you've flagged it. Now fuck off.' He leant forward to inspect the page on Jeremy's screen, but noticed that the lawyer didn't step away. 'Why are you still here?'

'There are some other small marks that could save us—'

He waved him away. 'Give them to Max. But if he and Geraldine want to keep something, it stays, is that clear?'

The lawyer took his place behind Max's chair and spoke over his shoulder. Ever more people were assembling there. So they could all see what he was doing, they formed a wedge with Max at its point. Their heads seemed to be pulled forward by the lit screen, as if it were a window through which they might climb.

The lawyer was saying, 'If we could make clear that the mosque completely denies...' and Geraldine was saying, 'Where's the line about how we've decided to keep working with the threat hanging over us?' and one of the reporters was saying, 'The bombing wasn't in Damascus itself, it was in...' and another was saying, 'The counter-terror acronym is actually slightly misleading; it's not really a public body, it's...' and Aamir Malik was saying, 'The West Acton imam's been there for eight years, and his age is...' and Will's head popped up from his reading to say, 'Max, in half the stories we've got the accomplice Muhammed Ranjha with an *e*, and in the others we've got Muhammad with an *a*.'

Max ordered, 'Check the cuts. What did we call him last time?'

Will hurried to look and alter, the soft pads of his fingers damp on the keys and the mouse.

The Editor told Jeremy to open the front page and began to call names across the newsroom. 'Walker, Gross, Feldstein, Murray, Thwaite, Geraldine.'

Will said, 'Muhammad with an *a*,' as Geraldine detached

herself from the group behind Max to join the other senior editors, who were rushing importantly together to form a semicircle behind Jeremy. The rest of the newsroom watched them. It was twelve minutes to edition and the outer departments' work was done. Almost every page had gone. The double column of paired pages was almost all in blue. The chief was calling, 'Kill eight, page eight is coming again, eight V-two.' One of the pages further back, twenty-two, the Blind Bulgarian, was still in red. The chief bounded over to Max, a damp dark wheel marked under each arm, and said, 'Max, darling, why the fuck has twenty-two not gone yet?'

The Editor, surprised and incensed by this unexpected interruption, boomed: 'Can't you see he's subbing the splash? Fuck off at once.'

The chief was bowled backwards and, before he could stop the words escaping, said, 'Yes, sir.' Some recess of Max's mind stored that for enjoyment later. But right then, he flicked Ctrl+Tab, the movement of thumb and forefinger unconscious. The splash was replaced in front of him by page twenty-two. In the five seconds he had, his eyes touched the headline, byline, captions, pull-quote, first par, last par. He brought the headline slightly closer to the text, made it a touch larger and aligned its edge with that of the first column. Then hit send and was back in the splash.

While the chief pairer said into his phone, 'We've got twenty-two. Twenty-two is coming now,' the Editor said to those he'd gathered behind Jeremy: 'Don't just stand there. Front-page headline, tell him what to type.' Jeremy's fingers hovered above the keyboard. The chief was shouting, his composure shot, 'For fuck's sake, get nine back, how the hell did that happen?'

The first front-page suggestion came from one of the

assistant editors, Alex Thwaite, who was feeling grave and statesmanlike after writing a Churchillian leader column. While Jeremy typed what he said, Thwaite's cigarette-roughened voice growled: 'Perhaps it's just:

TERROR
COMES TO
LONDON

'Stark, sombre, severe, with a strap underneath to explain.'

'Don't be ridiculous,' said the Editor. 'It makes it sound as if Cockneys are running around screaming.'

Geraldine tried, 'Then it's just:

TERRORISTS
PLAN BOMB
ATTACK ON
BEAST HQ '

'No, no, *NO*,' said the Editor. 'You aren't getting it at all. That's a reporter's headline. Those are the facts; what's the significance, what's the import? This isn't just about our newspaper. This is the biggest attack on the West in years. And "plan" is useless, too. Don't you think we could try to get at least a *little* urgency into it?'

Jeremy, elated by the power of what he was involved in, made a suggestion: 'Maybe it's:

ISLAMIC
BOMBING
LOOMS IN
LONDON '

'No.' The Editor dismissed it, though he didn't seem to think it unusual that Jeremy would speak up. 'That's just plod, plod, plod. Think of something better, and be quick about it, because you only have eight minutes to do it in. Feldstein, this is your job, isn't it? What have you got to say for yourself?'

'Um, I'm just thinking.'

'I know, I can hear your brain fucking clanking. Get on with it.'

Feldstein started to speak without knowing what he was going to say. It sometimes worked. 'Um...

MUSLIM

PLOT LOOMS '

'A plot can't fucking well loom, Feldstein, God damn you.'

Jeremy again deleted everything. Jack from the Art desk had arrived and was watching nervously. Once the headline had been decided upon, he would still have to adjust the lettering as well as the shapes on pages four and five to make the copy fit. All other pages had been sent.

The Editor said, 'It's not just an attack on the *Beast*. September the eleventh wasn't just an attack on the World Trade Center; it was an attack on America, on America's prestige, its symbols, its idea of itself. And now, why us? We aren't just a newspaper; we're one of the pillars of English life, an institution, like the army or the monarchy. This is—'

But he interrupted himself because Will had spoken. His words made breathless by the appalling implications of what he'd noticed, and by the ambitious excitement of having been the one to do so, he asked Max, 'If the terrorists are from the Punjab, why were the people Jez saw outside speaking Arabic?'

That stopped them cold. Max looked at Jeremy, Jeremy looked at Max. The Editor looked from one to the other. He hadn't realized that Jeremy was the sub in question. At his desk, the chief turned from his computer, and stood up. The clocks ticked inexorably towards 9:45.

Jeremy said the only thing he could: 'I don't know the difference, do I? I thought it was Arabic, but it could have been anything.'

Max said, 'I'll take it out. Will, check six–seven to see whether it's in there, too. Get the pages back if you have to. Fast as you can.'

Will felt the Editor's eye linger on him for a moment before, with the clarity of the fear that had slapped them all, the Editor said, 'I have the headline:

MUSLIMS
DECLARE
WAR ON
BRITAIN

'With a strap underneath: "Bomb attack imminent in central London".' Feldstein nodded; that was why Charles was Editor. To Jack the Editor said, 'It's yours. Get on with it.' And the designer ran back to his desk.

There were less than four minutes left. The Editor strode after Jack, saying, 'As big as possible.' The pod, and everyone else in the newsroom, heard him continuing at the Art desk: 'Move that strap closer to the headline; you could drive a bus through that gap. Quickly now!'

Will said to Max, 'The second spread's clear.'

A full two and a half minutes later, Jack shouted across, 'Max, you've got the page.'

By now, everyone but Max, even the chief and the pairers, even the Editor, had stopped working. The newsroom stood and watched him silently. The subs twisted in their chairs or followed what he was doing on their screens. The double column of paired pages gleamed blue but for pages one, four and five. The chief pairer was at Max's elbow, turning a red biro in his fingers and saying, 'One minute.'

Everything was now in his hands. The work of hundreds of reporters, stringers, snappers, editors, designers and subs was complete but for the keystone he had to place. Never had he been calmer, more lucid. His concentration was total, meditative, emptied of all but the splash and the time. His mind held the copy suspended within itself and did not see but felt where something was amiss. All he knew were the columns, the flow, a tweak to the third par, the time; the ache in his fingers went unfelt and the phones went unheard as Max outpaced the clock.

Twenty-four seconds before deadline, he inhaled, coming out of it, and hit send.

The pairer spun on his heel and called across the strange quiet. 'Pages one, four and five coming now. You've got the splash.'

His assistant looked, moved, clicked, and spoke into the direct phone he'd been holding to his ear in readiness. 'One, four and five are through. The splash is through.' Then he added, 'Thanks,' put the phone back on its cradle and said, 'It's gone. We're off stone. The paper's away.'

FOURTEENTH CHAPTER

ASSEMBLED around the subs' desks, but much reduced in number and uncertain now that the struggle was over, the *Beast*'s staff looked to the Editor to lead them. He, however, was in inaudible consultation with Geraldine. The subs stood up at their desks or whispered to one another. The pairs of onliners at the doors wandered in little circles or swung their arms uneasily. The phone at Newsdesk rang and was answered. As the heady imperative of getting the paper away slowly faded, the fears it had suppressed began to re-establish themselves. While they'd been embodying the *Beast* in full roar the crowd had been vast and invincible; now they felt again the fragility of being only one easily punctured bag of skin.

But then the Editor finished what he was telling Geraldine and addressed them like a general amid the wreckage of his enemy. He said, 'Well done, everyone,' and they burst into a relieved cacophony of clapping, cheering and banging on tables. The Editor took this as his due. Once it was tailing off, he spoke over them, and they fell silent to listen:

'You have done something great today. You have defied terror.' There was a second round of cheers, quickly hushed. His tone was different from the tub-thumping he'd done before edition. There was a melancholy in it, the victor's sense of incompleteness. Nevertheless, he went on: 'We have become a target because we have fought in long and unwavering defence of the principles that England holds dear, or ought to: our liberty, our decency, our sovereignty and our sense of justice.' He looked into their faces and even those who thought him a tyrant were stirred.

'Often have we had to stand between this country and subjugation; to unelected technocrats in Brussels, to the secret courts of our own government, to a metropolitan elite that holds the rest of the country in disdain, and finally, to that elite's cowardice in tolerating the extremists in our midst.'

He held out a hand towards Jeremy. 'Come over here.' Jeremy was tilting back his chair, his mind still running, and snapped forward when summoned. For the first time in the decade and a half he'd worked there, he felt everyone's attention on him.

He went up to the Editor like an Oscar winner to the podium, barely managing to stop himself grinning. The Editor sombrely shook his hand and said to the crowd, 'I do not need to remind you that the price of liberty is eternal vigilance. And, through his vigilance, Mr Underwood has not only saved this newspaper from physical destruction but has also given us the opportunity to demonstrate that news-papers themselves are in anything but decline. Chief sub, three cheers, please.'

The chief, keeping his face completely blank and perhaps just standing ever so slightly, almost imperceptibly, to attention, called out, 'Hip-hip!'

And everyone but the chief, the Editor and Jeremy cried, 'Hooray!'

'Hip-hip!'

'Hooray!'

'Hip-hip!'

'Hooray!'

Max relaxed into unmodulated pride for his friend.

Putting his hand on Jeremy's shoulder, the Editor continued: 'And our vigilance will not end with this splash. They will hurl whatever else they have at us. So tomorrow we will move somewhere we can better defend ourselves. As a few of you will know, the *Beast* has long maintained a fortified newsroom in Berkshire for the eventuality of attack. We will decamp there in the morning. At last, we will clear out of London. No more of this place.' With a huge sweep of his hand, he cast London aside.

'We will return to the heartland, to make our stand among the people whose champions we are. Back to the meadows, the lanes, the hedgerows and the country churches, the hills and the hundreds, the village greens, the guildhalls, the real England.'

He'd finished, but it was too much for them to take in and this time there was no cheering. A fortified newsroom in Berkshire? For how long? And their families? But the Editor had no more to tell them. He went back to his office, and they parted for him. His staff felt somehow out of sync. The scene was already historic, its significance too large to grasp in the living of it.

Then someone began to yell from one of the doors, and everything went back to normal. It was the Editor of the *Impartial*, who'd apparently seen the *Beast*'s first edition on ClipShare. A slight, foppish, middle-aged man in a delicately tailored, midnight-blue suit, he was being grappled by two boys from *BeastOnline* and kept jumping almost out of their grasp as he shouted: 'What if it had been tonight? What if it had been tonight, you fucking fruitcake? I'll have you prosecuted for this, you hear me, Brython? I'll see you in jail for this.'

But the Editor had no interest in hearing; he was already back in his office, informing the police of the planned bombing. And the *Beast* loped on. Corrections and developments had to be dressed into the second edition. There were body counts to be updated, new denials to append. An online version of the splash had to be okayed for publication overnight. The details of the retreat to Berkshire had to be worked out and disseminated. No freelancers would be required; only staff whom the *Beast* could fully call its own. The Berkshire *Beast* would be leaner than usual, and the freelancers would just have to find somewhere else.

As their duties came to an end, the reporters began to disperse, to pack, and to wonder. The second edition went in another, less intense, frenzy of shouting and rushing and page-killing. Then the subs, too, started to pull their bags and satchels out from under their desks and lift their coats from the pegs on which they'd hung them at lunchtime.

Will left the building euphoric with self-importance. He'd saved the paper from embarrassing itself in the splash and been noticed by the Editor. He was sure Rosie had seen it. And not only that, but as he strolled through the atrium he found it swarming with stressed and terrified hacks from the *Impartial* and the *Trumpet*, trying to get the story for themselves. Lost-looking security guards in black suits were vainly attempting to corral them; and beefy policemen, still in their motorbike leathers, kept asking who was in charge. Will moved through them as one long in the know.

But by the time he'd sat for half an hour in the stuffy tube, and walked heavily up the steps on to the street at Bethnal Green, the last of the adrenaline had worn off, leaving him exhausted. All the extra energy his body had advanced him for edition was now overdue, and he ached. He trudged along the empty, lamp-lit streets to his flat and, as every evening, it seemed far further from the station than it had that afternoon. At least his meander could be on the road itself. There were few cars; the city had already had its evening.

He tried to keep around him the bright figures of the Editor and the chief and Max, but they flickered and fluttered off along the dark streets away from him. He could sometimes conjure them in talk with his housemates, but it meant having to explain so much; and at any rate when he got in this evening they were already asleep. He clicked on the bulb in the narrow kitchen and carefully shut the door so as not to wake them. The fridge hummed in the deep quiet that settles on a house after everyone has gone to bed, and the overhead light gleamed on the laminated counters and the shiny floor. From the fridge he took a plastic bottle of milk and that lunchtime's leftovers, clumps of tomato-reddened penne. As he ate alone at the table, he found himself losing his hold on what precisely all the day's exertion had been for.

Nonetheless, he felt better once the food was in his system, just a little empty, his brain burnt out. He tried to imagine this place they were going to tomorrow, but couldn't form any coherent picture of it. He roused himself enough to write a note to the others explaining that he was going away. One was training as a lawyer and the other taught in a nearby comprehensive; they would probably be gone by the time he woke up. He smiled through his fatigue as he began his note with the words, 'In case you haven't already seen it on the news...'

Thirty miles away, in the commuter village of Kemsing, outside Sevenoaks, Jeremy softly opened the door to his bedroom. Louise had fallen asleep with the light on so that he'd know to wake her when he came in. He was already back among the mental furniture of home – the traffic, the commute that had lengthened since the *Beast* moved from Wapping to Kensington, the signs that Kemsing's house prices were continuing to rise – but tonight he brought with him something more important.

Rather than crawl in next to Louise so she could unknot his tie with sleepy fingers, he sat against the headrest and crossed his shoes on top of the duvet.

She shifted towards him without opening her eyes, sprawled a hand across his belly and asked, 'How was work?'

He told her about the paper's big story, omitting his own part in it out of an unexpected unwillingness to brag. As he talked, she became ever more wakeful until finally she sat up in alarm, saying, 'What? What? Tell me that again.'

'Like I said, it turned out there was a plot to bomb the newspaper. But I don't think it'll happen now. And we won't be there anyway. We'll be in this place in the countryside.'

'But they would have bombed it with you inside it! What were the security people doing? Where were the police?'

'Well, we didn't tell the police till after edition.'

'You didn't tell the police?! What's the matter with you? It was that crazy Editor of yours, wasn't it? I'll kill him myself! God knows he'd deserve it. What was he playing at?'

He didn't want to hear the Editor criticized tonight and tried to draw her down against himself. But she pushed him off and cross-examined him until he'd gone through it again, still eliding what he himself had done. Many of her questions – what exactly this place in Berkshire was, how long he expected to be away for, when he would be able to call – he didn't have an answer for. But, as they talked, her bright fear for him gradually faded to matters of practicality: who would take the girls to school, for example; and whether she should cancel her dinner plans for Thursday evening.

Not until much later, once they'd undressed him and switched off the light and were lying unusually interlocked in the dark, did he whisper that the person who'd spotted the terrorists was him. Then there was another round of questioning, quieter but fiercer, in which she said, 'You just don't know any better sometimes. You just act like you don't have a care in the world, or anyone who would miss you if something happened. You should have come home as soon as you even guessed how serious it was.'

But, later, she regretted that, and kissed him on the face and whispered, 'How funny, my little Jeremy being the big hero. Aren't you just the bravest, my lamb.' And now that she finally understood how satisfied he was, he sank towards sleep. He didn't bother telling her about the demotion; he'd almost forgotten it himself. After all, he'd been cheered by the whole newsroom. Instead of merely making the daily trade of labour for salary, today he'd actually done something. And she was right: it had been dangerous. He hadn't thought about it at the time, but yes, now that she'd said so he could see it himself: today he'd been *brave*.

Far off in North London, Max and his wife were having sex. He'd returned home wreathed and mantled in glory and, as he moved in her, his wife called to him, 'Maximus, oh, Maximus!' It was a nickname he wouldn't admit that he'd ever heard (not even to her) but to his ear it rang out like the chanting of a crowd.

And afterwards, once his panting had ebbed, he was able to tell her, with relish, that he would miss the entirety of her parents' visit. He would be too busy defying terror; they could take themselves out for lunch.

In South Kensington, the Editor prowled the cavernous gloom of his empty house. The streetlamps cast a grid of shadow on to the wall beside him, and a dark spray of leaves swayed across it. His heels clicked on the immaculate wooden floor, but he cared nothing for whether it was immaculate or not – his housekeeper kept the place furnished – and his head was full, as always, of tomorrow's news. He was deeply moved by the thought that these terrorists were inflicting fresh trauma on the survivors of the 7/7 attacks. Moved and resolute. He would not let their suffering go untold; a Saturday feature, perhaps. A heartbreaking interview with a 7/7 widow.

Once he'd paced off that thought, he descended to the one room in the house he really thought of as having anything to do with him. The cellar had been arranged as a personal study ever since the house was chosen by his then wife, whom he'd now almost wholly forgotten. He'd furnished it as his father's had been: rich with leather, dark wood and down-shaded lamps. Just visible beyond the circle of lamplight were archiving cupboards in which he himself, when on holiday, filed the news sections from the *Beast*. The pages, neatly suspended though they were behind their rows of doors, gave off a remnant of predatory intent, like a wolf's pelt.

The Editor opened the cupboard directly behind his desk, pushed the pages aside with the back of his hand and lifted from its hiding place a wooden shoebox his father had given him. He put it on the desk, beside the framed photograph of his son, and sat down. Inside the box were warped photographs, some cheaply made medals for service in Africa and Italy, a few letters on translucently thin paper, a plain grey cardboard box of ammunition and his father's service revolver. With two hands, he reverently took the heavy, dully gleaming pistol from the box and began, as on many a reflective evening before, to clean and oil it.

He found himself in an unusual mood. The melancholy that had begun after edition settled heavily on him as he carefully pushed the stiff, narrow brush through each of the six chambers. The day's excitement now felt like a last hurrah. This story had legs, and would keep running, but he couldn't imagine that he would ever again preside over a splash like the one that would be on newsstands in the morning. He was glad to have had it. He wouldn't have wanted simply to wane towards the point where his body and his weariness overcame him. And it had been quite a hurrah. Perhaps even the high-water mark of his career. Lucky to have it so close to the end.

Among the small group of national-newspaper editors, he was already the last of his own kind – the old-fashioned newsmen who could calculate newsprint by the bale and knew the weight of a barrel of ink. Those who'd actually worked on Fleet Street, and done so in its long noontime, when the pubs were thronged with hacks, and the *Beast*, the *Brute* and the others in the pack between them sold more copies every day than there were households in Britain. He remembered the zenith itself from his childhood, when his father wrote for the *Brute* and a single edition could shift more than nine million copies. Nine million! Even tomorrow's wouldn't manage much more than two.

He pushed the long brush through the barrel, turning it slowly in his hand with the rifling. There was hardly any dirt. It was a long time since the gun had been fired. He should make sure that it still worked.

The *Brute* now was on its knees, not able to pay enough journalists to get enough good stories to get enough circulation to bring in enough income: the terminal spiral. The *Beast* didn't even attack it any more. That, too, was a tragedy, to see a century's ferocious competition reduced to pity. He laid the brush aside.

Of the papers that were still fighting, there was just one that outsold the *Beast*: that upstart builder's rag the *Fun*, but it was just topless girls and smutty jokes, hardly a newspaper at all. And even it had lost half a million readers in the past five years. Moreover, the *Beast* had decisively outflanked it. Because only he, he alone, had seen right away and with total clarity that the internet would usher in the end of newspapers, and understood then that the race, which didn't seem even to have begun when he founded *BeastOnline*, was to the death.

Now *BeastOnline* was the most-read news website in the world. More readers than the BBC, more than anything produced by the Americans. It reached ten million a day, and rising. Already, *BeastOnline* was cannibalizing its mother, breaking stories that could have waited for the print edition. But why wait? News was best when newest. And *BeastOnline* had the brazen chutzpah of the coming thing. The print edition was starting to lag behind. He'd saved the *Beast* by destroying it; that was his legacy. But he didn't want to live to see *BeastOnline*'s final victory, and regretted that he probably would.

Using a rag kept for that purpose, he worked the metal with oil, exploring its cavities and protrusions, then with another rag rubbed it to a dry shine. He rolled the empty cylinder to hear its lubricated clicking. His other hand squeezed the ammunition box so the cardboard lid stood up, and he opened it with his thumb. The heavy bullets nestled inside like sleeping bees. Feeling the pleasure of how snugly they fitted into the spaces they were made for, he slipped six of them into the chambers, and clicked the gun shut.

He wished the internet had a single head, so he could put the gun to the back of it. But it didn't. His time was over. There would be no more gentlemen of the Press. There was no place in the coming era for that old romance of notepads and shoe leather. Feeds, content, copy and paste; he'd shown the way, but he could not follow.

That was perhaps just the nature of things; the unceasing change that had already done for the typesetters and that would one day do for websites, too. But the terrible, perverse waste was that the mahout atop *BeastOnline* would not be his son. Despite having the news in his blood and being saturated with it as a child, Edward denied his patrimony. He'd become a director of music videos. Even when the Editor expressed it to himself this baldly, he couldn't quite grasp it. Music videos? Tarts gyrating in bikinis? Even after years it was still shocking.

He moved the framed picture into the centre of the lamplight and turned it side-on to himself. Standing up, he reflected that the boy had always been headstrong, contrary, intolerant of authority. All good qualities in a journalist. But this year he'd refused even to come on their annual father-and-son ice-fishing trip to Greenland. And this despite the fact that he, his father, had in something approaching desperation offered to bend the rules of right and wrong for him. If Edward agreed to join *BeastOnline*, he would of course have to go in at the bottom, but the Editor had guaranteed that the boy would be on the back bench within three years. Three short years! It had taken him nearly twenty. And the boy hadn't even considered it.

The Editor, having reached the edge of the room, turned on his heel with ceremonial self-consciousness, as if for a duel. He lifted the revolver in the steady, two-handed grip his own father had taught him and, without hesitating, shot the framed photograph through the face.

Of the artificial thunderclap that leapt from the barrel, nothing was heard above ground. On the broad, night-time street of white-fronted houses and under the artificial shadows of the trees, all was still.

In the newsroom, too, everything was quiet. Rosie was the last sub there. She was on the late shift and had just finished proofreading the third edition. As the newsroom emptied, the ceiling lights, which were activated by motion sensors, had clicked off, the darkness settling at the newsroom's edge and then closing in.

After edition, she'd been hoping for a word from Max on the Blind Bulgarian story – to the effect that even though things had gone close to the brink she'd been right to be meticulous. But nothing. And, as nothing came and came, she'd had to turn her eyes to the truth: she'd frozen up; the story had been taken from her. Getting the story right in the right amount of time was why she was there, and she'd failed to do it. She cried at her desk, glancing around to make sure no one could see. Then rubbed her face and ran her fingers through her thin hair; she'd developed a little dandruff with the stress.

She told herself to toughen up. She'd known before she started that the *Beast* was going to be hard; that was why everyone said it was good training. Really she wanted to write elegant, thoughtful features for a Sunday magazine, perhaps the *Stentorian*'s, stories that would make the readers cry. But lots of the best people started out on the *Beast*. Toughness must be part of what they learnt here. She told herself to be more like Will. He didn't let things touch him. When things became pressured he became not less but more accurate; faster, surer. That was the sort of person who made a success of it.

Her phone rang. The taxi was outside. Still worrying about whether she'd missed something in the proofread, she gathered her bag and coat and went downstairs. The subs' empty desks and chairs sat illuminated a while longer. Then, but for the single lamp burning eternally at Newsdesk and the pallid glow of the screens manned overnight at *BeastOnline*, the lights went out.

WEDNESDAY

FIFTEENTH CHAPTER

AT A little after eight the following morning, Assistant Commissioner Nigel Willis of the Metropolitan Police slowed his car and turned it carefully over the bump at the entrance to the petrol station where he bought his newspaper. His eyes felt dry and his head tight; he'd been up late co-ordinating raids on the houses of Kayani and his gang, and on their mosque. It had been after three by the time he stopped the interrogations because everyone was exhausted and they were getting nothing. This morning he'd heard the whole story again on the radio, in a discussion that had been running since before he left the house: the *Beast*'s building was surrounded by armed police; the government had raised the national threat level to 'critical'; the Prime Minister had convened a meeting of COBRA and declared that an attack on the Press was an attack on the institutions of democracy. But Nigel had an unhappy suspicion and wanted to check the original article for himself.

He parked beside the concrete payment shack appended to the forecourt and walked across to the bank of thick grey plastic cubes that held the papers. Instead of picking up his usual *Stentorian*, he looked through the transparent lids for the *Beast*. There was only one left. He lifted it out, the backs of his fingers touching plastic, and went in to pay. As he waited, he read the front page and noticed that the man in front of him in the queue was already reading the inside. When he reached the counter, the attendant, with whom he never exchanged more than or a nod or sometimes, around Christmas or during the World Cup or the Ashes, a 'Morning', asked him, 'Is this the last one?'

'Um, yes it is.'

The attendant, who was wearing a green BP cap and matching polo shirt, shook his head. 'Incredible, isn't it? I'm keeping one as a souvenir – the day the Muslims declared war.'

Nigel gave a non-committal smile, wondering whether he might have to start buying his paper somewhere else, and took the *Beast* back to his car. He spread it awkwardly on the steering wheel and skimmed through the heavy black type to the passage he was searching for: how the *Beast* had actually come by this information. He'd already heard how one of their reporters had stumbled on the plot, but there, just as he feared, the article quoted in confirmation 'an anonymous senior source at Scotland Yard' with his own words about 'an attack in the next few days' and information from 'people in the terror community'.

Nigel scrunched the newspaper shut and said, 'Oh, piss on it!'

Those 'people' had actually just been Dan Felsenburg, who was subordinate to him but with whom he ate lunch. Dan had rung just before that bloody reporter from the *Beast*, to ask whether he'd heard anything about an attack like this. When he'd rung Dan back after the story broke, to ask where *he*'d heard about it, he said that he'd got it all from questions put to him by a reporter at the *Beast*.

Nigel scrunched the paper into a tighter bundle and closed his eyes so as not to see it. He could sense the nearness of absolute humiliation. Already he could imagine going into his next quarterly appraisal carrying a mistake that had been front-page news; actually, he wouldn't even make it to the appraisal; he would have to resign. And then what? Private security consultant? He was certainly senior enough to find something – he'd been sounded out at a conference just a couple of months ago by a firm in Dubai – but the thought of it was obscurely degrading: taking money from a rich man or a corporate manager and having to act as though their concerns were important.

His mind automatically teased apart layers of possibility and laid them out separate: just because he'd misinformed the *Beast*, that didn't mean they weren't right about this plot. The prime piece of evidence, after all, wasn't from him: one of their reporters had seen what he believed to be bombers and, for what it was worth, there was nothing about their burqas that violated the Kayani group's descriptions. In that case, he might be safe. He needed to identify which possibilities were true before anyone else did. If the self-important odd bods from MI5 got there first, it would be out of his hands for good.

As he drove off the forecourt and in the direction of the Yard, another layer of possibility occurred to him: that there was a bombing planned, but not by Kayani. He tapped the car's little touchscreen to call Dan, who picked up at once. 'Morning, Nige.'

'Morning.'

They spoke over each other, Dan's voice louder: 'Are you on the way in?'

'Yep, I'm just in the car. Is there anything new from the cells?'

'We're just about to get started again. They're just getting fed. I think we should be back in there in the next half-hour. Was there an angle in particular you wanted us to work?'

'No, no new angle. But just to make sure I've got this right – has any of them given us anything that indicates they had prior knowledge of the attack?'

'About where the bombers might have been preparing?'

'No, just anything that indicates they'd heard of it before we arrested them.'

'Umm, well, no. It's pretty frustrating really. The bombers must have been careful about keeping up a Chinese wall. Maybe it'll be easier now they're tired, but what we really need is this Met source who's in the *Beast*. Who is that? Is that one of ours?'

Nigel rolled his eyes in disgust at this situation. 'Daniel, I don't have to tell you what constraints operational security can place even on inner-departmental information sharing.'

'Oh,' said Dan. 'So we're on to them.'

'We haven't got them.'

'Of course.'

'In fact, to be totally frank, I think it's fair to say that not very much was done about it before last night.'

'Right,' said Dan grimly. They'd often spoken about other teams' failure to be proactive.

'We need to get these people found *today*. Pull bodies off anything you need to; everything else can wait. I'm going to call the commissioner now for more manpower.'

'Great, that's what I was thinking, too. Because it's been all over the news that the *Beast* are leaving their offices. Our guys might use their bomb somewhere else.'

'If there's a bomb.'

Dan was surprised into momentary silence, then said, 'What do you mean, *if* there's a bomb?'

'We don't just accept things on the *Daily Beast*'s say-so, do we? What evidence have we actually got? A news report, some rumours going round the department.'

Dan let this thought ramify, and asked slowly, 'So what are you saying?'

'The department's been lucky so far. No one's been hurt. Nothing embarrassing has happened. But we need those people found and we need them questioned.'

SIXTEENTH CHAPTER

AS JEREMY steered his car along the deeply grooved route to Copper House, he suspected nothing of the turn Willis's investigation was taking. Overnight, his sense of the Burqa Bombing story had settled into an unfamiliar optimism. It had been with no small pride that he told the girls at breakfast he was sorry he wouldn't be able to drive them to school because he had to go away for a week on a big story. He'd seen that they were impressed and, with a feeling that it was magnanimous of him to be concerned with family arrangements on a day like today, he was suddenly moved by the thought that he was their father.

In the car he listened to Radio 1, where Hugh Ames was talking about his, Jeremy's, story. For once he didn't feel the least bit tired. Yesterday he'd worked right at the newspaper's molten core and some of its heat and power had transferred themselves to him. He felt again something that in his slow disappointment he'd begun to believe he never had: the excitement of the news, the hectic barging speed of catching a story and the belief that journalism, no matter how threadbare and put upon, was the finest profession known to men. He himself could not say how he'd managed to spot the bombers for what they were. It must have been some kind of exquisitely honed sensitivity, the hunch of all hunches. The years of drudging had paid their dividend.

Ames interrupted himself for an update just in: the Met was drafting thousands of extra officers from Kent, Surrey, Essex and East Anglia, hugely expanding the scope of the operation. At this very moment, uniformed police were going door-to-door looking for clues and raids were taking place on the homes of those linked to the terror gang.

But Ames wasn't talking about the brave determination of the police and the *Beast* to root out terror. Instead he counted up the incidents of Islamophobic violence that had been reported just this morning. Three young Muslim men in Luton had been badly beaten up by what was rumoured to be a group of ex-servicemen, someone had smeared excrement on the door of a mosque in Cardiff, Twitter was *seething* with stories of intimidation and hate speech, and a whole row of halal butchers in London's East End had had bricks thrown through their windows, one wrapped in the front page of the *Daily Beast*.

Ames addressed his studio guests: 'So, I think we have to ask, don't we, aside from the very real danger of terrorism, what role is played in all this by provocation? The *Daily Beast*'s headline this morning, "Muslims declare war on Britain", has already attracted dozens of complaints to IPSO, the Press-standards authority, one of them from Julian Winfield, the editor of the *Impartial*, who has also reported it to the Met as incitement to religious hatred. Now, we all know there's little love lost between the *Impartial* and the *Beast* at the best of times, but since that headline hit the newsstands this morning there's been this spate of shocking anti-Muslim violence. So I think we have to ask the question, who is doing more to incite terror in this country, Islamic extremists or the *Daily Beast*?'

As the first guest, a political columnist on the *Conscientious*, told Hugh that she thought he was absolutely right, Jeremy hummed with contentment. He was riding too high to be twinged by the three boys beaten up in Luton, and this earnest, safe BBC indignation was precisely the tone that the luvvies took when their feathers had been well and truly ruffled. It was how the establishment spoke whenever the *Beast* got too boisterous for its sensibilities. The BBC must feel off the pace today: the *Beast* had the story of a generation and all they could do was comment on it. Ames himself had done a couple of years on the *Beast* before going straight, and Jeremy had been drinking with him a few times. He might look out Ames's email address and tease him a little.

Amused by that thought, he stopped listening. It had rained in the night and dark patches of damp still leant in shadow-shapes across roads and pavements. Wisps of spent cloud drifted over the city. The traffic was light. It was a good morning.

When he arrived at Copper House, he saw that the police had set up a cordon across the streets around the building. A black cab ahead of him made a U-turn in the road and headed back the way it had come. He noticed a few snappers loitering on the pavement, one of whom he recognized as a freelance who'd gone to the *Respectable*.

There were knots of armed police in paramilitary-blue jumpsuits and matching baseball caps, their hands on the submachine guns slung across their chests. They stood separate from the ordinary policemen in fluorescent-yellow rain jackets and peaked black hats, one of whom signalled him to come forward. A chicane of orange barriers had been laid out for a hundred yards or so before the cordon itself and, as he manoeuvred cautiously through it, Jeremy realized, his stomach turning over, that it was to slow down car-bombers.

He was stopped by a tense officer about his own age who started telling him he couldn't get through here. But Jeremy showed his pass for the *Beast* and the policeman said, 'Oh, I'm sorry, sir.' He waved at his colleagues to move the barrier aside and gave Jeremy a nod of respect, man to man.

He parked in his usual spot underground, then went out into the tree-canopied square behind the building. A crowd of people from the paper was gathered there, nervously pushing their mini-suitcases back and forth and breathing cigarette smoke into the morning air. Holding their suit-bags over their shoulders by the thin metal coat-hangers, they were gabbling and slapping each other on the shoulder in unnatural excitement.

He found the subs in a group on the pavement nearest Copper House. Max swaggered across to him looking not just unperturbed but almost purring with his own composure. There was a cigarette between his fingers and a black trench coat over his usual black shirt and black trousers. His case and suit-bag were leant neatly against the wall. 'Morning, Jez,' he said, offering him his packet. 'We've just been talking about you. See anyone we should be worried about?' Jez took a cigarette. 'How about him?' He pointed out an armed policeman talking into the walkie-talkie Velcroed to his chest. 'Is he an Islamist sleeper agent?'

Jeremy, flattered, squinted at the policeman and said, 'Nah, that one's just fiddling his expenses.'

Max held out his lighter, shielding it with his other hand for Jeremy, who asked, 'So what the hell's this place we're going to? Is it really a bunker?'

'I'd have to double check this is true,' said Max, judiciously smoothing his hair, 'but I don't think it's actually underground. More like a secure newsroom. They built it in the Cold War so they could still get the paper out if the Russians nuked London. The point is that our jihadi friends, or any new jihadi friends we've made this morning, won't find it just by Googling our address.'

'But someone must have been there before.'

'I think Frank has. A few of the—'

They abruptly had to shift sideways as a train of porters swung around the corner carrying packing boxes. Plants, lamps and framed pictures protruded from the brown cardboard. Max and Jeremy watched as one porter put down a box – all of them had 'Beast on Sunday Editor's office' written on them in permanent marker – and opened the back of a van. Another porter had a rolled-up rug bending thickly over his shoulder, the protective mesh on its underside making a pale overlay to the deep colours within. Behind him shuffled two others, their arms and faces taut, taking tiny steps under the weight of a life-sized golden baby elephant.

The chief sub bounded over to them, his fat bald head quivering on his shoulders. 'Rats!' he exclaimed with relish. 'Rats, running down the gangplank, getting off the ship before it sinks.'

'Look at that thing,' said Jeremy, watching the *BoS* Editor's golden elephant be heaved up on to the lip of the van. 'What else do you think he's got in there?'

'That's none of our concern, Jezdemona. Let the rats run away, and the ones who're left, however incompetent, must be hacks. Lauren hasn't turned up, that gutless backstabber.'

'Lauren?' Jeremy was taken aback; he'd thought she had the tenacity of ambition.

'No, and neither has Jack from the Art desk, that yellow-bellied mummy's boy. And a few milksops from Features, Diary, the gentler departments. They'll never work on Grub Street again. But what about you, Jez, spotted anyone else with your X-ray news-vision? Got your jihad goggles on?'

'Nothing so far,' said Jeremy, much pleased by how things were turning out. He supposed he had his job back.

'Now would be the time, though, wouldn't it? All of us bunched close together outside the building – imagine what a nail bomb would do. Wipe out half the newsroom. If I was a jihadi, I'd be at an upstairs window in one of those houses right now, warming up my throwing arm.' They glanced uneasily at the opaque upper windows in the block of flats nearest them. 'The sooner we get out of London, the better. You don't notice how packed it is with Muzzers till you start looking. And we don't want to give the *Strumpet* a great front page: "*Beast* staff massacred; chief sub tells of survivor's guilt".'

Max looked at his watch. 'At least it would be too late for them to get it into their first edition.'

Jeremy said, 'But Frank, aren't we going to have every hack in London watching everything we do? I just saw at least a couple of snappers outside the barriers.'

'No no no no *no*, it's all different now. We've got unmarked police escorts from here to Berkshire. A few of our esteemed colleagues from the *Brute* tried to tail the first buses to go off this morning and Plod sent them to cool their heels in the cells at Ladbroke Road. You see, little Jezzy, you're in the big leagues now.'

Jeremy was impressed. He'd have to tell Louise. It might reassure her a little. Then again, it might not.

The chief thrust his chin at Max, saying in a tone almost

of reprimand, 'I take it you saw one of your headlines was on *Front Page* last night.'

'Oh yes?' said Max, pretending that he hadn't watched it with his wife. 'Which one was it?'

'The one about Kate Kloss and Edith Bohler. "You can't have your Kate and Edith too".'

'Hm,' said Max the Magnanimous. 'They're not great at choosing them – that wasn't the best yesterday. And you know, the kid had a good one.'

'What, Will?'

Max shrugged as if to say that knowing the names of rookie grunts was none of his concern.

'Dr Filth?'

'No. The one about the psychic parrot. "Polly sees a cracker". Unusual headline.'

The chief didn't smile. 'Too silly a story for *Front Page*. Too obviously bullshit. Psychic parrots? How full of crap would a newspaper have to be to print something like that?'

He clapped Jeremy on the arm and was already off to interrogate the chief policeman about whether they'd searched the surrounding houses. Once he'd vexed as many policemen as he came into contact with, he began to wind up the already skittish crowd. By the time their bus arrived, they were yelling and whooping with volatile hilarity. As they stowed their luggage, they shouted:

'Big bag, Nick, how many bombs you got in there?'

'What's that scruffy piece of shit suitcase? It looks like you've dragged it all the way from Syria.'

'Who let this man in here? He's obviously a female jihadi in disguise. Police! Police! Take him away!'

'Did that cop just whisper "*Allahu Akbar*"? Did he just whisper "*Allahu Akbar*"? Bomber! Bomber!'

The crowd surged nervously.

'Last chance to run away! Go find where Lauren's hiding and get in next to her.'

'I wouldn't hide next to Lauren; she's probably shat herself already.'

And there was a resounding cheer, to his acute embarrassment, as Will, the only one who'd come in casual clothes, assuming they'd change when they got there, heaved Rosie's pastel-pink suitcase into the side of the bus.

They boarded, aiming ostentatiously breezy greetings at the two armed policemen awkwardly riding shotgun in the front seats and at the phlegmatic driver, who'd seen worse. They argued excitedly about which seats would be safest if the bus was blown up and pretend-fought about who got to sit nearest the exit. While they were still squabbling, the bus juddered and moved off, to a chorus of hurrahs from the back. While the driver manoeuvred past the barriers and on to the main road, the chief braced himself in the aisle and, conducting with his hands, led everyone but Max and the policemen in roaring out:

'It's a long way to Tipperaaaary,
it's a long way to go.'

They beat time on the big plastic windows with the flats of their hands, and bawled:

'It's a long way to Tipperaaa-aaary,
to the sweetest girl I know.
So goodbye Piccadiiiiiilly,
Farewell Leicester Square...'

The bus accelerated heavily up the hill, passing smart antique shops, the flat white faces of stuccoed rows, and restaurants named after towns in Italy and France, then turned left at Notting Hill and on to the highway leading west out of London.

The chief dropped hard into the seat next to Jez, who was by himself because Max had decided to sit behind the driver and study the morning's papers. Will was in front of them and jumped in his place when the chief grabbed his shoulder. The chief cackled. 'Don't be so jittery, greenhorn; we'll be safely in the Home Counties soon enough. Look at this.'

The chief's whole face was red with the pressure in his capillaries and his boisterousness had become a little frenetic. Under his gruesome exhilaration he looked very tired. He flourished something at Will. It was an accounting ledger with a faded maroon cover and a newspaper cut-out of a dog Sellotaped to the front. 'The *Beagle Logbook*,' announced the chief, standing up again and holding it aloft to make sure everyone noticed. 'The *Beagle Logbook*, boys and girls, volume twenty-eight.'

The others cheered. Only a few of the older ones knew what he was talking about, but for the moment their spirits were so high they would cheer anything. The chief flourished it again and thudded down the steep stairs to the bus's toilet, to leave it there.

Will asked Jeremy, 'Is it something for this place we're going to?'

Jeremy, feeling very amused and comfortable, said: 'No, it's the *Legal Bogbook*. All the complaints and cases against the paper. It was always in a toilet on the sixth floor and everyone used to say that just looking at it would get you sacked and sued at the same time. I didn't know it still existed.'

The chief re-ascended, breathing heavily, and let himself

plonk back into the seat next to Jez. Some of the older subs were already sending an overexcited junior down the stairs to fetch it. Jeremy asked, 'Is it alright for us to have that out?'

'Look around, Jezmerelda, we're in emergency measures. None of the normal rules apply.'

'I didn't know it was even still being kept up.'

With the back of his hairy wrist, the chief dabbed sweat from his temples. He said, 'I've been doing it.'

'But where's it been – not in that same toilet?'

'It's been kept at a secret location so none of those wide-eyed little Johnny-come-latelies from *BeastOnline* can start blabbing about it.'

'Do you mean it's been in your house?'

A burst of laughter interrupted them. The subs had started to read the *Beagle*. The chief had actually imagined they would descend into the bus's tiny interior cave to consult it, but he was satisfied nevertheless. To Will he said, 'Half the *Beast*'s soiled old knickers are in that book, along with the names of who soiled them. You're usually not even allowed to know it exists until you've done your first decade before the mast. So make sure you study it before this kind of quality journalism dies out for good.'

At that, his tiredness seemed to overwhelm him and he slumped back fatly in his seat, letting the noise of the subs ricochet around him.

The bus reached the edge of London and the roads widened. The periods of continuous motion stretched longer and as the bus found its place in the steady procession on the motorway the excited subs started to grow soberer. The anxious hilarity of departure wore off. Conversations quietened and became serious. Several remembered to send messages to their families. Jeremy texted Louise that everything was fine and they even had a police escort. The *Beagle* was passed from row to row and finally it came down the pecking order to Will.

He opened it and found the pages were stiff with glued-in sheets of printed A4. Turning haphazardly, he read: 'In regard to the case of Oliver Bruntsfield, real name Oliver John Martin, the popular singer in whose swimming pool a man was found dead during a party, we have given an undertaking not to print the following remarks by a responding policeman, from, "That bent bastard definitely did it" down to "The guy's arsehole was like the Japanese flag". Please contact the Legal Department with any queries.'

The chief roused himself. He shifted his bulk forward and folded his forearms on the top of Will's seat. 'Great stuff, isn't it, grasshopper?'

'What are you reading about?' Jeremy, too, looked over the seatback.

The chief said, 'The Olly Bruntsfield quotes from Plod.'

Jeremy winced. 'Uff. I wish I'd never heard that.'

Will asked, 'Is this... I mean, is this really true?'

'Of course it's true, young grunt. In fact, you can be more sure it's true than anything that makes it into print, because it's taken some of Britain's finest legal minds to keep it from getting there.'

'But Bruntsfield got off, didn't he?'

'I'll say he got off.'

They laughed, and Jeremy said, 'Do you remember that one from Plod when they found Maria Elmersson naked in bed with her wrists cut? How did it go? Something about her gashes and—'

The chief spoke over him. 'It was the forensics, after he'd examined her, and he said: "That's the first time I've seen a woman with three gashes – and all of them bloody."'

They laughed, Jeremy wincing again, and Will joined in when he saw it was alright. He turned the pages as the chief, regaining some animation, told more stories. Will's eye fell on isolated sentences: '... and therefore advise against publishing even the anonymized version suggested by Ms Enderling, "Troubled Hollywood actress who came to London for the theatre turns tricks at fashionable club/restaurant", and reiterate that the picture series obtained is not legally conclusive.' '... but his lawyers insist that they will sue over any hint, however oblique, of the Gay Pop Mogul's "Son" Is Really His Nephew story, especially as...' 'They claim that the Duchess has never frequented or "moonlighted" in any capacity at the Horns table-dancing club, Shoreditch, or any other similar establishment, and on the day of the alleged sighting was on an official engagement [This cannot be independently verified. However, you MUST contact the legal department before taking ANY action on this story].'

Reading greedily as he recognized the names, Will tried to fix in his memory every detail of this initiation into some of the newspaper's secrets. He asked the older men, 'How far do these books go back?'

'There was an archive,' said the chief. 'But I don't know where it went. I once, when I first worked here, saw a *Beagle* with all the Nazi stuff from the thirties.'

'When you first came,' asked Jeremy, 'did you work with John Dyson?'

'He interviewed me!' To Will he said: 'The knackered has-been who got banged out yesterday. How old must he be now? Probably losing his teeth already. He's been semi-retired since you were in nappies. But fucking hell, he was from a different time; you knew him, didn't you, Jez?'

'Not really, to be honest. I think he was already officially retired when I came here. He was doing some subbing for extra cash, but I don't think he liked it very much.'

'No, he wouldn't have, bit beneath him to actually do any work, especially something as menial as subbing. He was comment editor on the *Chronicle* before we swallowed it up. But, fuck me, he really was from a more gentlemanly time.' The chief was smiling. 'The interview he gave me was in El Vino's, off Fleet Street. There's only lawyers in there now, but in those days the place was heaving with hacks, all of them in there from lunchtime onwards, knocking them back – even Dyson, who always pretended he didn't really drink. We wouldn't let you do that now, would we, youngling?'

Will shook his head, listening.

'For the interview there was him and a few of the other top guys from that time: James Rose, Tom Griffiths, who got sacked from the *Strumpet* for putting the Editor's byline on a story about a rollerskating dog, Mark Rennie, big Andy Pyke, fat Andy, the Fat Controller as once was, whose son Clint turned out to be an idiot and had to get a job making things up for the *Lark*. They were all there.

'So we get stuck in, and not pints, it was before people started wanting booze to taste good as well as get them pissed, so it was all this disgusting sour red wine. I'm still just a freshly hatched little punk, so I puke my guts out under the table. Nobody notices. Tom's staggering around like he's got Parkinson's, which he does now, the poor bastard. I don't know what year it is, let alone what time or how long till edition, when Dyson slaps a hand on my chest like this' – the chief splayed his fingers where those others had been thirty years before – 'holding himself up. And he says' – the chief put on a stiff toffish voice – '"I wouldn't take this job if I were you; it's driving me to a crack-up. But I'm sure you sub like

an angel, so if you do want the bloody thing, you can have it."
I said yes, and they went in to lay out the paper.'

He and Jeremy were misty with nostalgia. 'Imagine that now. You probably sent in your CV and did tests and spoke to HR, didn't you, pipsqueak?'

Will bobbed his head. 'I didn't, but all the trainees did.' He'd never seen the chief so freed of his usual violent mania, and he took the opportunity to ingratiate himself. 'Did it really use to be like that?'

'Oh yes,' said Jeremy, wanting to explain the surprise that had gathered in him over the years about how *different* things had become. 'Everything's so corporate now, but I caught the tail end of the real Fleet Street. The guy I trained under, Nick Robertson, used to insist, actually insist, that everyone kept a four-pack under their desk for the afternoon. And that was after a couple at lunch. He finally went—'

But the past was welling up in the chief, and it spilt out of him. 'On Fleet Street, we had a pub *inside* the building. You'd call down on the internal system, ask them to put a pint and a chaser on the bar – on your tab. Then pretend you were going to the loo, sprint down the stairs, neck them both, and sprint back up. Dyson once, after a few trips, sprinted up one flight less than he should have and had to get dragged out of one of the magazines for trying to make them tell him where they'd hidden his desk.'

The chief paused with pleasure as a vision of the drunken Dyson appeared to him, then said, 'You can't even imagine how it was then. Some of the old guard were still wearing green visors and arm garters, and they used to bore me shitless about how *they*'d caught the tail end of the real Fleet Street, when copy still came in by fucking telegram. But being on a paper then was like being in the best gentleman's club in the world. Now you're expected to fucking work for a living.'

Jeremy said, 'If you can get the work,' and the chief's pleasure ended. Will wanted to keep him talking, so he asked, 'But what I've never understood is how you used to do the subbing without a computer. So just, how did you make things fit?'

Jeremy looked to the chief, deferring, but the chief seemed to have lost interest. He looked across Jeremy and out of the window, past which sunlit countryside was unspooling like coloured celluloid past a shutter. Jeremy said, 'You had to know the width of all the letters and then add them up to fit the space. But actually I remember when I was starting out at the *Sentinel*, when you used to have carbons – a sheet of carbon paper you'd put behind the page you were typing on to make the carbon copy – and I—'

The chief interrupted. 'That's why when you copy someone into an email, which is all you know, it says "cc" in the box, or why – what you young fucks don't realize is that all these names actually came from somewhere. When we spike stories, you used to have an actual spike. When the paper's off stone, there actually used to be a fucking great big perfectly flat stone that you actually laid out the pages on.'

He stopped – and Jeremy, after giving him a moment, finished his anecdote: 'So, when I was starting out at the *Sentinel*, I couldn't get the hang of lining up the carbon with the normal paper, and I remember thinking, "I'll never make it in journalism; it's just too technical for me."'

Will laughed, but the chief said, 'It's all over, the newspaper era. What a big national paper used to be... Every paper used to have its own library, can you imagine that? And that was recent enough to be in my time. In the war, the *Beast* built Spitfires. Think about that. Out of tins sent in by the readers. And now they have to make extra money by selling us sandwiches for lunch. Jez and I were around for the end of real printing, with actual type, and you'll be around to see the end of print altogether. And it'll go fast, Will. I mean, John Dyson, what he was to us...'

Jeremy said: 'It's the end of the old late shift.'

'It's the end of everything.' The chief shook his head, his frown pushing deep wrinkles up his forehead. Then he sighed and flopped back into his seat again. In a voice they'd never heard before, he said, 'Fuck it.' He looked at Jeremy. 'I'm leaving. I'm going to the *Fun*. Production editor. I signed the contract last night while they were gagging to know what had been going on.'

'But...' said Jeremy.

'I'm fifty-four, Jez. Ten more years. The old world's gone. We're all just desk-monkeys now, and I reckon the *Fun*'ll see me out quietly.'

SEVENTEENTH CHAPTER

NEAR the small Berkshire town of Thatcham, the bus carefully eased itself up a woodland road too narrow for centre markings and finally arrived at a pair of high chain-link gates set back into the trees. As a pair of armed policemen came forward to open the gates, the elder of the two men hiding in a ditch across the road began to take photographs. He'd already shot all the earlier buses and now he'd got this one, too: a line of seated hacks in profile at the windows; the policemen ushering the bus inside; the bus nosing around a corner and out of sight.

He banged the bottom of his fist against the soft verge; his guess had come good. To the younger man lying on his belly beside him he said: 'This is fantastic stuff, Gavin, absolutely fantastic. How're we doing on getting inside, has Nikki texted back yet?'

Gavin was sulking. With a martyred expression, he rolled a little and hoiked the phone out of his pocket. There was a WhatsApp message from his brother, but nothing else. 'No,' he said. 'Nothing.'

The elder man stared at him. 'Gavin, what's the matter with you?'

'You could have told me we were going to be lying in a ditch.'

'What?'

Gavin's voice grew petulant. 'Then I wouldn't have worn my suit. If you'd said, I could have worn something else. Now it's completely covered in mud. And you're not wearing a suit.'

Adrian glanced down at himself. It was true that he'd decided to wear some easily replaceable trousers, with an old jumper over his shirt and tie. 'Don't *gripe*, Gavin,' he said. 'Do you think those pros in there are *griping*? No, they're probably making contacts and getting leads; they've probably *already* unearthed some great local stories we've been over-looking for months.'

Gavin was not persuaded. He muttered, 'Yeah, maybe, but I bet they don't have to buy a new suit every day.'

Adrian looked at him with misgiving. Perhaps Gavin was not cut out to be a journalist. The only reason he'd given Gavin a job on the *Echo* in the first place was that he was the son of his first girlfriend, to whom he still felt warm and obliging. And it wasn't as if he had many jobs to give out. They'd just been forced to add '*& Advertiser*' to the masthead: *The Newbury and Thatcham Echo & Advertiser*; he'd had a hell of a time on InDesign trying to make it all fit.

He tried to be understanding. 'Gavin, I'm sorry about your suit. I'm sure it'll come out.'

'It won't, look at it. On the *Beast* they probably have a clothes allowance.'

Adrian drew in his breath, but said, 'OK, we'll see what we can do when we get back to town. But for now, let's remember that this is the biggest story in the history of the *Echo*.

Not just that, it's the biggest story in the *world* right now, and it's on *our* patch. I think that's worth a grass-stain or two.'

'I don't see what the great story is. It's just a bunch of people working in one place instead of another place.'

Adrian paused to frame his comments constructively. 'The way you've got to think about it is: what were we talking about the other day, when we were on the pet-doppelgangers story?'

'Um...' Gavin thought. 'About how we couldn't write the story till we'd found one of the doppelgangers?'

'Exactly, that's exactly right. Until we'd found one *or not found one*. Doppelganger found, or doppelganger mystery. It's the same here. We don't know what the story is, but we *do* know that there's a great story in there somewhere. And when we damn well get in there, and dig around, and find it, the *Newbury and Thatcham Echo & Advertiser* is going to be first in the world for news. First in the *world*. Imagine that.' Adrian was getting excited again. 'And your name can be one of the ones on the byline.'

'Fine,' said Gavin. 'But Nikki still hasn't texted back. She's probably at work.'

'Well, can you look up the number of where she works on your phone?'

'Yeah.'

Some of Adrian's irritation escaped him. 'Well, Jesus, Gavin, do it then. Call the hairdresser, ask to speak to Nikki, find out if her husband's on shift. For all we know, he might be that bloody policeman right bloody there, just desperate for a chance to let us inside.'

To Gavin it seemed unlikely, but nevertheless he Googled 'Shear Bliss Thatcham'. While the phone was ringing, Adrian started to talk again about how this could be the turning point in the *Echo*'s fortunes that he'd long predicted. It was all Gavin had heard all morning and he was glad to cut Adrian off with a gesture; someone at the hairdresser's had picked up.

Inside the belt of trees tied loosely around the bunker, Jeremy lowered a foot from the bus to the tarmac and then let his weight follow it. Back in the open air, he took the opportunity to light a cigarette. In front of him a row of buses gleamed in the sunshine and beyond them squatted the lair where the *Beast* had gone to ground. It was a low, wide, boxy, concrete building that could have been a school, except that there were no windows. Apprehensive policemen patrolled it, their wrists cocked high on their submachine guns. Outside the wide, single-panel door, like that to a vault, an officer-grade policeman with a pair of assistants was checking the subs' ID cards against a list.

Jeremy followed a general movement towards the building, trundling his wheelie suitcase behind him. Everyone seemed oppressed by the sight of all these policemen and by their anxiousness. Jeremy walked slowly, still thinking about what he'd heard. That the chief was leaving, that he *could* leave, shocked him. The chief had lived on the *Beast*'s back so long he'd grown into it like some malevolent parasite. The idea that even he'd lost his belief in it – in the middle of a story like this – and that he now wanted to go out *quietly*... It raised Jeremy's fears about his own future from their shallow sleep.

But he reacted to them with a kind of indignation. It felt almost treasonous of the chief to be defeatist when Jeremy's story was commanding the whole world's attention, and he wondered briefly whether the chief was just afraid. How could anyone imagine that the *Beast* was in decline when the prime minister had convened COBRA, the Met was turning out in force and the story was getting blanket coverage on every channel, every website, every Twitter feed?

'Hoy, dreamboat!' The chief was hailing him. He was standing beside the policemen at the door and shouting, 'Quick sharp! Get your name checked off or you'll have to sleep outside where the jihadis can get you.' The ranking policeman shot him an irritated glance that only sharpened the chief's appetite for provocation. 'Hup hup, get inside where it's nice and safe before one of those lone wolves starts spraying bullets at the entrance. We don't want you to get left outside with the cops.'

Jeremy caught the policeman's eye and made an apologetic show of compliance as he presented his pass. While his name was being found, he noticed that the officer's badge was from Thames Valley Police. He was surprised any Berkshire cops had guns. He'd sort of thought that cops outside big cities spent their time directing traffic and carrying shopping for old ladies. The officer drew a line through Jeremy's name and said tautly, 'Thank you, Mr Underwood. Move inside please.'

'Yep, come on in, Jez,' said the chief. 'The cops are feeling shirty because the Editor won't let them in the building.' Jeremy spared himself noticing the policemen's reactions. 'He doesn't want to expose the free Press to state interference, so they're having to do their shits in the gardeners' outhouse.'

There was no acknowledgement of what they'd spoken about on the bus, but he seemed less self-satisfied than usual, more reckless, baiting the policemen instead of ordering them about. Jeremy moved his gaze away from the chief, so as not to need to say anything, and saw that the bunker's door was a foot thick, inset with rods that could extend into the opposite wall.

The chief saw him looking and said, 'Isn't this place fantastic? It's almost a shame the Kremlin never sobered up long enough to land a nuke on Westminster. Bam-flash, London gone, BBC gone, Fleet Street incinerated, all of us on shift pulverized, everybody in zones one and two just little heaps of white ash being pissed on by radioactive rain. And the next morning, when you're in your house in Hampshire going crazy because the telly's black, the radio's just static and everything's fucked, what arrives on the doorstep but your *Daily Beast.*' There was reverence in his voice. 'All run off the presses in the cellar of this building and distributed by the van fleet they keep in Thatcham. Front-page headline:

RUSSIANS
DROP THE
BOMB ON
LONDON

'Subdeck: "Millions dead. War declared. Counter-strike razes Moscow and St Petersburg. PM says: We will not give in to terror."'

'That's—'

The chief could not be halted. 'World-exclusive picture of the moment Big Ben went down. Twelve pages of coverage inside. Comment: "Is England better off without the metropolis?" Health: "Ten top tips for avoiding radiation sickness." Personal Finance: "What this means for property prices in the Southeast."'

Jeremy wanted to ask why the chief was leaving, if he loved the *Beast* so much. But he asked nothing and, as they walked, looked around at this place where they'd arrived. The walls and floor were bare concrete, as if in a military base. Above their heads, the ceilings were low enough to touch and the glowing strip lights were encaged in wire. The walls had, however, been decorated with black-and-white photographs blown up to the size of news pages: a mountaineer in woollen clothes and circular goggles planted his foot on a snowy ridge, above the caption: '*Daily Beast* Yeti Expedition, Tibet 1956. Reporter Gary Wadeson makes tracks for Kangri Rinpoche'. Then Humphrey Bogart in an armchair reading a large-format *Beast*, pipe stem held casually in the corner of his mouth. The caption read, '"Bogey" enjoys his *Daily Beast* on the set of *Casablanca*, Hollywood 1942', and the headline on the paper was 'Rommel Stopped at Alamein'.

But today's story, his story, was the equal of anything from this golden past. Jeremy glared at the creased flesh on the back of the chief's head as he followed him around a corner into the fortified newsroom itself.

There was the same racket as in Kensington, but the newsroom was smaller and, like the corridor, constrained by a low ceiling, rough, blank, windowless walls and a poured-concrete floor. The furniture looked as if it had been there since the seventies; the desks metal, the chairs unpadded. But the computers were newish and there was the same crowded maze of desks, the same phones and talking and typing and the same TV channels fuzzily projected on to the wall behind the back bench. Jeremy was obscurely moved by this persistence of forms, until he noticed that the newsroom was uneasy and that groups of people were actually watching the screens.

All the channels were telling the same story with variations of the same images. The shot they kept coming back to was of a paper shop gutted by fire, with a blue-and-white line of plastic police tape fluttering in the foreground. Around the charred holes of a display window and a narrow door the brickwork was blackened, as if by an untidy child colouring outside the lines, and on the pavement beneath were feathery black flakes of burnt newspaper. The thick blue plastic *Daily Beast* awning had partially melted in the heat and the camera, with the newsman's taste for symbol, kept returning to where the *Beast*'s white crest had warped and run.

But what people were watching were the ticker lines. The BBC's said, 'Shop owner killed in "retaliatory" arson attack after anti-Muslim violence'. ITV's was 'Shopkeeper burnt alive in pro-Muslim attack in Luton' and Sky had 'White shopkeeper burnt alive in anti-*Beast* firebombing'. In another of the shots every channel kept switching to, a group of bearded Muslim men in long shirts and embroidered skullcaps were yelling and holding up hastily daubed signs that read 'Burn the *Beast*'.

Burnt alive. Jeremy glanced nonsensically over his shoulder at the entrance to the newsroom, where there was only a Diary girl hurrying outside, phone in hand. Burnt alive. He was suddenly glad he wasn't in London, and that the walls here were so thick.

The chief muscled through the uncertain crowd to the subs' bench. He heaved his wheelie suitcase flat on to a desk, unzipped the lid and popped it open. Lying on top of his clothes and held in place by crossed elastic straps was the road sign 'EC4 Fleet Street'.

The chief pushed one of the chairs against a square pillar at the end of the back bench and warily hauled himself up on to it. As people nearby saw what he was doing, they began sombre applause. The rest of the newsroom noticed and the chief, playing to the crowd, held the sign above his head like a boxer displaying his title belt. Everyone began to clap and whistle. Then someone banged on his desk, others joined in, and the tone abruptly dropped into utter seriousness. The *Beast*'s staff pounded the desks till they shook and staplers and telephones jumped up like rain off the pavement.

The chief, slowly swivelling to show them all the sign, shouted, 'No surrender!'

The crowd roared back, 'NO SURRENDER!'

'No surrender!'

'NO SURRENDER!'

'No surrender!'

'NO SURRENDER!'

The chief turned to duct-tape the corners of the sign to the crude concrete, and a chant was taken up and hollered out: 'BEAST! BEAST! BEAST! BEAST!'

Then it was done and, as the chief, almost overcome, bent to lower himself off the chair, there was a loud final cheer and relieved laughter.

Jeremy wanted to say something to the chief, but had no idea what. For someone who was supposed to be at the centre of all that was going on, he felt as if he were struggling to get up to speed. Before he could try, the chief slapped him meatily on the shoulder and said, 'Come on, Jezzum, look alive, you raddled old hack, for as long as you can. For all you know, we had an al-Qaeda arson squad half an hour behind us on the M4. We've got to get your bag on your bunk so they know whose is whose if we all get barbecued.'

The chief was already moving off, and Jeremy and some of the other subs followed. He led them down another long concrete corridor with dormitories coming off it. The doors were standing open and Jeremy could see rooms like those in a barracks: metal bunks, thin orange duvets and grey metal lockers. To the doors had been Sellotaped sheets of A4 printed

with the names of departments: Features, Diary, Showbiz...
On one door, though, someone had instead affixed a sign prised
from the lower level of the car park under Copper House:
a blue square with the white legend 'SUB BASEMENT'.

Inside the subs' dorm, a thin, slightly translucent sheet had
been strung across one end of the room to screen off a space for
the girls. Max had saved the bunk above his own for Jeremy
and a folded set of garish orange linen was sitting on it ready
for the bed to be made. Max had hung his jacket and shirts fr—

////////NEWSFLASH////////

Chief Inspector David Kemnay of the Specialist Firearms
Command prodded a droplet of sweat from the corner of his
eye and whispered into his phone: 'I'm afraid there's no way
to be sure, sir. We think it's just Mian's family in the house,
but there could be anyone in there.'

From the other end of the line, Nigel Willis said, 'Hold off
till you get a clear chance to arrest them both. What are they
doing now?'

'Still going back and forth between the house and the car,
loading it up.'

'Is there any indication they're loading the vehicle with
explosives or weapons?'

'Impossible to tell. It looks like sleeping bags, a tent, cereal
boxes. But again, there could be anything inside those packages.'

'But there's no danger to the public? The area's secure?'

'Officers behind a wall and in an upstairs window opposite,
two unmarked vans, all round the back of the house, other
houses evacuated.'

'Good. We need to make these arrests as quickly as is safe, and get them into questioning. MI5 are on the way, but keep them at a distance. If they take any of the evidence, we'll never—'

'Wait, Mian's got into the driver's seat. The other one's closed the door to the house. It looks like—'

'Make the arrest! Make sure that—'

Kemnay had already signalled and his men, in helmets and body armour, were already rising out of their hiding places or jumping down from the back doors of the vans, pointing their submachine guns and shouting over one another, 'Out of the car! Down on the ground! Out of the car! Down on the ground!'

Mian, inside the car, moved in a way he shouldn't have and one of the guns spoke a sharp percussive pop. In the same instant, many more followed and the car's windshield burst into a shower of shatterproof glass. Choudry had turned to flee back into the house and the bullets caught him in the side, knocking him off his feet and over a waist-high iron gate.

A group of Kemnay's men leapt past him towards the front door and from inside came a crunch and shrieks as more policemen smashed in through the back. The front door was flung open and Kemnay flinched, but it was only a pudgy old woman in house clothes with a thick grey plait falling over her shoulder. Kemnay tried to make out what the men inside were saying over the radio, but all he could hear was her starting to howl.

////////////////////////

Max had hung his jacket and shirts from one end of the bed and beneath it he was laying out a neat row of shower gel, hair gel, shaving foam, upright toothpaste. Beside these was a stack of books: the authorized biography of Lord Copper; an investigative journalist's account of the phone-hacking scandal; *The Principles of Rhetoric*.

Jeremy hoisted his bag up on to the bunk. On the bare wall beside it was another framed photograph: a young pilot with his goggles perched up on his leather flying cap, grinning as he rested one hand on the wing of a Spitfire. The caption read, 'Wing Commander Peter Murray with his machine, Spitfire MH342, built by subscription from readers of the *Daily Beast*. Lost in action 16 June 1942. In memory of The Few.'

He silently climbed the short ladder to his bunk, then twisted awkwardly and sat down next to the pillow. 'Burn the *Beast*'. And a man already burnt alive. He recoiled from that thought and, taking the cigarette carton from his coat pocket, began turning it in his hand. And the chief was leaving. Maybe it *was* time to get out.

But that thought opened up in him a kind of despair. On the monthly transfer from the *Beast* depended the mortgage, the catchment area, the girls' schooling. If they had to move somewhere cheaper, the schools would get worse and would probably be no better than his own. And that would mean that the Underwoods weren't engaged in a generation-by-generation ascent to ever greater ease and leisure and sophistication, but just flailing, scrabbling, writhing vainly in the mud.

Max plucked the pleat in Jeremy's trouser and beckoned him to lean forward. Unlike the grave faces worn by everyone else, his demeanour was distinctly smug. He said, 'Listen, I spoke to Frank for you, and now that Lauren's wimped out and you're the big hero, you can have your old pod-leader job back. While we're here, though, I'm going to have a specialist Burqa Bombing pod and you should be on it. So you're with me till we get back, then you're pod leader again.'

It was no more than he deserved. And even if Max was being facetious, the 'big hero' couldn't think about departure while still in the thick of the action. The Press would not be intimidated by one little firebomb, or one man's departure. No surrender. He gratefully put his thoughts aside and said, 'OK. That's good.'

'We'll have to take Will and Rosie as well for now, but we'll keep them on the straight and narrow, won't we, eh Jezza?' Max twitched his trouser leg again, as if expecting more of a reaction.

'Listen, Max,' he murmured, so that the others in the room wouldn't hear. 'I've got to tell you something. I spoke to Frank on the bus and he's leaving. He's—'

'He's going to the *Fun*. Back-bench production job. I already know. Will told me.'

'Oh right.' That was why Max was so pleased.

'He's not a bad kid, that one. We'll make a sub of him yet. Shame he's such a suck up.'

Jeremy grimaced. 'He is a bit.'

'Now come on, the shift doesn't start for a couple of hours. Some of the others are a bit shaken up so we're—'

'I'm not surprised. "Burn the *Beast*" – it's not a great reaction to a story, is it?'

'No,' said Max. 'Not what we would have wanted.'

'What kind of person does that?'

Max tilted his head to one side. 'Well, it's not clear that they realized he wouldn't be able to get out.'

'If you chuck a firebomb through someone's window, what do you expect?'

'You're right. And I suppose that's why we don't have any windows here. But listen, some of the others are a bit rattled as well, so we're going to go to the pub in Upper Bucklebury and settle their nerves.'

'Is that a good idea? I thought the whole point of this place was to stay inside it.'

'You'll be alright. You're not so famous yet that you'll be recognized. And anyway, we're not in London any more; we're in England. There are no jihadis here.'

EIGHTEENTH CHAPTER

IN THE kitchen of the Cottage Inn, Upper Bucklebury, Adrian and Gavin were interviewing a local Muslim for the *Echo*. It wasn't going well. As he pulled warm pint glasses out of a dishwasher and stacked them screakily on a metal counter, Ayub Benjelloun, a slight, fluid man in his early twenties, with curly hair, wispy sideburns and a strong Thatcham accent, told them, 'My family's from Morocco. What have a bunch of inbred Pakis got to do with me?'

Adrian considered that while a waft of salty steam from inside the dishwasher drifted on to him. 'Fair point,' he said. 'But the coverage talks about British Muslims, not British Pakistanis. How do you feel about that?'

'Could you not find any Pakis in Bucklebury, is that why you're asking me? What about the guy who runs Costcutter?'

Adrian had already thought of that, but it had turned out Mr Agrawal was a Hindu. 'So you don't like being lumped together by the Press? How do you feel about the *Beast* being just down the road?'

Benjelloun pushed past him to fetch a tray of dirty glasses.

'Aren't you meant to be on their side? Or are you a different kind of journalist?'

'We're from the *Echo*, the—'

'I know. The one with all the adverts in the back.'

Adrian suppressed his thoughts about that and said, 'Yes, that's the one.'

'Can you sell anything you want in there?'

Adrian said with dignity, 'You'd have to ask the ad-sales team. I can give you his number.'

'But does anyone actually sell anything that way? Why wouldn't you just put it on eBay?'

Adrian stared very briefly at a fixed point. 'I suppose it's because it's local. Then you don't have the postage problem you do if you sell something to someone who lives further away.'

'Hmm.' Benjelloun went to push past him again, but said, 'Do you want to just pass me those glasses?'

Adrian looked at Gavin, who was supposed to be taking all this down to practise his shorthand. Adrian could see that on his spiral notepad he'd written, not in shorthand:

Zante flights x 2   = £400
flat for ten days   = £300
food and drink   = £50 a day = £500
                    = £1200
FUUUUUCK!!
get suit money
from Adrian?

'Gavin!' he snapped. 'Pass Mr Benjelloum those dirty glasses.'

'It's Benjell*oun*. With an *n*.'

'Sorry. Mr Benjelloun. Can you pass him the glasses, Gavin?'

With a dolorous sigh, Gavin closed his notebook, laid it on the counter and began to move stacks of dirty glasses across to where Benjelloun could reach them. Feeling Adrian's glare, he muttered, 'This isn't what I thought journalism would be like.'

'To me,' said Benjelloun, 'it looks a lot like working in a kitchen.'

And to Adrian's dismay, they both sniggered.

Towards them through the dappled sunlight on a woodland lane strode a dark-clad little group of journalists from the *Beast*. The chief had blustered them past the police, demanding whether they really wanted to prevent the free Press from investigating whatever it wanted and then, when they tried to insist that the journalists stay inside, asking whether they'd like to explain that to the Editor.

Will wasn't worried about being beyond the bunker's walls. Although he knew it was irrational, he felt protected by being the junior among these men. If someone was going to be burnt alive, it shouldn't really be him. And it was elating to be taken up into their group. In the bunker the chief had shouted across to him, 'Saddle up then, recruit, you're coming, too. And bring your friend.' Now the summer air lay warm on his skin, the leaves above his head swayed gently and his eye rested on variations of bark, moss and foliage, relieved for once of the city's smooth planes and right angles. There was some respite from his solitary competition against the massing crowds, some real, many imagined, above whom he would have to clamber if he was to have anything he wanted.

So he did not speed up to walk next to Rosie, though opportunities to talk to her outside the newsroom were few.

Instead he thought dreamily about the vanished typesetters the chief had invoked on the bus. Wasn't the dad in Updike's Rabbit books a typesetter? Will thought he remembered that Rabbit senior worked in linotype, which certainly sounded obsolete. And when was that set? The 1970s? The sixties?

He found himself walking next to Turkish Liz, whom he liked despite her being middle-aged, in a different department and of little use to him. As when speaking to the chief, he wanted to set her off, so that he could absorb her: 'It's good to get out of there,' he ventured. 'The atmosphere was getting pretty full on.'

'Atmosphere? People just don't want to get firebombed by some brainwashed muppets from Acton.'

'No, no, I guess not. Do you think it'll be alright here?'

'I don't think any of this is alright. We're in the middle of nowhere with nowhere to go if they work out where we are. There's only one fucking street here in case you hadn't noticed. And have you ever seen a picture of someone who's been burnt? I mean really burnt. Where their face has started to cook? Let me tell you – if you had, you'd wish you hadn't.'

'So do you think we should go back to London?'

'We should never have fucking *left* London. The *Beast* might think the countryside is lovely, but have you ever heard of anyone who works on the paper actually *going* to the countryside? Maybe Brython – he's a true believer – but not me; I've never gone to the countryside since the day I arrived in Britain.'

'Which bit of Turkey did you come from?'

That interrupted her mood and she cackled, then called out, 'Oi, Max, your rugrat just asked me what bit of Turkey I'm from.'

Max turned and walked backwards for a couple of paces,

saying, 'Don't murder him before anyone else does. We'll need all the bodies we've got this evening.'

Just as Will was becoming embarrassed because he didn't understand, she said, 'I'm not from Turkey at all. I'm Greek. Greek Cypriot. My family was booted out in the invasion. So: Turkish Liz. What a bunch of cunts.' She shook her head, pleased by the mark of belonging.

Will looked at her. He thought Greeks were supposed to have straight noses rather than hooks. But he supposed there'd been so much intermarrying there wasn't much ethnic difference any more. 'That must have been awful,' he said politely, 'having to leave your home and come over here.'

'Damn right it's awful here. You should hear the stories my snappers bring back when they have to go to the countryside on a job and can't help meeting the readers. They're all nicey-nicey racists on the outside like everyone else, but by the time we've been in the pub a few hours some old gent in a tweed suit'll be asking permission to suck you off in the loos.'

To make sure he fully understood the depravity of country folk, she started to tell him the anecdotes she'd heard from her snappers. Will guessed that the reason she talked about sex so much was because she wasn't getting any; and wondered whether she had her dark eye on him. He listened, dismantling her tales to understand how the photographers worked, how you spoke to them and how you got them to do things.

Soon they reached the first few cottages and then a road sign announcing Upper Bucklebury. Small houses looked out at each other from under low roofs of curving clay tiles speckled with moss. The street was narrower than a normal road, with slender pavements, and a little crooked. Trees opened like umbrellas over some of the houses. There must be a medieval church around here somewhere, and a village green.

But before they saw any more of Upper Bucklebury they found the pub. It was two buildings, a small whitewashed cottage and a larger red-brick house that had been built against it. Outside were picnic benches enclosed by a white fence and on a pole at the front was a double-sided illustration of the pub's name, showing the cottage in some Berkshire dreamtime of golden hay wains and piebald cattle. The pub's name – the Cottage Inn – was printed in gold lettering underneath; and the subs automatically competed to make the best joke about cottaging. Liz said to Will, 'See what I mean?'

They clattered inside. There was a step down and Will ducked under the lintel, blinking in what seemed like gloom after the day's brightness. The ceiling was held up by dark wooden beams with stiff cracks running along the grain. There were a few locals on stools at the bar and, at a small table in the corner, two oddly flummoxed-looking men sitting behind a laptop. The younger had grass stains all down the front of his suit.

The chief pushed through to the bar and in the quiet since they'd come in addressed the landlord: 'Hail there, Moonshine Sally, six pints of your cheapest piss for the rabble and one of your finest ale for me.'

Max leant forward to add, in a mollifying voice, 'Make that seven pints, please.'

The chief glared at him and put his black expenses card down on the bar. 'And we'd like to open a tab.'

The landlord, a deep-chested man in a synthetic short-sleeved shirt, started pulling on one of the long wooden levers behind the bar and said, 'I don't know how it is where you come from – London, I should think – but just so you know, I don't serve piss in my pub.'

'You've got Carling,' said the chief, with the glib momentum he'd had since admitting that he was going to leave. 'That's just piss with extra water.'

The landlord eyed him. His regulars maintained a wary quiet, watching the muted flatscreen TV in the corner and pretending not to have noticed the new arrivals.

'Um, excuse me,' said Max. 'I'm sorry about him. He's a bit worked up.' The chief fixed Max with ardent hate. 'You see, we're from—'

'I know who you are. You're staying at the facility down the back road to Thatcham.' He pointed at the TV. 'I've been watching the news all morning. They've deployed four thousand officers just in the capital.' Inside the TV's shiny black frame they could see a demonstration at Trafalgar Square. The crowd were holding up black placards printed with a white slogan: #BeastReader.

The chief said, 'Good for circulation, this terrorism. Look at all the new readers we've got. But it doesn't look like we've got as many people in our protest as Charlie Hebdo had. How many's that there, a few thousand? They had more than a million and they weren't even a proper newspaper.'

The landlord said, 'A damn sight more than were at that Muslim protest saying "Burn the Beast". It's obvious what side the country's on. That was only a few extremists.'

'It's the extremists that are the problem, though, isn't it, barkeep? Or how many terrorists does it take to chuck a bomb? I just wish they'd get on with it so I could go into my final retirement.'

The landlord glared at the levers and kept pulling pints. The beer rushed white into the glasses, settling amber as it deepened. The chief took them as they were passed across the bar and distributed them in order of seniority, saying,

'Keep up the good work, Jez,' or 'Keep on defying terror, greenhorn,' or just, 'Max.' Liz asked for a double vodka and tonic instead.

The TV switched from the demonstrators to a photo of the man who'd been killed in his shop. The journalists and the regulars fell silent and watched. The photo showed a sunburnt man grinning heartily in holiday clothes and twisting in his chair to meet the camera's gaze. He was wearing a novelty Australian hat decorated with dangling corks and raising a plastic goblet of some orange cocktail. Around him were what must be his extended family, cousins perhaps, similar-looking kids and adults in shorts and hats and sunglasses. The ticker line read, 'First pictures of shopkeeper burnt alive in anti-*Beast* retaliation'. The journalists drank their drinks and fear shifted in them.

'Could have happened anywhere,' said the chief. 'Even in a nice place like, ooh, Upper Bucklebury.'

'You certainly stirred things up with that article,' said the landlord. 'They're saying there's gangs on the streets in Luton and Bradford with knives and crowbars, white and Muslim.'

'If we weren't on every English jihadi's bombing wish-list before, we're certainly at number one now. Maybe best to run us out of the village before the burqas turn up.'

'That might well be true,' said the landlord. 'But the PM did a speech there, at the demonstration. He said we're all standing side-by-side with the *Beast*. The whole country. Shoulder to shoulder. To show that that's not what Britain's about.'

'But it's not the kind of shoulder-to-shoulder where he might get blown up as well, is it?' said the chief. 'He means the kind where he gets to go to Trafalgar Square without being heckled and be a statesman for the afternoon.' He put on a mock-posho's voice: '"We will not let them divide us; we will unite behind my leadership." It's probably how he imagined being PM when he was just a little lad in Savile Row shorts. He thought one day he'd have the chance to say: "We shall fight them on the beaches, we shall fight them in the fields and in the streets and in the marginal constituencies, and we shall *never* lose the next election."'

The journalists laughed loudly, but the landlord pointed the remote at the TV and the screen went blank. Looking at the chief, he seemed to be deciding something. Then he forced a certain geniality into his manner and said, 'I'm sure you've all had enough of that. You'll be a bit shaken up, bit overexcited. Bit of gallows humour. Only to be expected. That first round was on the house. Who wants another?'

The journalists were flattered. They tilted the ends of their pints into their mouths and put the empty glasses on the bar with much thanking and joshing. The landlord said to the regulars, 'Drinks for you, too, chaps. We're all together at a time like this. Same again?'

At that, the regulars, too, were pleased and began to shake hands with the journalists. One of them, a shy little man with a bald dome, round spectacles and a maroon cashmere jumper, lifted his voice enough to tell the journalists, 'You see, we've been, well...' From the bar in front of him he lifted a folded copy of that day's paper, grown baggy as the inside pages shifted out of alignment. He let the bottom half drop to show them the front page:

**MUSLIMS
DECLARE
WAR ON
BRITAIN**

The journalists made a small cheer and the chief asked him, 'So you're a reader?'

'Not *only* the *Beast*. I'm not one of those people who never looks at another newspaper. But, yes, I do have a subscription.'

'And have you signed up to *BeastPlus*, the reward scheme, like a good reader?'

'Yes, yes, I have, actually. Just for the wine mainly. They have some good offers sometimes.'

'Good lad,' said the chief. 'Keeping us all in pints.'

The landlord, pulling the drinks, said, 'You know, I was a policeman when all this was happening before, with the IRA.'

'A cop?' said the chief.

'A policeman.'

'The Micks were a better class of terrorist, weren't they, more our kind of people. Wanted to kill everyone else, not themselves. Everyone can understand that. You should ask Jez about them; he likes Ireland, don't you, Jez?'

Jeremy waved him away. 'I went there once on holiday and I'm never going again.'

'They killed MPs; people forget that now,' the landlord said. 'Airey Neave, Ian Gow, Tony Berry. They nearly killed Mrs Thatcher, too, of course. I was there, in Brighton, not in the hotel itself, but on duty.'

'Putting your life on the line?' said the chief.

'I wouldn't say that, but doing my bit, like we all are.' The other journalists lifted their glasses to this compliment. 'But it's newspapers that are the target now, isn't it? There were those Danish cartoonists, then that magazine in France and now the *Beast*.'

Jeremy said, '*Charlie Hebdo*.'

And the chief, thinking of how he was abandoning his newspaper, said in an access of bravado, 'I hope some jihadis do pitch up here looking for trouble. The *Beast* will rip them to shreds.'

The shy man asked, 'Do you think so, because—'

'Of course! Just look at today's paper.'

'Ahm, actually, I did want to ask you something about that.' And somewhat awkwardly he spread the newspaper on the bar in front of the journalists.

NINETEENTH CHAPTER

'OH, SORRY,' said the regular. 'My name's Gilbert by the way.' He paused as if unsure what to do next and, though everyone had shaken hands before, offered his hand to the chief.

Will rolled his eyes at Rosie, wanting it to be just hacks together. But the chief took Gilbert's hand in both of his with exaggerated bonhomie, declaring, 'A pleasure to meet you, Gilbert. Always a pleasure to meet a reader. I'm Frank Forshaw, the chief sub-editor, and these are some of my reprobates. What can we do for you?'

Gilbert didn't quite know how to take this reference to reprobates. He nodded at the other subs and found his place in the newspaper, which was opened to the map of concentric red circles around Copper House. He said, 'Now, of course there are things you can't write, as it were, directly, because of slander and things, but reading between the lines' – he glanced up to check that this had been noted – 'it's obvious that this mosque in Acton is teaching Syrian terror tactics to impressionable young men in London. And what I'd like to know is how on earth they get away with it. There must be a huge organization, huge amounts of money, international travel... How has that not been closed down?'

'Cells,' interjected the landlord. 'They'll be divided up into cells, won't they?'

'Cells, my arse,' said the chief. 'They probably put a collection plate round at the end of each service, saying, Come on: dig deep for Syria. At least a tenner each. And they pray five times a day, don't they? That's a lot of tenners.'

'But – but if they're somehow openly collecting money, that's appalling,' said Gilbert. 'What's stopping the police from arresting them all on sight? Is it red tape?'

'They probably haven't even noticed yet. Too busy giving out speeding tickets.'

'Now hold on a minute,' said the landlord.

But the chief didn't hold on. 'Who knows, we might even be subsidizing them the way we did the Taliban. Paying them for information about some other bunch of nutters.'

'No!' exclaimed Gilbert. 'Do you think that's true?'

'Might not be a bad idea to fund them and their training camps,' said the chief. 'Get them into the middle of nowhere with lots of explosives, maybe they'll blow themselves up while they're practising.'

Gilbert was very disappointed. From where he was standing, terrorism was not a laughing matter.

But the landlord said, 'You don't seriously think the Met is funding terrorists? The point is, even if they're not split up into cells, you'd be surprised how hard something like this can be to actually pin down so that it'll stick.'

'Well, the police certainly do seem to find it difficult. But a tired old hack like Jez here can get it done without even missing deadline.'

Gilbert tried to bring them back on to common ground. Putting his hand on the newspaper, he said, 'I did want to ask, though, is it very bad in London now, with the Muslims? All morning the news has been talking about these mobs chasing each other in Luton and Bradford, but is it very bad where you are?'

'London's full of Muzzers,' said the chief. 'One in three Londoners is now at least part Muslim and the rest are Russian oligarchs. Didn't you know that?'

Gilbert clucked his tongue. 'No, no, I don't mean... immigration. I just meant the violence. There are Muslims everywhere. We have some here in Bucklebury. Barry employs a Muslim right here in the kitchen.'

Despite themselves, the journalists tensed. The landlord immediately cautioned them, 'Now, don't get excited.' Jeremy became aware of how far they were from the bunker's protective walls. And the chief said, 'So is this what's going on, Bootleg Betsy? You're harbouring a Muslim back there. That'll be why you're such an expert on sleeper cells. You're not letting him cook with gas, are you? He doesn't have any spare propane canisters lying around back there just looking for a fire to start?'

Spreading his palms on the bar and leaning his weight forwards on to them, the landlord said, 'I won't have the people who work for me accused of things. Ayub's a good lad. He's not some sort of fanatic.'

'On the other hand,' said Max reasonably, not quite knowing what to make of what he was saying, 'the people who worked with the 7/7 bombers all said they were nice, quiet people.'

At that, Gilbert became flustered. He shifted forward as if to speak, but seemed to think better of it and, looking down his glass at the thick amber disc in its base, murmured, 'Hmm.'

The landlord just about kept his temper, and said, 'Listen, gents. You're shaken up, and rightly so. You've been threatened; a man's been horribly burnt. But you need to calm down.'

Jeremy said, 'No one's saying he's a terrorist just because he's a Muslim.'

But the chief didn't stop. 'You should know, Jez, you're the Islamist sniffer dog, aren't you, rooting out jihadis like a pig snuffling through shit. But don't you think it's worth finding out why, of all the pubs in all the towns and cities in the whole of England, he gets himself a job in an out-of-the-way village that just happens to be half a mile down the road from the *Beast*'s secret offices?'

Will's head began to thump the way it did before edition. *Was* it suspicious? On the face of it of course not. But everything at the moment was different from the face of things. And maybe it *was* odd to come all the way from wherever he'd come from to a place like Bucklebury, where the only thing nearby was the *Beast*. Of course there was almost certainly nothing to it. *Almost* certainly not, that was obvious. But not certainly not. And didn't their very suspicion necessarily mean that it was suspicious? He drank from his pint, but his mouth stayed dry.

The chief asked the landlord, 'How long's he worked here? Where did he come from?'

The landlord shuddered a kind of incredulous laugh, but his anger was reaching the surface. He said, 'I think that's probably about enough, don't you? Ayub's a good lad and has nothing to do with what's been going on. If you don't like it, you can find somewhere else to drink.'

'And how are you going to admit you were wrong if this place gets burnt down with you in it?'

The landlord appealed to Jeremy. 'If you're the expert, you can tell him this is ridiculous.' Maybe it was. This terrorism stuff was like boxing a gang of shadows; any one of them might really be a man in black. He had that vertiginous feeling again, of a terrible reality intruding. He tried to listen to the long-honed news-sense that had let him make the spot the day before, but got nothing. He said, 'I suppose it wouldn't hurt to find out some more.'

To everyone's surprise, Rosie, who felt that this was getting surreally unpleasant, spoke up, 'But he *couldn't* be a funda-mentalist even... even if we had any reason for thinking he was, which we don't. Strict Muslims are against alcohol and he works in a pub. It's completely... It doesn't make any sense.'

'That's right,' said the landlord, as if that settled it.

The chief saw the angles as he would on any story. 'Bit suspicious, that, don't you think, grubling, a fundamentalist Muslim working in a pub?'

'Oh, bloody hell,' said the landlord.

Gilbert looked up from his now-empty pint glass, which he'd been rotating on the bar. 'Now come on, Barry. It's not unreasonable to ask a few questions. These men were almost killed yesterday and—'

'Don't *you* start with this.'

Gilbert, abashed, let go of the glass, but went on: 'I just don't think it's—'

'You don't know what you're talking about.'

Gilbert's mouth worked with suppressed speech and, as it did, the chief bellowed, 'Oi, Ayoob! Come out here!'

The landlord banged the flat of his hand on the bar. 'Oi! If you shout at my staff again, you're out, standing together or no standing together, you hear me? Actually, you know what...?'

But behind him, the kitchen door was pushed ajar and Ayub leant out of it. His double-breasted chef's jacket hung loose as an empty sail and he'd put on his round white cap, which pressed down on the black locks that escaped from under it. He asked, 'Hello?'

'Get back in the kitchen,' ordered the landlord.

Ayub stiffened and his long black brows rose into two ridges, pushing a vertical furrow into the light brown skin between them. 'Didn't someone just ask me to come out here?'

'No,' said the landlord, but the chief said, 'Yes, I did.'

'Oh, yeah?' Ayub showed no inclination to retreat into the kitchen. The landlord said, 'These *gents* are from the *Daily Beast*.'

Ayub's features contorted. 'Oh, you've got to be kidding me.'

The journalists and the regulars all twitched up to a new degree of alertness. The chief asked, 'What do you mean?'

Behind the journalists, in the corner of the room, Adrian was on his feet, frantically signalling to Ayub, cutting his hand back and forth across his throat.

Ayub shook his head. 'I hate journalists.'

Jeremy's cigarette fingers trembled and Gilbert stood up off his stool, becoming a little shorter. The chief, as immaculately calm as a police marksman, asked, 'Why's that then?'

Ayub stepped out fully from behind the swing door. 'Same reason as everybody else: they harass people for money.'

'Like Muslims at the moment.'

'Yeah, like Muslims.'

'How long have you worked here?'

'Enough,' interrupted the landlord, trying to regain control of the situation. 'Don't answer that. You've had your fun, now let him get on with his work.'

'Now come on, Barry,' said Gilbert, mustering himself to

withstand his friend's disapproval. 'It's not an unfair question to ask.'

'Will you do me a favour, Gilbert, and stay out of this.'

'I will *not* stay out of it,' he said, blushing hard. 'I don't want to be burnt alive in the pub...' Ayub's brows jumped in astonishment. 'Or you know, blown up or machine-gunned or run over with a truck or whatever it is they're doing now. I'm not saying you're a terrorist, Ayub,' he clarified. 'Of course not. Just that it's not unfair in these circumstances, when people are being killed in normal towns in England just like this one, to ask who's who.'

'Wow, Gilbert, that's the last time I make your sunshine toast for you. And you,' he stared at the chief, 'you're a fat racist.'

'Hey,' said the landlord. 'Don't you get riled up.'

The chief spread his hands genially. 'What's race got to do with it, effendi? You *are* a Muslim, aren't you?'

The landlord said, 'He's answered your questions, which is more than he had to. And he's told you no, so back off.'

The chief asked his audience, 'Is that how it works? Someone says he's not a fundamentalist and that's it, you believe him? Maybe they should do the same test at airports. "Good morning, sir, are you a terrorist? No? Alright then, sorry to bother you, let me give you a hand with that bag." You're the expert, Jez; does that sound like a good plan to you?'

Jeremy had no idea what was going on. He said, 'Errrm...'

Rosie spoke up again: 'Jeremy. You know that this is – that he's obviously not—'

'Put a cork in it, sweetheart,' said the chief.

'Let the girl say what she wants,' the landlord ruled. 'Go on, love. Finish what you were saying.'

She began to explain, but the chief cut her off: 'We can talk more about your investigative skills back at the bunker, but for now why don't you shut the fuck up and let the real journalists try to stop us all getting burnt alive.'

Rosie gaped like a coshed fish. Will shifted. Although he thought meanly, just to himself, that ruffling someone maybe unfairly was a fair price for making absolutely sure about this, he said, 'I don't know, chief. Maybe—'

'You pipe down, too, whippersnapper.'

'I just think that actually Rosie has a—'

'When I want my subs to think, I'll let you know.'

'Maybe you should let them think more often,' said the landlord. 'What the girl said was right. Ayub *does* work in a pub, this pub, and sometimes even,' he went on triumphantly, 'when he's in the mood for it, has a drink with us at the end of the shift, don't you, Ayub?'

His employee, whose body had been becoming rigid, like a lone child's before a semicircle of bullies, was un-sprung by mere annoyance.

And the chief was not halted. 'That means nothing,' he said. 'The Taliban were smoking smack in the breaks between beheading unbelievers. A half-pint of bitter doesn't prove he's not got a bomb vest on under that jacket. I'd like to see him eat a bacon sandwich.'

Ayub ripped apart the two halves of his chef's jacket, un-popping the line of buttons down the front. Holding open the two stubby white wings, he showed them a grey T-shirt falling close around his slender torso, with two dark ovals of sweat at its seams. Ayub's hands were shaking with force, making the white cloth quiver. He said, 'What do you think of that, fat man?'

The chief said, 'So he's not got a bomb vest on right now. What were the chances of that anyway? I think eating a bacon sandwich is a better test.'

Ayub dropped the flaps of his jacket. 'Are you *serious?*'

The chief said, 'Eat a bacon sandwich then.'

Rosie said, 'This is *crazy*. Lots of Muslims don't eat bacon. Neither do Jews. It doesn't mean someone's an extremist.'

The landlord said, 'No one's eating anything. I'm closing the kitchen. I've had enough of this. Ayub, I think it's best you take the rest of the day off. You'll still be paid for the shift. On you go.'

'What, *I* have to leave because *they*'re a bunch of racists?'

'Yes, that's right. Now go on. Enjoy your afternoon off and I'll see you tomorrow.'

Ayub moved as if about to object, but then relaxed all at once and shrugged. 'Fine. See you tomorrow. See you, too, Gilbert. Watch out I don't sprinkle anthrax on your chips.'

Gilbert frowned at the bar.

Not acknowledging anyone else, Ayub pushed through the swing door, which clapped back once, twice, on its stiff hinge, and settled shut. Gilbert checked his watch as if he had a reason to leave. But there was a certain consensus of relief that Ayub was gone.

TWENTIETH CHAPTER

THE next moment, a vituperative argument broke out between everyone at once. Each fought to make his or her point about what they'd just seen and, to varying degrees, participated in. Jeremy wondered gloomily whether yesterday's reappearance of his journalistic powers had been a one-off. Will tried to calculate what it would cost him with the chief to have argued for Rosie, however briefly. But all made as much noise as possible, as if driving out shame.

The landlord kept telling the chief, 'I hope you've had your fill. I hope you've had it,' but the chief turned away from him. His phone was vibrating in his pocket and, as he pushed out past the edge of the little crowd, he crushed it awkwardly against the side of his head. He covered his other ear and listened. After a few seconds, he took the phone from his head and announced, 'Shut up! Oi, be quiet!' He spoke over the dwindling argument: 'Lads, two of our favourite terror trannies have been shot to bits in Ruislip. One's dead, the other's full of holes and I hope being waterboarded as we speak.'

A cruel thrill ran through Jeremy. Max quickly checked the BBC website on his phone – there was nothing yet.

'Middle bench and Liz, straight to the newsroom. Grunts, half three as usual. Hop to it. I'll pay the tab. How much is it, Moonshine Mandy?'

The landlord said very distinctly, 'I don't want your money. Get out, and don't come back here. You can tell your mates, too. Everyone from the *Beast* is barred.'

'What happened to standing together against Islamic terror? Because if you're not in favour of freedom, you're against it.'

'Out. And if I see you anywhere near here or near my staff again I'm calling the police.'

'Well, thanks for the drinks. Next time we come, we can talk about why you had to leave the force. Did the prisoners keep falling over and hitting their heads? Or was it that the woman suspects' clothes kept falling off?'

The landlord's fury was inarticulate until long after the journalists were out through the door and hurrying back along the lane towards the bunker. Not one of them could resist glancing back to see whether they were being followed. Ayub may have seemed not to be a terrorist, but that didn't mean no one else was.

By the time they passed the Bucklebury sign, *BeastOnline* had the story of the shooting up – riddled with typos and factual errors, but first in the world and including a photograph: a car pocked as if by a local meteor shower, the tyres flat, the windshield a rectangular hole, the entire frame listing into the road, and on the tarmac by the driver's door a spattering of dark juice. The journalists walked faster.

Will found that Rosie had come to walk beside him. She spoke quietly: 'It's just getting more and more out of hand, isn't it? These two getting shot, and the guy in the paper shop, and people on the street with baseball bats, and that just now, even though of course he's not – it's like it's all starting to come out of the woodwork, isn't it? And the worst thing is that I almost feel a bit glad; not glad they've been shot, but that they're, you know, out of action.'

Will's sense of invulnerability, after a wobble in the pub, was now resurgent, as if he'd just survived something. Running to a kind of high, he said, 'Yes, it's horrible, but you know, I think it'll all be fine.'

'It's like something from another country. The police shooting people on the street. It's not like England at all. It's like the Middle East.'

'This is Berkshire, not Beirut.'

Rosie didn't smile. 'We didn't expect there to be bombs in Kensington either, or a man being burnt alive in Luton.'

'No, no – of course not. Obviously. I just, I don't know, I just think it's going to be OK. Maybe not for those guys when the police get to them, but the bunker's pretty safe, isn't it? I mean, it is designed to withstand a nuclear holocaust, after all.'

'Yes, I know. It's just... I find it weird any time seeing policemen carrying guns; and now there are loads of them all over the place, even here in the middle of nowhere. I know it sounds stupid, but I just didn't think we were that kind of country.'

'We're not. It's just two guys who've been shot.' Will felt tremendously worldly. 'In the US, the police must shoot more people than that every day. And one of them's still alive. If he tells them where the other two are, the police can go arrest them and it's all over.'

'Hardly. What about all these vigilante posses out looking for Muslims – they're not just going to put their baseball bats away and go back to work. And that just then in the pub. That was horrible, the way they were bullying him. Do you think he's alright? I can't believe they sent him home.'

Will wondered again whether he would have to make up with the chief. Was there a chance the chief would respect Will more for opposing him? It was unlikely. He said, 'I'm sure he's OK. But if he didn't hate us before, he does now.'

'So does half the country.'

'At least it's not really half. Muslims are only, what, two or three per cent? And almost none of them are in Berkshire. It's more likely that someone'll lynch that chef.'

'Oh God, isn't that just exactly what would happen?'

'Come on, it's not him the Buckleburians would be after, if they were after anyone, is it?' He failed to suppress a grin. 'They can't have ever met such a legion of horribles as us.'

'*I*'ve never met such a legion of horribles as us.'

'Oh, I don't know. You've got your skinheads, your neo-Nazis, the KKK...' She didn't smile. 'But it's traditional, isn't it? Callous hacks.'

'I suppose I just don't think journalists have to be as bad as their reputation.'

Will said smoothly, 'Readers get the journalists they deserve.'

'It's more complicated than that.'

Will heard an implication that his thinking was simplistic, and was stung. 'But the *Beast* is actually... What liberal Londoners hate about the *Beast* isn't the *Beast* – it's that it has the same opinions as most of the rest of the country, which Londoners actually hate. And it's the majority of the country that doesn't actually get heard, when they're—'

He interrupted himself as the chain-link gates came into view. There were more armed policemen than before and they seemed nervier also. They clustered around the returning journalists, seeming almost angry with them and demanding to see their staff cards. As the chief leisurely brought his out, one asked what they'd been doing outside the compound anyway.

'Oh, not much,' the chief said blithely. 'Uncovering a potential jihadi cell. What have you been up to?'

'What?' the policeman said stupidly.

'They're operating out of the pub in Bucklebury. The landlord's running the whole thing, he's got a bomber in the kitchen. Might be a good idea to check it out, don't you think?'

Will caught Rosie's eye and they shared a thought: the chief was too much sometimes. It wasn't even funny. He went on, 'Better be quick, lads. Every jihadi sleeper cell in England'll have been activated by now. It'll look pretty bad if you don't even catch the one just up the road.'

The policemen looked at each other and while one went out of earshot to talk into his radio the others hustled the journalists through the gates. Rosie went ahead of Will and waited for him. Once he was through, they walked next to each other around the bend in the driveway. The buses had gone and the bunker was alone behind its tarmac. Liz said loudly, 'Oh, that's just fabulous. Now we can't get back to London even if we want to. What a bunch of geniuses.'

Will and Rosie were dawdling. She said, 'I don't really want to go back in there till we have to.'

He realized what he was about to say and, like a running deer that breaks upon a gully, his heart leapt. 'We could take a little perambulation round the building. We could go for a walk in the woods before we go back in. It might be good to get some fresh air. Clear our heads a bit for the shift.' An instant of quiet flight, the trajectory unalterable, the hoofs skipping their regular beats.

Rosie treated that suggestion as if it were perfectly natural. 'Yeah, good idea, but do you think that's allowed – to just wander around?'

Bluff reassurance was an attitude that Will had down pat. 'Oh, I'm sure it'll be fine,' he said. 'The police are here for our sake, after all, aren't they? We could just go along through the trees here.'

They were about to turn left off the tarmac but, just as they were about to step off the verge, Rosie stopped and lifted her voice, 'Liz, we're not due in yet. Do you reckon it's alright if we go for a wander once round the building?'

Liz bunched her lips. 'Do whatever you want. In my day, we spent half the afternoon in the toilets. Just don't expect us to come and find you if we're getting out sharpish.'

Max added, 'Shift starts at half three. Don't mess with anything important.'

Pretending not to have understood what Liz meant, they stepped under the trees and were away. There was no path, and the ground was clear except for knuckles of root protruding through it, so they let their whim guide them. The leaf canopy above them was brightly illuminated, but among the slender columns holding it up the light was crepuscular. The tone of their talk softened and became more intimate; they spoke less of the *Beast* and the readers and more of themselves and each other.

Rosie told him, 'You're doing really well here, especially considering how short a time it's been. That spot last night was really good.'

Will acted dismissive and, though he knew this wasn't what she was talking about, said, 'That Muhammed, Muhammad thing? Anyone would have seen that.'

'No, the thing about them not speaking Arabic. That was

an important spot, and the Editor definitely realized. I saw him notice you.'

A warm surge of satisfaction rolled through him. 'He was probably just thinking—' He puffed up his chest and boomed, 'Who the fuck gave you permission to talk in my newsroom? I've been Editor of this newspaper since you were still shitting into your diapers.'

Rosie had seen many do it better, but she laughed anyway. 'Seriously, though, it was good and, you know, I've been here longer than you and compared to you it's like they've hardly noticed I exist.'

Will had become unused to straightforward praise since leaving university tutorials. He shrugged and said, 'I don't know...'

'Honestly, you seem good at playing the game and everything like all the other cynical, ambitious young guys you get in journalism, but... That really was horrible in the pub, wasn't it?'

'Really horrible.'

'I didn't expect you... It was good that you tried to stop the chief from bullying him.'

He became truly embarrassed, and said, 'But it was you; you're the one who was trying to stop it.'

'Well, maybe, but you did, too.'

'Oh, hardly.' And because his mind ran on: 'I wonder how pissed off the chief is going to be.'

'What, you think they won't like you any more because you disagreed with them? They love you up. They're always sitting next to you on the bus or inviting you to the pub or telling you their stories.'

Will didn't want this now. 'No, no...'

'For real. I've been here a year and a half and when they

notice me it's only because they think I'm the wrong kind of person somehow. I sometimes think the chief only remembers he gave me a job when I try to book a holiday.'

Will's grip on himself relaxed enough to let him say what he thought without editing it first: 'It's probably because you're always doing that rabbit-in-headlights look.' He popped his eyes wide and drew down the corners of his mouth. 'They're probably just thinking, "Whatever she's scared of, I don't want to know about it."'

It could have gone either way, but Rosie laughed and the laughter was freeing. 'It's true. I did freak out a bit last night.'

'A bit? You looked like you were going to pass out right off your chair.' Rosie was still laughing. 'But I would have freaked out, too. That must have been the most bollocks story ever printed. None of it stood up, none of it at all.'

'I know! The blind woman who wasn't blind!' She covered her face with her hands. 'Oh, that was bad! Oh, it was so bad. But still, I can't believe I let it get to me like that. I was up all last night lying in bed worrying about it.'

Will let this reference to her bed go uncommented. 'It's amazing, isn't it.' He dared something: 'How you think it's just a place you go to work and all of a sudden it's seeping up from your subconscious. I... I end up dreaming about Max or the chief quite a lot. Not as much as at first, but still – how sad is that?'

She laughed again, 'Pretty sad. I do it too. All the time.' Her mind flicked to the dandruff she'd developed and she couldn't stop herself touching her hair just above her ear.

'And you know, I was trying to explain to my parents, who obviously can't believe that I would work for the *Beast*, that it's kind of absolutely awful and vicious, as you'd expect, but somehow sometimes quite fun at the same time.'

'Would you really call it *fun*? You're lying there having what I assume are anxiety dreams about it.'

'Sure, you're right. Of course it's super-stressful. But when there's a huge story, like this one, and you do well with it...' He let the sentence drift off, remembering that she hadn't been doing well. 'Or when you've got a big scoop about blind Bulgarians.'

She clapped her hands over her face again. 'Oh, God, don't remind me! It made it so much worse that Max kept calling it that.'

'Maybe it *was* the Bulgarian who was blind.'

'It would have made as much sense as anything else.' She shook her head. 'There was something really dodgy about that old woman as well. Why do you think she let us think she was properly blind?'

'Blind robbers, lying old ladies, are you sure at least some journalists aren't as bad as their reputation?'

She glared, warning him but not warning him.

Their wandering had led them to the compound's perimeter. Cutting through the woods was a stand of ten-foot chain-link fencing, topped with an unwinding spiral of razor wire. It was out of place, arbitrarily dividing trees from trees, and reminded Will of the solitary lamppost in the forest in Narnia. He asked, 'Shall we do a circuit?'

She nodded. 'Mmhmm.'

They walked along in silence, the decision to go on having made each very conscious of the other at their side. After a while, Rosie said, 'I can't believe Lauren didn't come today. I texted her but she didn't text me back. That basically means she's quit, doesn't it?'

Will made an awkward face. 'Looks like it.'

'I totally thought she was going to be the *Beast*'s first

female chief sub one day. But they're never going to let her come back, are they?'

'I mean, I think the way the chief sees it, not turning up today's pretty inexcusable. It doesn't really make you look like what he would consider a born hack.'

'You're the one who got sacked by the *Stentorian*, or didn't you?'

Will raised his eyebrows at her. Touché. 'Yeah, I did, I got made redundant the week after I finished my traineeship.'

'I'm sorry, I was just kidding. That's such a bad way to treat you, especially when they've trained you. And I bet there were loads of lazy, not-even-very-good middle-aged people who kept their cushy jobs on four times what you were getting.'

'To be fair, quite a few of that lot had already gone.'

'But they can take it. They were around in the gravy days; they've all already got their big houses in West London and cars and cottages in France and money for school fees. And when they retire on their guaranteed pensions, you and me are going to have to pay for them.'

'No gravy for us, only gruel. And even the chief is leaving – can you believe that?'

'Well, I'm not sorry he's going.'

'No, me neither really. But does it ever feel to you like we've come in at the end of something? Like before it was all japes and expense accounts and martini lunches and now we're here just to do a bit of donkey work while we wait for it to be over?'

'I don't really want to drink martinis for lunch, but I do—'

They heard a heavy thud, a cry of pain and the wild ringing of the chain-link against its metal uprights.

Their gazes jumped to each other. The ringing quickly abated, leaving a yet more frightening quiet. Rosie turned to run towards the bunker. But Will, the greater instinctual journalist, whispered throatily, 'Come on,' and ran not away from but towards the noise.

Rosie, aghast, followed. Struggling in her high heels, she fell a little way behind and Will came alone upon the tear in the fence. Close to one of the poles, a long swathe of mesh was curling over itself into the compound, the metal links bent and snapped. On the other side of it, three roundels of chopped tree trunk had been stacked against the pole, though one had slipped and was lying on its side. Scuffed into the ground beside it were the footprints and knee-marks of the person who'd tumbled off the fence when it tore.

Rosie arrived breathlessly. 'Oh my God, did someone try to break in?!'

'Yes, look over there, the wood!'

Rosie was casting about for danger. Will, through his fear, his attention darting frantically from tree trunk to tree trunk, knew that there was an opportunity in this. He tried to think.

'Oh my God!' she exclaimed again. 'We have to get out of here! They could be anywhere! Do you think it was the guy from the pub?'

'I don't know. We've got to get inside.'

'We've got to tell the police! Where are they?'

'No, we've got to tell Newsdesk. No. Max. It's Max we've got to tell. He's going to be the next chief; we can't go over his head.'

There were too many alarms screaming in Rosie's head for her to make sense of what he was saying. 'Let's go then!'

She slipped off her shoes and bolted for home. Will was left standing, momentarily furious; it should be him to bring in the news. He sprinted after her, catching up as she reached the edge of the tarmac. He stopped as she pulled her shoes on, looking back through the trees, and then jogged beside her as her heels clopped on the blacktop; he did not want to be seen to have left a girl behind. He could hear her panting in the hot stillness and he was thinking: Max, yes; not Newsdesk or the chief. Max was the person to tell. And when they were back under the shadow of the building his stride lengthened a little, so that he was a few paces in front when they plunged, blinded, into the inner darkness.

TWENTY-FIRST CHAPTER

FOR the second time in five minutes, Nigel Willis went over to the water cooler further down the sterile greenish hospital corridor, held his plastic cup under the spigot and depressed the little blue lever before remembering that the cooler was empty. Hardly noticing his mistake, he scrunched the cup in his fist and, as he walked back towards where he'd started, began to straighten it out again, his fingers quickly working kinks out of the plastic.

Choudry hadn't given up anything about the plot. He'd given up where he thought Kayani and Ranjha were. He'd given up the imam at the West Acton mosque. He'd given up more names of those who'd organized their travel to Syria. He'd even given up two cousins who hadn't been under suspicion. Only tremulously alive, handcuffed to the rails at the sides of the bed and jacked awake with whatever it was they'd injected into him, he'd readily whispered any detail they asked about. But he'd given up nothing about a bomb plot against the *Daily Beast*. He just kept saying that there was no plot or that, if there was, neither he nor Mian, who'd been killed by police bullets on Nigel's order, nor Kayani nor Ranjha, whom Nigel's men were now chasing down, knew anything about it.

Nigel looked around to throw the cup away and remembered that there was no bin. There was nothing in this corridor but the officer sitting on a chair next to the door to Choudry's room. Dan Felsenburg was in there still, going over things just one more time, endlessly. His persistence scratched across Nigel's mind like a nail. He was having to force himself not to scream at Felsenburg to leave the man alone. Because the appalling truth was that, as Choudry denied and denied that there was any plan to attack the *Beast*, Nigel was starting to believe him.

And Mian had already been killed, by officers acting on Nigel's instructions. Choudry might die, too. And this was turning into the biggest counter-terror operation the Met had ever undertaken. Thousands of men pulled in from sur-rounding counties. All other crime as good as unattended. Hourly press conferences with the commissioner, who was on his way here with someone from the very top of MI5 wanting an update in person. He'd also warned Nigel to expect a phone call from the home secretary herself.

Nigel could feel the strain physically, as if the muscles in his arms and legs were being stretched by a weight, fraying, ripping from their bone pegs. And he was so tired. He was brittle and shaky with tiredness. His thin thoughts sketched the same shape of things over and over again. He'd drunk so much coffee he could feel it coming out in his sweat. His suit felt hot and damp. He was probably dehydrated.

He went over to the water cooler and, as he reached to depress the little blue lever, realized what he was about to do. Making a sound that fortunately emerged as a high-pitched shout but was really at least half sob, he hit the transparent water barrel with the flat of his hand. It rocked heavily in its place, but didn't fall.

The officer at Choudry's door stood up in concern and said, 'Don't worry, boss. We'll get them.'

TWENTY-SECOND CHAPTER

A DIARY girl texting in the corridor jumped aside to let Will and Rosie pass, still blinking and stumbling, and then they were around the corner and into the clamour of the newsroom. They rushed between the desks to where the subs were sitting. Max saw them, shifted the pencil to the other side of his mouth, and said, 'Feeling keen? You can practise your headlines on the NIBs page if you like. See if you can beat one of mine.'

Will leant forward, closer up in Max's face than he'd ever been, and whispered between breaths: 'Someone tried to break in – the fence is down.'

Pure fear passed across Max's expression very quickly, loosening his mouth and untying the focused lines around his eyes. Then it was past, and he was himself and saying, 'Where?'

'Outside. I can show you.'

They were still almost intimately close and an understanding was communicated between them. Will knew he'd gone to the right person.

Max said, 'Wait here,' and strode towards the Editor's office in the same state of preternatural calm that he inhabited on deadline. Will and Rosie were left breathless, perspiring and oddly unhurried as the *Beast* whirled to confront this attack on its flank. Rosie wiped a few strands of hair that had become stuck to her temple. In the hollow at the base of her neck, Will could see the skin beating.

He played protective and asked, 'Are you OK?' He found he was less jangled as soon as he'd assumed an attitude.

Her head bobbed rapidly. 'How did they find us here? I thought this was supposed to be secret. Do you think it was that guy from the pub? Or that he tipped them off?'

It flashed across Will's mind that he'd have had good reason to – maybe he'd tweeted where they were – but in a tone that reassured one of them he said: 'I wouldn't worry about it. We're completely safe in here.'

She lurched closer to hiss, 'Don't worry about it?! Have you—'

Just then they saw a hastily assembled posse bearing down on them: the Editor, the chief, Max, Geraldine, all the senior reporters and two snappers. The chief was lavish with ill-concealed rage: 'Rosie, darling, I'm terribly sorry to interrupt your chit-chat, but—'

The Editor spoke over him, not breaking his long stride, 'Take me to them.'

Rosie was too taken aback to say anything other than, 'Um.'

'Look sharp, damn it.'

'You – do we... You want us to go outside?'

'How else are you going to show me? Who are you anyway?'

Will said helpfully, 'I know where it was. I'll show you.'

'Get moving then.'

As Will led them outside the posse crowded attentively around him, asking him questions. He answered, at the centre of things. Rosie followed them back outside and tried to think that this was a normal thing to do.

As they came in sight of where the torn fence sagged over itself, the Editor said, 'Stay back, everyone. Don't contaminate the scene.' They eyed the trees for whether any had a man behind it. After only a few dozen yards the trunks had overlaid one another sufficiently to have hidden anything at all. No one spoke. The journalists listened, not knowing for what, but heard only stillness, rustling leaves and their own breathing.

The Editor said, 'Snappers, all this needs to be documented.'

Geraldine, who was thrilled by being back in the field, as in her cub days, added unnecessarily, 'Don't move a blade of grass till it's been photographed. Ben, Stephen, go twenty yards down the fence, climb over and see if you can pick up their trail. And whatever you do, don't jolly well get shot.'

A couple of the reporters smiled at that and the Editor, too, seemed pleased.

The photographers paced careful semicircles around the scene, squatting and snapping and periodically holding their cameras in the deeper shade of their bodies to check they'd got the shots: the mesh curling like a breaking wave, the roundels of chopped wood, the distribution of scuff marks on the other side. One of the reporters walked figures of eight with his phone to his ear, trying to reach a forensics expert they'd used before. As the others urgently theorized in hushed voices about what had happened, the Editor looked and looked and looked. In his presence Will's feeling of imperviousness approached a frontline euphoria.

Stephen tucked his tie between two buttons on his shirt and draped his suit jacket over the razor wire on top of the fence. As Ben interlaced his fingers to give him a leg up, the head policeman arrived with a posse of his own, their raised submachine guns darting glances through the woods. He marched straight up to the Editor, his face as mottled as an old drinker's, and demanded, 'What do you think you're doing?'

The Editor put on the patrician manner he showed to outsiders. 'I,' he said, 'am doing what you have failed to do: protecting this newspaper and this country from extremist violence. What is the use, I ask you, of allowing your men on to this newspaper's compound if they will not even perform duties so basic as patrolling its perimeter?'

'That's ridiculous. The—'

The Editor spoke inexorably over him, his enormous voice not rising but holding the policeman fast. 'Does it surprise you that the concentrated might of Thames Valley Police, incompetent as its reputation may be, has been beaten to the story by two of the most junior journalists on my staff?'

'None of you can be here. This a crime scene. There are potentially dangerous—'

'I, for one, am not surprised. Time and again the police service has demonstrated its inability to keep up with this newspaper. If we had relied on the work of your colleagues yesterday, the plot may not have been uncovered until it was too late. And if we had relied on yours today, perhaps this break-in would have been successful.'

'The *Beast* wasn't exactly speedy with its information yesterday, though, was it? Stop me if I'm getting this wrong, but isn't it true that no one rang the Met about the bombing until ten o'clock at night? When would you have told us about this – next week? I want your reporters, whoever witnessed this, to give us a full statement right now.'

The Editor measured him by eye, and said, 'The idea that

the information this newspaper gave the Met yesterday was inconvenient because they'd already gone home for the night is frankly shocking. So, here is what—'

There was a clashing of metal as Stephen heaved his weight up on to the fence, the tips of his shiny black shoes scrabbling for purchase between the links.

'Hey,' shouted the policeman. 'Get down from there. This is a crime scene.' While Stephen ignored him, the Editor said, 'Let me remind you that you are here at my invitation and that—'

The policeman interrupted him, 'How about perverting the course of justice? How about that? Full statements, right now, by—'

'It's apparent to everyone that justice only has a chance of being done because of the information provided by this newspaper. If you interfere in its work, I will have you ejected from this private property and then ring every media organization in England to warn them that the state is indulging in censorship.'

Geraldine, who was inexpertly pressing buttons on her floral-patterned iPhone, threw in, 'Cops kicked out after bungling *Beast* probe.'

That embarrassed the policeman in front of his subordinates. 'It doesn't matter. No one goes anywhere or does anything without the police present.'

'But my God, that's exactly what I'm suggesting,' said the Editor. 'That man is going to look for a trail we've picked up. Yes, that's right. Almost certainly the would-be intruder. Some of your officers had better help his colleague over the fence and go with them. An armed presence could be the difference between life and death.' He'd already decided to move his father's pistol to a soft leather holster he could wear under a jumper.

The policeman was a little perplexed by this seeming shift in what the Editor meant. He said, 'The police need to have a complete overview of everything that happens. We need to know exactly what's going on at all times. And if anything else happens, you – your reporters – will have to take police instructions for their own safety. No questions asked.'

'My thoughts exactly. Hadn't we better get on with it? There's the trail. Let's follow it.'

The policeman hesitated a little longer, then said to his men, 'Fred and Alex, help them over the fence and go with them.'

'Good. Those of us opposing these murderers have to work together now more than ever, and share our information. We'll need *Beast* reporters present when you start making raids.'

The policeman tried to protest again, but Geraldine, who was now holding her phone horizontally on her palm, said, 'Charles, if you face the hole in the fence, you're pointing straight at Bucklebury.'

The Editor's blood leapt. 'Do you hear that? That place needs to be fucking ransacked! They need their doors kicked in and those jihadi cunts dragged out by the hair. And you...' He rounded on the policemen, one of whom was nervously re-sticking the Velcro holding his pistol to his thigh. 'You can tell your colleagues that if any of them leak this story, that if any of those cunts so much as tells his cunt of a wife what he's been doing at work, I will personally ring the home secretary and have him fucked every way I know how.'

The policemen murmured, and their officer talked at the Editor about precisely how he imagined this embedding of reporters would work. But Brython didn't care. His heart was singing. He'd caught the exciting feral whiff of a story on the loose.

Brython watched two policemen, their submachine guns

shifted on to their backs, join their hands into a step to help Ben climb over the fence. Less agile than Stephen and obstructed by a belly that had pulled his shirtfront out of his belt, he brought one knee up on to the top bar and wobbled, neither over nor not. The policemen raised their hands to soften a fall while Stephen gave advice from the other side. Swearing loudly, Ben swung his weight past the point of balance and dropped, loudly ripping the lining of his jacket and landing painfully on his hands and knees. The policemen followed easily. They pointed their guns' noses deeper into the woods and the little group stalked towards Upper Bucklebury.

In the midst of all that had to be thought about and acted upon, the Editor was overcome by a sense of immanent destiny: his last hurrah would be magnificent. He realized now that there had been a slim cavil of disappointment about yesterday's scoop: it had been handed to him for nothing. Now a story needed to be hunted and the hunters were off their leashes. He could hear bright bugles. He could feel fierce joy swelling in his chest. The last hurrah of print would be the *Daily Beast* running this story down: dramatic and exclusive pictures of the moment brave cops break jihadi cell in rural Berkshire; a scoop that would start, 'The *Daily Beast*'s reporters were on the scene last night as...'

The *Daily Beast* first in the world for news, and in print.

TWENTY-THIRD CHAPTER

TERROR, the unmistakeable scent of terror, enveloped them as they went back into the newsroom. The *Beast*'s staff were breathing it in and out; and it hung thick as fog around them. The news had circulated that someone had found them here where they'd supposed themselves safe. They were still trying to work but went quieter when the Editor came in, hoping for a speech that would make them feel as powerful as they had last night. But the Editor went straight through to his office and his journalists shifted and muttered and looked at one another.

At the subs' desk, Jeremy and Liz buttonholed Max before he could get back to his seat, and he could feel the others listening too. Jeremy accused, 'Do you think it was that Muslim kid from the pub? Did he tip someone off?'

And Liz said, 'I reckon we get the fuck out of here and back to London. I've booked a minibus from a rental place in Thatcham. I'm taking my desk, so there's space for seven more. Who wants in – Jez?'

'Maybe it's not such a bad idea. Better than getting burnt

alive out here in the middle of nowhere. What do you think, Max?'

He realized that it was him they were asking and not the chief. To test them, he said, 'Why don't you ask Frank what he thinks? He's in charge.'

'Fuck that,' said Liz. 'We all know he's going to the *Fun*.'

He was, and there was no way Max was going anywhere. He said, 'This isn't like you, Liz. You're old Fleet Street. You've seen worse than this.'

'No I fucking haven't. Old Fleet Street is punches in pubs, not being burnt alive. Have you seen what fire does to a person? Because I've got loads of pictures; I'll show you.'

She spun to call some up on her computer, her sharp black bob swinging around her face, but Max grabbed her lightly by the forearm. 'Hey, hey, listen for a second,' he said. She arched an eyebrow at his hand and he let go. 'First of all, these walls here are reinforced concrete. What are they going to do, flick matches at them?'

'Do you want me to show you what it looked like at *Charlie Hebdo* after they went in there with machine guns?'

'No one could get a gun in here; you've seen how many cops there are outside. And secondly, how's it going to look if we're at the centre of the biggest story in decades and we don't even manage to get the paper out?'

That gave her pause.

'Someone's knocked over a fence and what are we going to do, print blank pages? Imagine what a laughing stock we'd be. The *Beast* gets handed the story of a generation and doesn't even manage to write it down.'

She reluctantly shook her bob, capitulating, and said, 'Oh, fuck you, Max. Fine. With any luck I'll get raped before they shoot me, just as a sweetener.'

Max wasn't going to comment on that.

'But I'm keeping this van on standby – and if anyone comes through those doors, it'll be nothing to me if you get a seat in it or not.'

Max nodded, feeling paternalistic; this was how it would be when he was chief. Liz went back to her desk, but Jeremy sidled closer and said quietly, 'Maybe she's right, you know. Maybe we should get out of here.'

Max was in no rush to listen to Jez and his renewed pessimism. But he said under his breath, 'OK, bring your chair round next to mine.' And while they sat, and Jeremy shifted closer to give the pretence that they were working on a headline, Max looked around the newsroom. One of the Health reporters had braced her head between her knees, as if for a plane crash, and was doing breathing exercises. The shabby-dignified veterans on Politics were not very surreptitiously passing around a hip flask. On his own pod, Rosie looked about ready to cut and run. Will was trying to reassure her. The boy was useful. Max pulled down his hunched shoulders, stretching them into better posture for a moment, and said to Jeremy, 'I see the fairer departments are starting to show the strain.'

'Fair enough, don't you think?' Jeremy said at a volume below the level of anyone else's hearing. He was thinking of what fire would do to him and felt his whole body try to flinch at once, as if the skin were puckering. He was suddenly aware of what bad shape he was in, his belly protuberant, his lungs shrivelled with smoke, his right arm and shoulder knotted tight from typing. He said, 'I don't even just mean for myself. What would it be like for Louise and the girls? They're only fourteen and twelve; imagine how it must fuck you up if your dad gets killed when you're that age. Maybe

Liz has got a point and we should be getting out of here while we still can.'

'What happened to Jez the jihadi-finder general? I thought you were the plotter spotter extraordinaire.'

'Huh.'

'What?'

'Didn't you hear what Frank said in that pub? Jez the jihadi sniffer dog, rooting through shit? That's the way it always is here, isn't it? You bring in the biggest story anyone's ever seen and at first it's all "X-ray vision, Jez the jihadi spotter", then it's sniffer dog and, by lunchtime, it's all back to the usual shit.'

'Do you want the Editor to give you three cheers after every edition?'

'No, it's just: what's the point? You make an amazing spot and then before you know it everyone's already on to the next thing. I've not really got anything to do with the story any more.'

Max hid a smirk: typical Jez. 'That's just Frank, and why are you listening to him anyway?'

'But even Frank's getting out and he keeps an archive of the *Beast*'s legal letters in his own house. This is just the last nail in the coffin. It's over.'

'What's over?'

'The *Beast*, newspapers, all of it. And you're happy because you're climbing higher up, but it doesn't matter because the whole ship's going under.'

'Bullshit,' said Max. 'There'll always be a *Beast*. People are always going to want news. Maybe not like the old days, maybe not in print every day, but how many people still paid money for the paper this morning? Two and a half million? And what are you going to do instead? Get a job in PR and sub press releases for Renault?'

'At least at Renault I bet you get to go home at five and no one tries to set you on fire.'

To Max this was heresy. For once his measure left him. 'But you're a *journalist*, for fuck's sake. It's not some job you can just quit.' His voice dropped even quieter. 'Look at that grunt Will – Oxbridge-educated, probably went to private school, clever kid; could be a hedge-funder, could be a diplomat, could be anything. But what does he want to be? A sub on the *Beast*. You've already got that job. And not just that – you're standing there smoking a cigarette when the story of a generation comes up and asks you for a light. And you're right: it *is* dangerous, you really might get hurt; but there's no hack anywhere in the world who wouldn't give a lifetime of safe work to be in your seat today, you big fucking toddler.'

Both chastened by this uncharacteristic loss of calm, they said nothing for a moment and their eyes wandered on to Max's screen. When Will and Rosie had run in, he'd just been subbing a NIB about the discovery of a rare case of Hitler's personal 'Führerwein', which he'd headlined:

|THIS'LL LEAVE A NAZI |
|TASTE IN YOUR MOUTH|

Jeremy said, 'I suppose I just think my life can be better than this.'

'You selfish prick.' Max went to berate him further, but the anger dissipated before he spoke. There was no heat in his voice when he said: 'Don't you realize that in twenty years' time we'll be old men on a documentary saying, "I don't know how Jezza did it." Journalism students are going to be looking at their textbooks and reading "Chapter One: Watergate", Woodward and Bernstein; "Chapter Two: the *Daily Beast*'s

Coverage of the Burqa Bombings", Jeremy Underwood. My name won't be in there, but yours will.'

Jeremy did like the sound of that. Maybe it *would* be a waste of his years of drudgery not to stick around; after all, those miserable years had given him the news-sense that uncovered this in the first place. 'I suppose,' he said. 'I also just think that—'

But Liz called across him and everyone who heard the odd flatness of her voice listened in: 'Max, we've got a tip: the other two in Kayani's gang are on their way here.'

Uproar in the newsroom. Terrified journalists jerking this way and that. The Health reporter dropping off her chair and crawling under her desk. Dozens of people trying to call the same Thatcham taxi firm at once. Some pulling on coats and stuffing things into handbags. Phones ringing unanswered. Rosie clutching her keyboard to her chest as if she were going to use it to defend herself.

Then the Editor was among them and shouting through the noise to Liz, 'Where are they?'

Clutching the phone's mouthpiece to mute it, she shouted back, 'On a bus, in burqas, on the M6.'

'How far away?'

'We don't know exactly, but still in the North, or at least the Midlands. I've got a snapper and a reporter getting into a car in Manchester.'

'What's the route of the M6?'

And Geraldine, who'd found him through the chaos, told them, 'Bradford!'

The Editor said, 'By God. Bradford, Luton, London, Berkshire – the whole country's going up in flames. And they're coming thick and fast. How do we know about this?'

'A tip from a guy who's on the bus. But I can't get anything sensible out of him; he thinks he's going to get taken hostage any minute. I'm trying to get him to send a map pin.'

The Editor didn't know what that was, but it didn't matter. 'How does he know they're terrorists?'

'He says it's obvious.'

'Your people need to stand that up. Why would they come by bus?'

Geraldine said, 'The 7/7 bombers came to London by train. But why does Pictures have this? Why didn't it come to Newsdesk?'

'He wants to sell us a snap.'

The Editor said, 'We need to be absolutely sure. Who knows how many other cells have been activated? With those already at the fence it looks like we may be hit by a concerted attack.'

The pressure of fear on Rosie squeezed out a squeak. 'We'll be surrounded!'

The Editor was startled and looked down at her. Liz drew her hand across her eyes, and her hand was shaking.

Geraldine told Rosie, 'Don't be ridiculous. We can't be surrounded by half a dozen people.'

But at the word 'surrounded', the uproar around them grew out of control. The Editor ordered the newsroom, 'Quiet there.' But his staff took no notice. Terror made them reckless. They shouted at the Editor, tugged at their friends' sleeves, told them it was time to get out. The Editor's handsome head surveyed his newsroom; this insubordination was unheard of. Liz said, 'Why *don't* we go back to London? If they're closing in on us here.'

Geraldine rounded on her: 'Leave the newsroom at five hours to deadline?'

The Editor's great voice thundered across the chaos: 'Listen to me!' To make an example, he singled out Rosie. Pointing at her, he told his staff: 'Do not listen to this counsellor of surrender.' Rosie jolted as if electrocuted. 'This is precisely the kind of cowardice that the terrorists want to force us into; and if we allow them to do so, they have already beaten us.'

The noise did not die down. The Editor's words were not going over. Rosie's complexion lost its colour as the blood left her head. She went dizzy and moved to stand up, to get up and out, anywhere, to fresh air. But the Editor put his big hand on her shoulder and pushed her back down into her seat.

'What would have happened if Britain had given in to fear in 1940, when our small island kingdom stood alone, and stood firm, with all Hitler's legions arrayed against it? What would have happened had we listened to the appeasers and the Quislings in our midst?' A sob escaped Rosie, and her hands grabbed her mouth as if to hold it closed. Jeremy sought Max's eye to confirm: they were staunch hacks, staying where they were. Max nodded and Jeremy made a slight wince on Rosie's behalf. Max wasn't interested. The Editor was right. And if this broke her, it was better to find out now that she couldn't take the strain.

The Editor orated above them, not winning over his staff. Several people were actually leaving. 'They will never – can never – defeat this country by force of arms. Terror is their only weapon. If we do not give in to it, it does not exist. This girl, this—'

Suddenly, Will, as cravenly as he could, spoke from behind the Editor: 'Excuse me, Mr Brython, I'm... I'm very sorry to interrupt, but I was wondering whether there was anything we should do right away. Would you like me to tell the police?'

The Editor was thrown off his stride. Without thinking,

he said, 'Of course not. Can you imagine what a hash they'd make of things?'

Someone in the crowd shouted, 'You've lost it! We'll all be burnt alive!' And the crowd panicked. They realized that the Editor was no more than a sixty-year-old man in a suit, and that the *Beast* was just a job. Those who'd already grabbed bags and jackets surged for the exit. Others abandoned their things where they lay. The Features editor wavered, then ran. The Diary desk deserted *en bloc*. Only Newsdesk and the subs were still holding together.

The Editor fell back on the most important principle that journalism had taught him: anything that works. He reached under his jumper to draw out the pistol he'd stowed there and his fingertips found the smooth grip warmed by his body. But, as he was about to slide it out and fire into the ceiling, a means of gambling less occurred to him. His quarterdeck voice rang out: 'A million pounds! A million pounds to anyone!'

That slowed them down, drilled as they'd been in following the money, in knowing: *cui bono?*

'You heard me! A million pounds to anyone, immediately and in cash.'

Many of them, the whole Diary desk among them, were too far gone to care. They crowded through the doorway, knocking down a portly young Sport sub with mutton chops, who scrambled desperately back to his feet and away. A long-serving political correspondent, in the sudden knowledge of freedom, turned on the threshold, clinging to the wall, and shouted, 'I'll write your obituary, Brython. I'll write your obituary!'

The Editor marked him for later retribution. He told the rest, 'You know I have the money. And I give my word as your Editor that anyone who receives so much as a scratch or bruise as a result of an attempt to break into this bunker will receive a million pounds in apology from me personally.'

Someone said very loudly, 'You can't just buy us off.' But many thought, a million quid just for a bruise? The danger must be non-existent. A man as astute as the Editor wouldn't throw cash away like that. And imagine what it would be for a broken leg.

'I assure you that you will be defended just as we will defend the liberties for which this country stands. If it is true, as it appears to be, that terrorist reinforcements are coming to join those already at our gates, then a grave hour indeed has struck.' He surveyed the journalists who'd stayed with him and was deeply moved. 'If, tomorrow morning, it seems we can best secure our safety by returning to London, then to London we will return. But this great newspaper will not be silenced. We will seal the door of this bunker. We will outlast the storm.'

There was a quiet in which the phones rang, the fuzzy screens moved on the back wall and the journalists who'd stayed felt the stirring of a certain kind of grumbling stoicism. Liz looked at her watch and said, 'If we're going to get this story, we'd better get on with it.'

Geraldine said, 'The *Beast* stands firm.'

There was a murmur of agreement, as if from parliament's back benches, and several repeated: 'The *Beast* stands firm.' How the Editor loved them then. He had more to say to them, about how this newspaper had never missed an edition even during the Blitz. But instead he briskly put them back in order. 'Desk editors, get your people moving. We need some copy through to the page. Work out where the gaps in manpower are going to be. We'll have to drop the Diary spread entirely – so Features, we'll need more from you. And Geraldine, run this story to ground.'

The newsroom's enormous toothed wheels creaked, shuddered, and, slowly, stiffly, began to turn.

The Editor spoke so only Geraldine and Liz could hear. 'Geraldine, tell the deserters that the police will drive them into Thatcham in their vans and that any leak, even to a policeman, is a contravention of the Official Secrets Act, which carries a maximum sentence of imprisonment. Send some reporters to escort them. If the police try to get out of driving, tell them we don't want a horde of Muslim cabbies on our doorstep. Liz, are you still on the phone with your contact?'

'Yes.'

'Get him to look out of the window and read the distances on a fucking road sign. We need to know where they are and how long we've got. Also the bus timetables. They'll have to change somewhere, Oxford maybe, or Birmingham, if they want to take a bus to Thatcham or Newbury. Find that out. And I want you to find out exactly how your contact claims to know that they are terrorists. Then Geraldine, have your people seal the door.'

TWENTY-FOURTH CHAPTER

AISHA and her cousin Leila, whom Jeremy had seen outside Copper House the day before, fast-walked down a long, stuffy, sleeve-like tunnel reaching out from one of Heathrow's terminals, went through the industrial atrium at its end and stepped into the aeroplane that would take them home.

A few hours earlier, Aisha had flumped on to the sofa and turned on the TV, glad to have a break from sightseeing. At first she'd only half-followed what was happening on screen. But understanding had crept up, then seized her all at once: the Whole Foods sign, lunchtime yesterday, two figures in burqas. The police had already shot two Muslims.

She shouted for Leila, who came and saw. And Leila, who, despite her interest in new restaurants and fashion magazines, had a sensible heart, told her to book the next two seats to Abu Dhabi while she scooped her jewellery into a bag.

By unspoken agreement, Aisha and Leila omitted to put on their burqas when they left the flat. It was the first time Aisha had been uncovered in public since she was a little girl and her face felt as raw as after a plaster is torn off. No one looked at her. Leila didn't seem to notice being uncovered, almost as if she'd forgotten that this was supposed to be unusual. Aisha was beginning to think she'd underestimated her cousin.

They found their seats, fastened their belts and did not speak until the plane's rear wheels made their unnatural lurch and gave up contact with the ground. Safely off British soil, Leila spoke over the engine's muted howl: 'I never really liked it that much there, anyway. The air was so dirty.'

'Me neither,' said Aisha. She'd already taken *Game of Thrones: A Song of Ice and Fire* out of her handbag. She ran her thumb down one softened corner, letting the translucently thin pages escape upwards one at a time, and thought with a glimmer of innocent childish malice how sorry her father would be that the holiday he'd forced her to come on had turned out so badly.

TWENTY-FIFTH CHAPTER

THE Editor did not return to his office, but went from section to section, rearranging his staff to close the gaps left in the ranks by those who'd run away. The *Beast* really was on a war footing now. He felt like Baden-Powell in besieged Mafeking, putting fake soldiers on the walls to trick the Boers. While the bus grew in his mind like an approaching meteor, he moved unhurriedly between the desks and pods, inspecting the troops. The desk editors escorted him around their sections; he asked questions and remembered names, promoted a new Features editor and flattered them with his belief in their steadfastness. Many glanced at him when, with a hissing and then a hollow clunk, the air supply was turned up and the outside door swung shut.

Once he'd toured all the outer desks, he finally came to the centre and said, 'Enderling, Constantinos, Forshaw. You, too, Max, and you, Underwood.' Geraldine, Liz, the chief, Max and Jeremy clustered around him as he put a blank flatplan on Max's desk. Glancing up, he said, 'Frank, it looks as if every one of your subs is still here.'

The chief tried not to show his pride. 'They hate their lives anyway. Getting killed by jihadis is a step up for them.'

The Editor regarded him with irritation, his sense of moment too high-flown for newsroom banter. He said, 'Liz, what do we know? Does it stand up?'

'Our source is sure they're terrorists, absolutely sure, but he's bricking it. He can't say why he's so sure.'

'So we don't know.'

'We can have a proper look when our boys catch up to them.'

'Where are they?'

'I can't say exactly. Somewhere near Birmingham.'

The Editor looked at his watch. 'But by God, if they're still in the Midlands they might not even get here until after ten o'clock.'

Geraldine understood what he meant and was horrified as she hadn't been by the prospect of attack. 'But if they're not here in time, we—'

'Anything we print will be hopelessly out of date by morning,' he said bitterly. 'While every smug cunt on breakfast television is interviewing the families of the jihadis who've been arrested outside our own building overnight, we'll be sitting there with a front page that says, "Terror bus inbound. Nothing known."'

'We could get something in the later editions.'

'Oh, the later editions! For fuck's sake, Geraldine!'

Geraldine kept her mouth shut.

'Cunting cunt,' said the Editor, gathering himself. 'Cunting fucking cunt. Cunting fucking motherfucking cunting cunt.' He breathed out.

Jeremy put his thoughts forward. He was a specialist in this, after all. 'Um, Charles, why don't we tip off the police before the bus gets here? They'll pull them over and arrest them and we'll get that story?'

The Editor took this suggestion. 'We might have to, Underwood. But something like that will leak at once and every stringer and snapper in the Home Counties will be there five minutes behind us.'

'So we'll have a story,' said Geraldine in frustration. 'But we won't have the scoop.'

Jeremy said, 'Isn't this going to leak anyway, though, from one of the people who've left?'

'If they dare,' said the Editor, 'I'll have them fucking murdered.' His fore-thinking mind had already formulated a protection against leaks: he would ring the editors of the other nationals and tell them that a few kooks had been trying to break into the *Beast*'s compound; that the police were involved and that acting on any hysterical tips they might get would not just be embarrassing, it would put lives and national security at risk. They could, he thought, be pushed into feeling that they were doing their bit. He wouldn't bother with Julian at the *Impartial*.

He said, 'And even if it doesn't leak, if those dolts from Thames Valley Police screech up with their sirens on, these jihadis, if jihadis they are, might explode the bus and everyone in it.' Jeremy couldn't help thinking that at least it wouldn't be exploded *here*.

The Editor looked at his watch again and pensively said, 'Cunts.' He was imagining a front page with a big photograph, probably taken at night and floodlit – two figures in Islamic black putting their hands up as the police encircled them – and the exclusive headline 'Bombers caught outside *Beast*'. That would be a worthy end to the newspaper era.

But he said, 'What else do we have?' They huddled over the

flatplan, discussing alternatives; and, as on the night before, it felt as if laying out the paper conferred mastery over the events it described.

The Editor labelled the front page and the first four spreads – nine consecutive pages clear of adverts – Burqa Bombings. He said, 'Pages one, two and three will be the splash with whatever breaks in the next couple of hours, folding in the other developments.'

Geraldine said, 'After all, it's not as if we haven't got any stories. It's as good as a war.'

The Editor said nothing to that, but Geraldine wasn't wrong. The police were raiding Bucklebury, looking for the Muslim in the pub, and sweeping the woods between the village and the bunker. The Met's special force of 4,000 officers was essentially occupying suburban West London, although the *Strumpet* was well embedded with them, and would presumably be first to anything that broke. The Met's bosses and military intelligence were interrogating Dikhlat Choudry, the one who'd been shot but survived. Apparently he was still giving up all kinds of information. Geraldine had a source who was passing it on verbatim.

'On three, we'll also have two shorts.' The Editor's pencil delineated two boxes, horizontal and vertical. 'One for the Dramatic Shootout with Mian and Choudry, briefly because it's been everywhere since lunchtime, then a single col—'

/////////NEWSFLASH//////////

Paul Gilligan twitched the camera hidden in the satchel at his side. His hand was starting to ache; he'd been tailing this gang of what he hoped were hot-headed young Muslims for three hours and was beginning to lose faith they'd ever do anything newsworthy. Nor did he have any idea where he was. He'd never been to Leicester before – only driven up that morning when he heard there were white and Muslim vigilantes carrying weapons on the street. He'd found a gang of chavs first and got a few shots of badly concealed knives and piping, but when he sent them to Liz at the *Beast* she'd said she was getting the same stuff from everyone. It had been four days since he'd sold a picture.

He'd stuck with the chavs a little longer, with no joy. There'd been an exciting few minutes when they'd started throwing packets of bacon at a crowd of Muslims outside one of the mosques, but they'd legged it as soon as they heard sirens. And, for all their swagger, there seemed to be a high reluctance to actually use the weapons they were toting.

So he'd abandoned them and managed to find this lot: fourteen of them now that they'd picked up a few friends on their patrol. All of them under about twenty-five, with skullcaps and ragged beards; some of them in those Muslim pyjamas, others in jeans and shiny shirts. A few chain-smoking and swigging thin cans of energy drinks. They were quieter than the chavs but, unlike them, had also seemed to have some definite intent. So far all they'd done was lead him away from the shopping centre where he'd picked them up and into these anonymous terraced streets. He was beginning to think he should try to find the chavs again; maybe they'd get drunk.

But, as he wondered whether he'd even be able to find them again, the small mob slowed down, spreading into the road. Two young white women in short skirts and skimpy tops were coming hesitantly along the pavement towards them.

Paul stretched his fingers inside the satchel, rolled his

knuckles and brought the digits back to their places on the camera. The girls were cheap. Hoop earrings, make-up, ponytails. Slags from the estates, on the way out somewhere.

The Muslims started jeering at them, and one of the girls wanted to go back. But the other girl, a greasy blonde, refused to turn around. She took her friend's hand and marched towards them. The first few Muslims moved aside, leering at them. That was a picture. Paul lifted the camera and started rattling off near-identical shots: the cheap girls walking defiantly through the mob; the angry, taunting, lustful faces all around them.

Then a hand reached for the blonde's ponytail, to pull it back. Confusion broke out. The girls started shrieking and tried to run. Hands grabbed at them, blocked them. One of the men flicked a large black cloth out of a bag. The blonde tried to twist away from it, but was still held by the ponytail and a hand caught her shoulder while another, missing, hit her in the face. Through the viewfinder Paul saw her features contort. Grabbed and held, she began to wail as the black burqa was pulled over her head. And before it swallowed her up, Paul's camera caught spreading below her nose an unmistakeable spill of blood. The shutter clicked rapidly. Paul felt the tingle of a great shot.

'One for the Dramatic Shootout with Mian and Choudry – briefly, because it's been everywhere since lunchtime – then a single column about the use of deadly force by the police.' The Editor lettered 'splash', 'shootout' and 'deadly force'.

Max asked, 'Do we know what the line's going to be?'

The chief said, 'What do you expect? Boohoo, the poor old terrorists got shot?'

The Editor asked, 'Have you seen the copy?'

'It's a comment piece from one of the cops who shot that Brazilian a few years ago: tragic necessity; terrible for the cops involved.'

Glancing at the Editor to make sure he was watching, Max contradicted the chief, 'Shouldn't we reconstruct it as a news piece? "The prime minister last night offered his support to officers", etcetera, using the quotes from our man further down.'

Before the chief could speak, the Editor said, 'Yes, make it news. There's too much comment in these pages anyway. Terror's the subject of the op-ed as well. Aston's writing it now.'

Geraldine was impressed. 'The PM?'

The Editor nodded dismissively, thinking of other pages. Every PM made at minimum an accommodation with the *Beast*, and Aston struck him as a self-involved little boy. The only person he mentally referred to as 'the prime minister' was Churchill. 'Yes, Aston's going to say that they can only beat us by dividing us, then go on to free speech and unity in the global struggle against Islamism; and the payoff line is going to be, "Today, we are all *Beast* readers."'

'Are you going to tell him about this bus?'

'Certainly not. Who knows what that autist might do. Next spread, four–five, the Met's Terror Hunt. A map with graphics and snippets about sightings, arrests, where our forces are distributed. Then six–seven, the newspaper man horribly burnt alive and next to it the Great Muslim Debate: our foremost thinkers on what do we do about Islam. Geraldine, who do we have so far?'

'Our lead is top historian Ben Croton on Islam's violent origins and how we've got to either win the clash of civilizations or start buying prayer mats. Then Booker-winning novelist Robin Gibbs saying something clever about how the Muslims in his neighbourhood never talk to anyone else. Baroness Ahmad says it's time to ban the burqa; an economist says lots of jihadis are on benefits; and the Lord Chief Justice says half the inner city is run on Sharia law.'

Max carefully took the pencil from his mouth and made another suggestion. 'Does it need a piece condemning Islamophobia?'

The chief said with derision, 'Do you think we're going to headline the spread "Down with Islam"?'

Max remembered him blurting 'Yes, sir' to the Editor the night before, and openly smirked at him. 'No, but the *Impartial*'s already reported us to the Met for incitement to religious hatred.'

'Who gives a fuck about the *Impartial*? They've got fewer readers than our Gardening section.'

'No one gives a fuck about the *Impartial*. But there are vigilante kids on the streets with knives – if a Muslim gets stabbed, we're going to look pretty bad if we haven't covered ourselves.'

'What do you know about how we'll look? Last time I checked all you were in charge of was one of my pods.'

The Editor generally liked it when his subordinates fought; it sharpened their minds. But there was no time for this now. He ruled, 'Geraldine, find a left-wing civil-liberties campaigner, preferably white, to say that freedom of religion and of conscience is one of the founding tenets of this country. And that Britain does not single people out on the basis of their creed – this isn't Germany, or Russia. Also, put in a news piece reporting the *Impartial*'s potentially libellous accusation.

'Otherwise, Max is right: if a Muslim is killed, we lose control of this story. On one side there would be the *Impartial*, the *Conscientious* and the rest of the liberal media saying that we stirred this up; and on the other us, the *Respectable* and the *Stentorian* saying we didn't. Then we are not directing the story; we are *in* the story – the last thing we want. And what are our pages if not a forum for robust debate? The *Beast* has nothing to fear from the truth.'

The fourth and last Bombing spread would be what they called a smorgasbord: a picture of the terrorist Kayani as a teenager, playing cricket on a village green like a real English boy; the news piece about the *Impartial*; messages of solidarity from publications around the world, complete with their mastheads – the *Kansas City Star*, *Die Frankfurter Allgemeine*, *Il Corriere della Sera*, the *Jerusalem Post*, the *Straits Times*, the *Sydney Morning Herald* and many more. Once the Editor had sketched the layouts on the flatplan, he checked his watch again and said, 'Get the paper made. Liz, I want to know the instant your people find that bus.'

They went to work, but around them terror was gathering again. It was as if the air itself were thickening – filling with strands of anxious thought that held them like insects in a web, each one's twitching further agitating his companions. They kept glancing away from their desks, up at the clock, at Liz and at the bright bank of screens projected on to the back wall.

Will was relieved to be assigned some copy. To sit quietly while the terrorists came for them felt increasingly insane. He'd been given the hastily knocked-up news piece about the *Impartial*, but his mind ran across the letters too quickly to grasp them.

He looked across at Rosie. Patches of redness stood out under her eyes and on her cheeks; and, though she no longer seemed about to bolt, she didn't seem to be actually doing anything. She'd been assigned the softest story, about Kayani playing cricket, under the headline 'Why do they hate us?' He wanted to ask whether she was alright, but thought that she wouldn't want to speak to anyone after the humiliation of crying in the newsroom. It occurred to him with a pang that this might be the end for her at the *Beast*.

He looked again at the opening of the story and again the fuzz of words sped meaninglessly past his eye. But gradually, reading and rereading, he began to distinguish the black marks. The first paragraphs read:

> The *Impartial* has sparked outrage after it was accused of political point-scoring in a time of national crisis for criticizing the *Beast*, say MPs.
>
> The newspaper, which is owned by Russian oligarch Vadim Andropov, has filed an incendiary complaint with the Metropolitan Police, accusing the *Beast* of incitement to religious hatred, and another with IPSO, the regulator, about the *Beast*'s alleged failure to report what it knew about yesterday's attempted bombing to police in good time.

There was a lot to do, and a NOTE TO SUBS at the bottom: 'Outrage to follow. Am calling MPs.' The only quotes so far were from the *Impartial*'s complaint to IPSO and from the policeman who appeared to be in charge of hunting the terrorists. Assistant Commissioner Nigel Willis had said:

> 'The Metropolitan Police Service has reached the conclusion that there are no

grounds for pursuing a complaint against the *Daily Beast* newspaper for incitement to religious hatred.

'Further, although it would be inappropriate to comment on an ongoing IPSO investigation, the MPS has no complaint of its own to register regarding information released by the *Daily Beast* newspaper and will not be conducting any inquiry.

'Lastly, allegations that the *Daily Beast* has been obstructive to MPS operations are spurious; and I would remind the public that spurious allegations direct limited police resources away from crucial operations.

'On the contrary, the *Daily Beast* has uncovered valuable information about a highly dangerous extremist cell that the MPS has been hunting for some time. The vast and sophisticated Met operation to bring these men to justice would not have been possible without help from the *Daily Beast.*'

Will was somewhat settled by that, especially when he saw that the copy slightly cheesily described this guy as 'courageous copper Nigel Willis'. He knew it was sentimental but he was heartened to think that the *Beast* and the police were laying aside their reciprocal mistrust for a greater good. And the prime minister was going to say: 'Today we are all *Beast* readers!' The *Daily Beast* was certainly looking a lot more desirable on his CV now.

The story was not a page lead, so Will set the first par to 8.5- rather than 9.5-point type, removed the indentation, held shift for caps and rewrote:

> A NATIONAL newspaper has been denounced for using a national crisis for political point-scoring after it filed a 'spurious' complaint against the *Beast*'s coverage of the Burqa bombings.
>
> The Russian-owned, Left-leaning

He checked the style guide. Yes, 'Left' was capped up.

> The Russian-owned, Left-leaning *Impartial*, which has a circulation of less than 70,000, claimed the *Beast*'s coverage amounted to incitement to religious hatred – a claim the police have dismissed.
>
> A complaint of this type involves complex legal arguments and can cost thousands to investigate. Xx
>
> Xx, MP for Xx, said: [OUTRAGE GOES IN HERE].

He worked on, whittling the paragraphs to sharp points. The work calmed his fright and he kept his mind on it, as if each paragraph were a stake in the *Beast*'s defences. He noticed that he'd doubled 'national' in the opening par, and fixed it. The missing outrage was emailed to him. Curtis Arbuthnot, Tory MP for Bexleyheath, had given the reporter:

> 'These accusations are outrageous. Not

only do they cynically attempt to smear a professional competitor at a time of crisis, but its coverage, by accusing the *Daily Beast* of being "inflammatory", insidiously implies that the *Beast* is to blame for the attempted attack on its offices because of its fearless reporting on radical Islam in Britain today.

'That implication shows the *Impartial* to be an enemy of the very freedoms on which its callow calumnies depend. Its editors would do well to learn a lesson from their colleagues on the *Beast*, who would have every right to despise the *Impartial* but have already amply demonstrated that they would risk their lives to defend it.'

The other MP they'd called was from Labour, so that Will could write, 'MPs from across the major parties united last night in condemning…' It was Michael Davidson, Sheffield South, who'd said:

'They must be bonkers. I'm no friend of the *Beast*'s politics, but you can't deny that they're on the frontline against this medieval totalitarianism, and fair play to them. This isn't the time for that kind of point-scoring.

'The *Impartial* should apologize and make "We are all *Beast* readers" their front page tomorrow. Because at the moment they're siding with the terrorists.'

Just as he was putting the piece into revise, much stabilized by a job done, Liz sent one of her juniors to fetch the Editor. Max looked at her and she said, 'Yeah, we've caught up with them. And they're still fucking miles away.'

TWENTY-SIXTH CHAPTER

IN THE race between deadline and the loaded bus, the deadline approached faster. Liz stood leaning over the pictures laid out on her desk, the open phone line clamped to her chest, and kept glancing up at the clock behind the back bench. Its black pointers rotated tirelessly, one lapping the other, while the bus languished in the orbital systems and traffic-calming measures on the outskirts of Birmingham.

The Editor strode out of his office with an air of decision and asked Liz for the third time in half an hour, 'Where are they?'

The whole newsroom listened in as she moved the phone to her ear and said, 'Ken, where are you now...? They're south of Birmingham and on to the M40... seeing signs for Sherbourne, Bishop's Tachbrook – Warwick, they're just by Warwick and Leamington Spa. The bastards definitely won't get to Oxford till after half nine, let alone here.'

The Editor had known that this would be the case but had left room for the possibility that something about their trajectory would change: a loosening of traffic, a lifting of the pace.

The chief sidled warily over to him and said, 'Charles, just so you know, we're starting to cut things pretty fine on production. If we don't decide on a splash soon, it'll be a bit of a scramble making edition.'

The Editor knew that, of course. But that the chief had seen fit to mention it meant that the rest of the book was still a long way off. He ordered, 'Geraldine, put together what else we've got. Five minutes…' and went back to his office to think.

That the jihadi reinforcements were still far away slightly reassured the newsroom. But the bus and the deadline still came unceasingly closer and the nightly adrenaline flowed fast. It was becoming hard to concentrate. Liz muttered curses as she worked. Will's mind kept losing its hold on the letters displayed by his screen. Every few seconds he looked up, looked around, lost his place, forgot what he'd been reading and checked the screens projected behind the back bench, half-expecting to see footage of the jihadis arriving at the building he was in. They hadn't got off when the bus stopped in Birmingham, not even to go to the toilet or stretch their legs. It still hadn't been confirmed that they *were* jihadis, but that didn't seem like a good sign.

Jeremy was speaking in his head, saying, come on, super-sub. Come on, Jihadi Jez. Keep your fingers moving. Crunch down that par. Run those two sentences together. Woodward and Bernstein would have got the paper out.

Max was settling into himself, becoming still, while the chief became ostentatiously unfazed. As he came to give them copy, he flicked a print-off on to Jeremy's desk, saying, 'Pass that around, darling, but it's probably better if you don't let the Editor catch you with it.' He carried on to Max: 'And for you, Sub-Editor Barbie, the dramatic account of the other terrorists getting shot is in.'

The print-off was a gargoyle-ish caricature of the Prophet Muhammad drawn by the paper's cartoonist. Muhammad had dropped a dildo-shaped time bomb and was wincing as he was painfully sodomized by Charles Brython. The caption read, 'Fuck you, too, Muhammad!'

The joke couldn't get through to Jeremy and he held the picture as if it were incomprehensible. The chief said, 'I wouldn't be surprised if the old pervert really did take it up the shitter. You know he got himself married to a nine-year-old. If he was alive now, we'd have had him banged up for being a paedo.'

But before he could demonstrate his fearlessness any further, the Editor returned. Jeremy flipped the picture upside-down and put it under his keyboard. Every reporter, every sub, every section editor and graphics man and picture researcher watched the Editor pace across to Liz's desk and order Geraldine to join him. He said, 'Liz, any change on the bus?'

'Nope. They're still trundling along towards us.'

'So they won't be here in time for edition. Geraldine, what else do we have for the front page?'

'Actually,' Liz interrupted, 'we've just got something else in. From a snapper in Leicester.'

She spread the shots on top of the other pictures on her desk: on a shadowy street under metallic skies a ponytailed young blonde with huge hoop earrings was wailing upwards as fierce Muslim hands pulled a dense black cloth over her head. It looked as if it were swallowing her whole. And below her nose and across one cheek was an unmistakeable smear of dark carmine.

Liz said, 'A Muslim gang's been sticking white women into burqas.'

Geraldine was amazed. 'Bloody hell! This is fabulous. It's got to be the splash.'

'It's an outrage,' said the Editor.

'Yes!' cried Geraldine, eyes shining. '"Outrage as Muslim gang beats British woman and forces her into burqa. Fears of retaliation as tensions mount." And the girl's not at all bad-looking, either.'

The Editor glanced at Geraldine as at a guard dog you must remember never to let near the children. 'Where is she now?'

Liz said, 'She fought them off. The Muzzers didn't really know what to do with her once she was in it. She's at home.'

Geraldine said, 'You're getting all the stories today, aren't you? If you carry on like this I'll need to start sacking my desk. But we need this as a picture exclusive, don't we, Charles?'

'Yes, pay whatever you have to.'

Liz said, 'I already have. Everyone else knows it happened, but only we've got the picture. I had to promise the snapper every favour we can offer, but we've got it. I've sent someone to babysit him from now till tomorrow morning.'

'Bravo, Liz.' Geraldine shook her head in happy disbelief. 'This is great stuff. The girl's a complete tart by the look of things.'

'A woman beaten bloody on a British street and forced into a burqa,' said the Editor. He was appalled. 'We need a name, an interview.'

Geraldine said, 'Liz?'

'The snapper followed her home, but the family won't let him in.'

The Editor said, 'We need the interview exclusive. Pay whatever you have to. This is *our* story and we're certainly not going to be ham-fisted enough to fumble it.'

Liz shrugged angrily. 'It was in the middle of the street; what do you want me to do?'

'So are we going to get the interview?'

'We're still negotiating with the family, but I doubt anyone else has managed to get—'

'She's negotiating? That means she's talking to every cunt with a Dictaphone between here and Edinburgh. Fucking cunt. What's happening in Bucklebury?'

Geraldine said, 'We've got half of Newsdesk out there with the cops but they haven't really turned anything up yet, I'm afraid. We've got a lead on this notorious Muslim who works in the pub, and we've raided a Costcutter, but it's all been made more difficult; apparently, the subs started some kind of fracas at lunchtime and made sworn enemies of the locals.'

The Editor stared hard at the chief, who pretended not to have heard. While Liz listened to what was going on she, to her own surprise, silently prayed – actually prayed – that the bus would not get here, please, that the terrorists outside would not get in, that she would get back to London, that she would not die here.

The Editor said, 'And I take it those incompetents at the Met haven't found a fucking thing either?'

'They haven't. But maybe that's the story: police bunglers fail to find anything on biggest-ever operation. Public money wasted by—'

'Shut the fuck up for just a *moment*, could you, Geraldine, while I try to think of something to print that won't be complete shit.' Geraldine was entirely un-deflated but stopped talking. The Editor glanced at the relentless clock. It was all coming apart in his hands: the *Daily Beast* – first in the world, in print. It was all coming to nothing.

'And the one who was shot. What are we getting from the interrogation?'

'Any other day it would have made a great splash. Today, I wouldn't really think so. He's held out on the Burqa Bombings – tougher than they expected, it sounds like – but he's given up all kinds of colour about Syria, terrorism, being in the radicalized crowd. We could do it as a Dramatic Scene – dying jihadi interrogated in hospital bed, blood seeping through bandages, weak coughs, race against time to extract what he knows while outside the chilling terror plot ticks towards its terrible conclusion.'

'Anything about their connections to other terrorists?'

'He's given up a whole address book, but they're all in Syria and could just be a list of minicab firms for all anyone knows. Also, the Beeb have got at least some of all this, too, I'm afraid, Charles. They're broadcasting stuff that could only have come from him. They're probably just arguing with their lawyers before they start trowelling it on to every channel they've got.'

'So the whole of tomorrow's dramatic race-against-time interrogation story is going to be on the *News at Ten* tonight?'

'I very much doubt it. Looking at their stuff, I think they've got access to a cop, but they haven't seen the transcript. So they'll have to do "unconfirmed reports" and "speculation" and probably no quotes. So we're beating them there.'

'But they'll have all the news lines?'

'Yes, I suppose they will but—'

'God *damn* it, Geraldine! This is the story of our lifetimes, perhaps the last great story ever broken in print – *our* story – and you want to splash on some fucking colour piece that everyone already knows about.'

'Then how about our exclusive pic of the tart being forced into a burqa?'

'Next to our exclusive picture on the newsstand the *Stentorian* might have an exclusive interview and ten pictures.'

'But none anywhere near as good,' Geraldine said. 'Our picture's sensational. Women attacked in the streets. Militant Islam on the march. Police overwhelmed.'

'Yes and the readers will have a good look at our exclusive fucking picture and then buy the fucking *Stentorian*.'

'Well, we've got the picture of Kayani playing cricket; no one else has that. And the copy's tremendous stuff. His parents came over from the Punjab to work; his dad's a member of the Tory party, entirely pro-British. From patriots to Islamists in one generation, could be a splash: "Why they hate us – the jihadi generation growing up in England."'

'No, no, *no*! This story's still live, for Christ's sake. We don't want an investigation; we want breaking news. Those murderers are still out there, maybe only a few hundred feet away.'

'And that's the angle where no one can touch us. Attempted attack on the *Beast*'s base. Perimeter breached. Terror in idyllic Berkshire.'

'But you haven't fucking found them yet, have you, Geraldine?'

'We've made a good start. We've been to most of the—'

'I don't fucking care.' He considered for a moment. 'So we're not first on anything useable except the bus. No one else has that, Liz?'

'I haven't been off the line with our source since he called.'

'So we're sure no one else has it?'

'As sure as it's possible to be.'

'And what do we know about these terrorists?'

Liz shook her head. 'Fuck all.'

Geraldine said, 'We could put a picture of the bus together with the bloodied tart on the front; tie it all together.'

'Except we can't get a decent shot,' said Liz.

The Editor asked, 'Can't you see them through the window?'

'We've tried that. But even taking the glare off all it looks like is someone in a burqa sitting in a bus.'

'And by the time our rubbish fucking bus picture is on tomorrow's newsstands with no real news underneath it,' said the Editor, 'they'll have been arrested by those fucking halfwits from Thames Valley Police, probably live on Radio Oxford, God *damn* it, those motherfucking cunts, *cunts*, cunting cunts!' He squeezed his great fists. 'Perhaps we ought to call the BBC ourselves, and the police, and tip them both.' Geraldine went pale. 'After all, an attack on the *Beast* is an attack on us all. The *Beast* has called for unity in the face of terror; perhaps now is the time for us not just to report, but to lead, to demonstrate to the world that the cost of unity is the sacrifice of individual advantage – a price anyone should gladly pay to protect British lives. So that, when people look back on the *Beast*'s achievements in these momentous days, they will point not to yesterday's scoop, but to today's relinquishing of a scoop, and say, *This* was their finest hour.'

Geraldine unconsciously pushed her bracelets up her forearms, so they stuck. 'Or,' she said, 'there is another way.'

The Editor looked at her with something bordering on love. They understood each other. 'Yes,' he said. 'There is.'

'We did it with Archbishop Morton.'

'Near Tiverton.'

'And with those fraudster brothers, the Sheridans.'

'Outside Wolverhampton.'

Liz said, 'You can't do that with a busload of people.'

'Don't you see that this is a war? They've activated cells all over the country. We're in a state of emergency.'

Liz said, 'There could be sixty people on that bus.'

The Editor didn't answer. He and Geraldine were each working through the same idea. Then he asked, 'How much money do your men have with them?'

Liz relayed the question into the phone, then said, 'Between them just short of two thousand.'

'How reliable are they?'

'They're reliable.'

'And you? We can't afford any hesitation. If you can't do it, Geraldine can.'

Liz felt from all around her the newsroom's desperate hope: that the *Beast* would protect them. She surrendered to it. 'Fuck that,' she said. 'We're not just going to lie here. If you fuck with the *Beast*, the *Beast* fucks back.'

'Good,' he said. 'Now, when your people squeeze the bus over on to the hard shoulder' – Geraldine drew in her breath – 'it will be of the essence that the terrorists don't see the snapper. Everything depends on that. If they realize they're being photographed they could blow their vests, take hostages, anything. So while the reporter gives the driver a thousand immediately, holding the other thousand in reserve, the snapper has to run into cover somewhere he can shoot the bus.

'That is of the essence,' the Editor said again. 'And it is your responsibility to make sure he understands that. The reporter and the driver can pretend he's noticed something wrong with the bus; that's why they're stopped. The driver asks everyone to get off for a few minutes while they're on the hard shoulder and, when they get off, our snapper gets the shot of them lined up against the side.' A complication occurred to him. 'Which side are the terrorists on – inside or outside?'

'Outside.'

'So they won't see the car?'

'No.'

The Editor nodded and said, 'Lucky. Brief your people, but tell them not to do anything until I say so. Warn your source about what's going to happen. Keep him calm. Impress upon him that it's crucial that he gives nothing away, for his own sake.'

While Liz rattled her instructions into the handset, a hush settled on the newsroom. Only Max kept working, untangling clauses, compressing paragraphs, inching the paper closer to edition. He said, 'Will, Rosie, how's that copy coming along?' and, though he sounded unnaturally loud, they hardly heard him.

The Editor stood as if alone. Before him shimmered a wondrous image: the newspaper ahead again, ahead of every TV channel, every website, every blog and tweeter in the world on the story that every single one of them was chasing. An impossible thing, really. One last full-throated roar before the newspaper curled around itself to die. And if it went wrong, the liberal media would cut chunks out of him and the *Beast*. No one would defend him. If they blew the bus, that would be the end for him. Downfall. Ignominy. The thing he'd put his life into tainted, turned on, cowed.

The clock ticked towards edition. A new degree of greatness beckoned. At the centre of this crushing pressure, a wild thrill of delight ran through him. He remembered something from his schooldays:

If you can make one heap of all your winnings
And risk it on one turn of pitch-and-toss...

He felt strangely free.

On the M40 outside Banbury, the bus grunted and snorted with adjustments of speed as the reporter's car pulled out to come alongside.

In the newsroom, the Editor said to Liz, 'You can tell them to begin.'

Liz was holding herself so tightly she could only be laconic. Into the phone she said, 'Alright, Ken, on you go, and start uploading pictures the second you can.'

Geraldine murmured, 'Bombs away.'

The Editor felt a sharp unexpected pang for all he was gambling, and said, 'Tell them to be careful. They must not – absolutely must not – spook the terrorists.'

Liz looked at him in surprise, then said into the phone, 'Ken? The Editor says fuck this up and you're both sacked. Now drive in front of him already and tell Dan to wave the money so the driver can see it. Tell him to wave his Press card as well...' She listened. The Editor and his newsroom watched her.

'What's he doing? What? ... Wind down the window and signal to him... Just signal that you want to talk and show him the money... What do you mean he's freaking out? Has Dan shown him the money? ... Don't fucking frighten him, just make nice and get him to stop... Just point, point, push him on to the hard shoulder and show him the money... Drive closer and shout to him... Get close enough to shout to him... What do you mean he's speeding up? How can he speed up if you're in front of him? ... We *want* him on the hard shoulder... But how—'

At this, the Editor's large frame twitched and, a second later, he stepped forward and snatched the phone from Liz, yanking the base on to its side. He spoke into the handset: 'What's going on? ... Back off then; he's only panicking because you're panicking him... Signal that you're not a threat and show him the money... I don't give a fuck about the speed limit... *How* fast? ... Just show him the money. Have you shown him the money? Why aren't you showing him the fucking money, you cunt? What are the two burqas doing? The driver's what? ... He's what? ... He's...?'

His head jerked away from the receiver. He stood as if stunned, the phone useless in his hand. His great voice mumbled, 'The bus has crashed.'

Pandemonium in the newsroom. Everyone shouting at once. Geraldine with her hand over her mouth. The Editor paralysed.

Liz grabbed the phone from him and, covering her other ear against the uproar, yelled into it, 'Ken! Ken! How bad's the crash? What the fuck's going on?' She listened, then spoke as if speaking a judgment: 'The bus has gone through the barriers and rolled down the verge. It's on its side. What do you want to do?'

Muscles clenched at the Editor's jaw and temples. His handsome face flushed red. There was an instant in which he quaked for what he'd done. But he'd stood at the helm for so many years that the helm itself now held him steady. He took the phone. 'This is Charles Brython; who's this? ... Dan, if you want to stay out of jail, do exactly as I tell you. Get over there and start taking pictures. Get the first shots through and on my desk in the next five minutes. Is that understood? We'll take care of the police. Now give the phone to Ken.'

As Dan was handing it over, the Editor said to Geraldine: 'Have one of your people ring Oxfordshire Police and tell them to expect a call from the Met about a top-secret incident outside Banbury. You get on to our man Willis in the Met and tip him off so that he brings this under his counter-terror operation. Tell him we don't know exactly what's happened and can't yet say for certain whether there was a hijacking.

'Ken? Yes. What we need you to find out is... Yes, I understand people have been killed, and I want you to help the survivors, but first I want to know: are the terrorists alive and able to talk? And is the driver alive? ... Ken? Ken! Stop fucking snivelling, I thought you were a newsman... Alright, good, now get over there and find out: are the terrorists alive or dead?'

TWENTY-SEVENTH CHAPTER

WHEN it rolled down the verge, the bus had gouged a great brown swathe out of the ground above where it now lay. The corner of the roof that had plunged briefly into the soil had been crushed almost flat, bursting all the windows along the side that now faced the sky. Some passengers had been thrown clear and, as Ken slipped and stumbled down the steep slope from the car, he saw these figures lying in their own little elongated pools of shadow. Some rolled listlessly, others were still; and Ken inadvertently let out a soft moan. Even if he'd thought his first aid would do any good, there were too many for him to know where to begin.

He jogged clumsily across the grass, his limbs misbehaving, his tie flapping, towards the felled metal creature, and wished Dan had not hung back for wider shots, letting him go on alone. It was incongruous to see a bus on its side; it seemed larger than they usually did, like a dinosaur brought down in mid-stride. From the movies, he half-expected it to catch fire and explode, but in the tangled, broken black mess of pipes and shafts on the undercarriage he could see no spark;

only a reserve of thick oil gloopily emptying itself into the scraped earth.

This close, the bus was no longer silent. Through the irregular but constant whooshing of traffic on the motorway above him, he could make out voices. He ducked to see whether he could enter through the space where the front window had been. The aisle, turned through ninety degrees, looked tight and tiny, a crawl-space into a morgue. He noticed the driver's bruised corpse at his feet and recoiled, stumbling a few paces backwards. The driver was slumped on one arm, as if he'd thrown himself down for a snooze, and his snapped collarbone, strangely yellowed, jutted up through the cheap and shiny material of his uniform shirt. Ken spun away and looked back towards Dan, who was still keeping his distance. Ken tried to shout, but only a hoarse rasp came from his throat. He cleared it and tried again, 'Dan! Oi, Dan! How many wide shots do you even need? Get over here!'

Emboldened by anger, he turned back to the bus. Using its bent struts for footholds, he clambered up away from the dead driver and on to the bus's side. The panels felt thin and popped like the lids of jars under his hands and knees, but they held. From this gantry he looked down through the window-spaces into the bus's belly. Inside, it was already twilight. It seemed few people had been wearing seatbelts and each row of four formed an empty well-shaft at the bottom of which shifted and groaned the mixed-up bodies of the dead and injured.

Ken, feeling dizzy, carefully swivelled to shout back at Dan, but couldn't see him. He must have come closer, but Ken felt surreally alone beneath the sky. He gathered himself and crawled on. The bus was growing noisier; the survivors at the bottoms of these pits were beginning to cry out in pain.

He saw a porky middle-aged woman in a dress still strapped into her seat and dangling lifelessly from the belt. Someone who appeared to be her husband was standing on the lower seats and trying to free her. Looking up at Ken, his nose flattened and blood running down his chin from snapped teeth, he mangled the words: 'Help me get her out.' A terrible stink rose from the body and Ken knew the belt hadn't saved her. Unable to reply, he kept crawling, looking for the black cloth of a burqa.

He found them a few rows back, motionlessly tangled up at the bottom of a row with a young ginger man in a tracksuit. Ken kneeled upright, jimmied the phone from his pocket with trembling hands and told Geraldine. 'I've found them.'

'Well, are they alive?'

'I can't tell.'

'Go and have a better look then.'

Ken said nothing.

'Did you hear me, Ken? See what state they're in. There's no point just spotting them from across the room.'

'Yes. OK. I'm going.' The muscles in his arms and legs shivered. An urge to lie down dragged at him, to somehow get down on to the untouched grass and fall asleep on it. He looked down into the bus and then lowered himself inside.

Thinking he must not faint, he must not faint, or he would fall on to them, he climbed down the seats until his feet were beneath the aisle. The seatback he was standing on had been snapped like the man's teeth. There was no movement from the jumbled limbs below him, but from all around came sobs and voices and a smell that clogged his throat and made his diaphragm heave. He could see the sky above him, but did not climb back up to it. He manoeuvred himself until he could kneel in the wrecked aisle and reach down to the bodies.

He touched the fold of burqa nearest him and snatched his hand away wet. Warm blood had seeped through it. His hand began to shake, but he reached again and, quickly, before he could feel anything, pulled back the first black hood.

A few seconds later, in the newsroom, Geraldine cried, 'Dead! The terrorists are both dead!' And the newsroom exploded in relief. Sheer, plain relief swept away their unanswered questions about precisely who and what had been involved. The journalists whooped and raised their fists and shouted, 'Come on!' The *Beast* had struck back. Will banged his desk. Max and Jeremy nodded to each other with deep under-statement. Turkish Liz mimed a penis cumming into the air. Geraldine, her floral-patterned mobile held between ear and shoulder as she haphazardly banged all that Ken said into the computer, sang out again, 'They're girls! My giddy aunt, if they're involved with the others we might be on to a sort of jihadi Bonnie and Clyde. But with two Bonnies! Now chop-chop, Ken, come along – open their handbags and see if you can find their names; we're right on deadline.'

The Editor, with the unhindered speed of someone who now had only one course of action, had called for paper and was standing at the slanted Art desk, redrawing the pages. As the flashing pencil sliced clean lines across the sheets, he said: 'The splash will lead on the bus then go into the woman in Leicester – one story; a bus picture on the front – turning straight to two–three, where we have the burqa picture. All the other burqa spreads go one spread back. We're having five clear terror spreads now. Pages two–three-in-exile go on to twelve–thirteen with weather and lottery. On three we want information on the victims. Geraldine, Liz, we need names, ages, pictures in happier times, human details.

'Four–five is the dramatic interrogation plus raids on Bucklebury, not named. The old four–five, the Met's terror hunt, moves back whole on to six–seven. The new eight–nine is the burnt shopkeeper and the Great Muslim Debate. Drop the economist and the chief justice – get more from Ahmad and make it the Great Burqa Debate. She wants to say the burqa's a cloak for terror, a relic of medieval misogyny, and has no place in modern Britain; then our lefty civil-liberties campaigner wants to say that the state can't dictate what we wear, that individual liberty is the basis of a free Britain and that banning the burqa would be simply racist. Then the cricket smorgasbord moves back whole on to ten–eleven.'

Every instruction activated subs, designers, reporters, pairers, and the racket of production leapt into the air. Brython's staff shouted across one another:

'Weather and lottery on to page-two-in-exile, please!'

'Pervert pilot exposed needs a hundred-word trim!'

'Send that page, darling!'

'NIBs page is away! Forty-two is away!'

'Thirty-nine V-one, thirty-nine is coming again!'

'Anguish of the public-school rape victim goes to seventeen!'

'The terrorists' names are Farhana Rouhani and Begum Thorpe. One of our bonny bombers is married to a Brit. Get reporters on doorsteps – hop to it. We'll need family quotes for the second.'

'Frankenfish Oil in bold ragged, please! And put it above Cancer Risk for Macho Teens; make it all a Health sidebar.'

The squat bulk of the chief powered towards Max's Terror pod. 'Are you happier now, darlings? What did your uncle Frank tell you about people who fuck with the *Beast*?

But you may have noticed there's still a paper to get out. So pay attention.'

He slapped down a copy of his own flatplan, with the changes marked, and Max was already talking across him: 'Will, Art desk have filed the rag-outs to go next to your *Impartial* story – mastheads with a sentence or two under each. Check it all makes sense.'

The chief said, 'Copy's in for the Terror Hunt. Also the rewrites for the Great Muslim Debate are in.'

Max said, 'Jez, you know your tart in a burqa story is being grafted on to the splash, so you can leave that on the operating table for now.'

'OK, and I'm done with the interrogation.'

The chief told Max, 'Twelve–thirteen need a trim because they're getting a weather and lottery sidebar.'

'Where's the Cops with Guns copy? It happened hours ago.'

The chief shouted across to the Newsdesk. 'Sweethearts! Where are the Cops with Guns?'

'Right here! Just tidying it up.'

'Maximilian here can do that. Send it right over.'

Max said, 'So I'm waiting for that, the details of the bus victims, raids on Bucklebury and the splash.'

'And the Editor'll want us on time again tonight.' Max was already getting on with it. From his pocket, the chief pulled a sheet of quarter-folded A4 that had curved to the shape of his thigh. 'We're also having a sweepstake on how many dead on the bus. Count stops at midnight tonight; fiver entry, one guess, winner takes all. Who's in? Max?'

Max just said, 'They weren't all terrorists, Frank. Will, you've got five minutes for those mastheads. Then pick up both Muslim Debate pieces and get straight through them. Quick as you can.'

The chief said, 'Rosie, sweepstake?'

Rosie, from whom the terror was still draining away, just shook her head. She said to Max, 'I've finished the Kayani cricket story.'

The chief asked, 'Will?'

Will couldn't help grinning, but knew what Rosie would think of him if he took part, and said, 'I'm alright, thanks.'

'Jez? You're not a bleeding-heart greenhorn. You'll want in on the action.'

In the headiness of relief, Jeremy asked, 'What's the pot?'

'Already up to a hundred and twenty and Newsdesk want in as well.'

'A hundred and twenty?'

'Getting towards what one of these grunts gets paid for a shift, which isn't that much less than you.'

'Errm, what's everyone guessing?'

'I can't tell you that, young Jezuit! Not till you've guessed yourself. But come along, little Maxi here'll be getting impatient.'

Max was assigning copy as fast as he could and glared at Jeremy to hurry up.

'Alright then, I guess eighteen – no, seventeen.'

'I have to press you, sir, is seventeen your final answer?'

'No, eighteen. No, seventeen; definitely seventeen.'

'Excellent choice, darling. I'll collect later.'

Max needed to give someone the Met's Terror Hunt. The main run wanted only a few flicks of the scalpel, but the map was studded with boxes into which each chunk of copy – 'Police shoot Amir Mian'; 'Kayani sighted on waterfront' – would have to be finessed. It was ticklish and he sensed rather than noticed something false in it. Jez was busy; Will was busy. 'Rosie,' he said. 'Can you pick up the Terror Hunt spread?

Make sure you double check all the times are right. There's something fishy about them.' At least, he thought, always strategizing, if she fucked this up he would be rid of her.

He said, 'Jez, can you get this Dramatic Shootout out of the way so—'

His words were blown aside. The Editor had begun to inspect the pages towards the back of the book and his blood was up. 'Who the fuck drew this page?! Can't you *see*, man, that it's precisely the same shape as the one before? I don't give a fuck if it's just moved; this is a daily newspaper not a monthly magazine. If you can't stick the pace, then fuck off. Give me that pencil. I don't care if the page has gone, you'll have to get it back.'

The Editor's staff were warmed by his wrath. Having been in fear for their lives, they greeted these old terrors like old friends. After all, what did a tongue-lashing from the Editor mean but that everything was going back to normal? And between them buzzed the word that he'd released into the atmosphere: *hijack*. It spawned and multiplied, whirring from desk to desk – 'Do you think they hijacked it because they saw the pap?'; 'If someone decides to hijack a bus, you know there's nothing to stop them' – and these hijackings, each no more substantial than a breath, swarmed and filled the air, becoming incontrovertible in their ubiquity.

'Imagine being on a bus when it's hijacked; how fucking scary that must be.'

'Those poor bastards, just getting on a bus somewhere and then this.'

'It could have been any of us.'

'Well, it couldn't have been me. I'd've taken the train.'

'That would have been even worse, wouldn't it? And lucky, really, that it didn't happen on a busy street.'

They pulled together with the re-found strength of oarsmen who are pulling out of danger. Will's heart began to sing again yesterday's song of being one among many. Questions and answers sped between him, Max and Jeremy like the shuttle in the loom. He only wished that Rosie would be a part of it; she was leaning in to her screen as if trying to stare into its depths.

Behind him Geraldine was still on the phone to Ken, speaking extra loudly so the newsroom could follow what she was saying, like radio commentary on a lap of honour. 'Is Dan still getting shots of the survivors? Tell him to hurry; the pics won't make sense as a group if some of them are in the dark... And the driver's not dead, is he? Just unconscious. Can you wake the old dozer up? ... Oh alright, but if he doesn't shuffle off this mortal coil I want you to talk to him... Then go have a look who the others are... Look in their pockets; they must have something... They have credit cards, don't they, even in the north? ... I don't give two shits if you don't want to do it. How else do you suggest we find out who they are? ... And you'd better get on with it before the cops turn up and take you in for pinching watches, you old scallywag... Alright then, top man, quickly now... Gabriella Bagot, excellent. Liz, are you hearing this?'

Liz, feeling unusual affection for Geraldine, and indeed everyone around her, told her deputy: 'Get on Facebook, get on Google Images – we'll deal with copyright later. Gabriella Bagot, she's the first one. Headshots, age, job, survived by, some colour.'

Geraldine carried on speaking down the phone. 'Tim Thompson, is that Thompson with a *p*? ... Of Ashton-under-Lyne... then Colin Godfrey, of Skelmersdale... Paula O'Keeffe, of Ongar... God, who's ever heard of these ruddy places... Robert Connolly of Bolton – alright, we know that one.

Olivia Murphy, also of Bolton... Tristan Wellington – bit of a smart name, isn't it, for someone on a bus from Manchester. Where's he from? ... Devon?! Curiouser and curiouser. Maybe he's a QC having a torrid affair with a northern slapper. Is he wearing a wedding ring? ... Oh, there's a kid as well, *magnifique*! They don't carry ID, though, do they, more's the pity. Perhaps a library card? ... Oh, for Pete's sake don't get soppy; you've only got a few minutes... That's a good fellow... A bank card?! At his age? The way people spoil their children... Gary Connolly? So do we think he's the son of Robert Connolly and the woman, Murphy, the two of them living in sin? Were they all near each other? ... Right, right, but can you see a resemblance? Oh, I see, completely bashed in? How bloody tragic.'

While she spoke, the subs worked alert but calm, more concentrated and yet more detached than on a normal evening, with a kind of clean good hollowness like that after tears. And as night gathered around their bunker, just as it did, not so far away, around the living and the dying and the dead, they typed and trimmed and polished, categorizing the complex varieties of pain, disaster and wrongdoing into page lead and sidebar, spread and panel, headline, stand-first and picture caption.

Max revised Rosie's story about Kayani's English upbringing. Almost automatically he improved 'Kayani, the youthful suspect who has become a figurehead for the gang' to 'Kayani, the gang's baby-faced poster-boy'. He deleted her choice of pull-quote: 'He was never in trouble in school' and reverted to dummy copy – Thisisapullquotethisisapullqu – while he scanned the text. Then he wrote: 'The middle-class boy who hated Britain'.

He glanced up when in his peripheral vision he noticed

Geraldine jolt forward and say into the phone: 'Is it Thames Valley or the Met? They should know this is part of the Met's operation. There aren't any reporters with them? ... *Wunderbar*. There's nothing on the wires yet either, so no one else will have so much as a whisper of it in their first edition. Make yourself useful to the coppers, point out the would-be hijackers and see if you can extract some quotes... Yes, yes, we already have people going to their doorsteps... Alright, don't argue with them for now, is that all the names? ... So that's... sixteen, including the two hijackers. Is that right? Have you ticked off the bodies? ... So the count's at sixteen. By golly, what a splash!'

TWENTY-EIGHTH CHAPTER

'IT'S in! The splash is in, Maxi darling,' the chief shouted above the din of the newsroom. All around him, his colleagues were flying through their work. Their words formed themselves as quickly as they could type; their eyes were keen, their judgement certain, their hands swift and steady.

Even with less than half an hour to edition, Max did not simply bounce the splash copy onwards to Jez, but snatched a clear moment to sieve it through his mind. One reporter had written the top while another had started halfway down – and both were still filing paragraphs as they finished them. They'd adopted the *Beast*'s highest-flown register: 'innocent lives catastrophically interrupted', 'the fatal momentum of mistrust' and 'outbreaks of violence the length and breadth of England'.

They had a quote from a survivor of the bus's plunge: 'I didn't even see the hijacking; it was all so fast.' And their source, too, was still alive: 'They were suspicious; I knew it when they sat down. I told myself I was just being paranoid, but I wish I'd called earlier.'

Max said, 'Jez, the splash is yours. More pars coming as they're written. Where are you with the Dramatic Shootout and the Interrogation story?'

'Shootout is in... now. Interrogation just needs a couple of lines taken out of it.'

'But other than that it's ready to go?'

'All done.'

'I'll trim the fat then. You put it down and get into the splash.'

The layout kept shifting as Jeremy worked on the copy, the page reloading itself with slow computerized blinks every time Art desk displaced its columns. Photographs of the dead, cropped neatly square, were dropping into a four-by-four grid. To vary the design, the first box had been turned over to caption copy and the picture of that victim – Gary Connolly, twelve, of Bolton – had been enlarged to the same size as the grid and put alongside it. A pale, red-haired little boy, he was twisting away in disgusted glee as the young copper-and-cream spaniel he was holding tried to lick his face.

The Editor was striding towards them, his quarterdeck voice ringing out: 'News editors! Caraway, Gross, Feldstein, Murray, Thwaite, Enderling! How is it possible that no one has thought to write a splash headline?'

As the senior editors hurried to gather behind Max, the paper's South African lawyer unwillingly propelled himself once more into the ruckus. His sweat-slicked yellow hair stuck out from one side of his head, his twitching eye was squeezed shut and he was clutching a printout of all the Terror copy, on which he'd highlighted sentence after sentence in minatory orange. 'Excuse me,' he said, opening his eye long enough for it to spasm. 'Charles?'

The Editor glared down at him. 'What is it?'

Splaying his fingers across the uppermost sheet and forcing

himself not to gabble, the lawyer said: 'I'm just very concerned. First of all, in the splash, we're calling these two women – um, Farhana Rouhani and Begum Thorpe – terrorists, and accusing them of either deliberately crashing the bus or causing a fatal accident, but what evidence have we got to stand that up? I'm looking through the copy, but other than an assertion from—'

'Haven't you been taught the first principles of the law? They're dead, and you can't libel the dead. How on earth have you managed to keep a job on a national newspaper without even knowing that?'

'Yes, but it just takes one person to complain to IPSO about irresponsible—'

'One person? Can you comprehend how many people are going to read this newspaper tomorrow?'

The chief was calling out, 'Thirty-one, V-one, thirty-one is away!' Max spoke to his pod: 'Will, in Cops with Guns, he says he's twice had to pull the trigger in the line of duty. Is that two shots in one incident or two incidents with an unspecified number of shots?'

Will spoke without ceasing to type. 'Two incidents. An armed robbery and then a suicidal City worker.'

'Good. Rosie, where's the Terror Hunt?'

'There's something wrong with the times. It doesn't make sense.'

'Then get the reporter over. Unless you want the reader to think we can't even get that right.'

Rosie flinched and spun out of her chair towards the Newsdesk.

The lawyer was saying, '… and in particular some of the details in the Interrogation story, where we're talking about Choudry's injuries.' He read highlighted phrases from the printout. '"One bullet clipped the bone in his upper arm, spraying chips through the surrounding tissue" or, here, "punctured his liver, leading to internal bleeding that—"'

Geraldine interrupted: 'Sounds as if he's got off pretty lightly.'

'The point is that this is obviously confidential medical information. I just – how did we? – there's nowhere this could have come from except his doctors and medical records.' He despairingly held up a sheet on which paragraph after paragraph had been orange-highlighted. 'It's not even just that it's confidential, and the potential for fines – I don't know how we got it, but it's not just that; there might well be grounds to argue, when it comes to trial, that all this would be prejudicial. Printing this could mean that when this guy's in court, the case is thrown out for—'

The Editor's voice went off like a depth charge: 'For FUCK's sake! Keep the *fuck* up. The same news lines are all over the BBC. This isn't a moot you're in now. We *will* print the truth, and if our justice system turns out to be so catastrophically mismanaged that this murderer goes free, we will hold them to account.'

The lawyer looked up at him doggedly, as if about to make another objection. But then the tension went out of him as if out of a rope gone slack. He rotated very slowly, as though he might fall, and reeled away between the desks.

The Editor said, 'Good.' He would concern himself with legalities tomorrow. 'You men' – he included Geraldine in that – 'haven't you written the front page yet? And why haven't I been shown the other pages?'

One of the pairers hurried across with a loose sheaf of printed A3 drooping over his arm. 'Stand there!' commanded the Editor, and the pairer held up the sheets as if on a tray. The Editor inspected each at arm's length while beside him his advisers tried to write the front-page headline. '16 dead in terror crash'; '16 killed in terror hijacking'. The pages to which the Editor had no objection he let fall, and they draped themselves like loyal hounds over his feet. But, on the others, he reworded headlines, swapped pictures and adjusted the text with his unerring ear for the true voice of the *Beast*. Each time he did, the chief shouted 'Kill twenty-four!' or 'Hold eighteen!' and the pairers picked up the direct phone to the presses and said, 'Kill twenty-four! Twenty-four is coming again. Twenty-four, V-one.'

Trying to block all this out, Rosie questioned Ben, the pudgy reporter, who was looking at her screen: 'It says here that the police caught Kayani's cousin hiding under his car at 10:18 this morning.'

'That's right.'

'But that can only have happened after they interrogated Kayani's brother.'

'Yes, he tipped them off.'

'Then how can they have only raided the Kayani family house at 11:35?'

'That's definitely right; I got it straight from the police who were there.'

'But how can they have arrested the cousin before they got the tip-off?'

'Oh, I see what you mean. Let me just check.'

He flipped open his notebook and ran his eye across the squiggles and hieroglyphs of his shorthand, which he always found difficult to read back. Rosie wiped her palms on her thighs and flicked her gaze at the clock. Somehow it had jumped forward. Eleven minutes to deadline. The chief called out, 'Page sixteen! Sixteen is away!' They were almost at the Terror pages. She tried to calmly reread the text on her screen.

Max, noticing her look up, said, 'Rosie, where's that spread?'

'It's almost there, just sorting the times.'

'Get it in. That spread's got to go. Will, so does that comment piece.'

'I'm just putting it down. Do we have a style on hijab?'

'On what?'

'Hijab – the headscarf rather than the burqa.'

'Our style is headscarf.'

'OK, done. The story's in revise.'

'So you're clear?'

'Yes.'

'Jez, do you need him?'

'Yep, Will, can you check the name of the police force in Luton?'

The chief appeared and said, 'Max, sweetheart, Newsdesk have got quotes from the slag they wrapped in a burqa. I've assigned it to the page as an add.'

Max ran his hand once, quickly, over the gelled furrows in his hair. 'What's in it?'

'Nothing to change the angle, and not exclusive. Just a statement with reaction, but it's good.'

'OK. Jez, that has to go in high up. Will, check names and facts.'

Will snapped back the answers as he found them, thrilling to his own ability to hold its pace.

The Editor told his advisers: 'I want this headline written. What have you got?'

Max brought up the front page on his screen and, while they tried, carried on revising his pod's copy in a window at the bottom. The numbers called out by the chief were falling rapidly towards the front of the book. Without looking up,

Max said, 'Rosie, I need that story. Do what you have to do. Put it down now.'

Rosie wasn't putting it down, but Max had to switch back to typing the headline attempts that came from the group behind him:

**16 DEAD IN
NEW JIHADI
ATROCITY**

It was far too vague, but still the Editor was not wholly displeased. It had the solid ring of hard news: sixteen dead in a terror attack on British soil and the *Beast* was breaking the story in print. While he considered, questions flickered quickly around the pod. Will told Jez: 'It's Bedfordshire Police.'

'Not Constabulary?'

'They used to be called that, now Police.'

'And the burnt shopkeeper's from Luton?'

'A part called Bury Park, where the Muslims live. Bury with a *u*.'

'Age?'

'Forty-eight.'

Max said, 'In the pro-Muslim comment piece, are all burqas banned in France?'

'Anything that covers the face. So hijabs are OK.'

Will laughed with the elation of making jokes right on deadline and Rosie asked her reporter again, 'But how can they have gone after the cousin before they got the tip-off?'

He pushed his glasses up his snub nose and shrugged. 'Maybe they got another tip-off from someone else.'

Rosie's fingers had leaked a grubby curve on to the keys and the mouse. It was as if there was a bubble trapped in her throat that stopped her breathing. In her head the only words she could form were, 'If they can't even get that right; if they can't even get that right...' and out loud she said, 'But that doesn't make any sense!'

'We're right on deadline; can't we just fudge it?'

She almost shrieked, 'I know we're on deadline! There's no way to fudge it. It's all about the times. Can you check your notes again? Maybe there's a—'

The Editor was saying, 'Now show it to me with the picture of the bus. That's it. Now what's the line?'

Thwaite suggested: 'Is it:

**16 KILLED AS
FIGHTING BREAKS
OUT ACROSS THE
BRITISH ISLES ?'**

'Too many words,' said the Editor. 'And it makes it sound like an enormous fucking bar brawl. No, it's:

**16 KILLED
AS BRITISH
CIVIL WAR
BREAKS OUT '**

'Civil war?' said Thwaite. 'But we had war on the cover this morning.'

'Armed gangs on patrol, women beaten and forced into burqas, two people shot, a man burnt alive, sixteen killed by the other side, an attempted invasion of our compound – if it's not a war, what the fuck would you call it?'

Geraldine spoke up: 'Should we have eighteen killed in the

headline, with the shopkeeper and the one the cops popped this morning?'

'No, it's too confusing. What it wants is a strap underneath explaining that—'

And Max said: 'Now, Rosie, I need that story right now. Just put it down if you can't finish it.'

'I'm almost there, just a—'

And Will said to Jez: 'That cross-head about Rouhani, Terror Family – might it not make readers assume the two on the bus are actually related to the original four, especially because—'

'What should it be then?'

'Terror Network.'

Max said: 'Change it.'

The pages were being sent one right behind the other. The outer desks had already reached the stillness after deadline. The first of the Terror spreads went, the chief calling it out exultantly, 'Ten–eleven V-two! Ten–eleven is away!'

And Rosie, the pressure in her mind almost intolerable, broke through. 'It just can't be right. It must have been 11*p.m.* when he tipped them off. It must have been the night before.'

The reporter's podgy cheeks blew out and he said, 'Oh yeah, sorry, it was 11p.m., not a.m. It was the night before.' And as she saw it, the error became absurdly small.

'Definitely?'

'Yes, definitely. That's my mistake. Good spot.'

'Rosie,' said Max. 'Right now!'

'I've just sorted it. Give me a minute to tidy it up.'

'You've got thirty seconds.'

The chief called out, 'Eight–nine V-three coming now.' And the pairers called back, 'Eight–nine V-three.'

'Eight–nine is away!'

The Editor asked Max, 'What's still to go?'

'Splash, Interrogation, Terror Hunt. Interrogation is just going.'

The chief called out, 'Four–five is away! Six–seven and the splash still to come.'

The Editor was reading the splash over Max's shoulder. He pointed at the photo of Gary Connolly with the spaniel clambering over him. 'Why is that dog not named in the caption? The readers want to know the name of the dog.'

Turkish Liz, caught out, looked at her staff. 'Get the dog's name.' Six picture researchers reached for their keyboards and their phones.

Max said, 'Rosie, no more time. Put it down or I'll push you out of it.'

'OK, it's done, it's down.'

Max's eye touched the headline, stand-first, captions, date-lines over the boxes. 'Are these times right? I'm going to send it.'

'Yes, they're right.'

Max sent the page and in the same instant two picture researchers cried together: 'Teddy!' One went on, 'The dog's name is Teddy.'

Max wrote it in, then zoomed out so the Editor could see the whole spread on the screen.

'Alright,' said the Editor. 'Send it.'

Max pressed Send, the chief glanced over it, pressed Send and called out, 'Pages one–two–three. The splash is coming over!'

They were late, by a minute or so, when the pairer called into the enormous quiet, 'One, two, three are gone. We're off stone. The paper's away.' Rosie expelled a long cataract of pressurized air. Salt had crystallized at her temples, her fingers were shaky, sweat was going cold on her back and she'd have to throw away her blouse because of the stains under the arms, but she felt that she'd finally earned her seat.

TWENTY-NINTH CHAPTER

THAT night, once the reactions of the victims' families had been incorporated into the second edition, along with the news that a seventeenth victim, Nicola Dillon, had died in an ambulance on the way to hospital, and once some immediate details from the police raids on the Rouhani and Thorpe houses had been incorporated into the third, and the paper finally put to bed, the *Beast*'s staff celebrated. With the reckless confidence that came from having withstood to victory, they persuaded the chief to take hold of the heavy circular handle sealing the door to the outside, and unseal it. They filled the narrow corridor behind him, a shifting, agitated mass, giggling and hushing each other as he turned the smooth mechanism hand over hand. Invisible steel rods withdrew from their tubes in the opposite wall and the big door cracked open on a soundless hinge.

The chief swung the door inwards on its pivot, walking backwards, and waved the horde past him, cackling, 'Fly, my pretties, fly!' They shuffled through and, once past the bottleneck, sprayed into the soft outside air. The floodlighting on the tarmac tapered their shadows into long thin streaks and they waved their arms as they crossed it before slipping under the trees into velvety, welcoming darkness.

The living woods around them breathed out the scents of bark, sap, moss and mulch, moist soil turned by feet and the sweetness expelled by flowers as they closed. As Rosie swaggered beside Will, they sucked up the summer-night feeling of warmth after dark and, when she stumbled over a root, she grabbed his arm not at all accidentally.

The *Beast*'s staff set up in a spot where the susurrant canopy above them gave way and the stars dangled just out of reach like heavy fruit. White moonlight fell across the top of the clearing, illumining the trunks on one side and cutting across the journalists' shoulders as they moved in and out of it. Someone had brought a surprisingly loud iPod speaker loaded with fifties rock 'n' roll and Features had contributed a motley collection of drinks they'd discovered inside one of the storerooms: bottles of brandy, vermouth and Campari whose faded labels carried outdated designs.

Rosie swigged from a spherical bottle of Chambord and talked over Will. She wanted to talk, to talk and talk, to let run free the words and thoughts leaping lightly out of her. She wanted to drink more and have more of everything – more cigarettes, more brandy – and to tell again the story of how she'd punched her way through to deadline. When she told the part where the reporter blithely, maddeningly, said, 'Maybe someone different tipped them off,' she laughed with the heartiness of someone who'd come unscathed from a brawl.

Will was bewitched by her. He watched her small slight figure sway and gesture in the dark and wished that they were alone together in the woods. He wanted to touch her somehow, on the arm perhaps, but before he could gather the courage the music changed and she grabbed his hand and said, 'Come on, let's dance.'

The younger, looser-limbed journalists spun each other while the boulder shapes of the older stalwarts stood around the edges in groups. They gave facetious advice to those stacking up brushwood for a fire and debated whether the Editor would be investigated for triggering the hijack.

The chief bustled into the ring. He'd been to make another inspection of the damaged fence and returned ebulliently convinced that the terrorists responsible would be hunted down in the morning. Spotting Jeremy loitering next to Max on the edge of a conversation, he homed in, spreading his arms and crying, 'Look who it is! Tonight's champion – the man with the talent for terror, the bane of the bombers, the jinx of the jihadis, the hammer of Boko Haram, the defeater of al-Qa-eeda, Mr Jeeeeremy Underwoooood!' While the others laughed and looked over, Jeremy tried not to sag; he knew what was coming.

The chief clapped him meatily on the shoulder, announcing, 'Seventeen dead! Beautifully done, Mr Underwood; the sweepstake is yours. Two hundred and fifteen pounds, ladies and gentlemen, so let's have a cheer for the hack with the direct line to Jihad HQ, the man who knows where Osama Bin Laden is really buried, and what really happened on—'

'Listen, Frank. I'm alright actually. Give it to someone else.' Jeremy lit a cigarette.

'What are you on about?' The chief pulled out a thin fold of banknotes. Jeremy could barely distinguish them in the dark, but the chief began counting the notes from one hand to the other. 'Twenty–forty–sixty–eighty–a hundred. One-twenty, one-forty, one-sixty, one-seventy, one-eighty, one-ninety, two hundred. And three fivers.' He splayed these like playing cards, then put them back on the pile and held it out towards Jeremy. 'That's more than you'd get for a freelance shift, isn't it?'

'I don't want it.'

'What do you mean, you don't want it?'

Jeremy couldn't help thinking it was unfair; plenty of others had placed bets as well. It was typical of his luck that he'd actually won. 'I just don't want it. Give it to someone else. Who came second?'

'It's a sweepstake, Jez, there is no second place. Winner takes all.'

'Then whoever was closest. Or give it to charity or something.'

'Charity? What do you think this is, the Women's Institute?'

'No,' he said. 'It's just, I just don't want it.' He pulled on his cigarette, the circular smoulder at its end flaring and drawing closer.

The chief understood and became derisive. 'Oh, don't want to take the nasty cash because the nice people got hurt? It doesn't have any actual blood on it, if that's what you're squeamish about. It's been used to buy newspapers and pints and now you're going to use it to buy petrol or more fags or whatever you want.'

'Nah, no thanks.'

'Get a present for your kids then. Two girls, isn't it?' Jeremy did not want the chief talking about his daughters. 'Nice little present or something, 'cause their dad's been away.'

'Listen, Frank, I—'

'They must be sad without their daddy. They must be worried about him. They probably—'

'Fine.' Jeremy cut him off. 'Fine. Give it here.' He reached for the wad, but the chief crowed 'Yoink!' and jerked it away from his fingers.

Jeremy would not play the game of grabbing at it, but simply held out his hand until the chief, after a couple of feints, put the money on his palm. The chief made as if to headlock him and said, 'Always got a gripe about something, eh, Jez? What are you doing tomorrow morning? We should have a talk.'

Jeremy wasn't listening. His mind was full of the greasy feel of the banknotes between his fingers. He saw in his mind the pictures that had come through of the bus lying on its side like a shot racehorse, with bodies of its passengers strewn around, some already in bags. He decided to call his wife.

Managing to escape from the chief, he stumbled out of the circle and into the denser dark beneath the trees. Hidden twigs leapt to catch his arm or touch his cheek, ferns brushed his ankles and every few moments he re-blinded himself by staring into the luminous rectangle of his phone screen. There was no signal. He blundered around a little longer, swearing less and sighing more, until he gave up. His foot had knocked into a recumbent log and, after using the glow of his phone to inspect the wood for sliminess, he sat down.

He dejectedly lit another cigarette and let the darkness around him settle. The dim shapes of tree trunks and thick branches detached themselves from the surrounding blackness. He thought of taking the banknotes from his pocket and flinging them into the night, which would swallow them as if they'd never been. But it seemed a melodramatic thing to do.

He wished he'd been able to get through to Louise. He could have told her about it if it had been right away, but now he knew he wouldn't. Especially because it was rare for her to think highly of what he did all day; and this bus disaster wasn't, as it were, unconnected from his miraculous spot. If he was honest with himself, the crash and his great moment – it was all of a piece. He just wished he hadn't won the sweepstake. But the story itself was good, he had to remember that. There might be some pretty tasteless humour in the newsroom, and this sweepstake was about as bad as he'd seen, but he had to remember that that was just the noise that happened while something important was being done. It was about stopping terrorism, people being killed on buses or in tube trains like on 7/7. It wasn't just about him.

Eventually, through being chewed over and over, these thoughts lost their sharpness. He wished Max were here. Sighing again, he heaved himself to his feet and wondered unconnectedly how long he'd been sitting here. He could still hear voices and, no longer needing to hold out his hand as a bumper, shuffled his way back towards the others. As he approached, he caught the scent of smoke and saw rich orange light splashing through the irregular wooden pillars, casting behind them flickering poles of shadow.

His colleagues, even some of the older, more curmudgeonly ones, were dancing around the fire. While the iPod on the tree stump played 'Shake Your Tail Feather', Will and Rosie were doing the twist, miming snorkelling and swimming while they gazed happily at each other. Max had his elbows tucked into his sides and was waggling his bottom back and forth like a happy duck. His eyes were closed in the easy satisfaction of a man who knows he is going to be promoted. The chief, his squat bulk hunched forward like an ape's, was dancing the mashed potato. Geraldine, a bottle of rum in one out-flung hand, was teaching Turkish Liz a kind of wild hornpipe, which Liz, her arms held stiff above her head, embellished with pseudo-Cypriot flourishes. The only person actually bent over and shaking his tail feather was the South African lawyer, who had had a lot of crème de menthe and appeared to be crying.

Jeremy did not dance and did not want to. He found a stumpy bottle of Glengarry whisky and sat down heavily with his back to a tree. When the song finished, Max came over and carefully sat down on the ground next to him, panting a little. Neither spoke but, by the time the bottle had gone to and fro between them, Jeremy felt that it was alright; he was no worse than anyone else, maybe even a little better, and Max was the most loyal friend a man could ask for.

Back in the bunker, standing truly alone but habituated to his solitude, the Editor inspected himself in the mirror. He was stripped to the waist and rubbing Vaseline into the livid marks that the underarm holster had chafed into the side of his ageing chest. The pistol itself gleamed dully on the porcelain backboard of the sink. Folded up beside it was a water-spotted print-off of the *Brute*'s front page; they'd got an exclusive interview with the tart forced into a burqa. His own paper was so far ahead that he could be pleased there was life in the old *Brute* yet.

He'd read the interview through while on the phone to the prime minister, whom he'd counselled to take firm action and reassure the frightened populace – but not to violate the Englishman's ancient liberties. After all, this wasn't Germany, or Russia. Upon hearing this warning, the PM had called him 'statesmanlike' and asked whether he would consider accepting a peerage; Brython wondered whether this slick little City boy had ever seen a real statesman.

He worked the sticky jelly into the mottled red outline

of the holster straps and asked his conscience about the 'hijacking'. Had those women really been about to hijack the bus? Perhaps the police now interrogating their families would discover something but, in truth, he doubted it. No one would ever know for sure. But he was sure that the crash had been precipitated by the *Beast*. He asked his conscience: had he done wrong?

The answer came straight back: no, he had not. There was a war on, between Christian England, the Christian West, and the forces of barbaric Islamism. The attacks were only the most obvious aspect; there were the burqas, the child brides, the oriental ghettoes, the honour killings, the fanaticism – all that was not the real England. Those foreign horrors had to be kept out, along with those who bore them. Shakespeare had said it best: that the English Channel was supposed to serve as a wall against the envy of less happy lands.

Did that mean his own personal conscience was unstained? No. It was stained alright, stained and spattered. But it was the duty of the strong to suffer those stains, like crusaders who had to break the commandment against killing. The taking on of sin was one sacrifice among many, gladly given. And sacrifice was ennobling. He would accept the peerage. He would use it, as he did everything, for the public good.

Some of this public was at that moment gathered at the Cottage Inn, condemning Brython's beloved *Beast*. One of the policemen who'd been on duty at the compound – and was from Bucklebury himself – relayed what those hypocrites were up to now: they'd unsealed the doors and were having a party outside, with no regard for the terrorists it might attract, not to mention the obvious stupidity of building a fire in the middle of a wood. And even that wasn't all of it: when Chris, the night commander, had asked them nicely – very nicely, even – to put it out and go back inside, that same vicious little foulmouthed fat man who'd been making trouble in the pub had told him to F-off and go back to patrolling the fence.

The landlord gave the judgment he'd been refining to his patrons all afternoon and evening: 'They're not worthy to be called a British newspaper. To speak the way they did to me, to someone who's served this country, served against the IRA. And the way they treated Ayub as well, it's unacceptable.'

Ayub, who had not, as it turned out, gone home after the subs' visit and had now heard this many times, lifted his half-pint to pre-empt any more praise.

Gilbert clapped him cautiously on the shoulder and said, 'Really, though, it was disgraceful.' They'd all lied to the police on Ayub's behalf and said that he'd gone home to Thatcham, making Gilbert feel a little like someone bravely hiding a Jew from the Gestapo. But things still weren't quite right between them. 'The way they got us all riled up, that's their stock in trade, isn't it?' He didn't quite dare ask Ayub whether he agreed, so directed himself to the landlord. 'Really, Barry, it's not right. Why *don't* we get the police back and tell them the whole story?'

The landlord shook his head dismissively. 'There's no point bothering the lads in blue. They're handcuffed themselves.'

The off-duty policeman put in, 'You should see what it's like in there. Their Editor says, "Do this," and we all have to do it. They've got us right in their pocket. It's fucking embarrassing.'

The landlord said, 'And the thing is, too, they haven't technically committed any crimes. The law's got nothing to say against someone being a nasty piece of work.'

It was now that Adrian, the editor of the *Thatcham and Newbury Echo & Advertiser*, made the move he'd been planning: 'Barry's right. It's not criminal charges that deal with this sort of thing; it's exposure to public scrutiny, letting people know what they're really like.'

There was a lot of nodding. 'If people knew what they're really like,' said Gilbert, 'they wouldn't be in Trafalgar Square saying they're *Beast* readers, that's for sure. They'd never buy it again. I'm certainly never going to.'

'*You* should do it,' the landlord told Adrian. 'Put it on the front page of the *Echo*.'

'I'd like to, I'd like to very much,' he said, feeling as brilliantly Machiavellian as the great Charles Brython himself. 'But I don't know if there's quite enough on them.'

'Not enough on them? Were you in the loos or something when they were in here?'

Adrian wobbled his head non-committally. 'I was listening,' he said. 'But they'd just say it was a bit of arguing in a pub and everyone would think it's only natural that they're a bit wound up – and who's to say what really happened.'

'Who's to say?' The landlord was almost speechless. 'It was more than a bit of arguing! It was more than... And you saw what they did to Ayub!'

The others were pained.

'I did, Barry, I did. But to really get them, to really show people the truth – we'd have to get inside the building. If that was doable.' There was a fluttering inside Adrian's ribcage as he waited for the right person to speak.

'They've gone and opened the door themselves,' the policeman said defiantly. 'You can walk right in. Along with any terrorists you meet on the way.'

'Won't I get stopped?'

'Not if I took you.'

'Would that be alright, to take me and him?' He jerked his thumb at his young colleague, Gavin, who'd badly twisted his ankle falling from the *Beast*'s perimeter fence. He was sleeping it off on a narrow banquette behind one of the tables.

The guard thought for a while and then said, 'Fuck it. As long as you say you just sneaked in yourselves. If they're stupid enough to leave the door open, they should get what's coming to them.'

The landlord, impressed, said, 'Good man, Dave.'

Gilbert felt too overwrought by this drama to say anything, but picked up his pint in approval.

Not long afterwards, Dave finished his pint and didn't ask for another. Adrian put his laptop in a cupboard in the kitchen for safe keeping. Gavin was woken up, tetchy and needing the loo. And then once they'd all had a quick but solemn nip of whisky on the house, and Adrian had shaken hands with everyone, the three intruders set off down the dark lane towards the chink that the chief had opened in the armour of the *Beast*.

THURSDAY

THIRTIETH CHAPTER

'WAKEY, wakey, sleeping Jezzy,' whispered the chief from very close by, and Jeremy jerked into consciousness, his eyes popping open then squinting in the bleak overhead light. He swallowed and blinked, sliding towards the wall and away from the chief's ogre-ish head. Everyone else in the dorm was still asleep. Wrapping the thin orange duvet more tightly around his bulbous torso, he mumbled, 'It's not time yet.'

'Oh, but it is time, Rip van Jezzle. I've got a job just for you.'

Jeremy's hangover was descending on him. He probed it like a painful tooth. It hurt. 'Can't you get the grunts to do it?'

The apparently un-resting, unrelenting chief displayed no trace of having recently been held in the humane softness of sleep. His striped blue shirt was fresh; his paisley tie kinked as ever where it met the bulge of his gut. It was as if last night's bacchanal had never happened. If anything, he looked pleased with himself. 'This one's all yours, jammy old Jeremy, so get the fuck up.'

Jeremy rolled face-first on to the pillow and groaned into it. 'Alright,' he said. 'Just let me have a shower first.'

'Good lad. The block's at the end of the corridor. Meet you back here in twenty minutes.'

'What time is it now?'

'Seven thirty.'

'Oh, fucking hell, Frank. Half seven? Can't I have another hour? What time did we even come inside last night?'

'Twenty minutes, showered and shaved. Or those greedy reporters will have eaten all the breakfast.'

Although Jeremy was reasonably sure that the canteen wouldn't let that happen, the suggestion did add an irritating anxiety to his hangover. He waved the chief away, so he wouldn't see his vest and boxer shorts, and clumsily lowered himself down the stepladder.

In the shower's heat and steam and noise, he supported himself with a hand splayed against the cool tile and let the water rush over his head and down his swollen belly. He wished it could spray straight into his skull and rinse it out like a mug. His throat burnt and his lips pinched: he'd smoked too much last night and he could feel the black fog sitting in his lungs like a gas in a jar. At least that slight disgust postponed the moment when he would have to find out whether it was possible to go outside and smoke today.

He waited for the paracetamol to seep into his headache and saw again what he realized he'd been watching in his head overnight: the dead little ginger boy with his dog, freed by Jeremy's mind to play outside the picture's edges. But Jeremy had not killed him. He was not responsible. Some shame settled on every man, just from having to live, and if you tried to brush it off it would only hang in the air and settle again.

He met the chief outside the dorm and trudged dutifully where he led, uninterested in where they were going. His cheeks were tight where he'd scraped off his stubble. He'd realized while shaving that he needed a new blade and hadn't brought any. As he wondered how long they would stay here, he felt something flat and compact in his pocket. The sweep-stake money. It was only money. Every tenner in England must have been involved in something untoward at some point – drug deals, paying for sex, or even just... The chief brought him up short. 'Why's that door open?'

Jeremy stared unthinkingly at the door in question. It angled a few inches from the frame and all that could be seen through the gap was the darkness of an unlit room.

The chief said, 'If some intoxicated hack has been at the stores, he'd better hope the jihadis get to him before I do.' He swung the door to the side and clicked the switch. Light jumped into the room and showed broad grey metal shelves bending slowly under boxes of blocky olive-green torches, of batteries, portable radios, signal flares. There were blister-packs holding Swiss Army knives, tough jugs of bleach, sheaves of Ordinance Survey maps with a tray of compasses beside them. Further down were first-aid kits, anti-radiation tablets, tin-foil blankets. On the lowest shelf were hazmat suits, neatly folded so the air-filtering masks were at the top and the attached rubber boots dangled off the front. Two of these had been put on the floor and the centre of each loosened heap of fabric had been crumpled by a round object.

Jeremy asked, 'Have people been sleeping in here?'

'Looks that way, doesn't it, Jezebell-end?'

The chief squatted beside where the sleepers must have lain, inspecting the concrete. Where their feet might have been, he pointed out: 'Mud. See that? Probably doing more than sleeping. Sexual congress, by the look of things.' With prudish disgust, he stood up out of his squat, wobbling slightly with the effort. 'Must have come in last night after the party that never happened. It might have been those two grunts from your pod; did you see them cosying up to each other in front of the fire that was never lit?'

Jeremy could hardly imagine or remember such exuberance of desire that you would sleep on a concrete floor rather than in a bed. It reminded him that he hadn't got through to Louise last night and that she'd be worried and angry when he finally did. He didn't give two shits whether someone had slept in here or not.

The chief gingerly tipped the sullied suits into an upright plastic barrel in the corner of the room and slapped the dirt off his hands. 'Nasty,' he said. 'Bet it was those grunts.'

'Maybe,' said Jeremy. 'The kid was in his bunk this morning, though, wasn't he?'

'True.'

They spoke no more until they'd gone up a flight of echoing stairs to the first floor and into the canteen. It was small, almost perfectly square, and loud with the scraping and clanging of cooking, crockery and talk. Along one side was a serving hatch where canteen staff in hairnets and white jackets tilled their patches of yellow egg or glistening sausage. They reminded Jeremy of the Muslim kid from the pub, who must still be out there somewhere. The thought didn't make him feel any better.

He took a tray and a *Beast* from their respective stacks and slid them along the metal rails while reading the front page:

**17 KILLED
AS BRITISH
CIVIL WAR
BREAKS OUT**

Strong headline, he thought with gloom. The body count had been updated for the later editions, and the picture was like a punch to the solar plexus: the smashed bus lying on its side with night falling around it; tangled metal, torn grass, zipped-up body bags. It was one of the best front pages he'd ever seen, let alone worked on.

He sighed and loaded up a plate with as much fried food as it could carry. His stomach churned but he clambered through the seats to one opposite the chief. They ate for a while, the chief reading the Burqa Bombings spreads and Jeremy turning his paper over to look at Sport. He let the salty, fatty food absorb his hangover and his thoughts. Once the chief had checked over all the News pages, marking infelicities for which subs would be reprimanded later, he folded the paper and quietly said, 'So, Jez.'

'Yeah, Frank, why the fuck are we up so early?'

'The Editor wants everyone, subs included, in the newsroom soon as. And I've got to give you your special assignment before the others start crawling all over everywhere.'

'How can there be any subbing to do now? The reporters haven't even written anything yet.'

'Keep your voice down.'

Jeremy glanced around. There were plenty of others eating at the long tables, alone or in groups, but none of their people. 'Why?'

'The job I've got for you's not here.'

Jeremy understood at once, and lowered his voice. 'You mean it's at the *Fun*?'

'Clever girl.'

'What is it?'

'You know I'm going to be production editor over there, a back-bench job?'

Jeremy nodded.

'Well...' The chief leant his bulk conspiratorially closer. 'My first task is to appoint a deputy production editor. It's a good gig, Jez. Matching the pages, making sure they get sent properly, keeping the pairers right, that sort of thing. You could do it even more deeply asleep than you are here. And the best thing is they do a nine-day rota, so you only have to work about half the number of evenings. Rest of the time, you get out at five o'clock. And because it's in London Bridge, it'll be nearly an hour off your commute.'

The possibility of actually getting out of the *Beast* awoke in Jeremy. But he stayed sceptical. 'How's that possible, leaving at five? Don't the pages all still go in the evening?'

'Yeah, except this job – these jobs – are to oversee production for the online and digital editions as well: iPad, smartphones, all that stuff. They want to...' The chief clasped his strong fat hands around each other. 'Bring it all together.'

'But I don't know anything about all that.'

'You don't have to. It's the easiest thing in the world; it's not even really journalism. All you've got to do is copy and paste and then make things fit. Or not even that, because these kids they've got making the editions do the copying and pasting for you. What they want old lags like you and me for is to keep an eye on them and make sure they don't lose their little minds and start writing "gherkin" instead of "Gurkha" or "minge" instead of "minister".'

'So you'd be teaching them as well.'

The chief nodded, conceding that. 'But you'd like that. I bet you liked it on the *Sentinel*, showing the rookies the ropes.'

Jeremy conceded in turn. 'Mmhmm.'

'And you get on with the whippersnappers we've got here.'

'Yeah, I suppose, but what's the money like over there?'

'For you, about the same, maybe a smidgen more. For me, untold riches, darling. Enough to go private when I start slobbering into my bib.'

Jeremy waggled his head. This was all so much to think about. 'What do you want *me* to do it for?'

'Jesus, Jez.' The chief sat up away from him, then swooped back again to hiss: 'What the fuck's wrong with you? You should be saying, Thanks, Frank; you've really looked out for me on this one. Where do I sign? When print goes under, half the lifers in here'll be coming to you to beg for shifts.'

Jeremy did like that idea. But he wasn't going to let anyone talk any lightness into him. He scooped a row of beans with his fork, pronged a roundel of sausage and lifted this load carefully to his mouth.

'Also...' The chief leant yet closer, his tie almost making contact with his plate. 'You hate it here. You've hated it for years. You've gone too soft for it. You don't enjoy it any more. You haven't even really enjoyed everything that's happened in the past couple of days. For me it's different. I don't want to stay and watch the old girl get put down. Might get jealous.'

The chief had run slightly astray of his point and they both looked at their plates. Jeremy said, 'The job does sound good.'

'Good? What more do you want? And your boss'll be your old pal Frank, who'll let you get away with murder in memory of many happy years on the *Beast*.'

There was another pause, in which only Jeremy looked at his plate. The chief asked, 'Well, should I tell them you want it?'

Reluctance to answer anything at all drew Jeremy's words out slowly. 'I don't know, Frank.'

'What don't you know?'

Jeremy was so tired; and this all just seemed like so much

hassle. He would probably be just as tired somewhere else. Things were more or less the same everywhere, weren't they? Even if what was happening in front of your eyes shifted and changed, it was all still just sound and light, a projection of fuzzy images like that on to the back wall of the newsroom. And behind the pictures there was only the cold wall, concrete and immutable.

'I don't know,' he said again. 'This story, you know, I don't like to say it, Frank, but I'm a pretty big wheel in it, aren't I? I might finally get promoted.'

The chief was flabbergasted. He went to speak but no words came and he soundlessly shut his mouth again, like a great greedy fish. Then he asked, 'What the fuck?'

Jeremy shrugged helplessly. All he wanted was for the chief not to be talking to him.

'Promoted to what? You think they'll give you chief sub ahead of Max?'

'No, no, of course not.'

'And you can tell your greasy little pal from me that I don't care what he does after I'm gone but he can keep in his place while I'm still here.'

Jeremy looked at his plate, where a last baked bean was sliding across the greased ceramic.

The chief was still incredulous. 'You don't think you're going to get promoted. A raise, at most, maybe. You're just going to sit here and let them shit on you until the whole thing goes under.'

Jeremy stabbed at the bean, which crumbled under a prong. 'I suppose so.'

'You suppose so?'

'Listen, Frank, thanks, really. I appreciate it. But I've got to go call my wife; I couldn't get hold of her last night.'

The chief threw up his hands. 'Fine. Go and talk to her,

you mad bastard. Maybe she'll snap you out of it. And hey, listen, I've got to find someone sharpish, so don't think you can moon about and then say yes whenever you feel like it.'

Jeremy nodded at this and went down to the newsroom, where the reporters were already chugging coffee and rubbing their eyes. He deliberately didn't check the TV screens for updates while he leant back in his seat and called Louise from his desk phone.

She said, 'Hello?' hesitantly, not recognizing the number and, as soon as he'd spoken and she began to talk, he wished he hadn't called. He would have been able to speak to her if he'd got through last night, but now he didn't want to talk to anyone. The pressure of what she had to say to him had apparently been building since he left home yesterday and he sat inert inside his clothes and his bulk while she belaboured him with words: there were soldiers at Kemsing station; how could he have said it wouldn't be dangerous? They had to decide whether to take the girls out of school.

He didn't want to decide about anything. He just wanted to do his drudgery in peace. Most of all, he wanted just to go back to sleep, preferably for a thousand years, and wake up when everyone and everything – Louise, Frank, the dead boy, the *Beast*, even his daughters – would be unable to bother him any further. A yearning gathered in him: to be buried far down below the surface of the earth, where no sound could reach him, where he would be utterly forgotten and would utterly forget himself, oblivious as a rock.

Now Louise was getting angry because he wasn't answering her questions. 'I don't see why you don't just leave and come home where it's safe. It's like you don't want to.'

Stay, go, charter a car with Turkish Liz, walk out on the job he came to every day...

He glanced up at the screens projected on to the back wall: soldiers in camouflage clothes and blue latex gloves were searching through brown people's suitcases at King's Cross; a double line of riot police with helmets and shields pushed back a roiling Muslim crowd; a group of black-suited MPs knelt to read the messages on a glinting mound of cellophane-wrapped bouquets; forensics experts in white scrubs went busily in and out of what looked like a wedding marquee, from which protruded the smashed muzzle of the bus; and a squat green tank, its long barrel sniffing the air, reversed soundlessly into position next to a taxi rank at Heathrow.

'Louise,' he said. 'If we give up, that means they've won. If we want to live in a free country, we've got to not give in.'

'Oh, you know I hate it when you do this.'

'Do what?'

'You're not really saying anything. You sound like the paper. You're not actually telling me anything, you're just making words.'

'Are you saying it's not a question of national—?'

'Oh, spare me. Why did you ring me when you didn't want to talk? Can you call me back later please? I'll figure out what to do with the girls today. I'm not going to send them to school.' And she hung up.

THIRTY-FIRST CHAPTER

TO ADRIAN'S incredulity, he noticed that Gavin was still picking at the by now almost-invisible grass stains on his lapel. That Gavin could be thinking about his suit when they were inside the *Beast*'s secret base astounded him. He ought to be as rapt as a fox in a hen-house with plump defenceless stories flapping all about him, but instead he was thinking about his outfit. The lad would never make it as a reporter. Adrian hissed, 'Leave it alone.'

They were standing in a corridor and pretending to peruse the framed pictures from the *Beast*'s glorious past. Gavin sullenly swivelled his head towards Adrian to complain, 'It's never really going to come out.'

Adrian looked at the lapels. The stains were now no more than shiny discolorations of the grey material. Under the jacket was the white shirt Adrian had had to lend Gavin when he himself had changed into his suit jacket yesterday afternoon. It was the spare shirt he kept in his car, a routine maintained from his reporting days, and now it was creased and crumpled from Gavin's sleeping in it. 'Of course it'll come out. You just need to get it properly dry-cleaned. We'll deal with it tomorrow, alright? You're just making it more conspicuous.'

Gavin turned back to the picture. 'Fine.'

'Now come on, Gavin, we've got bigger—'

A lugubrious middle-aged man with a paunch and fresh razor-burn shambled around the corner. Adrian and Gavin quickly focused on the picture in front of them. It showed an adolescent chimp wearing a fez and studying an issue of the *Beast* triumphantly headlined:

ARGIES

BARGED

OUT OF

STANLEY

The caption read, 'Bernie, unofficial mascot of Royal Marines 45 Commando, reads the *Daily Beast*'s account of victory in the Falkland Islands. *Beast* reporter Brendan Walters was the first Englishman into Port Stanley, entering at the head of the heroic liberators.'

Adrian leant closer, careful not to let his eyes jump to contact with the man now passing them. But even as he pretended to read, the giddiness of the clandestine overcame him. He'd heard that anecdote about Walters before and now he was right in the middle of making an anecdote to match it. Or almost match it. The first man into Port Stanley! The *Beast* really was fantastic. Even this nothing-seeming man traipsing behind him – what dazzling wheezes he must have pulled off in his time!

Jeremy, for his part, merely glanced at these two unknown men who'd so blatantly stopped talking when he appeared.

He didn't recognize them, which was unusual, but there were always people plotting and machinating in the corridors, and who was he to know every skulker and skulduggerer with a job here? He didn't even want to listen to what they were saying; his day was already bad enough without getting mixed up in anyone else's. And that morning's developments in the story – the army moving in to guard train stations, airports and town centres; a Muslim crowd in Bradford turning on the police – had provoked the newsroom into nervous aggression. Worst of all, someone had burnt down another paper shop, albeit without killing anyone this time. He'd already heard Geraldine telling someone on the phone, 'If the rotter so much as mumbles *Allahu Akbar*, you have my blessing to pre-emptively kick his head in.'

He carried on past them and, once his scuffing footsteps were out of earshot, Adrian spoke in a voice pressurized with excitement: 'We have to have our wits very, *very* much about us, Gavin. Anything could happen now we're in here.'

'OK,' said Gavin. 'It's not that great though, is it?'

Adrian couldn't understand. 'What are you— what do you mean?'

Gavin shrugged in a way that made Adrian glad he'd never had children. 'I thought it'd be like a Bond villain's base in here, all flashing lights and touchscreens and, you know, airlocks, and super-slick. But it's basically a bit crap, isn't it? It looks like Thatcham Community Centre.'

'Gavin. We are inside what may today be the most powerful news organization in the world. Its staff are geniuses of news. They've just smashed a jihadi bombing ring that MI5 couldn't find and broken a story that's being talked about right now in every country that even *has* the news.' He allowed some of his happiness to show itself. 'And we, you and me, the quiet modest little *Thatcham and Newbury Echo & Advertiser*, are going to turn the tables and report on *them*.'

'So far we can report that they've got torches in their store cupboard. And that sleeping on the floor with a boiler suit for a pillow is actually pretty shit.'

Adrian was so exasperated he lightly slapped the bare wall with the flat of his hand. 'Let's go and find the newsroom then.'

'Yeah, let's get on with it. I've got to go into town this afternoon and get my ankle looked at.'

Adrian decided simply to act as if Gavin had never said that. 'Which way do you reckon it is?'

When, last night, they'd crept into the bunker's bright interior, Adrian had memorized the turnings they took and made Gavin repeat them back to him in case they were separated. But as for finding something else...

'Let's try the way that man went.'

They walked after Jeremy, Gavin still limping slightly from yesterday's fall off the perimeter fence. Adrian was sure he was exaggerating. He tried to ignore it and search the scene for telling details. Gavin was looking only at the framed photographs they passed. He said, 'Some of these are pretty sick. Wouldn't it be amazing if one of them had like a secret vault behind it and then a whole other bunker underneath this decoy one?'

Adrian almost despaired of him. But he told himself that, to be fair, at least the lad was using his ingenuity. 'Yes, it *would* be amazing. And really...' He shook his head with wry amusement. 'You never know with a paper like the *Beast*. I wouldn't put anything past them.'

'Like having a second bunker?'

'Well, no, I don't think that. Just the excavation involved, the cost…' He relented: 'But I suppose if they have one secret bunker, why not two?'

'Yeah, who knows what kind of crazy shit we'll find in here.'

'Exactly! That's it, Gavin, that's exactly it!' Adrian was delighted by the phrase. 'Crazy shit,' he repeated, 'that's it exactly.'

They came to a stretch of corridor that had many closed doors set into both sides, with a department name Sellotaped to each one. On the label marked 'Diary' someone had graffitied in slanting blue biro 'BLOWJOBS £10 ALL DAY!!' Gavin was intrigued.

Adrian could not see one that said 'Newsroom'. 'So,' he asked, making sure to involve Gavin, 'what do you think?'

'That one's got a proper sign on it that says "SUB BASE-MENT".' Gavin pointed. It was true. A sign in blue-and-white plastic. Adrian said, 'So that'll be the entrance to the secret sub-bunker.'

Gavin smirked. Adrian thought it might be the first time he'd made a joke that Gavin had (almost) laughed at. Gavin usually never even seemed to recognize his jokes as such.

'Maybe it's a missile silo, or like a big control room with loads of scientists, and the prime minister and the Editor of the *Beast* making plans to take over the whole of Britain.'

Adrian let slide that the PM was *already* in charge of the whole of Britain. 'There's certainly an entire printing press in here somewhere.'

Gavin shrugged, not totally indifferently. 'I guess that could be cool. But are we going to look in the sub basement or what?'

Adrian suavely stepped to the side of the door, clowning like a dad at a children's party. 'After you, 007.' Despite himself, he could hear the *GoldenEye* theme music in his head. He and Gavin were like secret agents, secret *news*agents. No. That didn't work. Secret agents of the news. Putting one over on their opponents' empire just like plucky little Britain outwitting the Soviet Union.

They positioned themselves on either side of the door.

'Ready?' asked Adrian, resisting the urge to mime holding a Walther PPK.

'Ready,' said Gavin.

Adrian pressed down the handle and with a push sent the door swinging away from them. They peered inside. It was a dormitory.

'Oh,' said Adrian.

'It's not a basement at all.'

'No.'

'So where do we go now?'

'Let's just have a little poke around here first. Who knows what we might turn up?'

They went in, feeling for the first time that they were trespassing. There was little for them to see: bunk beds dressed with painfully orange linen, thin duvets corkscrewed around themselves by departed sleepers, the corners of sheets flapping from under their mattresses. The lower bunk directly in front of them, however, was tautly made and had beneath it a neat row of books – a biography of Lord Copper, *The Principles of Rhetoric.*

'Brilliant!' exclaimed Adrian. 'Just brilliant. Look at that seriousness. I bet no one on the *Echo*'s reading about rhetoric.'

Gavin, tiring a little of all this, lifted a finger in pantomime of 'Eureka!' and said, 'But maybe...' He tiptoed over to the made bed and – with a cry of 'Gotcha!' – ripped back the duvet. Underneath was nothing but the orange sheet. He blew air out of his mouth. 'Seriously, though, what are we even going to find in here? It's not like they've actually got a missile silo; it's all just people's stuff.'

'Well, whatever happens,' Adrian had laid all this out in his head overnight, 'in tomorrow's edition we'll have "World Exclusive: Inside the *Daily Beast*'s Secret Berkshire HQ". No one's going to walk past *that* without picking it up. Then beside it a picture of the police at the gate; that'll be the front page, so that when you open the paper it's like going inside. Then our report on what it's like. Maybe that's "spartan conditions", "mass dormitories", or maybe we find something more, some documents. Like maybe they've been given sensational instructions on what to do in an attack. Or they've written touching last letters to their families in case they're killed. I don't know, but we won't know until we've looked around.'

They began to go through the little piles of possessions beside the bunks and to lift things out of bags to look further inside. At first they were cautious, reluctant even, held back by the taboo against touching things that didn't belong to them. But gradually a feeling for it came over them and they pulled open cases, unravelled clothes and plunged shoulder-deep into rucksacks.

Then Gavin said, 'I think I've got something, boss.' Tweezing it between finger and thumb, he held up a pair of boxer shorts patterned with penguins and intoned, 'World Exclusive: *Beast* caught with its pants down'.

Adrian's laugh came out as a snort. He said, 'Come on, put those back.'

Gavin bent over to replace the patterned boxers in the bag he'd taken them from but stopped midway. 'Hold on,' he said. 'There's a document in here as well.' Adrian looked around while Gavin ceremoniously unfolded a handwritten sheet and, holding it out in front of him, began to read: '"My dear R..."'

'My dear what, sorry?'

'It's just the letter R.'

'Oh, right. OK. Shorthand, probably. Maybe an emotional farewell to his wife.'

Gavin re-centred himself. '"My dear R, I'm too happy to sleep and so I have to write to you. Your closeness – knowing you're in a bunk only a few feet from mine, is—"'

'Stop, stop, stop,' interrupted Adrian in embarrassment. 'That's just someone's personal letter.'

'Sounds like two of them are shagging. Do you think this is an all-male dorm?'

'That makes no difference at all. Put it back. Although, there's nothing in there about how sad he'd be if the other one got blown up, is there? Or how worried he is about the other one?'

Gavin scanned down the page. 'It's pretty hard to read.'

'He must have been writing in the dark. With the torch on his phone.'

Gavin continued to the bottom and turned the page over. As he squinted at the progressively smaller, messier script, a plummy female voice hailed them from the door. 'What the bloody hell are you two doing?'

Adrian saw a bush of sand-coloured hair, a blue jacket and a summer dress printed with enormous pale flowers. He started to put together an excuse, but she carried on over him: 'Don't you know that everyone's supposed to be in the newsroom already? Or did you think you rather felt like doing a bit of malingering instead?'

Adrian took his cue. 'We were just tidying up a bit first.'

'Tidying up! What are you, maiden aunts? Or is it just that subs really are the most hopeless gang of pedants?'

Geraldine glared at them as if expecting an answer. Adrian played his part, mumbling, 'We just thought it'd be better if things were in order.'

She threw up her hands in disbelief, jangling her bracelets. 'And this place is *still* messier than a Turkish bordello! I hope you're better subs than you are *femmes de chambre* or there'll be no point filing any copy at all. Now hop to it, back to the newsroom.'

Adrian and Gavin glanced at each other. They went through the door and into the corridor. Geraldine stepped back to let them out. They looked at her expectantly. 'For the love of Pete, I'm not going to walk you there as well. You'll have to manage that on your own.' She shooed them in the right direction. 'Go on then – chop-chop – start walking.'

THIRTY-SECOND CHAPTER

WILL flinched when he noticed Gavin and Adrian near the centre of the newsroom. Among the thronging, hurrying hubbub, they drifted across its lines of motion. The younger, his suit stained, was limping, and Will's mind flashed from recognition to a reflexive guess: they were the men he'd seen in the pub; it was probably them who'd tried to climb the fence; the younger one must have fallen and injured his leg.

This intuition set him trembling with excitement. His heart murmured and he had to grip his mouse and keyboard so no one would see his hands shake. This was a career-making catch, if he could bring it in. And all around were dozens of as yet oblivious reporters who would like to bring it in themselves.

The intruders were trying to appear as if they belonged there, pretending to discuss some print-offs the older man was holding while their eyes travelled all over the inside of the newsroom. For jihadis they didn't look very fanatical. It seemed so unlikely that they were terrorists. Of course, Will had never seen any before, but these just did not look like men about to start killing. Keyed-up, yes; tense, yes; but not murderous. In a few years he could be the youngest editor in the country.

Max was the wrong person to go to this time; it would become a catch from his pod, ergo his catch. And the rewards Max could give were still small. Will would go straight to the Editor. He would talk to the Editor himself and tell him – but who were they? The older one looked like the manager of a provincial supermarket. He was taking the pretence more seriously than the younger one, splaying his fingers to the surface of the sheets he was holding as if explaining something. The younger one, who stood taller than his boss, was openly glancing around. They might be saboteurs, or undercover policemen who were testing their colleagues, or some kind of protestors. But surely not jihadis.

He realized it didn't matter. All that could be investigated later. The thing now was to make the catch before anyone else noticed them. He had to go to the Editor's office. He glanced at Rosie, who was absorbed in the story she was working on. Last night, with her, it had been like when the flint of a cigarette lighter is rasped in a room long filling with gas; he'd gone up with a whump. He hadn't realized it had been so long since another person touched him. Now her black-and-white work clothes had re-straightened themselves into a professional casing; the buttons buttoned, the shirt no longer flapping open above him. She shouldn't mind, he hoped, that he was going to leave her here in the newsroom, but he didn't think there was any danger and, once he was travelling upwards, he could carry her with him.

The two intruders, still feigning their discussion, had drawn level with the back bench and stopped. Will had to twist slightly in his chair to see them there, over Jeremy's shoulder, but kept his head straight so as not to draw attention.

They now appeared to be conferring for real and, as Will watched, they naturally, very naturally, as if it were the most natural thing in the world, sauntered towards a grey-painted door off the side of the newsroom. Will gripped his mouse. The older man pushed down the handle, pulled back the door and ushered his subordinate inside. As soon as he'd passed through, the older man followed him in and shut the door behind them.

Now, now, this was the time, while they were in there, before they could go somewhere else. Half-rising, he said to Max, 'I've just got to nip out for a second.'

Annoyed by this unprofessionalism, Max said, 'Make it quick.'

Will nodded deferentially. Without looking at Rosie, he hurried towards the corridor that led to the Editor's office. As he cut through the newsroom, he saw everything as he imagined the intruders must see it. The soft, white-haired reporter Maurice was asking one of the Features girls, 'But she must be famous for something more than having a large rear end'; Turkish Liz was spreading out printed-off pictures of the hijackers' families, who'd been arrested overnight; Geraldine was almost horizontal in her chair, her wedges crossed on the edge of her desk, and was drawling into her floral-patterned phone, 'He's the archbish, you hopeless clot; his line should be that Muslim community leaders must start taking responsibility for their flock.' One day soon, all this might be Will's.

But he must not mess this up by getting ahead of himself. He cut through everything and into the narrow corridor. Here were framed pictures of men the *Beast* remembered – company men, chief subs and production editors from thirty years before – photographed with pints and captioned with nicknames. As he passed them almost at a jog, he recognized

John Dyson, whom he'd seen banged out two days before, and he thought: I will be banged out when my time comes; my picture will be here when I am gone.

He hurtled past the editor's PA, who was exhaustedly resting a mug against her forehead and too slow to stop Will rapping loudly on the door marked 'Charles Brython, Editor'.

'Come!'

Will slipped inside and closed the door on the PA's protests. What he found slightly disappointed him: instead of a separate world of luxury and status, there was just more bare concrete, a wide desk strewn with layers of print-offs marked up in blue pencil and, behind it, hugely, the Editor himself.

'Who the fuck are you?' he asked, and jabbed a button on his desk phone. 'Emma, can you explain to me why—'

Will hurried out, 'I'm sorry, Mr Brython, but it's important.'

The Editor paused and said into the phone, 'Don't worry, I'll take care of it myself.' Then said, 'Well? Get on with it.'

Now, actually having the Editor's ear, Will became temporarily star-struck. 'It's that... I've just seen... I'm not sure exactly who.' His thoughts coalesced: 'The building's been infiltrated.'

'WHAT?! How do you know?'

'I've just seen them. But—'

'Good God, man! They're inside the building?'

'In the newsroom, but—'

The Editor surged to his feet, knocking his chair back against the wall behind him. He reached up under the dark-blue pullover he was wearing beneath his jacket and brought out a pistol. Will stumbled backwards, instinctively lifting his palms. 'Don't play the fool, damn you! Put your hands down! How the fuck did they get inside? You say they're in the newsroom?'

'They went through a door just off it, by the back bench, I think it's—'

'It's a meeting room.' The Editor was coming round from behind his desk, his great chest rising and falling. 'Cunting mother of cunt. They're probably prepping a bomb. Mother*fucker*, come on!'

In two strides he was at the door and pulling it open, holding the pistol vertically like an officer about to go over the top. His PA jumped in her seat when she saw it, spilling pale tea across her keyboard.

Will went after the Editor, ignoring her again, and managed to get out, 'I don't think they're jihadis. I recognized them.'

Not slowing his stride back the way Will had come, the Editor demanded, 'Who are they?'

Hurrying to keep up, Will said, 'I saw them yesterday, at the pub in Bucklebury. One of them, today, he's got a limp, like he hurt it falling off the fence. I think he's the one who tried to break in.'

'Muslims?'

Even from slightly behind the Editor, Will's gaze would not detach from the pistol, which he saw was old-fashioned, narrow, something from the war. 'No, no. I don't think so. They're both white, in suits. Maybe they're some kind of protestor.'

The Editor ignored his speculation. 'Ages?'

'The younger one, with the limp, is about twenty, the older one's in his forties, I would say. But I really don't think they're dangerous.'

'What the fuck do you know about it? They've been tailing our staff and now they've broken in to the most sensitive building in England, and you want to tell me they're not dangerous! How did you spot them?'

'I recognized them, from yesterday.'

'And you're the one who found the break-in, aren't you? Why is that?'

Will acted humble. 'Lucky, I suppose.'

'Big stories have a habit of finding good reporters. What is it that you—'

But then they emerged from the corridor into the newsroom and the pistol wreaked terror around them. Brython's staff gasped and shrieked and the pistol cleared a path for him. Those nearest abandoned their desks and ran, shielding their heads. Those further away dived off their chairs and into cover behind desks and filing cabinets. The chief stopped mid-bustle and stared at them as they passed. Liz grabbed her camera. Will could see Jeremy agog, still in his chair, Max pulling him down. Rosie was already out of sight.

The Editor strode along behind the back bench, past spinning chairs and dropped phones, the last of his senior staff fleeing around him, and stopped twenty feet from the innocuous door. The TV projector sent blurred colours and lines wobbling across his shoulder and face. Geraldine rushed to his side. Someone was sobbing.

With the back of his free hand, the Editor waved his people further away. They retreated, leaving a wide unhindered corridor of air between the Editor and his target. He told Will, 'Listen at the door for whether they're still in there. But for Christ's sake don't walk into my line of fire.'

THIRTY-THIRD CHAPTER

WILL put his ear's whorled cartilage to the door, leaning close enough to make out the brush-lines in the grey paint, his head directly in front of the Editor's pistol. He could see the newsroom watching him from its hiding places. Several people were writing shorthand or filming with their phones. Liz had come closest and was on one knee, taking pictures. Jez was standing beside her, hastily pressing buttons on a small video camera. The muscles at the root of Will's ear tingled with the effort of listening, but he could hear nothing beyond the blood at his temples and the dry breath in his throat.

The Editor asked his newsroom: 'Has anyone seen anyone coming out of that door?'

The journalists looked around at one another. From beside the Editor, Geraldine, giving it the stiff upper lip, asked, 'Charles, old stick, would you mind giving me a hint about what's going on?'

'Two men have succeeded in breaking into this bunker.' People ducked involuntarily, letting out strings of obscenities.

'They were last seen going in there.' The Editor ordered Will: 'Knock!'

Will flattened his body against the solid wall and stretched his arm so that his fist was extended as far as possible from his vital organs. A rapid double tap, then he jerked his hand back to his chest. The Editor's voice rang out: 'Surrender now and you won't be harmed! You have a story you want the British public to hear. Come out talking and we will tell that story in our pages.'

Inside the meagrely furnished meeting room, Adrian snapped his fingers with delight. 'That old fox, always turning things towards the next edition.'

And outside Will pointed and pointed at the door, mouthing: 'They're in there! They're in there!'

The Editor shifted one foot slightly forward, to make a steadier base, and took the pistol in a firmer, two-handed grip. 'This is your opportunity to tell your side of things. The public deserves to hear your account. We are in the midst of a national crisis and you obviously have something important to say. But your message will be distorted by the media unless you come out and explain it.'

Jeremy was still struggling with the video camera Liz had shoved into his hands. Something was wrong with the focus and he couldn't work out what.

Inside the meeting room, Adrian was bouncing on the spot with excitement. Never before had working on the *Echo* been so *dramatic*. This would be one of the great tales of modern journalism: two guys from a tiny local paper holed up inside the *Beast*'s bunker, putting one over on that Goliath. He cried out at Gavin, 'I've got it! We'll phone in the story from here! We'll phone it in! We'll dictate the copy. By the time they escort us out, *our* newsroom will already have it!'

Gavin was nervous and unconvinced. 'There's no reception in here.'

Adrian snatched his phone from his pocket. It was true: the bar-chart symbol at the top of the screen was empty and had a cross against it. 'Search then! Maybe there's a spot somewhere in this room!' Holding his phone aloft like a Geiger counter, he started sweeping it along the bare walls and into the corners, then above the thin conference table and the plastic school-chairs. Gavin reluctantly copied him, waving his phone in un-meticulous circles, but asked, 'Don't you think we should just let them kick us out? They sound pretty serious.'

Adrian didn't interrupt his search. 'You wanted more action! Now you've got it!'

'But seriously, don't you think we should, you know, call it a day? It's been great and everything, but haven't we maybe taken it far enough? And actually, if they kick us out, we can just go back to the office and write up the story.'

'Ha! You think they'd let us do that?' Adrian scowled. 'Who equips a meeting room without putting a phone in it? They won't give us an inch!'

Gavin stopped even pretending to scan the air. 'But how are they going to stop us leaving? They can't arrest us, they're not the police.'

'Oh, they won't let that stop them!' Adrian dropped to his knees and crawled under the table, moving jerkily as he swung his phone from side to side.

'Seriously though...' Gavin addressed the blank tabletop.

Adrian didn't reply. But, after a moment, he emerged from under the table and stood up, breathing heavily. He said, 'They're journalistic geniuses, Gavin. They'll do whatever they can think of. We have to do the same. There's no signal, so we'll have to try something else.'

In the newsroom, at the other end of the line that connected the door to the muzzle of the Editor's pistol, Geraldine asked, 'Who are these two?'

The Editor's gaze didn't shift. 'We don't know. They're white though.'

'Bloody hell. White jihadis. And we thought it was bad enough that that hijacker was married to a Brit. How on earth did they get inside?'

'Stand back now, Geraldine,' said the Editor. He'd noticed the door handle slowly angling down away from the horizontal. The door's left edge detached itself from the frame and began slowly to pivot outwards. The newsroom's staff hunkered down into cover. Liz's camera clicked and clicked. The door, once it had pivoted enough for a slim person to slip through, stopped moving.

Liz was trying to take pictures through the gap but wasn't getting anything. Will edged away from the door and knelt down behind a thick industrial printer. The Editor breathed out, settling himself further.

They waited.

Then the door was flung open and from behind it broke Adrian, accelerating towards Liz and Jeremy. He was carrying a plastic chair in front of him as a fender. Liz snapped, snapped, snapped. Jeremy stood immobile, the useless video camera still in his hand, watching this neatly suited little man bear down on him in a state of what looked like exhilaration. As Adrian was almost upon them, he hurled the chair and began a shout – which went unheard because, as he opened his mouth, a shot rang out.

The metallic whip crack was so fast it almost caught up with its own echo and the reverberation in the contained space was so loud that the journalists' hands twitched to their ears. An invisible force smacked into the left side of Adrian's chest. It spun him off his feet and backwards, so the second shot struck him square on, just above the heart, knocking him irrecoverably to the floor.

The chair he'd thrown clattered into Liz and Jeremy. Liz clumsily blocked it with a forearm while still taking pictures. Jeremy felt the chair legs scrape across his arm and collide with the side of his paunch, but didn't see them. In the instant of the shots, he'd been looking not at Adrian, nor even at the Editor, but at the wall behind him.

Across the fuzzy news channels had loomed the gargantuan black shadow of the Editor's pistol. The sight induced in Jeremy the shock of vertigo, a reeling through time.

He staggered as the newsroom erupted around him. He saw the Editor and Geraldine running closer; saw Will leaning dazed against the printer; saw two trembling hands stretched out of the doorway in a gesture of surrender; heard Geraldine bawling, 'Get him out here! Get him out here!'; and smelt something like scorched carpet.

And below all, on the floor, he saw the dead man. He was quite short, his brown hair cropped sensibly as it receded, his M&S suit dusty at the knees, his blue-checked shirt a little too casual for the *Beast*. The top button was done up and his tie patterned with tiny typewriters. His eyes rolled horribly part of the way back under their lids, which had fallen to different levels, like broken awnings. They did not flutter, nor stare, nor see, but were only balls of milky matter, thickening.

His arms were spatchcocked outwards as if he'd been miming a leap of joy when killed. But they didn't match the nothing expression on his face. The parts had lost what made them cohere. Averting his eyes from Adrian's chest, Jeremy saw that one of his trouser legs had ridden up; he saw the top of a forlorn school-type black sock, failing to cover the exposed, nearly hairless calf. Jeremy was ashamed to look at it.

Jeremy didn't let his eyes touch the wounds themselves; but, as he watched, a red puddle seemed to gather from beneath the body, seeping quickly out of his suit and advancing across the newsroom's slick concrete.

Then the Editor clattered in and was pushing two strong fingers into the side of the dead man's neck. Geraldine had dragged the other one from the meeting room and was yelling at him, 'Who are you? Who do you work for?'

The Editor stood up gravely, the fatal metal still in his hand. 'He's dead.'

The terrified young man moaned, 'We're journalists.'

'*Journalists?*'

'From the *Thatcham Echo*. We wanted to get the scoop. We broke in; I'm really sorry. He's...' Gavin went to point at his boss and dropped his finger as if burnt. 'He's the editor. Adrian Trent. I'm just a reporter. I'm just a trainee really; Adrian keeps saying I don't know anything.'

The Editor looked to Geraldine and said, 'Good Lord.'

'Charles...'

Brython held up a hand to stop her strategizing. He was suddenly very weary. In a flat voice, he said, 'I'm finished.' He *was* finished. There was no doubt. And it was just. He'd made this error and an innocent man was dead. He'd taken a risk, many risks, over the years and this time things had come out against him. A man was dead. Geraldine turned her face away from him. Brython was right: he was finished, because of this idiotic nobody bleeding out on the floor. Frustration urged her to kick the corpse. And already Brython was looking around the tumultuous newsroom like someone about to leave it for ever.

Amid the remorse and the pain of sudden loss, a small part of him was pleased. His many enemies – lords, tycoons and ministers of state among them – had been trying to bring him down since he was in early middle age; he was glad that the one to succeed should be a journalist. But even now his feel for the mechanisms of public life had not deserted him; and he said, 'Liz, we need a shot of me standing over the body.'

Liz, who'd been bottling in her words, shrieked, 'I've got a scratch!' She pointed at the back of her left hand, where the chair had drawn a thick red line. 'From the man you've killed, you fucking psycho. You said anyone who got so much as a scratch—'

'Yes,' said Brython with dignity. Geraldine was looking at Liz as if she'd lost her mind. But money didn't matter now. 'A million pounds. You'll get it. I keep my word. Now take the picture.' He arranged his features to demonstrate the great grief he wanted the readers to see he felt, and let the fatal pistol hang by his side. Jeremy looked down at his own forearm: it, too, was bruised.

Through the viewfinder, Liz saw the Editor standing monumentally with Adrian stretched at his feet: a news photograph that would become immortal as soon as it was taken. She took it.

Geraldine had understood what he was going to do. Bittersweet respect unbalanced her voice as she said, 'Tomorrow's front page.'

'World-exclusive interview with *Daily Beast* Editor Charles Brython, who tells candidly how he shot journalist Adrian Trent. Exclusive pictures of the scene and of Brython in handcuffs. Exclusive account of the shooting itself.'

'It'll be the most sensational story we've ever printed.'

'Yes. You'll have to order an even bigger run.'

'And we can leak it as much as we want; it'll only make more publicity for our scoop. They'll be tearing them off the shelves. No one else'll be able to get anywhere near it.'

'Except this boy.'

Brython and Geraldine examined Gavin, who stepped backwards as if to defend himself. As they moved, Jeremy saw that the dark puddle of Adrian's blood must have run up against Brython's shoe when he was posing over the body. The sticky puddle had congealed around its curve and, where grooves had been cut into the sole, oozed underneath to form three red ridges.

Gavin said to Geraldine, 'I recognize you! I saw you in the corridor! You pointed me in here!'

Geraldine was unperturbed. 'Yes, you duped me. Good reporting instincts. How would you like to be a reporter on the most important newspaper in the world?'

'On the *Beast*?'

'Yes, on the *Beast*. We'll even make you a senior reporter.'

Gavin asked stupidly, 'A senior reporter? What do I have to do?'

'Nothing. I'll get you a contract and a confidentiality agreement.'

Gavin didn't know what any of this meant. He automatically asked, 'How much will you pay me?'

She gestured bitterly at the corpse. 'It'll be more than he was getting.'

'But what about Adrian?' With that, he seemed to apprehend the enormity of Adrian's death and started to cry, mutely at first and then with uncontrolled gulps and sobs, his boyish shoulders shaking as he brought his hands in front of his face.

Geraldine said to her reporters, 'Put him back in that room

and have HR give him a confidentiality agreement right fucking now. Backdate it by a week. Is that clear? Charles—'

'Your byline will be on the splash, but I'm going to dictate it. Get ready to break the story online. No pictures, no location, no names except mine. Very brief, just that the Editor of the *Daily Beast* has shot someone dead and a statement that full exclusive coverage, pictures and interviews will be in tomorrow's print edition. Get that ready, then we'll ring our man in the Met at the same time, to report it. And find something to cover the body till they arrive.'

He considered for a few moments, his thoughts lucid and unhurried, then spoke louder, to address the newsroom and bring it to order. 'Quiet now. Show your respect.' The newsroom hushed. 'This is a heartbreaking tragedy. And the *Daily Beast* will accord our fallen comrade every tribute a newspaper can. We will print a black border around tomorrow's edition, on every page, and below the masthead we will print the dedication: "In memoriam, Adrian Trent, newsman", with his dates. Mr Trent has given his life in service of the noble profession in which we are all engaged. To break in to the most sensitive building in England in pursuit of a story, while the country is up in arms, is no minor feat of daring. We will remember his courage.'

Two reporters had stripped a thin orange sheet from one of the beds and they uncomfortably draped it, fluttering, over Adrian's body. The Editor remained silent until it was done, then said to Geraldine, 'Send someone to his family's house to present our condolences and record their last tributes to him.' He carried on to the newsroom: 'We will honour his memory in many ways and first among them will be our continued devotion to the news for which he died. You will understand that his story is my last as Editor of the *Daily*

Beast, and that this will be my final edition. You may never see another like it. I wish you all good luck.' No one reacted except Geraldine, who blinked hard, her eyes bloodshot. She supposed she would be Editor, but that prospect was no solace yet.

'There will be time for nostalgia later. For now there is work to be done,' he said, but nonetheless went on: 'Goodbye to you all. The burden of upholding this newspaper's proud standards now rests on you. And remember: I will be reading.' He lost the direction of his thoughts and looked down at his father's pistol. The dull metal gleamed at him. He supposed they would destroy it. 'Now then,' he said. 'Now everyone back to your places. Each story needs to have crossed my desk before we let the police in. Quickly now, if you're still newsmen and not just bystanders.'

Some of them righted chairs, moved towards their seats. The chief, who was already adding to his personal legend that he'd kept working with a body bleeding out on the floor behind him, translated the order into his own terms: 'You heard the Editor. Dry your eyes, you snivellers. Any of your lives would be improved by getting shot. Pod leaders, get your teams working!'

But Max recognized how malleable this moment was and pressed his imprint into it. He spoke up: 'Excuse me for interrupting, Charles, but is it a good idea to put an edition this important into the hands of someone who's already signed a contract with the *Fun*?'

No fury came to Brython, only fatigue. He asked the chief, 'Is this true?'

The chief's mouth worked. He went to yell at Max but instead he turned to Brython and accused, 'It's all over. The *Beast*, it's done for. And you're the one who just finished her off.'

Brython said nothing. And Geraldine, who took the chief's downfall as a small consolation, jumped in: 'Well, you treacherous oaf, we won't miss you. Are you going to go take a seat with our new senior reporter or are you going to let us have the police give you a beating first?'

The chief merely took his phone out of his pocket and flicked it aside to skitter across the concrete. 'When you come begging for a job on *FunOnline*, Geraldine, I'll give you one. Remember that.' And he walked unescorted to the meeting room.

Brython said to Max, 'Take over then, if that's what you want. Get them working.'

And Max, unsure whether his colleagues would obey him, called them by name. 'Jez, can you take over the Terror pod.'

But Jeremy was still seeing the shadow of the Editor's pistol loom across the fuzzy screens, a terrible reality intruding. This body, this job, this room... this was the life he was in. And life's only conclusion lay on the floor under an orange sheet.

'Jez,' said Max again. 'Take over the pod.'

Jeremy shook his head. 'No. No. Sorry, Max. I'm leaving. I quit. Sorry.'

Max held his gaze, asking with the privileges of their long friendship. Then Max looked away and Jeremy walked out, very simply, on his own feet.

As he went through the newsroom, he heard Max behind him call, 'Will, you're running the pod. Take my seat. You can handle it.' And Will, with shock still audible in his voice, replied, 'I'm on it, chief. Rosie, you're with me.'

The great toothed wheels of the *Beast*'s machinery again began to turn. One by one, the keyboards began to clatter. Phones rang, section editors demanded copy, noise rose from every corner. Geraldine stood at one end of the Newsdesk,

almost overcome by devotion as she served under Brython
for the last time, and commanded her subordinates above
the growing din: 'Get on the phones. Call all the papers, the
TV channels, even call bloody BBC Radio Berkshire, and give
them the teaser. In five minutes, this is going to be breaking
everywhere in the world.'

Brython was preparing to start his dictation. To compose
his thoughts, he examined the garish orange bed-sheet that
clung to the features of the dead man. It was stuck down
in two places with what looked like blackish glue; and the
side nearest him had been soaked through by the sticky
puddle beneath. He nodded grimly and, his quarterdeck voice
ringing out clear and powerful, he began, 'The *Daily Beast*'s
fight-back in the war against Islamic terror has claimed its
first casualty...'

ACKNOWLEDGMENTS

First and foremost, I owe a debt of gratitude to my agent Anna Webber. Also to the team at Head of Zeus: Neil Belton, Lauren Atherton, Suzanne Sangster, Blake Brooks and, through them, Adrian McLaughlin and Monica Hope. Several people read and commented on ideas and drafts, especially Cordelia Jenkins, Paul Pickering, Peter Leggatt, Kate Rundell and Simon Akam. One person has read more of my writing and offered more help than anyone else: Candia McWilliam. I also owe much to my colleagues in the newsrooms I've worked in and hope they enjoy this. Lastly, I didn't know Stella Powell-Jones when I was writing this book, but I'm thankful I know her now.